Forever Hilltop

Forever Hilltop

FEATURING

An Unlikely Blessing &
Surprising Grace

Two Books in One Volume

JUDY BAER

Guideposts
New York, New York

Forever Hilltop

ISBN 13: 978-0-8249-4529-9

Published by Guideposts
16 East 34th Street
New York, New York 10016
www.guideposts.org

Distributed by Ideals Publications, a Guideposts company
2630 Elm Hill Pike, Suite 100
Nashville, TN 37214

Cover and Interior Design by Müllerhaus
Publishing Group | www.mullerhaus.net

Printed and bound in the United States of America
10 9 8 7 6 5 4 3 2 1

DEDICATION

For Hazel Fosen on her 100th birthday. I love you!

An Unlikely Blessing

CHAPTER ONE

Uncle Alex! Look out for that...*pig*?"

Jared's voice trailed away as Alex Armstrong applied a heavy foot to the brakes of his aging gray van and came to a screeching halt. A pink pig sat on its backside in the middle of the two-lane highway, its black hooves splayed on the concrete. It turned its head and gave them a baleful stare from one small eye, but made no signs of moving. Alex craned his neck and saw that the porker had company—piglets scurried back and forth across the road, squealing.

"Looks like a truck tipped over." Jared pointed to an old pickup jerry-rigged with a makeshift cage that lay on its side a few yards ahead. The driver of the truck—a thin, spry man who'd seen seventy in his rearview mirror—and several other passersby flapped their arms, but the pigs ignored them.

A man in oil-stained jeans, a denim shirt with a frayed collar, and a billed cap that announced Red's Gas & Garage sauntered over to Alex's van, bent to peer into the driver's side window, and grinned a flashing white smile. "Sorry about the holdup. We'll get them rounded up soon as we can. I *told* Ole that this piece of junk pickup wouldn't move Twinkle Toes, but would he listen? No way. I knew that if the pig and babies all moved to one side, that tin excuse for a truck would topple, and look what happened."

"Twinkle Toes?" Alex stammered.

The fellow gaped at him and shook his head, like Alex had been hiding in the other half of the world. "He's taking her to tonight's petting zoo at the park. It wouldn't be the same without Twinkle Toes." The man nodded as if that explained everything and meandered toward the sow. He pulled the billed cap from his head and yelled, "You pink varmints are blocking traffic!"

"Like that's going to help," Jared muttered, but he never took his gaze from the chaotic scene before him.

The man named Ole, apparent title-holder of the dented pickup, rummaged in his jacket pocket and produced a dark, spotted banana days past its prime. He held it out and peeled it slowly to reveal a brown pillar of mush.

Twinkle Toes gave a soft, almost loving grunt, hoisted herself to her feet, and tiptoed toward the gelatinous muck. She reached her owner, opened her mouth, and made the banana vanish, peel and all. In a quick, practiced move, the elderly man slid a homemade halter over her head to trap her.

"If you guys would quit standing around gawking and help me get my pickup righted, I'd get her back in." A strong Norwegian accent frosted Ole's words. "The piglets will follow." The voice sounded familiar to Alex.

By this time the crowd had grown significantly, as traffic piled up in both directions. Alex took a step forward, ready to help. Then he remembered his impractical leather loafers. He wouldn't be able to get enough traction to make a difference moving the truck. Jared, city boy to the core, looked as helpless as Alex felt. Several men stepped up and, with much pushing and grunting, rocked the elderly pickup back onto its tires. Ole hopped into the box like a man half his age, shoved one end of a piece of three-quarter-inch plywood onto the ground, and turned it into a ramp. Twinkle Toes scrambled up the makeshift ramp. The piglets congregated by the back tires and were lifted one by one to join their mother.

Ole used a piece of rope to secure the door on the battered cage, rounded the truck to the cab, revved the engine, and crept off at a snail's pace.

"Ole is batty about that pig."

Startled, Alex jumped. The fellow who'd first spoken to him had returned. "Excuse me?"

"Oh yeah. He does presentations at schools, teaching grade school kids all about pigs. He tells them how pigs sniff out truffles and that they have to wallow in mud to keep cool because they don't have sweat glands."

"Oh." Jared shot Alex a befuddled look. "Weird. I guess you learn something new every day." He turned the crank to roll his window up.

The traffic jam was dispersing now that the excitement was over. One by one, the cars pulled away until Alex's van and the chatty fellow's truck were the only ones left.

"He even compares himself to President Harry Truman, if you can believe it," the man said.

Alex, who was beginning to feel as though he'd fallen through a rabbit hole and ended up in Wonderland, did a double take. "Excuse me?"

"According to Ole, Harry Truman once said that 'no man should be allowed to be president who does not understand hogs.'"

"I didn't know..." Alex stammered. How was he supposed to respond to that?

"I'm Dixon Daniels, by the way." The farmer thrust his hand through Alex's open window to shake hands. Before Alex could say more, the stranger wandered back to his own vehicle.

"What *is* this place?" Jared asked, shaking his head.

Alex glanced at the road sign not thirty yards from them.

WELCOME TO GRASSY VALLEY, NORTH DAKOTA.
CITY POPULATION: 1,254
A PLACE LIKE HOME.

Alex took a deep breath. "Well, Jared, I guess you could say we're home."

So this was it.

Alex Armstrong pulled his van to the side of the gravel road and stared at the panorama before him. He gazed across gently undulating fields, past a small, glittering azure pond painted brightly with late afternoon sun, and beyond a flock of marsh ducks coming in for a landing. The mallards' glossy-green heads glinted in the sunlight, and a tawny deer streaked from its hiding place near a stand of plump cattails as Alex fixed his gaze on a white outline butted against the horizon.

He squinted slightly and the structure took shape. A rectangle, with concrete steps protruding from the prow and an added-on shanty jutting from the stern, rested atop a slight rise in the prairie. A spire rose upward from the roof near the front of the building and seemed to disappear into heaven but for a wink of metal, a cross, piercing the sky.

"Is that your church, Uncle Alex?" Jared unwound in the passenger seat and stretched until Alex thought the seventeen-year-old might put his foot through the windshield. Sometimes Alex wondered how this lanky beanpole of a kid with feet the size of Volkswagens could possibly be related to his petite, proper sister Carol, but he'd been thankful for the companionship Jared had provided on the drive from Chicago.

Jared scraped his fingers through his already-tousled dark hair and peered at the vista before him. "It's like a photograph...or a movie set." He dusted tortilla chips from his lap and leaned forward. "It doesn't even look real."

Alex couldn't disagree with that. It didn't feel real either. He was a city boy through and through. What was tangible to him was the ivy-covered Christian college campus where he'd met the woman he'd planned to marry and had taught English for more than twelve years. Taught, that was, until the hand of God—a surprisingly heavy hand in this case—had turned him around and sent him off to seminary to become a pastor. There, he'd felt like an old man in a sea of youth. Most of his classmates were little older than the college seniors he'd taught for so many years.

Now here he was, a tenured professor turned inexperienced minister. His former fiancée dating someone else. Starting over at age forty-two. Gazing helplessly at his first assignment, a tiny, two-church North Dakota parish situated at a sparsely populated bend in the road.

Jared squirmed like an eager puppy in his seat. "Drive to the church. I want to see it up close."

Alex didn't move. Couldn't make himself. He'd known it would be small. He had been warned that this part of North Dakota was rural. But still, somehow, he hadn't expected this. The muscles in Alex's stomach tightened. It was the clench of anxiety he'd been fighting ever since the call had come and he'd been invited, sight unseen, to pastor this congregation. He was out of his element here.

Maybe God hadn't spoken to him at all, Alex thought, a sinking sensation in his stomach. Perhaps in his eagerness to get away from the pain of the breakup, he'd only *imagined* he was following God's will by coming here. Maybe this whole thing was a gross error in judgment on his part.

"Don't be like this. You told Mom and me that God sent you to seminary and brought you here for a purpose." Jared waved his hand toward the pristine white church. "So here it is. Let's take a look at it."

"It doesn't look much like a purpose," Alex muttered as he drove forward and pulled into the tidy churchyard. "It's barely as big as a shoe box." A cemetery with headstones in orderly rows sat off to one side. It must have been recently mowed, and not a blade of grass was out of place.

He'd have to investigate it later. Alex's senses were already tripping into overload. A riot of peonies and beds of petunias greeted them from well-kept flower beds along the foundation of the building. Old-fashioned flowers, he thought. His grandmother had grown peonies.

"Paul Bunyan's shoe box, maybe," Jared corrected him. "It must hold close to a hundred people."

"Sixty could pack in, maybe. Sixty sardines, I mean."

Jared gave his uncle an appraising look, and Alex clamped his mouth shut. His nephew probably thought he was a crotchety old geezer.

"I know, I know," Alex retorted to Jared's unspoken reproach. "I'm living my dream-come-true." Alex parroted his persistently cheerful sister's parting words as they drove away from her house in Elmhurst, outside Chicago.

"Mom says God puts people in situations that seem all wrong but turn out to be great somewhere down the road. Like how I used to hate mowing lawns, and now that I have a little summer business doing it, I really like it, you know?"

Bless Carol's heart, Alex thought. *She's raising him right.* Of course the kid was still supremely annoying on occasion.

Alex was being shaped for something. He had to be. God had asked him to walk by faith. And then God had trotted him here. The sky was so big here, the land so vast—so utterly unlike anything he'd ever known.

"This is cool." Jared opened the car door and jumped out. Everything was either "awesome" or "cool" to Jared, including hot chocolate, summer days, the Sahara desert, and tanning beds. He ambled loose-jointedly toward the church. When Alex caught up with him, his nephew was staring up at the lofty steeple, head tipped back, squinting into the sun.

"Actually, my dream was more along the lines of an associate pastor position in a church in a mid-sized city," Alex said mildly, trying not to reveal his anxiety even though his heart was tripping like a drum major in the Rose Parade. "Some place offering lots of programs and several services on Sunday morning. My dream would have had an attached preschool and day care. And, if there was a par-sonage at all, it would be within five minutes of a grocery store and post office. *That* was *my* idea of a humble way to start." The worst part was, he'd almost had it. And then Natalie—

"Who needs that stuff? Here you've got pigs, cows, and…tractors and…wild animals and stuff…."

Jared was trying. Alex had to give him that.

"There's something I don't get," Jared added. "Why is this called Hilltop Community Church? There isn't a hill for miles. Why isn't it called Grassy Valley Community Church? That's the name of the town we drove through."

"This church isn't located in the town of Grassy Valley. It's out here in the country, in Hilltop Township, hence, the name Hilltop Community Church."

"What's a township?"

"I had to look it up myself," Alex admitted, feeling a little sheepish that he had so much to learn. "It's a subdivision of a county, with a local government that takes care of things like road maintenance—a community within a community, of sorts. The people of Hilltop are tied together by their interest in this particular area, and the church is named after the township."

"Oh," Jared said. He snapped his gum and took the steps to the front door two at a time. He tested the doorknob and the ten-foot-high door glided silently open. "There aren't even any locks." A shadow flitted across Jared's features. "Different from our church at home, isn't it? Mom still talks about the fuss everyone put up when the council decided that we needed to lock the doors when no one was in the church office."

Alex remembered it vividly. He, too, had hated the idea of having someone seek solace in a church and be turned away by bolted doors; but after several acts of vandalism on the property, what else could they do? Theirs was an inner city congregation, a beacon of light in a poor, tough district, a church his family had loved for years in a neighborhood that had aged badly. But here were open doors to welcome anyone who might come.

Alex took a deep breath and followed his nephew into the building. He felt immediately at home in the high-ceilinged vestibule, as if welcomed by the generations who had worshipped here. The floor, worn from years of footsteps, was solid beneath their feet and polished to a high shine. Two ropes, one thick and meaty, the other slightly finer, hung straight down from the ceiling.

"Bells!" And before his uncle could stop him, Jared grabbed the thickest rope and tugged. Something grated, and the sound of a clapper striking the inside of a gigantic bell gonged out its song. Alex felt the sound reverberate in his chest.

"Cool." Jared dropped the rope and pushed through a pair of tall, white swinging doors into the body of the church. Alex followed more slowly, soaking in the scents of pine oil and candle wax, feeling as if he were at a precipice, looking upon the sheer drop into which he was about to tumble.

"It's like landing on another planet," Jared said.

"You've got that right," Alex murmured. Planet Hilltop Community Church. "I guess no one will mind if we go in and look around." It was peculiar to feel like an interloper in what was now "his" church.

"Didn't the call committee want to bring you here first?" So Jared actually *had* been listening when his uncle told him what had transpired prior to being hired. Alex hadn't been sure, plugged in as Jared was to a pair of headphones. He'd been busy listening to music and eating bag after bag of chips all the way across Minnesota.

"Let's take the risk."

The interior looked more like a replica in a museum than a functioning church. Ahead of Alex, Jared followed the ruby carpet runner down the aisle toward the altar, his size-eleven athletic shoes making a squishy sound as he walked. He tipped back his head to stare at the ceiling. "What's that stuff?"

Alex followed the direction of his nephew's pointing index finger. "Embossed tin. The real stuff." He glanced down and paused to run his hand along the back of a pew, a curve of wood with intricate carving. "This is a masterpiece. Every care was taken in building this place. It's incredible."

Thanks to sunlight flowing through the elaborate stained-glass windows depicting the highlights of Jesus' time on earth, every bit of the church glistened. It was as if they were standing inside a jewel box. From a painting above the altar, a kindly, loving Jesus with small children scattered at His feet beckoned them forward. *Come to Me, all you that are weary and are carrying heavy burdens, and I will give you rest.*

"Are you scared, Unc?" Jared's question hit hard at the queasy pit of Alex's stomach.

"Scared?" He paused. "I'd like to say no, but I suppose I am, a little. This"—he tipped his head toward the church and the fields beyond—"is foreign territory."

Here I am, Lord. You've taken me a long way from home in so many ways. It is like another universe. He took a deep breath and opened his eyes.

He put his hand on Jared's bony shoulder. "But I'm sure God will bless it in ways I can't even imagine." He added a silent prayer to the end of his statement: *Please?*

*A*lex and Jared swung around at the sound of a small scuffle in the doorway. A tall, athletic, sandy-haired man in denims strode into the church, followed closely by a pretty, pleasant-looking woman with deep auburn hair and vivid blue eyes. Alex and Jared froze where they stood, guilty as children caught with their hands in the cookie jar.

"You rang?" the man said. His hazel eyes shone with amusement. A lock of hair flopped into his eye, and he scraped it back with his fingers.

Alex and Jared stared at him blankly.

"You rang?" he said again, this time tipping his head toward the entryway. "You rang the church bell?"

"Oh…sorry. That was me." Jared flushed to the roots of his hair. "I didn't mean to disturb anyone. Out in the country like this." He glanced ruefully at Alex. Jared's cheeks grew ruddy as he scuffed the toe of his foot and lowered his gaze. "I thought that no one would hear."

"But that's the reason you ring the bell, isn't it? So it can be heard."

Alex felt sorry for his impulsive nephew. "We apologize. I hope you didn't drive all the way over here to check it out."

"It isn't exactly a cross-country trip," the sandy-haired man said dryly. He was of medium build but his arms were tanned and sinewy—a man accustomed to outdoor work. "Takes all of three minutes to get here, including turning the key in the ignition. We live on the first farm north." He tipped his head in the direction that was, apparently, north and thrust out his hand. "Mike Carlsen. This is my wife Lauren. And you are…?" He let the question trail into the ether.

Alex took two steps toward the man's wife. "Lauren? From the call committee? I believe we've already met. Via the telephone, at least. I'm Alex Armstrong, and this is my nephew Jared. He kindly agreed to keep me company on the drive out from Chicago."

"*Reverend* Armstrong! So nice to meet you in person!" Lauren gripped his hand in a warm, firm shake. Once she spoke, Alex recognized her as the brisk, cheerful woman with an easy laugh and a rich, refined voice that sounded smooth and inviting as a cup of hot cocoa on a winter's day. That warm, husky, mocha-laced voice was difficult to forget. "I didn't realize you were coming today."

"Jared and I took a few extra days to drive here. I hadn't spent much time with my nephew recently, so we did some sightseeing along the way." He glanced at Jared, who was once again staring at the church's interior. "I'd planned to call you from the road to tell you I'd be here a day early, but then decided that perhaps I'd do some exploring unannounced first."

"No problem. We're accustomed to early around here," Mike drawled. "No matter what time the church organist gets here to play the prelude on Sunday mornings, there's a gaggle of older people already waiting for the music to start. She suspects they arrive the night before and sleep in the pews just to get her goat."

Jared's jaw dropped and Alex looked startled. Then Lauren's rich, hearty laughter spilled out. "Mike, quit teasing! Don't believe everything you hear, Reverend. Mike's sense of humor sneaks up on you sometimes." She waved him away. "Have you eaten?"

"We ate lunch four or five hours ago, but we still have some bagels in the car. We'll be fine."

Lauren wrinkled her nose. "So you *haven't* eaten. We'll remedy that first thing. While you are looking around the church, I'll go home and fix a little something. Mike, bring them to our place when they're done."

"That's not necessary," Alex protested, "you don't need to bother—"

"You'll soon realize that very little is accomplished around here without a pot of coffee and a plate of goodies," Mike said. "Rule number one is that Hilltop Community Church and plentiful food go hand-in-hand."

"We moved back to my family home to farm after twenty years in Fargo," Lauren said. "I'd nearly forgotten how much of a friendship ritual feeding of others is around here." She patted her lean stomach. "But I got the hang of it again very quickly."

She turned to her husband, who was gazing at her affectionately. "Give me twenty minutes." Mike nodded and raised his index finger in the air as his wife turned to leave.

"I'd be happy to give you the tour unless you want to explore the church for yourselves," Mike offered.

"We'd like a tour," Alex said. "I felt like an interloper just walking in."

"That's what churches are for, aren't they? Walking in, sitting down, praying. No one is turned away here." Mike's lip twitched as if he were trying to hold back a smile. "Of course, newcomers do have to endure a lot of curious stares. I suppose it's the price you pay for walking into a place where everyone has known everybody else for a hundred years."

Alex wondered how long it would be until he was no longer considered a newcomer or if that would ever happen.

"When we moved here, I had to go through that rite of passage myself," Mike added, eyes dancing. His even temperament was apparent in his every word. "After all, I was a stranger and I had married a girl from the community. I had to prove myself worthy. Now it's your turn."

Alex swallowed thickly.

"Don't worry about it," Mike assured him. "The people here are eager for you to come. We've been without a pastor for some time. They are ready to love you. We worried that we wouldn't find another pastor for our little two-point parish."

Jared suddenly tuned in to the conversation. "What's a two-point parish?"

"Just a way of saying that I'll be responsible for two individual churches with two separate buildings and two congregations," Alex explained. "Each church is too small to meet the expense of a pastor on its own, but by working together they can afford one. In this case, me."

"Not just anyone wants to come out to a small, isolated spot like this," Mike said. "It's hard to find someone willing to take it on. Podunk, USA, that's us. The economy hasn't done us any favors lately what with high gas prices and all."

That, Alex mused, was worrisome.

Seeing Alex's expression, Mike hurried to add, "You see, you really are a gift from God."

An odd feeling settled in the pit of Alex's stomach. He tried to keep his tone casual. "How many pastors did the call committee interview before they chose me?"

Mike's eyebrows practically disappeared beneath that lock of sandy hair. "How many? Only you. Nobody else would even talk to the committee. Something about the location or some such thing."

Alex and Jared glanced at each other. Jared's face had gone white, and Alex felt the color draining from his own cheeks as well. *No one* would even *talk* to these people?

"Of course, Lauren and the others took that as a really good sign," Mike continued, unaware that he'd shot a dart of terror into Alex's heart.

"A…a *good* sign?" Alex wasn't sure he'd heard correctly.

"Sure. We asked God to send us the *perfect* person for Hilltop, and He picked you." Mike had more confidence in his voice than Alex thought warranted.

"Obviously He didn't want our minds muddled with a bunch of choices and opportunities to make a mistake. No, Reverend Alex, you were the only candidate, hand-picked and hand-wrapped by God. I *told* you that you are a gift to us."

"No pressure," Jared said with a grimace as they followed Mike into the basement.

The expectations for him couldn't be higher. It was a recipe for unbridled success or complete disaster. At the moment, he just didn't know which. They'd driven past several ponds on the way to the church. Alex hoped they weren't deep. He was afraid that someone might ask him to walk on water.

They spilled out of the narrow staircase passageway and into a large room filled with long tables, surrounded by metal folding chairs. Sheer lace tablecloths and bud vases holding artificial pink roses softened the hard edges of the room. Simple ruffled valences cozied up the high, narrow windows. Off to the left, through a pass-through, they could see a sparkling kitchen.

"We like to keep things nice," Mike explained. "God's house and all. The community has a lot of fussy housekeepers. No dust gets by them."

Alex imagined an army of women marching, gimlet-eyed, brooms held high, ready to mount a frantic attack on smudges and dust.

Big white enamel coffeepots and gold and black serving carafes were lined in rows on the counter, and although he might have imagined it, Alex thought the aroma of freshly brewed coffee lingered in the air.

"What's that?" Jared pointed to a porcelain sink over which an old-fashioned hand pump loomed.

"There's a well beneath the church that was dug when the building was built."

"You mean there's no running water?" Jared's eyes widened.

Alex recalled the half-hour shower Jared had taken at the hotel that morning.

"That pump isn't hooked up anymore. We just left it there when we remodeled the church basement—sentimental, I guess."

The teenager looked dubious. His expression read, *What could be sentimental about a pump?*

"Lauren likes to tell about how her grandmother used to wash dishes after a potluck. She'd pump the water into a kettle, heat it on the stove, and then use it in the sink. More than once she pumped up a little lizard or a garter snake. They just slithered right out. That's why, Lauren says, they carried water from home to make coffee."

"Gross!" Jared shuddered. For once, something wasn't cool.

Funeral bells, hand pumps and snakes, a church kept clean as any five-star restaurant's kitchen, only one candidate for the pastor's position…

What else would he find in this strange place?

"We'd better go," Mike said. "Lauren will be waiting. I wish we had time to drive by the Hubbard house. You'd enjoy seeing it. We'll do it another time."

Alex wasn't sure what was so special about the Hubbard house, and Mike didn't seem in any rush to tell him. No matter. He'd find out soon enough.

Mike, Alex and Jared rode together down the long, straight road to the Carlsen farm. The road was flanked by windbreaks made of rows of trees that Mike referred to as shelterbelts. The gravel driveway led into an open area where several buildings circled the working part of the yard. Mike pointed out the old-fashioned wooden granaries, a machine shop, a storage shed, chicken coop, and bunkhouse as well as a shiny cluster of round metal grain bins as they drove up. A red barn loomed large over a fenced-in pasture that, at the moment, was occupied by a caramel-colored Belgian draft horse, a miniature donkey, and two brown-and-white llamas.

"Llamas?" Jared's mouth hung open. "Here?"

"They're Lauren's project." Mike shrugged. "She wants to raise them and use the fiber for weaving. She's always got some new project she's working on." As Mike spoke, a gleaming red rooster perched on the top fence rail fluffed his feathers, stretched to his full height, and crowed a perfectly splendid cock-a-doodle-do.

Jared pointed to a small building on the far side of the yard. "Is that a pigpen? Cool!"

The four-square house was old—built in 1909 according to Mike—but solid and inviting. "There are several houses like ours throughout the neighborhood," Mike explained. "Sometimes they call this style a Prairie Box. When you used to be able to order an entire house from the Sears catalogue, these square houses were easiest to ship. The Hubbard house that I mentioned earlier wasn't one of those, however. The first Mrs. Hubbard had very specific ideas about the house she wanted built."

"What, exactly, is so special about—" Alex began.

"A house from Sears?" Jared interrupted. "Like a kitchen appliance or pair of shoes?" Jared sounded incredulous.

"Hard to imagine now," Mike said agreeably, "but then it made sense."

He led them into the house through a side door that entered directly into the kitchen. "Lauren's grandparents always saved the front door for 'special' occasions," Mike explained, "And now we always forget it's there."

Cherry cupboards lined the kitchen walls and in the center of the room was a large wooden dining table set with placemats, frosty glasses of iced tea, and a plate of sandwiches large enough to feed a small militia.

"Welcome." Lauren ushered them in. "We've got tuna, roast beef, and my husband's favorite, fried egg sandwiches." Lauren gestured them to their places around the table. "There's leftover macaroni salad too. Sorry I can't offer you more on such short notice. I took an apple cake out of the oven an hour ago, so we can have that. I would have cooked more had I known you'd be here for supper." She paused for a breath. "Or do you call it dinner? Around here, dinner is usually what's served at noon and supper comes at six o'clock."

"You can call meals anything you like when they're like this." Alex admired the feast, mouth watering.

Mike winked at him. "We *told* you nothing gets done without food around here."

"You'll be fine here, Reverend Alex," Lauren assured him. "If you like food, you'll be okay. People around here *love* to feed the minister."

Jared studied the food-laden table and muttered, "Awesome." Alex, however, could only imagine his waistline expanding.

"Please, take a place, sit anywhere you like," Lauren encouraged.

Mike was the last to sit up to the table. He looked at Alex expectantly. "Would you like to say grace?"

He was happy to do it. This request would be made of him often from now on, he suspected.

They bowed their heads. "Lord, I am grateful for this opportunity to share this meal with Lauren and Mike, and for their hospitality. Thank You for safe travel and delicious food. Bless the people of Hilltop, Lord, and guide me so that I may become the pastor they are hoping to have. Amen."

And thank You for a fresh start, Lord. Help me to make the most of it.

"Pass the sandwiches," Mike instructed, "and dig in. I never pass up a fried egg sandwich."

Jared took one of the sandwiches, laid it on his plate and peeked tentatively under the top piece of bread. Alex was amused to see that the egg yolk was broken and cooked hard and looked like a big white eyeball with a yellow iris. It was liberally sprinkled with pepper, and both slices of bread were thick with melted butter. This would be very new to his nephew, he knew. He doubted his sister Carol ever made this fare.

Mike took a bite and chewed, a smile on his face. "The only thing better is an onion sandwich, but Lauren won't let me have any of those."

"Onions and what?" Alex asked. He'd never heard of some of the things people ate around here.

"Onions and nothing—except butter and salt."

"Don't you need meat on the sandwich?"

"When you order a roast beef sandwich with raw onions, what do you taste?" Mike asked and helped himself to another egg sandwich.

"Onions mostly, I guess."

"Exactly. Why bother with the meat when you only taste the onions anyway? Sad to say, Lauren taught me what an onion sandwich was and then said I couldn't have any."

"Why?" Jared shoved his sandwich into this mouth and took a huge bite. He looked puzzled and his uncle tried to suppress a smile.

"I had to pick between onions and kissing my wife." Mike grinned impishly. "What else could I do?"

"Oh." Jared blushed until he was the color of the barn outside the window. "I get it."

Lauren patted the back of her husband's hand. "He made the right choice."

Alex couldn't stop the smile he felt spreading across his features. He felt a flutter of excitement and a lightness he hadn't experienced of late. At the moment he was feeling sorry for all those other poor fellows who had passed up this opportunity.

"So tell me about your sister church, All Saints Fellowship. I don't know much about them."

Lauren and Mike exchanged a potent glance, and a blush reddened Lauren's neck and rose all the way to her forehead. "I'll apologize in advance for them. All Saints is an ironic name, according to some people. Wags around here think 'All Sinners' might be a better moniker."

Alex laid his sandwich down. "I don't understand."

"Some think the problem boils down to pure jealousy," Lauren said with a sigh. "Although I think it's more complicated than that."

"Jealousy?"

"Hilltop is bigger by half, so it has half again as many offerings in the plate. We put a new roof on our church and shored up the foundation years before All Saints could afford to do it." Lauren spoke as she stacked empty plates. "Then we remodeled the kitchen and laid new carpeting. That ruffled a few feathers too. Our quilting ladies send a lot of quilts to overseas missions each year." She appeared pleased by this bit of information. "We do nearly one hundred layettes and they can barely manage fifty. But the worst of it is that we give three times as much to missions as All Saints, and it's given them an inferiority complex the size of Minnesota. That may be at least part of the issue."

Alex was reminded of the petty jealousies that often haunted competing departments in his college. "How do they know how much your church is giving? Aren't these gifts supposed to be given quietly, without trumpeting numbers to the whole world?"

"When you give alms, do not let your left hand know what your right hand is doing, you mean? The two churches have always shared a treasurer, and those things get out. Of course that doesn't take Alf Nyborg into account...."

The doorbell rang and Lauren sprang up. Before Lauren could reach the door, they heard the screen door slam and heavy footsteps on the stairs.

A small, stocky woman shot into the room like a rocket from a cannon. "We have to kill them all immediately," she announced. "Lauren, you've got to help me!"

The little woman appeared to be a series of squares, from her high cheekbones and square jawline to her blocky shoulders, rectangular body, and stocky legs. She even wore a pair of shoes with broad squared toes.

"Hello, Mattie," Lauren said pleasantly. She didn't seem the least bit concerned about the mayhem the older woman was advocating.

"Poison. We need poison." Mattie's eyes glittered with malicious glee. "Do you think Sam Waters sells anything at the hardware store powerful enough to do them in?"

"Coffee, Mattie?" Mike said mildly. "We're going to have apple cake with ice cream in a minute."

"I'm so upset I couldn't eat a thing, I'm sure." Yet she trotted to the table and sat down with a thud on a spindle-backed chair. She made a lot of noise for a little woman. "Just a sliver, please. And the tiniest dab of ice cream."

Lauren smiled and stood up. "I assume the rest of you want some too?"

Alex and Jared nodded mutely. Alex didn't know quite what else to say.

It was only then that Mattie appeared to notice them. "Company, I see." She looked them over like they were fresh produce at an open-air market. "Young man," she said to Jared. "You'd better have a double piece. You need fattening up."

The teenager stared at her, deer in the headlights.

Lauren came back to the table with a slab of cake and put it in front of her newest guest. There were two huge scoops of ice cream on top. Mattie didn't even blink. It seemed that the word *sliver* had an entirely different meaning here.

"This is our new pastor, Alex Armstrong, and his nephew Jared. Alex, this is Matilda or, as we call her, Mattie Olsen. Hers is one of the oldest families in the community."

"Pastor Armstrong!" Mattie patted at her hair, and gray sprouts erupted all over her head. Unfortunately, it made it look worse rather than better. "Welcome to the Hilltop community." Her words were now warm and buttery, and her complexion deepened to a ruddy color not unlike beet juice. "Oh my, I hope you don't think I was rude. I'm not usually so impolite. It's just that I've been so distressed and we really need to do the killing soon." She nodded as if that explained everything.

Her eagle eye fell again on Jared. "And young man, you really are too thin. What if you got sick? You'd have nothing to go on." She patted her own ample midsection. "Now I, on the other hand... I'll have you over for *rommegrot* one day soon."

"What's—"

She cut Jared off. "It's a pudding made with cream, you know. Very tasty."

Alex marveled that she'd gone from murder and mayhem to clogging Jared's arteries without a beat.

Mattie's head spun again, this time toward Mike. Her mouth curled downward and the edges of her brow knit together. "Why wasn't I told they were here? I should have known. I'm an *Olsen*!"

"They arrived less than an hour ago. We found them at the church looking around. Other than us, you're the first to meet them," Lauren said soothingly, obviously accustomed to smoothing this particular bird's feathers.

"Oh, well then…." Mollified, Mattie turned again to Alex. "If you have any questions whatsoever about the church or the community, come to me. I've been here a long time and my grandfather was one of the first pioneers in the area. I'm familiar with everyone and everything."

Alex had no doubt she was. Out loud he said, "Maybe you could start by telling me who you are planning to kill?"

Mattie reddened and put her hands to her cheeks. "Goodness, I didn't make a very proper entrance, did I?" She paused, and her eyes narrowed. "Ants. Armies of ants, multitudes of ants, *legions* of ants. In the back entrance to the church. We've got to do something before we serve the next church dinner or they will be crawling on every counter. I wonder if Sam has enough poison for the job. Who did I hear was going to Minot? They could get more poison there."

Anxiety flooded her features. "I saw a documentary on imported red fire ants. Do you know they swarm? And that their bites are painful? Dreadful little things, ants." She stabbed her cake with her fork.

"That kind of ant doesn't live in these parts, Mattie," Mike said calmly. "Besides, I rather admire the little things. They're hard workers, ants."

Mattie glared at him.

"Why don't you let me take care of the ant traps and you put your energy toward those angel food cakes you do so well?" he offered. Alex liked his calm, pragmatic way of dealing with this obviously excitable woman.

"Mattie can make an angel food higher and lighter than anyone

I've ever met," Lauren said, genuine admiration in her voice. She brought the coffeepot to the table, poured it into five mugs, and distributed them around the table. When she set a cup in front of Jared, he made a face. Alex gave the boy a warning look. Apparently everyone around here drank coffee.

"It's in the egg whites and the mixing," Mattie said. "And years of practice."

"No church dinner here is complete without a piece of angel food with whipped cream and berries." Lauren smiled a little as she dealt cake out to the rest. "And some devil's food cake just to balance things out."

"Huh?" Jared choked on his cake.

At least, his uncle thought, he hadn't said "Cool."

"Years ago the church dinner committee decided that people didn't need more than two choices for dessert," Lauren explained. "They decided on cake, white and chocolate. Some jokester concluded that, to represent the battle between good and evil, the cakes should be angel food and devil's food. We've loosened up on the desserts now—there are usually several choices—but there's always angel food and devil's food on hand as a tip of the hat to the past." She blew on her coffee to cool it. "There's a story for everything around here."

"And a lot of hat tipping," Mike added. "Wait and see." Alex was sure he would see.

After Mattie finished her cake and left in her Chevy Impala—on her way, no doubt, to bugle to the community that the pastor had arrived—they sat at the table in companionable silence. Alex found the big country kitchen both inviting and relaxing. There were half a dozen bird feeders just outside the big picture window by the table, and a bird clock—the kind that chirps a birdsong on the hour—over the door. Quilted placemats, purple violets with fuzzy green leaves, and a radio softly playing country music in the background all seemed so welcoming and so apt out here. So many people to meet, so much history to learn and, no doubt, a potential minefield or two to scope out, Alex mused. There was always at least one touchy, tricky parishioner who could rile the entire congregation. Who would that be? He was in no hurry to find out.

"You two look exhausted," Lauren said bluntly. "It has been a long day."

"Why don't you just crash here tonight and start fresh in the morning? The parsonage can wait until tomorrow."

Alex's legs and arms felt heavy with weariness, and he could see Jared was wearing out as well. "It's tempting, but we really should…"

"I'll take that as a 'yes.' Get your bags and bring them upstairs. I'll show you the guest room."

He was too tired to protest, Alex realized.

They retrieved what they needed from the van and followed Lauren up the stairs to a guest room. It held a set of antique dressers, a rocking chair, several studio photos from the 1800s, and an open armoire filled with colorful quilts. The bed was large and inviting.

Both he and Jared were asleep as their heads hit the pillows.

"Are you ready to see the parsonage?" Lauren inquired the next morning after a hearty breakfast of biscuits and sausage gravy. "I'll put some milk, eggs and bread in a bag, so you'll have a little something to eat until you get to the store in Grassy Valley."

She returned with an entire bag of groceries gleaned from her own cupboards including fruit, cereal, caramel rolls and a quarter of the apple cake. She handed the bag to Alex. "The parsonage is just across the slough from the church. Seems to work out pretty well. You can see all the comings and goings from your kitchen window."

"'Slough'?"

"That marshy wet area beside the parking lot."

"The pond, you mean?"

"Those birthing rooms for mosquitoes may be called ponds in the city," Lauren told him, "but here they are definitely sloughs."

The parsonage. His new home. It was twenty-four years ago that he'd moved into his first apartment in Chicago, right near the college. At the time, to a broke college student, it was the Taj Mahal. Alex had eventually graduated into a "real" house, but had never lived more than a few blocks from campus. He thought he was settled in the Chicago suburbs for life. Of course, he'd thought he'd be married too, but that hadn't gone exactly as planned.

"I hope you'll be patient with me as we learn the ropes out here."

"You will have to be patient with us as well," Lauren assured him. "This is a new dance and we're first-time partners. We're bound to step on each other's toes occasionally, but it doesn't mean we won't enjoy the music."

Alex wiggled his toes inside his shoes, imagining already how many ways they could be trod upon.

CHAPTER FOUR

Mike walked Alex and Jared from the cool, cosseting interior of the Carlsen house into outside brightness, where split-tailed barn swallows with rusty bellies and blue-black wings reeled overhead. The Carlsens' corrugated steel grain bins glinted sharply in the intense light, and the glare forced them to shade their eyes with their hands.

"It's a beautiful day to move in." As Mike pointed a finger in the direction of the church and beyond, a big black lab with glossy fur and a tongue the color of pink cotton candy padded up to them. Mike automatically bent to scratch him behind one ear. "Hey, Laddie. Good boy." He looked up at Alex. "You know where you're going, right? Hang a right after the church. Then it's the first driveway on the left."

"Aren't you coming?" Alex hesitated. He didn't feel ready to be set free to roam quite yet.

"I thought you might want some time alone first, this being your new home and all."

Alex could see the wisdom in that. He didn't have great hopes for his new digs, considering that they'd been standing empty for some time. It might be better to see the place without an observer from the congregation. That way he could regroup if the house was not what he was expecting. He didn't want to start on the wrong foot.

"Good idea. But feel free to stop over any time," Alex said. Not only did he already feel a kinship with Mike and Lauren, but he suspected it could get lonely here on the prairie, with homes sparsely scattered across thousands of acres of land. Alex was accustomed to keeping the side windows of his house shuttered so that he didn't look directly into his neighbor's kitchen. He didn't know what all this space would do to him. He'd read Rolvaag's *Giants in the Earth* and knew of Beret Hansa's spiral into madness alone on the prairie. It didn't seem quite so unlikely to him anymore.

"Don't worry." Mike laughed. "People around Hilltop don't have any reservations about that. You'll see. By the way, the key to the parsonage is under the front doormat. Around here that's where most people keep their keys."

What, then, was the use of locking one's door? Or was that another formality that could be dispensed with now that he was in Hilltop? Alex imagined hoards of curious onlookers crowding into his home to examine the titles of the books on his shelves and white-glove the tops of his counters.

He'd be sure to pick up a dust cloth. But they'd be disappointed by the books. All he'd brought with him were scholarly tomes—theology, history, and the many he'd collected in his years as an English professor. If they looked in his closets they'd find his extensive collection of running shoes and the obscenely large bags of Tootsie Rolls and Hershey's Kisses that his sister had given him as a going-away present. If he had a secret vice for others to discover, it was chocolate. Bars, benign, Alex decided, but still a secret he wanted to keep. If the single ladies of Hilltop and Grassy Valley discovered he liked chocolate, he'd be smothered in brownies before he knew what hit him.

He and Jared clambered into the van and Alex turned the key in the ignition. He'd left the key in the vehicle with the doors unlocked. He was already losing his city ways. Where he'd come from that was an invitation for someone to take a joy ride in his car. Here, it seemed that the worst that could happen was a low-flying bird making its mark on his windshield. Alex backed the car up slowly.

"Cool people, huh, Unc?" Jared leaned forward in his seat as if willing his uncle to go faster. "Lauren's a great cook too." Spoken like a true bottomless pit of a teenage boy. "Very." Alex drove slowly, unaccustomed to the pull and shift of loose gravel rather than smooth pavement beneath his tires. Fresh gravel, his friend and mentor Edward O'Donnell had told him, was the nuisance of many rural pastors. Usually there was little time to spare between services at one church and another. On gravel, however, there was no speeding without the danger of going into the ditch or having a pebble fly up and crack the windshield. More rocks in the road to negotiate—literally.

They turned off the Carlsens' lane and onto another larger gravel thoroughfare, a county road, according to Mike. Someday the community had hopes that someone, somewhere would come up with enough money to tar or even pave it, he'd said, but things were tight in the road department these days, what with people behind on their taxes and all.

They passed the church, its fresh white paint making it glow in the sunlight, and Alex impulsively turned in the opposite direction of the parsonage.

"What are you doing, Unc?"

"Mike told me that All Saints is this way. I thought we'd just drive by and take a look."

Alex patted his shirt pocket and dug out his sunglasses. The sun was bright and the colors so vivid that it hurt his eyes. The sky, but for a few puffy white clouds, was cerulean blue. The fields were a fresh bright green and the tilled fields, a rich, velvety black. They passed an occasional farm, most of them with large white houses and barn-red outbuildings. Once, a dog raced down the road after them, barking, until they passed the territory it was protecting. Alex felt as though he was driving through a Norman Rockwell painting.

After about twenty minutes, Jared started to squirm in his seat. "Are you sure you got the directions right?"

"Mike said we could see the building from the top of a small rise. I was sure this was…" Alex's voice faded as they ascended what could barely be called a hill. "Look! There it is!" He pulled to the side of the road and they stared off into the distance where a small church nestled into the flatness of the countryside. Fields of various shades of green made a patchwork design around it. From here it looked like a postcard scene, so quaint and pristine that it could have been an artist's rendition of the prairie. All Saints Church's shape was similar to that of Hilltop, but the building was much smaller than its sister, and squat rather than soaring.

"Cool!" Jared said. "If we're going to look at it, let's go." Alex drove cautiously into the churchyard, feeling a little like he was trespassing, but Jared had no such reservations. As the car rolled to a stop, Jared flung open the door and burst out of the vehicle. "Maybe they've got church bells here too."

"Please don't ring them this time," Alex pleaded. "I'd like to announce my presence differently here."

Jared reached the church, grabbed the door handle and pulled. Nothing. The door did not swing open in welcome as it had at Hilltop. This place was locked up tight.

"I thought Mike said churches were for walking into," Jared commented. "So what's up with this?"

"Apparently not everyone agrees with Mike's philosophy," Alex murmured. He saw already that the Hilltop and All Saints churches were going to be very different.

The parsonage was a sturdy two-story structure with a green shingled roof. It was painted bright white, its radiance broken up by deep green shutters surrounding double-hung windows.

Peonies, tiger lilies, hostas, and salvia grew around the concrete block foundation, making the house look as though it had erupted in the midst of a patch of flowers. There were several hanging baskets of petunias and begonias blooming on the front porch, and the grass had been very recently mowed. The windows were partially open, and sheer curtains floated on the gentle breeze. It was as if someone was expecting them.

So this was his new home, the one God had planned for him. The flowers made it look like Eden.

He drove around the circle of gravel that constituted the driveway in front of the house and stopped. The house had large windows and an open porch that invited the sun into the house. His last home had been on a busy street, the sidewalks filled nine months a year with college students. He rarely opened his windows and allowed traffic noise to enter. Instead, he ran his air conditioner all summer long and lived in sterile, climate-controlled comfort. Here, all that would disturb his peace was the sound of chirping birds, hardheaded woodpeckers hammering on the surrounding trees, and the scent of flowers.

And were those tomatoes and beans staked up in rows in the black patch of earth nearby? Alex climbed out of the car and walked around to the side of the house. A butterfly garden of black-eyed Susans, daylilies, purple coneflowers, and marigolds grew between the house and the separate single stall garage. The butterflies flitting in the midst of the flowers mimicked the nervous fluttering in his belly.

"Are you *sure* no one lives here?" Jared stared at the flourishing garden. "Maybe we're at the wrong place."

Alex looked out at the empty prairie. He'd followed the directions he'd been given. This was the farmstead closest to the church. "We couldn't be. There's got to be an explanation. Let's look inside."

Jared reluctantly trailed in his uncle's steps.

The skeleton key was under the mat, right where Mike had said it would be, and turned smoothly in the old-fashioned keyhole. Obviously the church didn't want to keep intruders out very badly.

The door glided open, and instead of the musty, closed-up smell he'd expected, he was greeted with the aroma of Pine-Sol and lavender. The entry was cramped but welcoming. A small rocker padded in chintz, a brass floor lamp, a coat rack and a small bookcase took up most of the space. They wiped their feet on the colorful woven rug and moved deeper into the house. Alex stopped abruptly at the kitchen door. What in the world...

Jared bumped into his back. "Hey, watch it!" Jared ducked around Alex, peeking into the kitchen, and froze. "Whoa!"

The kitchen had fresh white cupboards, Brazilian black granite countertops, a black-and-white tile checkered floor and pendant lighting. The cozy eating area held an antique pedestal table and six chairs placed just so on a round red rug with roosters crowing around the perimeter. A massive gas range hunkered in a corner.

"They might have gone a little overboard on the remodel. It was just completed last week. What do you think?"

Alex and Jared almost shot out of their shoes at the sound of another voice in the room. They turned in unison to see the fellow they'd met yesterday, at the sight of the piglet spill, still wearing the Red's Gas & Garage cap. He stuck out a grease-stained hand

and flashed a pearly smile in a tanned face. His shake was strong and firm, just like the rest of his person.

"Dixon Daniels. We met on the edge of town yesterday when Ole and Twinkle Toes tipped over. Sorry I didn't realize you were the new minister. I could have given you directions or something."

Alex opened his mouth, trying to think of what to say, when Daniels began to answer the flood of questions raging in Alex's head. "Mattie Olsen—with an *e*—called me as soon as she met you at Mike and Lauren's, so I came over here this morning to open the windows and mow the lawn." Seeing the perplexed expression on Alex's face, he added, "People tend to meddle in each other's business around here. You'll get used to it. Why, sometimes word gets out about what I've done before I've even gotten around to doing it."

The man nodded toward a glass vase filled with flowers. "Tried to cozy things up a bit. Hope you like it."

"Like it? It's more than I ever expected." Alex gestured toward a single-serve espresso maker on the counter.

"Lauren led the charge to get the kitchen updated," Daniels explained, the toothpick in his mouth waggling precariously. "I think she gave you the kitchen she wants for herself, but that's okay. You'll probably be doing a lot of entertaining, right?"

He would? Alex's mouth gaped open but no sound came out. Fortunately, Daniels didn't seem to mind.

"Are you sure nobody's been living here? There's a garden." Jared jumped into the conversational gap. "My mom grows tomatoes," he added as an afterthought.

"Does someone else use the land?" Alex ventured. But he was still thinking about what the man had said about entertaining. His culinary skills revolved around things with "instant" and "precooked" in their labels.

"No, there's plenty of land around here without borrowing some-one else's. The garden was Lauren's idea too. The call committee decided to plant one here last spring so that the new pastor would have fresh garden produce when he arrived."

"But you hadn't called anyone yet, had you?"

"No, but Lauren figured the committee was making a statement to the congregation." Daniels looked at the pair of puzzled faces. "You know, reminding them that God will provide. She wanted to encourage everyone to have faith that we'd have a pastor by the time the tomatoes were ripe. You got here just in time."

Alex's head was still spinning when Daniels added, "Of course, it's usually that way with God, isn't it?" He took off his cap and scratched his head. His mop of brown hair appeared to have been cut with a gardening shears. "He's never late, but He's not known for being early either. He's always where He needs to be though, just in the nick of time."

Alex couldn't argue with that. While he was pondering Dixon's comment, Jared poked his nose into a walk-in pantry to the right of the refrigerator and whistled. "Unc! You're set!"

Alex flipped on the light switch beside the door and looked to see what his nephew was staring at. Food, of course. Nothing excited Jared as much as food. But Alex could see why. There were rows and rows of it—pint and quart jars filled with ruby apple rings, pale and luscious pear halves, flawless peaches, and pickles of every kind and size— slices, planks and baby dills—as well as what he could only guess were pickled watermelon rinds. And the tomatoes! Fresh from the garden to the canner—stewed, chunked, pureed and made into salsa— even at the farmer's market he frequented in the city, he'd never seen such a variety of home-canned delicacies. There were clear canisters full of flour; white, powdered and brown sugar; and miles of store-bought canned goods—pork and beans, pineapple rings and cream of mushroom soup, to name a few.

"You won't have to buy groceries for six months," Jared observed. Then he turned a canny eye to his uncle. "And you're going to have to learn to cook."

"It looks like it." God—or the parishioners—were certainly giving him a huge push in that direction.

"This is crazy." Jared methodically opened drawers and cupboards filled with pots and pans, cooking utensils, everyday dishes and flatware. Even the salt and pepper shakers were full. "They really meant it when they said Hilltop was expecting you, Uncle Alex."

Dixon grinned. "I told you so."

A fullness in his throat nearly kept Alex from responding. This quiet yet confident welcome overwhelmed him in ways a lavish party or a marching band could not have. They were his people, caring for him already.

While the foyer, kitchen and dining room took up most of the front of the house, a living room, bath and former bedroom turned office ran across the back. There were large windows in the living room overlooking a lawn that sloped down to the rows and rows of trees that Mike referred to as shelterbelts. A perennial flower bed was filled with salvia and day lilies and an annual bed of nasturtiums, marigolds, petunias, moss roses and other varieties Alex couldn't identify.

"Not bad, Unc!" Jared moved forward to sit in one of two leather recliners in the living room and promptly leaned back to put his feet up. There were more lamps and bookcases and a long floral couch like those that were so popular in a previous decade. The pictures on the walls were predictable—a rendition of the Last Supper, one of Christ praying on the Mount of Olives, several florals, and the traditional Gainesboro Blue Boy painting that seemed to grace all of the homes of a certain era. For a moment Alex was transported back in time to his grandmother's living room.

"There was a committee of ladies who spruced up the parsonage. Edith Bloch, Stoddard's wife—he was on the call committee—and Flossie Kennedy worked hard on this," Dixon informed them.

Alex recalled Stoddard Bloch, a blustery gentleman determined to interject his opinion into the conversation at every opportunity. Alex had thought he might have served better on, say, the building committee, where his comments on "shoring up the foundations of the church," "hammering everything into place" and "sawing off unnecessary expenses" would be more appropriate.

"I remember Mr. Block from my interview. Who is Flossie Kennedy?"

"Flossie is Horace Abel's housekeeper and she lives there with her son Charles, who runs an Internet business."

"That's interesting. Hilltop is very diversified."

"Some people wonder why Charles never moved on but mother-and-son relationships are complicated. My mother tried to kick me out of the house when I was twelve and she barely puts up with me now."

Dixon's impish grin told Alex that he said it all in fun.

"What kind of trouble are you causing her?"

Dixon laughed. "It makes Ma crazy that I'm not married and neither is my sister Emmy. Mom's itching for grandchildren and no one's very enthusiastic about giving her any." He smiled cheerfully. "Now I'd better finish mowing that last patch of grass behind the garage. See you in a few minutes." He sauntered off, whistling again, his confident, easy gait seeming to match his breezy personality. If there was a more likable personality than Dixon, Alex mused, he had yet to meet it.

By this time, Jared had tried out the sofa and every chair and settled on the big leather recliner. He leaned back and stretched out his lanky frame in repose. "This is where you'll sit while you are reading," Jared stated confidently. "I can see it already."

"Am I so predictable?"

Jared nodded slowly. "Totally."

Alex wasn't sure he was flattered. "Well, perhaps I'll be less predictable out here. This is as good a place for new beginnings as anywhere."

"Right," Jared said doubtfully.

Alex took it as a challenge. He wasn't a predictable, tedious college professor anymore. And he wasn't engaged anymore. He was a spiritual explorer on a mighty exploit, so he might as well act like one. That would show Jared not to pigeonhole his old uncle too quickly.

Alex stopped dead in his tracks at the door to the former bedroom, which was filled with floor-to-ceiling bookshelves, a desk even bigger than the one he'd chosen for his home study in Chicago, and a small, realistic-looking electric fireplace with an elaborate mantel.

"This is exactly what I've always wanted in an office—cozy, inviting, a place I can fill with books," Alex finally murmured. "*This* is where I'll be spending my time."

Jared's enthusiasm faltered. "Books give me the creeps."

"You don't mean that," Alex said lightly, even though his nephew's statement had an unfortunate ring of truth.

"You've got a great crib here, Unc," Jared said, putting his stamp of approval on the place. "My mom has got to see this someday."

"You'll have to come together next time," Alex said as they negotiated the steps to the second floor. "A visit from my sister would be most welcome." He and Carol were only a year apart in age. They been raised as if they were twins and the bond between them had never wavered.

They'd barely begun to discuss Jared's next visit when Dixon appeared again. He was sweating from exertion and his hair stood in unruly spikes on his head. His ruddy features gleamed with perspiration and he wiped at his forehead with the back of his shirt-sleeve. "Mowing is all done."

"I don't know how to thank you…," Alex began.

"I do." Dixon's white, even teeth flashed in his tanned face. "Mattie Olsen put a container of iced sweet tea in the refrigerator and a plate of cookies in the breadbox. Some of that would be thanks enough for me."

"Gladly." Alex found the tea and cookies right where Dixon said they would be, and Jared brought out plates and glasses. They sat at the big round table.

"So, Dixon, what can you tell me about this place?" Alex asked, pouring Dixon a second glass of tea. He'd slurped down the first with barely a blink.

"Everything."

Alex started to laugh and then realized Dixon was serious. "I've lived here all my life. I know this place as well as the back of my hand." Dixon's blue eyes twinkled. "But I'm not going to tell you everything all at once. That would be overload. I'll be glad to dole it out on a need-to-know basis. It would be my pleasure to help you along until you have your footing here."

"Much appreciated," Alex said with relief. "I'll need a guide for a while."

"Happy to oblige. It's a good place, Hilltop. It was settled by Scandinavians—Swedes and Norwegians. There's always been some rivalry between them but they got together long enough to build the church. It's a carryover from 'the old country.' I understand Swedes and Norwegians have always exchanged jabs over their nationalities. The church helped to erase that. And Grassy Valley is a fine little town. We have our issues, of course, but everyone hangs together and we muddle along."

The fondness in Dixon's voice was apparent. A good sign, Alex thought. "Maybe you could start by telling me a little about yourself, Dixon. I think I can handle that much."

"I'm just a simple farm boy, that's all."

Alex doubted that.

"I farm the same farm my great-grandfather did. He homesteaded it in the late 1800s and there have been Daniels here ever since. My great-grandfather and his son, my granddaddy, helped build the church. They came from Illinois. My great-grandfather and Lauren Carlsen's were friends back then, newcomers, all of them." He shoved his hat to the back of his head and stared up at the sky, a signal, Alex was soon to realize, that Dixon had a story to tell.

"In fact, the way my granddad told me—he was only a little boy at the time—his parents came across the prairie in a covered wagon. A storm was brewing in the west about the time they arrived out here and it looked pretty desolate." He gestured toward the tidy rows of shelterbelts that marched between many of the fields. "Most of the trees around here came much later, and my great-grandfather and his wife could see the windstorm rolling in, wheeling and raging across the prairie in a fury."

Alex tried to imagine it, a single, lonely covered wagon on an empty prairie, a sky churning with black clouds, a whipping wind and a storm bearing down. In comparison, it was a little embarrassing to consider his own trepidation at arriving at this new place with a cozy home, a surfeit of food in the cupboards and newly polished windows.

"Anyway, my great-grandfather saw the trouble coming and let the horses loose. He's just gotten his family tucked into a gully when the wind hit and turned the covered wagon upside down. There it sat, wheels spinning, like a big turtle on its back—and him with a wife and five little kids lying in the dirt wondering if they'd been sucked into a nightmare."

"Whoa." Jared's eyes were wide.

"I'm ashamed to say I've never given the trials of the pioneers much thought," Alex admitted, "until just now." It was interesting—and a little sad—how insulated he'd been from the raw beginnings of this country.

"That's okay," Dixon said generously, "you'll be giving it plenty of thought out here."

They sat together at the table in companionable silence for some time before Alex ventured to ask, "How about you, Dixon? It sounds like you come from a long line of family men. Do you want to settle down and have a wife and children someday?"

Dixon's complexion grew ruddy. "Not yet. I've been looking at the ladies, but there are so many pretty ones that I just can't decide who to choose." Then he flashed that winning grin. "Besides, most of the ones around here feel like sisters. One of these days I'll just have to get out of town and look around."

A car's tires crunching on the gravel outside the house cut short Alex's response as he and Dixon both stood to peer out the window.

"Well, look who's here," Dixon murmured.

*A*lex had seen wrecks in his day but this took the cake. The car was as patchwork as the quilt on his bed, every fender a salvaged part of a different color. The doors weren't much better. One of them he deduced—from the tape holding it closed—didn't work at all. Duct tape was the obvious remedy of choice. It appeared on a cracked rear window, the trunk, and the roof and was also used to patch and mend several smaller faults and fractures.

The man who slowly exited the car didn't look much better. He wore thick denim carpenter pants. A pair of pliers peeked from one pocket. Another held a hammer. The tools looked heavy enough to tug the pants right off the scrawny hips of the wearer. All his clothes were too large, including his cotton red and navy plaid work shirt. Over his salt-and-pepper hair, the man wore the traditional headgear of the area, a billed cap advertising Red's Gas & Garage.

Dixon moved to greet the fellow as if they were long-lost brothers. "Jonas Owens! Where have you been keeping yourself?"

"I haven't been getting out much." The man's voice was flat and unenthusiastic.

"Came to see the new pastor, did you?" Dixon gestured in Alex's direction. "Here he is, and his nephew Jared from Chicago."

Jared lifted a hand in greeting. "Hi."

"Actually, I came looking for a cow. My best milker. She wandered off through a break in the fence."

Jonas stuck out his hand and as they shook, Alex felt the rough calluses of a man accustomed to hard labor.

"Pleased to meet you, Reverend. I'm Jonas Owens. Welcome to Hilltop. It's a good place to live."

"At least it was," Jonas added under his breath.

"Jonas's great-grandfather was another pioneer who came to this area about the same time mine did," Dixon informed Alex. "He built a prosperous wheat farm here." Dixon pointed off in the distance.

"What a long, rich heritage you all have here." Alex hoped this was the right response. "I can see I have a lot to learn."

Now his nephew's head bobbed in agreement.

"I'll say you do," Dixon agreed cheerfully. "Just so you know, it's best to be careful who you talk about around here. It's not like a city full of strangers. I'm sure a preacher wouldn't gossip or anything, but if you did, you'd likely be talking to someone's great-uncle or third cousin."

"Whoever belittles another lacks sense, but an intelligent person remains silent," Alex murmured, quoting Proverbs.

"You've got that right." Dixon clapped Alex on the back. "I've got to be going now. I've got a tractor torn apart and lying on the shed floor. I should probably put it back together before I forget where all the parts came from. I'll see you in the office for coffee tomorrow."

"You will? What office?"

"The church office, of course. Didn't they tell you that you had one? We aren't *that* far behind the times out here. It's the cubbyhole past the foyer on the south side of the sanctuary. If you didn't know it was there you might think it was a closet. Yesterday I installed a new coffeepot and put a pound of nice full-bodied Sumatra in the cupboard for you and me. I've got a hard-to-find Indonesian coffee that we can try next. And I make a pretty mean mocha too."

Sumatran and Indonesian coffees? Mochas in the church office?

"And three pounds of Folgers for everyone else. That's what they prefer. I try to introduce them to new things, but they aren't very adventurous around here, at least not with their coffee. Most everybody still prefers egg coffee if they can get it."

Egg coffee? Alex was still puzzling over that when Dixon said his good-byes and pulled out of the yard in his pickup. Jared wandered off in the direction of an unattached garage across the farmstead, leaving Alex and Jonas to stare at each other, each shifting awkwardly from foot to foot.

"So, Jonas," Alex began awkwardly, "I haven't seen your cow, but I'm happy to help you look."

Jonas shrugged. "Come along then."

Alex crawled into the wreck of a car, trying not to disturb the duct tape that held the seat together. He said just a little too heartily, "Tell me a little more about yourself."

Jonas shifted uncomfortably, as if Alex had just asked him to explain black holes. "Like Dixon said, there have been members of the Owens family around here for more than a hundred years." His voice trailed away, as if he'd lost interest in the conversation.

"I'm going to drive out on that lane." He pointed toward some clumps of grass. There was no discernable path that Alex could see but he was beginning to believe that one could inexplicably appear out of nowhere.

"I've found her down here before. There's good grass," Jonas said. "Hang on." He pressed on the gas pedal and the car exploded across the yard and into the field.

Jonas hit the first rut and Alex bounced into the air and came down hard. It was a tooth-rattling ride but at the end was Jonas's cow, a brown-and-white Hereford with a sweet face, placidly chewing a mouth full of grass. She looked up at them with soulful eyes.

"Now how will you get her to move?" Alex asked. The cow didn't appear to be in a hurry to go anywhere.

"I'll send my boys over to herd her home now that I'm sure she's here."

Jonas didn't look particularly happy that he'd found what he'd been looking for, Alex observed. Something more than the wandering animal had to be bothering him. They turned around and Jonas drove slowly back to the yard.

"Thanks for the ride, Jonas," Alex said as he opened the car door. "Next time she's missing, just call me and I'll go out and see if she's there." Alex paused before adding, "Is there anything else? "Something I could do for you?"

Jonas's forehead creased and a look of melancholy shaded his features. "Could you pray for me and my family, Pastor Alex? I'd sure appreciate it."

"Consider it done. Is there something special…?"

Jonas shook his head. "Just pray. God will know what it's about. And welcome again. It's good to have you here." Without another word, Jonas shifted his miserable excuse for a car into gear, and with some grating noises and a few gunshot-like backfires, he drove out of the yard.

Whatever Jonas Owens's problems were, Alex would find out eventually. Until then he'd do just what he'd promised. Pray.

Jared popped his head out of the old garage. "Hey, Unc," he yelled. "There's a lot of cool stuff in here, come and see this."

Alex crossed the newly mowed lawn and stepped into the dimness of the old building. There were dozens of North Dakota and

Minnesota license plates hammered to the walls in tidy rows and a veritable art gallery of oil-streaked old calendars—1957, 1958, 1959— and all the way to the present. Many had obviously been distributed by the ubiquitous Red's Gas & Garage. Some of them had penciled notations about the daily activities of their former owners—things like "pick up baby chicks at railroad depot" and "State Fair begins." One notation said "See banker." Some things, Alex realized, never change, especially troubles.

Mike had said things were tight in the road department because people were behind on their taxes. And there was Jonas Owens's down-and-out appearance and demeanor, not to mention the trouble at All Saints. Beneath the pastoral beauty here was an undercoat of financial, emotional and spiritual concerns that he did not yet understand.

The garage smelled of grease and oil and reminded Alex of his Uncle Bert's auto repair shop in Naperville. He'd spent many a pleasant afternoon there in the perfume of motor oil, surrounded by tool benches, car bays and the jokes and jibes the three repairmen shot back and forth like lightning bolts.

His uncle was considered a fine mechanic and was never lacking customers. People always need oil and filters changed, tires rotated, or fluids checked. Here, it appeared that he would be expected to do that himself. A farmer was a jack of all trades, Alex was learning, and independent in ways that were difficult for city folks like Alex to comprehend.

Alex was growing to appreciate the pioneer spirit that lingered here.

Nostalgia hit him like an ocean wave. He longed to become a part of this tight-knit place someday. He would make time to study this wall of calendars and to discover more about the people who'd lived here before him. And he would go to Red's and pick up his own calendar so that, at the end of the year, he too could contribute to this wall.

There were old wooden boxes the size of steamer trunks lining the back wall. Some had ancient cast-iron padlocks with keys still hanging in the undone locks. Other, newer padlocks' shackles dangled open, all inviting exploration. That would have to wait for another day, however.

"I'd like to look more right now, Jared, but I'd better have you help me carry my things into the house. I promised your mother I'd put you on the train back to Chicago tonight."

"I don't want to go yet." Jared's lips turned downward and the light in his eyes dimmed. "It's not as lame here as I thought it would be." Then he looked up at his uncle with a more cheerful light in his eyes and a smile on his face. "I should stay here for a while. I don't want you to be here all alone."

Alex shook his head. "Your mother will be waiting for you, and she won't be happy if I don't send you home on time." And, Alex thought to himself, if what he'd seen so far was a hint, he wouldn't be by himself for long. There'd probably be a caravan of neighbors parading through the church parking lot tomorrow to check him out.

He had brought enough boxes for a family of four, Alex decided as he toted the last of them into the house, and most of them were filled with books, papers and music. His clothing took up two large suitcases and there were household things and more clothing his sister was storing for him, which she would send later. It didn't look as if he'd need most of it, however.

Alex carried an armful of papers into the office, where Jared had just set down a box of books—fiction, biographies, autobiographies and books on spiritual matters. Jared looked up as Alex entered.

"Hey, Unc. When are you planning to do all this reading?"

"Most of these I've already read and will use for reference." Alex lifted a leather-bound volume by one of his favorite theologians. "And the rest? I suppose there will be some long quiet nights around here, especially this winter."

Jared's eyes narrowed slyly. "Maybe you'll meet a nice lady out here. There must be some single women around. I wouldn't mind having a new aunt...."

Alex glared at his nephew until Jared's voice trailed off. "Now you sound like your mother. 'Alex, find a nice woman and settle down,' 'Alex, you don't want to spend the rest of your life alone....'"

"My favorite is 'Find yourself a wife so I don't have to take care of you in your old age,'" Jared offered unhelpfully.

"My sister Carol has been trying to boss me around since the day I was born. It rarely works. I wonder why she persists." Alex sighed and plowed into a box of books that had not yet been arranged on shelves.

Carol had disapproved of the women he'd dated in college, deeming them all shallow. She was probably right—who wasn't a little shallow at eighteen or twenty? They were all like steel, only partially tempered. People needed a little more time in the fire to develop into the people they were to become.

But he'd expected more of Natalie, a sociology professor at the college at which he'd taught. He'd expected loyalty, love...and faithfulness. Alex had been badly disappointed on all counts.

He should have listened to Carol. Life might have turned out differently.

At five o'clock Jared announced, "I'm hungry. What's for supper? A pizza, maybe?"

Alex heard his own stomach growl. Or was it tires crunching on gravel outside? He walked into the kitchen to look out the window that overlooked the circular driveway. A gray 1987 Buick Regal in mint condition pulled up slowly to the house. When it had come to a complete stop, the passenger door opened and a small, timorous-looking woman in a navy skirt and pale green blouse emerged. In her hand was a quilted dish carrier. A portly, gray-haired gentleman exited the driver's side. He rummaged in the back seat for a moment and emerged with a large tin cake pan with a metal cover. The kind, Alex thought, that his grandmother used to use.

Hesitantly, the pair started toward the house.

"Looks like we have company, Jared, and they brought food."

Jared popped out of the back room like a jack-in-the-box. His sandy-colored hair was in disarray and sweat beaded on his forehead. He looked flushed and warm from exertion. "Food? I'm starving."

Alex couldn't agree more. Hopefully this was some of the country hospitality others had assured him he'd see here. He hurried to the door before his visitors could knock and threw it open. "Hello, come in. I'm Alex Armstrong and you are…"

"I'm Clarence Olson—with an *o*—and this is Lydia. She thought you might like some supper brought in, considering it's your first night here and all." Clarence wore a pair of dark navy trousers, a bright pink shirt with a white collar and Italian knock-off black loafers with silver horse-bit detailing. He was the peacock to Lydia's pea hen.

"That's very kind of you. My nephew Jared and I were just discussing what to have for dinner and here you are."

Lydia looked disappointed. "Dinner? I'd hoped you'd eat it tonight… for supper."

He had to remember that dinner was the noon meal here and supper was eaten in the evening or he'd confuse everyone.

"Absolutely. Will you join us?"

"Don't worry about it. Lydia made the same meal for Jacob and me," Clarence said. "It's in the oven at home right now. You just sit down and eat if you're hungry."

Alex could see Jared's head bobbing and he was eagerly rubbing his stomach. "Will you stay and visit if we do?"

The man tapped a finger with grease embedded under his nail on the nine-by-thirteen-inch pan. "That's Lydia's special German chocolate cake. I'd join you for a slice of that."

Clarence took a seat at one end of the table and sat there contentedly while Jared filled glasses with ice and water and Lydia scurried about serving massive portions of tater tot hotdish. Alex had the impression that if he'd first met them in their own home, it would have played out the same way, with Clarence being served and Lydia doing the serving.

"Can I say grace, Uncle Alex?" Jared asked, igniting an approving smile on Clarence's and Lydia's faces. "Dear God, " he began in the same conversational tone he used with the rest of his family, "thanks for this great food, which looks awesome. Love those tater tots. Thanks, too, for this cool place my uncle will be living. You really take care of him, God. Take care of all of us…please? In Your name, amen."

"Why, that was lovely!" Lydia burst out. "So…cozy and genuine." She appeared more at ease than she had moments earlier.

"So, Clarence," Alex wasn't sure how to phrase this. "I noticed that when you introduced yourself you said your name was Olson— with an *o*—and Mattie Olsen said her name was Olsen—with an *e*. What exactly does that mean?" Alex asked.

"Traditionally, because of the Danish influence on Norway, the Norwegian surname Olsen is spelled with an *e*. When it is spelled with an *o*, it's usually Swedish. Olsen—Olson." Clarence appeared proud to impart this bit of information. "Mattie's heritage is Norwegian and ours is Swedish. It's as simple as that."

Simple? Hardly. Alex dug into his food. He would need energy to keep all this straight in his head.

Finally he came up for air. "This is a great meal, Lydia. This was the perfect welcome for us. Thank you so much." He laid down his fork. "I wish I could cook like that. I'd open a restaurant."

Lydia's laughter pealed throughout the room, a pleasant, unexpected sound. "Then you'll have to have some lessons. There are a lot of good cooks around Hilltop and Grassy Valley."

Alex turned to Clarence. "And what do you do, Clarence?"

"I'm a retired diesel mechanic. I worked for the implement dealer in Grassy Valley for years. And we farm a little and have a few cattle." He crossed his hands over his stomach. The buttons and buttonholes of the pink shirt were sorely strained by the size of his belly.

"You mentioned a Jacob. Is that your son?"

Lydia choked on a sip of water and Clarence's face turned red. "Lydia and I aren't married. We're brother and sister. Jacob is our other brother."

Now it was Alex's turn to flush. "I'm sorry, I shouldn't be making assumptions. Maybe I'd better study the church directory before I embarrass myself more."

"It's quite all right," Clarence said generously. "The three of us have lived together on the farm ever since our parents died. Our father went in 1975 and Mother in '86. We get along just fine, Jacob, Lydia and me."

Alex caught a brief movement from the corner of his eye. Had Lydia flinched?

CHAPTER SIX

*A*lex watched Lydia drop her gaze to her plate.

"Tell me about yourself, Lydia," he encouraged, hoping to draw her out and not simply defer to her brother on every issue.

"There's not that much to tell. I enjoy cooking, of course." She flushed a little. "And my jams and jellies usually win blue ribbons at the county fair."

"No kidding? That's great." Alex sat back and crossed his arms over his chest. "I haven't been to a county fair since I was a kid and my grandparents took me."

"I'm planning to enter my strawberry-rhubarb jam this year. My rhubarb plants were exceptional this year." Her voice grew animated as she described the large leafy plants with edible red and green stalks, but the light in her pale eyes dimmed when Clarence interrupted to impart information about the spring's weather. As he talked right over her, Lydia's soft, round features hardened into a scowl. It occurred to Alex that Clarence's obliviousness to his sister's feeling's might easily churn up a rebellious spirit in the mild-mannered Lydia.

"Liddy is the youngest in the family," Clarence informed Alex, "born when our mother was in her late forties. At the time, it seemed like a calamity, an embarrassment, you know, having a child at such a late age, but it turned out to be a blessing." He turned a fond eye on his sister, who was blushing pink as the single peony Alex had picked for the table.

Alex wondered what it would be like to be considered the family "calamity."

"But Liddy here took care of both our parents until they passed away, and now she's invaluable to Jacob and me. Quite the little cook and housekeeper, that's our Lydia."

Alex felt a little sorry for Lydia, caretaker first for her parents and now her brothers. Before he could comment further, the conversation veered into territory more pertinent to Alex himself.

"Have you met the Holmquists yet?" Clarence asked as he took a bite of his cake.

"Not yet."

"You'll like Mildred and Chester," Lydia assured him. "Mildred was quite a looker in her day," Clarence added. Lydia sent him a disapproving look.

"She's in her eighties now, but I remember her when I was a boy. Our father told us that every single man between the ages of six and sixty wanted Mildred for his wife, but once she met Winchester Holmquist, that was it for everyone else. She never looked at another man."

"He was a handsome fellow too," Lydia added. "And polite! I've never met another man with such lovely manners." She flushed. "But you have lovely manners too, I'm sure, Pastor." Lydia folded her hands in her lap and sighed. "Such a nice love story. So romantic."

"Romance!" Clarence erupted. "Lydia, you're a perfectly good woman if you'd keep your head out of the clouds."

Lydia pursed her lips and ignored her brother. That was probably what had kept her sane all these years with him under the same roof—ignoring him.

"Has anyone told you about the Bruuns yet?" Clarence inquired. "One of them is a little"—he put his finger to his temple and made a circular motion—"crazy. And those Packard kids that run wild around here! Let me tell you…"

"What about your brother Jacob?" Alex urged, eager to get the train of conversation on an alternate track. "You haven't said much about him."

Lydia and Clarence exchanged a quick glance that Alex couldn't decipher. The garrulous Clarence became suddenly secretive.

"Oh, Jacob is a homebody. There's not much to say about him," Clarence said dismissively. "Is there, Lydia?"

"Jacob is a little shy," Lydia explained. "He's a hard worker but doesn't leave the farm much." She flushed a little. "And he's a big fan of my pies, especially the crème ones and my lemon meringue."

Clarence snorted derisively. "You spoil him, Lydia."

She straightened and thrust her chin forward. Alex could see the faintest flicker of fire in her eyes. Her diminutive frame seemed to gather volume, and her mousy brown hair fairly bristled with indignation. "You don't seem to complain about my strawberry-rhubarb crunch or sour cream–raisin pie, Clarence. Or the cakes, cookies and those orange scones I serve with cream…."

Jared coughed into his elbow to hide a smile. Alex used sheer willpower to suppress his. If Lydia *were* ever to decide to resist Clarence's brotherly bullying, it might be an interesting match to watch.

Lydia insisted on washing the dishes while the men had seconds of her tender chocolate cake.

"You don't have to do that, Lydia," Alex said, but she was already scrubbing at the casserole dish vigorously, putting her whole body into it. There were damp curls at the base of her neck. "Relax with us. It will give me a chance to try out the new dishwasher later."

Lydia opened her mouth to speak, but Clarence beat her to it. "She doesn't mind. Our Liddy has her hands in dishwater three times a day. She's used to it."

"Yes, Clarence," she said meekly, but rolled her eyes at Alex.

A portrait of the Olsons was coming into view. So far there were just hints of the officious Clarence, the quiet Lydia with her deeply buried feisty streak, and the mysterious Jacob. Lydia, most likely, was the glue that held their household together. But she was underappreciated and, like a good adhesive, nearly invisible, only noticed when it came unbonded and no longer worked.

"Have you got plans for the evening, Reverend?" Clarence inquired, readying himself to settle in and entertain the new pastor for the rest of the night.

"My nephew is leaving on the train for Chicago in a few hours." Alex glanced at Jared, who looked away. "How far, exactly, is the drive to the depot?"

"I'd plan for more than a hour. It's better to be there earlier rather than later. The train pulls in and out again so fast it barely stops."

"Oh my, we'd best be going." Lydia placed her dish back into its carrier. "We don't want you to be late." With a hearty round of handshaking and good wishes, Clarence and Lydia made their way to the car.

As they stood on the front step waving them away, Alex turned to Jared and asked, "Well, what do you think?"

Jared chewed on his upper lip for a moment. "I'm glad I won't be around when Lydia Olson finally gives her brother what's coming to him."

Out of the mouths of babes.

The Olsons' taillights disappeared over a slight rise in the road, and Jared turned to his uncle. "I'm sorry I have to go home," he admitted a little sheepishly. "I'd like to find out how this all turns out."

Alex picked up the broom leaning against the wall. "What do you mean?"

"This place is full of stories." Jared's brow furrowed. "The people we've met—Lauren and Mike, Dixon, that sad-looking man Jonas, and now the people who just left—they've all got stories, and we've only had time to experience the first page of each of them."

His nephew was right. Hilltop was a veritable library of reading material. Alex would have to peruse and eventually understand it all.

"You'd better put your stuff in the car," Alex called to Jared. "Since I don't know exactly where the station is, I'd like to start a little early."

Jared's head popped out the door that led to the bathroom, a tooth-brush in his mouth, and nodded. He disappeared again, and Alex heard the sound of running water. Shortly he reappeared, grooming evidently complete. "Are you sure we have to go already? I wish we'd come straight here rather than spending time at the water park and sightseeing."

Alex recalled how much talking he'd had to do to convince his nephew to make this trip with him to "beyond nowhere," as Jared had so succinctly put it. He clapped his nephew on the shoulder. "Then we should discuss when you're coming back."

Jared's shoulders sagged. "Talk to my mom. She's got this thing about missing school. She won't let me do it. I'd stay away from school entirely if she'd let me."

On their trip, his nephew had made several comments in the same vein, Alex observed. "I wasn't suggesting that. You'll have school breaks, and there's always next summer. Why don't you look at your school calendar and call me with some dates?" Before Alex could pursue it further, he heard a vehicle pull into the yard.

He moved aside the curtain to peer out. It was Dixon Daniels again, this time in a pair of khaki trousers and an indigo knit shirt that emphasized the blue sparkle of his eyes.

Alex opened the screen door, and Dixon sauntered to the door and stepped over the threshold. "How do you like your new place?"

"Great, so far. Lydia and Clarence Olson were here with an amazing supper. We're beginning to feel right at home." He turned to his nephew. "Right, Jared?"

"Yeah." The boy's face was long and gloomy.

"You don't look all that happy about it," Dixon commented. "I saw another guy recently with that very same expression on his face. 'Course, a horse had just stepped on his foot."

"Jared's not ready to leave," Alex confided. "I don't want him to go either, but we'll both have to answer to my sister if he doesn't show up at the train station tomorrow."

"Leave a sock under the bed," Dixon advised the teen. Jared cocked an eyebrow. "Why?"

"Seed. Whenever my family went somewhere, we always 'accidentally' left something behind—a piece of clothing, a pair of reading glasses, a toy. My mother said it was seed for another visit because we'd have to come back to pick it up."

Jared brightened. "Maybe I'll leave the iPod. It belongs to Mom, and she'd be out here in a heartbeat if I left it behind."

"Don't press your luck," Dixon advised. "I'd recommend a jacket or maybe a belt."

"Gotcha." Jared glanced at his watch. "I suppose I'd better check to see if I've left anything behind."

He disappeared up the flight of stairs three steps at a time, and Alex turned to Dixon. "To what do we owe the pleasure of this visit?"

"I just washed my truck," Dixon said, "so I thought I'd volunteer to give you and Jared a ride to the station. It will be a long drive home, especially when you're anticipating your first night at the parsonage."

A load lightened in his chest, one he hadn't even known was

there. This place with its wide open spaces, sparse trees and endless horizon left him feeling exposed and a little vulnerable. He knew how to maneuver himself about in a seedy neighborhood, but this…

"That's very nice of you."

"No problem. I just have to make one stop to drop off a chain saw that I borrowed from one of your neighbors. His name is Mark Nash. I'll introduce you. You'll like him. Mark's a good guy."

"I believe God provided me with a very human guardian angel, Dixon—you. I needed someone with whom to navigate this first bumpy patch as I learn my way around Hilltop Township."

Dixon looked startled and then amused. "I hope I'm not an angel. There's no room under my shirt for wings."

They put Jared's duffel bag in Dixon's truck and set out. Dixon pulled out of the yard and drove the two and a half miles to another farmyard. A man was in the yard, his head under the hood of an old Jeep. A lanky dog sat at his feet. The animal, skinny and long legged, looked to be part greyhound, but had fur the pale silvery gray of a Weimaraner. She had a white head and a dusky ring around one eye like the dog in *The Little Rascals*. She looked like she had been put together by a committee with opposing visions. Her long, straight ears perked up when Dixon's pickup entered the yard.

"That's Dixie," Dixon said, pointing at the dog. "Mark picked her up at a flea market when she was a pup. Kinda looks like she came from a rummage sale, doesn't she, a little bit of this and a little bit of that?"

Indeed she did. But her tail began to wag in a slow, fanning fashion that indicated welcome.

"Good dog, Dixie. Smarter than a whip. She knows every car and truck in the township and only barks at strange ones. Don't be offended if she barks at you the first time you bring that van down the road. She'll soon learn who you are, and then she'll be silent as a lamb."

Alex remembered his Uncle Bert's dog, Wally. Wally had had as questionable a lineage as this mutt but, also like this one, was intelligent and sensitive. Alex had pleaded for a dog many times in his childhood, but his apartment building didn't allow pets, so his pleas had always fallen on deaf ears.

"Do you have dogs?" Alex asked.

"Hunting dogs. Labs. Willie and Wonka. They're pretty rowdy, so I don't usually bring them with me in the truck." A faint blush crept over Dixon's features. "They're more like pets than most hunting dogs. Don't tell anyone, but they sleep in my bed at night. It's great in the winter. We have plenty of two-dog nights."

Seeing the confusion on Alex's face, he continued. "You don't know about dog nights? In Alaska, mushers bring their sled dogs into bed with them to stay warm. If it's really cold, you might need four or five dogs. Most people are familiar with a three-dog night, but that might have something to do with the fact that there's also a rock group by that name. Like I said, a two-dog night usually works for me."

"Of course. Why didn't I think of that?" Alex murmured. Chicago seemed farther away by the minute.

Alex catalogued that bit of canine information, opened the door and slid to the ground. He would have to find a more polished way to get out of these high vehicles. The seats must be three feet off the ground. Long-legged Jared leaped out far more gracefully.

Mark's head appeared around the hood of the Jeep. He was a man familiar with hard work, Alex guessed. His eyes were sharp with intelligence and his expression good-natured.

He sauntered toward them, wiping his hands on an oily rag that had seen better days, but somehow he'd avoided getting any grease on himself. He wore his jeans and denim shirt like they were business attire. He looked nothing like the farmer in bib overalls Alex had imagined before he'd arrived in Hilltop. "Hello, Dixon." Mark's voice sounded cultivated and refined. "Who have you got here?"

"This is the pastor, Alex Armstrong, and his nephew Jared. I'm driving them to the train station so Jared can go back to Chicago. I thought I'd return your chain saw on the way." He gestured toward a building behind the house. "I'll put it in the shop."

"Pleased to meet you, Reverend, and you too, Jared. Welcome to Hilltop." He studied them with sharp eyes, and Alex felt a little as though he was being run through an X-ray machine. Dixie, the dog, was staring at them in exactly the same way, sizing them up.

Then her tail started to fan wildly. Soon her whole rump was involved in the welcome. Alex and Jared had been approved.

"We've spoken on the phone once," Mark said. "I was part of the call committee." Before Alex could respond, he turned to Jared. "Do you know much about engines?"

Jared brightened. "A little."

That was an understatement. His uncle knew that he'd taken the family vacuum cleaner, sewing machine and lawn mower apart by the time he was six.

"Take a look under the hood. I've been tightening belts." Jared darted forward and disappeared under the Jeep's hood. "The fan belt is fine, but your alternator belt is still a little loose. Mind if I tighten it?"

"Here's a nine-sixteenth wrench." Mark put the tool in Jared's open hand.

With Jared occupied, Mark turned again to Dixon and Alex. "How's Hilltop so far?"

"Good." Alex shrugged. "The church, the parsonage, the people... all wonderful."

"Mark's great-grandfather homesteaded here in the late 1800s, like everyone else," Dixon explained. "He came from the 'old country' like most of the Norwegians and Swedes who settled around here. The original house is gone. Burned in a fire. Still, this is the family place." Dixon moved his hand in a grand gesture that encompassed the tidily mowed grass, the newer ranch-style house and lush fields.

"So you've lived here all your life?" Alex nodded to Mark.

"Off and on." Mark slid the rag into his pocket. "I went to college, spent some time in New York working as a stock broker, saw the error of my ways and came back to farm a few years ago. One of the smartest moves I've ever made." He laughed. "I decided that if I was going to be involved with bulls and bears, they'd be of the Angus and grizzly kind."

"I don't have the stomach for the ups and downs of the market," Alex said. "People's emotional highs and lows are one thing. The financial ones are quite another."

Mark smiled knowingly.

Alex had always been diligent about money, not for his own gain, but for pet missions and charities that he'd given to for years and that needed support now more than ever. "I admire people with financial savvy. You're on the board of trustees for the church, I hope."

Mark and Dixon laughed out loud.

"He's going to be good, I can already tell," Dixon said. "He's already trying to put people on committees."

"Just so you don't put me on the potluck dinner committee. My mother was in charge of it for years. She said she didn't know how the ladies did it, but some years almost everyone would bring desserts, and another it was all salads. She started buying hams to have in the refrigerator in case all that came in was Jell-O and buns."

"I'm anxious to experience my first potluck at Hilltop."

"You'll enjoy it," Mark assured him. "Once Hilltop gets a look at you, you'll be fed quite nicely, I'm sure."

Dixon sniggered and dug his hands deeper into the pockets of his khakis.

"What do you mean?"

"You're single. As soon as the ladies around here think there's someone without a wife who needs feeding, they'll be right on it. You can expect two or three casseroles a week, I'd wager."

"Yeah, and that's only from the married ones," Dixon added. "The single ones are even more attentive." He grinned. "Mark and I should know."

A sense of foreboding shimmered at the edge of Alex's consciousness. The last thing he needed right now was romantic involvement. Only months before his wedding, Natalie had announced she was in love with someone else. If Alex had had his way, he never would have even heard of Hilltop, but now he was here. God had given him what he had needed—a fresh start—and he wasn't going to mess that up just yet.

"Until the single ladies know if you are a *serious* bachelor or could possibly be husband material, they'll keep feeding you. There aren't many new men moving to the area, so every eye will be on you. Trust me, Mark and I have been through it."

"And you are *serious* bachelors, I take it?"

"That's the public face," Dixon said cheerfully. "Otherwise we'd have so much attention that we'd be like pigs fattened for slaughter right now."

"Thanks for the word of caution."

Dixon clapped a hand around Alex's shoulders. "The Three Musketeers, that's us. Our motto will be theirs, 'All for one and one for all.'"

Athos, Porthos and Aramis. The inseparable friends from Dumas's French novel *Les Trois Mousquetairs*. Alex felt warmed and welcomed by the idea.

"Hey, Unc," Jared called, emerging from under the hood. "What time does the train leave?" He wiped his hands on a rag on the roof of the car.

Dixon and Alex simultaneously looked at their watches. "We'd better get going," Dixon suggested.

They said their good-byes, and Dixon peeled out of the yard, gravel flying from beneath his wheels. Alex sat back, feeling pleased that he'd met two men who could become good friends. He'd worry about the concerned women of the church later. For now, it was a start.

"I wish I didn't have to leave," Jared said as he slumped in the back seat of the extended cab pickup.

"Your mother says you've got some work to finish at home. Besides, the start of school is only five weeks off." Alex's sister and her husband had scrimped and saved for years so that Jared could attend The Academy, a fine private school with an excellent reputation.

"I like the social stuff," Jared said vaguely, refusing to look Alex in the eye, "but not the rest." He obviously didn't want to talk about it.

Dixon pulled off the highway and into a town called Wheatville that Alex vaguely recalled from their trip out. It was large enough to have two fast-food restaurants, a big-box store, a truck stop, an implement dealership and, apparently, a train station. Dixon drove directly to a picturesque but aging brick depot with a two-story central tower and a covered platform supported by columns and trusses. It was a veritable historic jewel.

They walked inside, and Alex discovered that the inside was even more charming, with high oak wainscoting, plastered walls, arched ceiling and maple floors. Dixon immediately sat down in the waiting room and began to rummage through two-year-old magazines.

Jared looked around, his eyebrow raised. "Why's it so empty?"

"When these depots were built, they were very busy. Now depots have very little staff and are open only when a train is about to arrive.

I figure, though, that high gas prices will wake people up sooner or later and they'll start using the train again." A train whistle in the distance cut into Dixon's speech. Jared grabbed his duffel bag and headed outside to the platform. As the train approached, Alex threw his arms around his nephew.

"I'll let you say your good-byes without me," Dixon said and headed toward the pickup, leaving Alex and Jared alone on the platform as a searing bright light bore down upon them, accompanied by the roar of an engine. The wheels screeched as the train came to a stop.

"I'll be back as soon as I can, Uncle Alex."

"Next time, you'll stay longer. By then I'll be better acquainted. We'll have some fun, okay?"

The conductor waved at Jared, the only passenger boarding. With a quick look back, Jared stepped on the small stool the conductor had put on the ground and into the silver train. Alex watched him wave from inside as the train's heavy door closed in front of him. Then the train jerked to a start and was gone.

Alex stood alone on the stone paving outside the quaint brick-and-mortar depot, watching the receding train. The station manager turned out the lights one by one. Finally, only the uncovered incandescent bulb over the station door remained lit.

Alex felt an unexpectedly lonely feeling in his gut, and he felt a rush of gratitude that Dixon was waiting for him in the pickup, no doubt twiddling with the radio dials. But how many radio stations could there be out here? How much of *anything* could be out here, even radio signals?

He'd remained calm and assured until his nephew boarded the train, but now the butterflies in his stomach were reproducing at an alarming rate. Why, he wondered, had he thought it a good idea to give up the security and familiarity of a tenured teaching position for this?

Because he'd had to, he reminded himself. Although the door to marriage had closed, God had graciously opened a window on a new life. Alex had put Him in charge, and he wasn't going to pull away now. Though his contract with Hilltop was open-ended, Alex had promised to stay at least two years. Twenty-four months—what would he be thinking then?

When he returned to the pickup, Dixon was leaning back in his seat and using a pen to direct the invisible orchestra playing on public radio.

When he jumped into the car, Dixon dropped the pen into the middle console. "Don't mind me. I played a tuba in the band and never quite recovered from it."

Another surprise…a fellow with a bent toward classical music. Alex filed the bit of information in his head, which felt very full already. Before he could comment out loud, Dixon's pickup roared to life and they left Wheatville as quickly as they'd come.

"It's very dark," Alex commented as the miles sped by. There was no way to tell how much ground they had covered because there was little in the countryside beyond the headlights of the pickup by which to judge their speed. A few distant yard lights glowed dimly. They passed very few cars.

"Blacker than a black cat in a coal bin," Dixon agreed. "But look at the stars!"

Alex rolled down his window and tipped his head out to look at the sky, his dark, short-cropped hair ruffled by the wind. "It's like the planetarium back home. We never see stars like this in the city. There is too much light from streetlights, signs, buildings and cars to see more than the very brightest ones. Here it feels as if you could reach up and touch them."

"I can't imagine living without stars."

"I can't either—now. I was shortchanged." Alex enjoyed the cool, damp smell of the night air. "Even our family vacations were spent in cities. My mother wasn't much for green grass and the crawling critters that come with it. My grandparents had a cabin on Lake Michigan, but it was a very populated area so it almost felt like a small city as well."

"Can you see the Big Dipper?"

Alex craned his neck to see the distinct grouping of seven stars that created a rough outline of a large ladle-like dipper. "I can. There's the North Star. Polaris," he added, recalling his many visits to the planetarium as a child. "But what's that over there?" He pointed to the north, along what he knew to be the curve of the earth where an undulating curtain of pale iridescent green shimmered east to west across the sky. "It's beautiful."

"Aurora borealis," Dixon said. "Northern lights."

"Astounding." Alex was mesmerized by the ghostly presence of the shifting, flickering striations. He wished Jared were here to see this.

"Their visibility increases with your proximity to the North Pole. During the winter we often think we *are* at the pole. Only thing missing is polar bears and penguins. We have long nights. Lights are most visible then."

The diffuse glow was riveting, mysterious, like God's window curtains floating on a heavenly breeze. Alex didn't want to shift his gaze. "What causes it?"

"It's an interaction between Earth's magnetic field and solar wind." Dixon hesitated and then chuckled. "It's a little like what happens at Hilltop sometimes. Some people are magnets and others are wind. When they collide, something always happens that lights up the sky. Fireworks."

Alex closed his eyes. Now he couldn't even look at the sky without being reminded of the vast responsibilities of his new job.

Finally his curiosity got the best of him. "Are you going to tell me who you mean when you talk about magnets and wind?"

"Don't you want to find out for yourself?" Dixon's voice was teasing and his eyes glinted impishly in the greenish glow of the dashboard. "I'd imagine there will be quite a thrill in the discovery. Like a puzzle—who tends to get under everyone's skin, who the local troublemakers are, who's the queen bee in the church kitchen...."

Alex heard himself sigh. "I'm not a twentysomething pastor, and I want to make it work. With God's help I want to make this experience a blessing for everyone—even me."

"Music to my ears, Reverend. Frankly, I wasn't sure we'd ever get a pastor like you—still youthful and enthusiastic about growing the church. I thought we'd get someone shaken out of the blankets of retirement."

"Young and passionate? Dixon, you have a silver tongue." The rest of their ride seemed like eons to Alex. They drove through inky blackness cut only by the beam of Dixon's headlights. They discussed the weather, which Dixon assured him was glorious in the summer and fall and tundra-like in the winter, and conversed about the crops grown in the area—wheat, barley, oats, peas, corn and sunflowers.

"It's a tightrope we walk," Dixon commented. "Too much rain can be as bad for farmers as too little. It's a balancing act with nature."

"It must take nerves of steel to plant a crop and wait months to see if there's a return or not."

"Farmers are betting men. We're always rolling nature's dice, gambling on the weather and holding our collective breaths until the last grain is in the bin. Only then do we know if we've won or lost."

It was after one in the morning when Dixon pulled the Jeep up next to the steps to the parsonage. "Here you are, Reverend. You should sleep fast, because your day will start hot and heavy tomorrow. I figure you'll get at least one breakfast quiche and a pan of fresh sweet rolls by 8:00 AM. Put the coffeepot on early."

∾

Alex was glad he'd left a light on. As he came inside, he shed his shoes on the rag rug in the front entry and headed for the kitchen. There were no streetlights, and the darkness on the prairie was like nothing he'd ever experienced. Lydia had left the German chocolate cake on the counter, wrapped in foil, and he wasn't about to let it go to waste. He poured a huge glass of milk, cut a slice of cake almost the size of the salad plate he was using and ate it standing up.

When he had cleaned his plate, he took the stairs two at a time, and without undressing, lay down on the bed. He was asleep almost before his head hit the pillow.

Unfortunately, his night's sleep was fraught with dreams of Mattie Olsen on a murderous rampage, ants the size of mice invading the parsonage, Dixon and Mark building a barricade at the end of the driveway to stop the flow of quiches, and a long train whisking his nephew into the night.

On Wednesday morning he woke up exhausted.

He peered out the window to make sure that there were no gargantuan ants or a quiche-proof barricade. When he was sure everything he'd experienced last night was truly a dream, he showered, shaved and chose his clothing carefully.

What did one wear to work on the first day of being a pastor? A suit seemed too formal, and denim impossibly casual, so he settled on a pair of light-colored khakis, a blue and white plaid shirt, and a navy tie. Approachable, friendly and professional, he hoped, attire that sent a signal that said he was here to work and to be available to those who had hired him.

Then he sat down on the corner of the bed, shoulders sagging, hands clasped limply between his knees. For a moment, feelings of insufficiency nipped at him. But only for a moment.

"I won't stand for this," he announced into the silence and rose to his full six-foot height. "The *Lord* is my shepherd!" he reminded himself. He had that to claim no matter how much doubt and fear assailed him.

Alex walked into the kitchen. The sun was shining across the walls and the black-and-white kitchen floor, and Alex looked around with satisfaction and a little trepidation. The kitchen was so beautiful and professional looking that he felt a sense of obligation settling around his shoulders. No more Pop-Tarts and black coffee for breakfast. This was a new, fresh start. Suddenly he craved a bowl of steel-cut oatmeal and a banana.

He settled for a homemade, individually wrapped cinnamon roll from the freezer, an apple left over from his cross-country trip with Jared and a vow to do better nutritionally tomorrow.

He felt a little silly driving his van to the church, considering it was less than a mile from the house, but the property between the two structures was low and swampy.

Alex pulled into the churchyard and noticed something sitting behind the church that he'd somehow missed in his first tour—two tidy outhouses sitting side by side. He moved forward slowly, a little unsure about the etiquette for approaching an outdoor toilet. The doors for these intriguing structures were on opposite sides, which Alex could see would provide privacy, and crescent moons carved in the eaves provided vents and light. They were little different from the portable toilets provided for concerts and sports events in the city,

Alex thought. He knocked lightly on one of the doors and pushed it open. It was dusky, and motes of dust danced in the light seeping through the crescent moon opening. It was a two-holer, with a third, smaller hole meant for a child. The paper was kept in three-pound coffee cans, he noted; and, oddly, there were framed pictures from a Sears catalogue hanging on the wall.

Alex backed out of the small space. Impressive. It was as tidy and well cared for as everything else he'd seen. Even in the details, Hilltop did not disappoint.

He walked toward the small but immaculately manicured cemetery. It was rimmed with an ornamental black steel fence, the top of which was a series of extended spear-pointed pickets. Headstones of varying colors and shades of granite marched in neat rows across the pristinely mowed grass.

An unsightly plastic bag was caught on the fence in the far corner, so Alex walked the outside rim of the fence, pulled the bag down, crumpled it up in his hand and headed back in the way he had come. He glanced back over his shoulder and slowed his step. There was a large rectangle of dirt covered with weeds and crab grass that had sunk a few inches beneath the level of the ground around it. A grave? He retraced his steps and stared over the fence at the rough, patchy ground, reminding himself to ask someone why this relatively fresh grave had no apparent marker.

Stepping into the church was like stepping into a cool, silent womb. In the foyer, he turned to the right, through the pair of open doors to the nave, and felt his breath catch in his throat. The sun was doing dazzling things to and through the stained-glass windows. Ruby, scarlet, emerald, cobalt, amber, yellow, purple, orange and pink, the windows looked like bright gems. The light splashed through them and across the walls and floor. It was like being inside a kaleidoscope.

He dropped into the last pew and stared at the window depicting Jesus and the little children. Beneath the window on a brass plate read the words, *Let the little children come to me; do not stop them; for it is to such as these that the kingdom of God belongs. Truly I tell you, whoever does not receive the kingdom of God as a little child will never enter it (Mark 10:14–15).*

Alex loved children. Not so long ago he'd anticipated starting a family. He and Natalie had discussed it often. She'd been as anxious as he to have children. Not anymore, apparently.

No use dwelling on the past, Alex told himself grimly. It was time to meet the day.

He ventured into the back, and discovered that his office was little more than a large walk-in closet that had been created by simply building one room inside another. The larger room, Mike had told him, was once used for Sunday school and overflow crowds at weddings and funerals. It was now home to a series of coatracks, stacks of folding chairs, extra boxes of mouse poison, Christmas greenery and Alex's office. Two outside windows in the back wall of his space let in a pleasant amount of light.

A narrow desk ran parallel to the back wall. Alex was glad for that. He didn't relish being a vast desk's width away from people he counseled. There was so much to be read in a person's eyes, so many unintended flickers of emotion, that he wanted to be close to read the messages there. Off to the right sat a small desk that looked as though it had seen many students through high school before being donated here. It held a phone, a series of neatly laid out pens, and a large photo of a golden retriever. The dog's big licorice-drop nose and lolling red tongue were so well captured that they appeared to press against the glass of the frame.

A rolling computer stand and a dented beige file cabinet stood like sentinels on either side of a coffee cart. Alex found both caffeinated and decaf in the drawer of the cart, as well as an assortment of what his grandmother referred to as "store-bought" cookies—Pecan Sandies, Fig Newtons, shortbread, Nutter Butters and frosted lemon cookies.

The room was painted an innocuous pale gold color and the carpet was a mousy brown Berber, the kind of rug practical people bought because it "didn't show dirt." There were bookshelves lining available walls, all crowded with old hymnals and the detritus of pastors past.

"I can live with this," Alex said out loud. It was certainly no worse than his office at the college, which he'd shared with two colleagues, a monolith of a copy machine, and a steam cleaner for carpets that had appeared one day and never been retrieved.

Next he dug around in a plastic box on the bottom shelf of the tea cart for coffee filters. Dixon's Sumatra was there, just as he had promised.

He trotted to the basement kitchen to get water, and as soon as the coffee was brewing, Alex sat down behind his desk to try it on for size. The chair fit like a well-worn pair of shoes and he settled into it with a contented sigh. He was ready to work. But his flock must have smelled the coffee brewing. He might as well have made an announcement over a loudspeaker, because people began to arrive.

A blond woman with hair as wiry as a Brillo pad poked her nose through the office door. She sneezed.

"Allergies?" he asked sympathetically, having been sensitive to ragweed his entire life.

"Pollens, molds, dust mites, dogs, cats. Don't mind me." She put a large box of tissues and her purse on the smaller desk. "It's that time of year. Once the snow comes, I'll be fine. Sorry to be a little late. I had to drive my husband to work. His truck wasn't working and he has to be in early on Wednesdays."

She was slim, energetic looking, and of indeterminate age. Alex guessed her to be somewhere between forty and fifty, but he'd been wrong before. It was difficult to tell from the lumpy pink sweater and multicolored beaded necklace she wore or to see beyond the dramatic sweep of thick brown eyeliner circling each eye. With makeup that was more subtle, she could be quite attractive.

She noticed him studying her and her hands flew to her head. "Don't look at my hair!" she pleaded. "My hairdresser said it would grow out in six months. I'm never letting my sister-in-law touch my hair again, I'm telling you. It's a wonder that we're still speaking. I should have learned after that time she accidently colored it orange. Turning the other cheek should not apply to perms and color treatments."

Without giving him time to respond, she thrust out her hand in greeting. "You must be the new pastor. I'm Gabriella Andrea Dunn, your church secretary. People just call me Gandy, for short."

Alex took a deep breath, hoping Ms. Dunn had not sucked all the air out of the room with her introductory speech. "Alex Armstrong. It's nice to meet you, Ms. Dunn."

She scrunched her brows together. "It's Gandy. We aren't terribly formal here in Hilltop. We're all God's children, right? That makes us siblings. None of my siblings call me 'Ms. Dunn.'"

"Very well, then, Gandy." He rather liked her reference to being siblings in God. He hadn't thought of it quite that way before, but he relished the idea. "But you have a picture of a dog on your desk. If you have allergies…"

Gandy looked as him as if he were three bales short of a load. "I have allergies but I also have *priorities*, and dogs are *priorities*."

Alex cleared his throat. She was a woman who knew her mind. And Alex suspected she might know a whole lot about how things were done around this church. "Gandy, I have a question…."

"Ask me anything. If I know the answer I'll give it to you. If I don't, I'll find it for you."

"I was looking around outside and noticed the outhouses…."

"They're kept nicely, aren't they," Gandy asked with a note of pride in her voice. "Since we got the fire-breather, we've talked about tearing them down, but folks like them, especially in the summer months."

"The fire-breather?" Alex already regretted his inquiry.

"We don't have sewage or septic out here, so we've installed what's called a waterless incinerating toilet. When you flush, it ignites and burns up the…you know. It runs on propane. Works great, and we like an indoor biffy in the winter, but it's nice to get outside the rest of the time. Besides, it's a little alarming to flush a toilet and hear something give a roar and burst into flames right where you were sitting." She looked up at him expectantly. "Anything else you need to know?"

It took a moment for him to regain his composure. "About those pictures in the outhouse…"

"The ones taken from an old Sears, Roebuck catalogue? That was Inga Sorenson's idea. She thought it would be cute to have a memento of the past so she framed those pages. Get it?"

Gandy read the confusion on Alex's features and forged on. "Catalogues are what they used to use before toilet paper came along."

The light dawned. "Oh." Alex quickly changed the subject. "So how did you know I'd arrived? Or do you come in every day?"

"Mattie Olsen told me you were here, so I called Dixon to get the scoop."

Somehow that didn't surprise Alex. Word traveled as fast here as it did on the Internet.

"Then I'm sure you know more about me than I do about you. I wasn't even sure the church provided a secretary."

She snorted in a very unladylike fashion. "They don't provide one. Just me."

"But I thought you were…"

"I'm the church secretary all right," Gandy said amiably. "I'm just not paid to do it."

"We should see to that immediately!" It was a horrible oversight.

She waved her hands. "No, no! You don't understand. I'm a permanent volunteer, that's all. Money is tight around our house and most of what we have goes toward living expenses. I work at the church as my tithe, giving to God from what I have. In this case it's my work. We figure out what we earn a year and take ten percent of that. From that I determine how many hours I'll need to work in order for it to be our tithe. You should pray my husband gets a raise—then I'll be full time." She grinned happily and Alex saw that there was a bone-deep cheerfulness about the woman. Hardscrabble as her life might be, she'd taken lemons and made lemonade.

"Where do you live, Gandy? Near the church?"

"No, I live on the edge of Grassy Valley. My husband Mac drives a fuel truck for Red's. I feel like I'm part of Hilltop, though. I grew up here on Jonas Owens's place. Obadiah Owens was my grandfather. You'll meet my brother sooner or later." A shadow slipped fleetingly across her features like a cloud briefly obscuring the sun.

"I already did. He stopped by the parsonage."

"Really. *Hmm.*" The garrulous Gandy was suddenly subdued.

Before he could formulate a question about Gandy's brother, she pulled a plastic sandwich bag out of her purse. It was filled with small brown lumps dusted with something white that looked like chalk powder. She thrust it at him proudly. "Here, I brought you a treat—puppy chow."

He looked at the bag now in this hand. "But I don't have a dog."

Surprise and then amusement, spread over Gandy's sharp features and she laughed out loud. "It's for you, Pastor, not your dog!"

"But puppy chow…?"

"Taste it first, decide later." Gandy sat on the edge of the desk with an air of anticipation. Her thin body quivered with expectancy as she watched him cautiously study the bag.

Alex opened the bag and sniffed. The aroma of chocolate filled his nostrils. His eyes widened. "Is this what I think it is?"

"Try it, you'll like it." Gandy had her hands pressed together in suppressed excitement, obviously delighted to flabbergast the new pastor right off the bat.

Trust in the Lord with all your heart.... Reluctantly, Alex stuck his hand in the bag and pulled out a chunk of the light, airy stuff. Slowly he put it into his mouth and bit down. Then his eyes lit. "It is chocolate!"

"Crispy rice cereal squares, butter, melted chocolate, peanut butter and powdered sugar," Gandy told him. "It's my kids' favorite snack. I made a whole container just for you." She reached into the voluminous bag she'd put on the floor and brought out the treasure.

"It's delicious. Thank you." He dusted powdered sugar off his hands and the front of his shirt. "Do you give out your recipes? My nephew Jared would love this. I'd like to surprise him with it on his next visit."

Gandy looked him up and down like a meat inspector examining a hanging carcass. "You won't have to cook for yourself for a long while, I expect. There will be a lot of people wanting to help you put meat on those bones. By the way, there's a quiche on the back pew that Lolly Roscoe brought by. Do you want me to put it in the church refrigerator, or will you run it to the parsonage yourself?"

Alex was always grateful for his slim physique. He kept it that way by running and working out. His blood pressure rarely varied from 120/70, and he had a cholesterol level worth crowing about. He could see that he was a good physical specimen destined to become a fatted calf.

She turned away and busied herself scrawling something in longhand on a sheet of paper. Then, with a flourish, Gandy put the paper into Alex's hand.

"There you have it. Enjoy."

PUPPY CHOW
FROM THE KITCHEN OF GANDY DUNN

- ½ cup butter (some people leave this out)
- I cup creamy peanut butter
- 2 cups chocolate chips (sometimes I use semisweet chocolate, which is good too)
- Crispy rice or corn cereal squares (9 cups or a box worth)
- I pound powdered confectioner's sugar (experiment—you can probably use a little less)

Melt the butter, peanut butter and chocolate in a saucepan. Pour it over the cereal, tossing it gently until it is well coated. (Hint: I put the chocolate-coated cereal in a large paper bag, seal it and then shake it.)

* It's hard to ruin, Reverend, and I'd be surprised if you could.

This was his first recipe for his new kitchen. It pleased him more than he could have predicted. Maybe he would become a cook out here among so many good ones. Then he could knock his sister's socks off when she came to visit. But he'd have to collect more recipes than one. He made a mental note to ask Lydia for her German chocolate cake recipe. And another to learn to cook things that weren't chocolate.

Gandy clapped a hand across her mouth and her blue eyes grew large. "I'll bet I interrupted something important when I handed you that puppy chow. You were probably writing your sermon for Sunday. Don't pay attention to me. Just hand me the Bible readings and hymn numbers when you're ready for me to put them in the bulletin." She plopped down at her desk, took the plastic cover off the keyboard to her computer—an elderly machine that had been purchased in the dark ages of the computer era—and busied herself booting it up.

Alex felt like a slacker because the idea of writing his sermon hadn't entered his mind yet. He retreated guiltily to his own desk and turned to his own computer, which was considerably newer than Gandy's. What would he say on Sunday?

It probably wasn't wise to mention that he felt like he'd landed on another planet when he'd arrived. Was it only a couple days ago? It seemed like a lifetime already. He'd tell them how God called him into ministry and to Hilltop, and share his dreams for the church. This was his formal introduction to the church family, after all. He wanted people to know what they were getting.

For the moment, he would busy himself with reading a few past bulletins to see how things had been done. He would take the church directory home with him to study the faces and names he would soon encounter.

It was barely eleven o'clock when Alex felt his stomach growl and imagined that he smelled the aroma of cooking food. He looked up to ask Gandy a question and saw a trim woman standing in the office doorway holding a large casserole wrapped in a white dish towel. The sun was at her back and Alex had to squint to get a look at her face.

And what a face it was. The woman was painted within an inch of her life. Her skin was a flawless mask of color topped off by smooth, peachy cheeks. Her eyelids were burnished copper and the mascara she was wearing made her lashes look as long as palm fronds. Her lips reminded Alex of the ice at his local hockey arena after the Zamboni had gone by—multilayered and glistening. Only unlike ice, they were an orange color he'd seen only in a Caribbean sunset.

Michelangelo, Alex thought wryly, probably hadn't used much more paint than this on the Sistine Chapel. She trotted into the small office and, had he been standing, Alex might have been knocked off his feet by the scent of citrus and spice. Her perfume was stronger than the cleansers under his sink.

"Hello, Lilly, been cooking, I see." Gandy smiled at the woman. "Don't you look pretty? Been at one of those home makeup parties you give? You smell nice."

"It's Citrus Sunshine. Unfortunately I'm unable to get it anymore. I've quit selling makeup. Haven't you heard?" Lilly set the casserole on Alex's desk. "I've started selling jewelry. Going anywhere special, Gandy? Need anything new? How about gifts? Christmas will be coming eventually, you know."

Then the woman seemed to remember where she was and why she'd come. She turned to Alex. "Hello, Pastor, I'm Lilly Sumptner. I stopped to say welcome to Hilltop and brought you something for supper. I'll just tuck it in the refrigerator in the church kitchen. When you get home, just heat at three hundred fifty degrees until it cooks up again. An hour should be plenty."

"Hello, Lilly, this is a lovely gesture." Alex stood up to shake her hand, which was decorated with artificial nails that reminded him of bloodied dragon's teeth.

"My husband Chuck and I will have you over for dinner sometime soon," Lilly promised as she glanced at her watch. "Gotta run. I'm doing a jewelry party in Grassy Valley today and I can't be late. Very unprofessional." She took Alex's hand in her own. "We're glad you're here, Pastor. So very glad."

With that, Lilly Sumptner turned and left on a breeze of Citrus Sunshine.

Neither Alex nor Gandy spoke until the sound of Lilly's car disappeared in the distance.

"She's the party lady," Gandy said finally. "Always selling something. One day it's makeup, the next jewelry. No one knows what she'll sell next."

"Why does she keep changing products?" Alex shook his head. "That's not how it's usually done, is it?"

"She sells something until she runs out of customers. Then she starts selling something else. There aren't that many of us in the area, so she has to do that in order to keep us buying."

"I see," he said. That was unique marketing. "So rather than go outside the area and sell to a wider audience, she changes the product instead?"

"You could say that. It looks like she's using up her makeup inventory on herself, though. It was a little heavy-handed today. Lilly has a good heart, when she can get her head off business." Buying and selling, marketing plans and product selection. Lilly would probably have done well in business in Chicago, Alex mused, but instead she'd bloomed where she was planted, right here in Hilltop.

Lilly Sumpter's perfume had not yet dissipated when another visitor arrived at the church office. A small woman walked in carrying a jar of jam. When he first glanced up, Alex guessed her to be in her eighties, and she too was heavy-handed in the makeup department. She must attend Lilly's parties. Then he got a good look at her face. She had wrinkles like a topography map. Even with her trim figure in a bright blue housedress and her red lipstick and liberally rouged cheeks, she couldn't have been a day under seventy. And that was being generous.

"Rhubarb," she said as she plunked a pint jar with a Mason lid onto his desk. "I grow it in my backyard. I'll fill it for you again."

"Thank you. And you are…?" He gave the jar back and leaned forward, towering over the little woman.

She didn't seem to mind. "Tillie Tanner. Welcome, Pastor. We're glad you're here."

"You're right about that, Tillie!" Gandy chimed. "He's an answer to prayer."

Alex felt himself redden under the appraising eyes of the two women and was thankful when Tillie tapped the face of the large, man's wristwatch on her wrist. "Almost time for my soap opera. I'd better go. See you on Sunday, Pastor." Shoulders square and head held high, Tillie walked out the front door and down the steps to a car that didn't look a day younger than its driver.

Gandy glanced at the white-faced clock on the wall, leapt to her feet with a little squawk and grabbed her purse. "I almost forgot Debbie. You'll have to excuse me, Pastor, I have to take my daughter to the clinic for her allergy shot. I'll be back tomorrow to finish the bulletin." She eyed his desk for a list of hymns or readings for the Sunday service, but the desk was still bare.

"There's a medical facility in Grassy Valley?"

She snorted again. The sound, Alex began to realize, was her response to many things, usually those she held in low esteem. "There's a 'satellite clinic' staffed by the Wheatville Physicians Group, but it's not going to be revolving around here very long. Doc Ambros is making noises about retirement, and he's afraid that the Wheatville clinic isn't making plans to fill his position. He's afraid they'll close the satellite in Grassy Valley and we'll have no doctor at all. It's a shame. That will put us more than fifty miles from medical help. That's a long drive if you have an injured child or someone with chest pains. I'd like those doctors to break a leg out here and ride in a car for fifty miles to get it set!" She left the office, head high and back stiff.

Alex couldn't blame her. That was another thing he'd taken for granted. In Chicago, urgent care centers were located throughout the city, while here there was one elderly doctor for an entire community.

After Gandy was gone, Alex wandered into the nave and sat down in the last pew. *Am I doing this right, Lord*? As he sat there, a remarkable peace spread over him. He willed himself to remain still, not wanting this moment to slip away. He began to pray.

An hour later he looked up to find Dixon towering over him. He smiled at his new friend. "Have a seat, Dixon, I was just in conversation with the Lord."

"I don't want to interrupt any chat with the Big Guy," Dixon said. "I'll come back later."

"Please stay. I'm ready to get back to work. Is there anything I can help you with?"

"Not really, I just came to see if any quiche had arrived yet."

He got his answer when Alex flushed. "You called it right, Dixon. One arrived this morning."

"I told you so." Dixon's expression danced with mischief. "I hope you know that old saying isn't true."

"What old saying is that?"

"That real men don't eat quiche. They eat it, all right. They just don't *admit* it to anyone."

*A*fter Dixon left, Alex continued to study the stained-glass windows in the church. They depicted moments in the life of Christ—Jesus multiplying the loaves and fishes, surrounded by little children, shepherding His lambs. Christ's baptism was depicted with a white dove descending. There was a beautiful stained-glass rendering of Jesus praying in the garden and, Alex's favorite, Jesus walking on water as a sinking Peter reached out to Him.

Alex had always identified closely with Peter's weakness, and was comforted by Christ's love for His flawed disciple. It encouraged him, weak as he was sometimes, to carry on. He was so engrossed in studying the windows and what they represented that Alex didn't hear the soft footsteps behind him. A cool, bony hand fell gently on his bare forearm. His heart leapt, and a frisson of panic shot through him. He spun around to find someone behind him. Bony wrists protruded from his shirtsleeves and his cheeks appeared sunken.

The lanky man jumped back at Alex's reaction, almost as startled as Alex had been. "Sorry, Reverend, I didn't mean to alarm you."

"It's quite all right, Jonas." Alex stammered, his breathing returning to normal. "I was so engrossed in these beautiful windows that you could have driven an entire truck into the church and I might not have heard it."

"I'm here looking for my sister Gandy."

Alex took in the weary slouch of Jonas's shoulders and the hang-dog look on his face and felt yet another pang of sympathy for the man. Alex could see the resemblance between him and Gandy, especially the same pointed nose, rosy at the tip. Their personalities were where the two diverged. Gandy was chipper and upbeat, while her brother carried the weight of the world on his shoulders.

"I'm afraid that your sister has left for the day. Something about her daughter and an allergy shot."

Jonas looked more dejected than ever. "I forgot all about that. I'll have to catch her at home later. I just had some…questions." His face was shuttered from all expression.

"Tell me about your family, Jonas." Alex patted the pew next to him. "We didn't visit much on that hunt for your cow." A faint smile twitched at the corners of Jonas's mouth, and he lowered himself down.

"My wife's name is Barbara. She used to be a hairdresser in Grassy Valley before she started raising kids. She still works a day or two a week."

Alex remembered Gandy's Brillo-pad hair.

"Joe Jr. just graduated. Brett is fifteen. And Crissie, our tagalong, is eight."

"I hear your family has owned land here for a long time."

"In Hilltop Township everyone has been here since the beginning."

"Pardon me?" Alex didn't know what to make of this.

"Hilltop is the only township in the area in which the original families of the men who pioneered the land still own it. Every farm is owned by the grandson or great-grandson of the men and women who put down stakes here in the 1800s."

Seeing Alex's blank look, Jonas continued. "Congress passed the Homestead Act in 1862. For a small fee, a US citizen could claim 160 acres of public land, and a married couple could get 320 acres. Once the claim was made, they had to live on the land for five years, build living quarters and cultivate the land. Then it became their own. No land in this township has ever been sold. People around here are pretty proud of that heritage. Even my kids think it's interesting, and you know how kids are."

"What do you grow on your farm?" Alex asked.

"Wheat, barley, peas, whatever everyone else grows. The only difference is that I never get the yield everyone else does around here."

"You don't?"

"I don't use any chemicals on my crops. I summer fallow my fields, for example. I don't crop them every year, to preserve nutrients in the soil. Old-fashioned, I know, but it's the way my father and grandfather did it."

"Fascinating. Thanks for telling me. And," Alex added, "I hope to meet your family."

"Better meet them soon then," Jonas muttered, "before we aren't here anymore."

Jonas stood to leave, but Alex put a hand on his forearm. "Jonas?"

"Don't mind me, Reverend, I'm just down today."

"Want to talk about it?"

Jonas studied him appraisingly. "Let's just say things haven't been easy the past few years. Crop prices have been up and down. Three years ago I planted too early and my crop got washed out so I had to reseed. The next year I lost it all to hail. Last year my wife had appendicitis and ended up with peritonitis. She was in the hospital a long time and we didn't have very good insurance. Since she couldn't work, she had to close her hair salon. Guess you'd say we had a run of bad luck." A grimness settled about him that was almost palpable.

"That's tough," Alex murmured sympathetically.

"You don't know the half of it." He turned and lifted a hand to wave back over his shoulder. "Nice to see you, Reverend. You'll like Hilltop. It's a good place to call home." There was sadness in his eyes as he turned to go.

He would walk to the church occasionally, Alex decided as he got into his aging van at five o'clock to return to the parsonage. It would be good to give his heart a little exercise other than being startled by people creeping up on him in the church. It would also provide an opportunity to pray his way into the day before Gandy greeted him at the door, and it would provide him a chance to consider all that he was learning in these first days at Hilltop.

Jonas Owens stuck in his craw—a phrase he'd learned from Dixon. Or perhaps it was more like peanut butter stuck to the roof of his mouth. He couldn't get the man off his mind.

God is our refuge and strength, a very present help in trouble. Therefore we will not fear, Alex reminded himself. He would pray that Jonas experienced God's help in his trouble.

As he was about to pull out of the churchyard, he caught a movement from the corner of his eye. Something had scooted around the side of the small shed where, according to Gandy, the lawn mower and snowblower were kept.

Odd. Though he'd only gotten a glimpse of a form in that brief second, he guessed the figure was human rather than animal. While he had no interest in coming face-to-face with a fox, coyote, deer or moose, all of which Dixon said inhabited the area, a human was an entirely different matter. He turned his van around and drove slowly toward the shed.

The grass was matted around the building but Alex could see no discernible footsteps, at least not from a distance. He slipped out of the van to walk around the building on foot.

After circling the shed, he paused at the door to check the lock. It seemed fine at first glance. A simple affair held closed by a padlock. Alex turned away, chastising himself for a case of overactive imagination, but turned back when he heard an odd rustling sound, like that of large wings, emanating from the shed. A sliver of cold slithered along his spine, and the hairs stood at the nape of his neck. A single line from high school English popped into his mind. *Quoth the Raven, "Nevermore."*

Get a grip, Armstrong, he told himself. Here he was, a grown man, acting like a kid listening to spooky stories around a campfire. He looked at the lock again, more closely this time, and swallowed thickly. He poked at the padlock with his finger and it flipped open and dangled there. It only *appeared* to be intact. The building was actually unlocked.

Before he could consider it further, Alex swept the open lock aside and threw open the door.

The flap of wings echoed in his ears as a pair of glowing orange talons lifted from a roost and headed straight for his eyes. These were followed by a blur of blue-black feathers and an inhuman shriek that chilled his core. Alex threw himself sideways, and the creature landed on the ground where he had been standing. Screeching and complaining, the enormous black rooster with glossy feathers, rosy red wattle, and lousy personality fluffed itself into a huge feathery ball and ran off, squawking angrily. Then a small red-haired boy emerged, shooting out of the dimness of the shed, nearly knocking Alex to the ground.

"Now look what you done!" the child yelled, every bit as irate as the rooster. Hands on scrawny hips, the boy watched the bird sprint out of the churchyard, across the road and into a plowed field where the dark earth camouflaged all but the orange legs and bright wattle.

The little boy, who looked to be between eight and ten, spun around and glared at Alex indignantly. "What did you do that for?" the child demanded, rusty freckles standing out across the bridge of his nose. "Are you trying to ruin everything?"

Alex blinked, surprised to be put on the defensive. He spoke calmly into the furious little face. "I don't want to 'ruin' anything, but I have to ask, what were you and a rooster doing in the church storage barn?"

"What's it to you? You ain't the preacher or nothin'." The boy bristled indignantly. He had obviously claimed this as his own personal territory.

"As a matter of fact, I am the preacher." He stuck out a hand. "Reverend Alex Armstrong, at your service. And you are...?"

The boy's Adam's apple bounced in his throat as he swallowed. He was observably startled by this unexpected bit of news. "I didn't know they'd found a sucker...I mean pastor yet. My pa said they'd never find anyone stupid enough to come here where everybody is in financial trouble and he probably wouldn't get paid."

This was a new perspective, Alex thought, unsure how to take this bit of information. Finally he said, "That's in God's hands, not mine. But you *do* happen to have been in the church's shed, that bit is clear."

The child kicked his foot backward like a recalcitrant pony, managing to close the door with one swipe. "I'm not in there now." Then he scuttled sideways to get around Alex and make a run for it.

The teacher in Alex knew exactly what to do. "Young man, stay right where you are."

The boy recognized the authority in that voice and stopped. "You'd better tell me your name. After all, you know mine." Alex felt his sense of humor returning as he looked at the boy who appeared to be a cross between Huck Finn and Jared as a small boy.

"Willard Martin Packard, but everybody calls me Will."

Packard? He'd heard that name somewhere before. It took a moment but then he recalled Clarence Olson sitting in the kitchen with a scowl on his face saying, "Those Packard kids that run wild around here…"

"Nice to meet you, Will. Now I think we should look in the shed and see if that rooster did any damage." To Alex's surprise, the boy's remarkable pale blue eyes grew round with horror.

"He didn't do nothin', I'm sure of it." The child wasn't so cocky now.

"But *I'm* not sure. Would you open the door for me, please?" Alex was having a hard time keeping a straight face, but it wouldn't do to allow the boy to think that breaking and entering—even a shed—was acceptable.

"We knew it was almost empty." Words began to spill out of Will's mouth. "And they say churches are supposed to do good deeds, so we thought nobody would mind if we did a good deed in the shed. My ma always says God made humankind." He screwed up his face in thought. "'And let them have dominion over the fish of the sea, and over the birds of the air, and over the cattle, and over all the wild animals of the earth, and over every creeping thing that creeps upon the earth.' So we thought it had to be all right."

The little fellow could quote from Genesis! Alex's curiosity got the best of him. "Who taught you that verse?"

"Ma. So's we wouldn't pull the wings off flies or nothin'."

"I see." Alex steeled himself for what might be inside the shed. He was beginning to have a very bad feeling about this. Will opened the door slowly, and it groaned agonizingly on its unoiled hinges, making almost as much noise as the rooster had.

Alex took a deep breath and stepped in. The small but dusty windows let in a modicum of light, and it took a moment for his eyes to adjust. When they did, he realized that he was looking at something that was a cross between a pet shop and an animal shelter. There was another chicken, much smaller than the first, black but with more white in its feathers, roosting on a crossbeam. In a cage that had been recently supplied with fresh water and food was a gold and white cat with a nasty but healing gash in its side. Beside it slept two small gold kittens. In the final cage was—Alex swallowed thickly and backed away—an enormous black-and-white skunk.

"Don't worry about Rose," Will said, staring up at Alex. "My uncle took her stink bag out when she was little. She's a pet. I brung her in here to keep the others company. They're friends."

With friends like that, one doesn't need enemies, Alex thought. "I think you have some explaining to do, Will. Why are these creatures in the storage barn?"

Will pointed at the cat and her kittens. "My brother and sister and I found her bleeding and half dead by Bucky Chadwick's place. We figure he kicked her or set a dog on her. He does stuff like that. Says it's fun. He doesn't deserve any cats," Will said earnestly, his small face pinched. "Ma won't let us have any more pets at home, so we figured we'd start our own hoomain shelter right here."

"Hoomain...ah yes, humane shelter."

"We found the hen and rooster wandering by the side of the road and figured they fell off a truck or something so we brought them here too. We already found a home for the kittens, soon as they're big enough to take away from their mama."

Alex didn't know whether to laugh or cry. The child's earnestness was genuine, and the animals did look well cared for. The shed was relatively neat except for the droppings beneath the roosting area. No other damage had been done except to the broken padlock. It couldn't go on, of course, but what would they do about it?

"I'm afraid they can't be left in here indefinitely. And you know, I'm sure, that it was wrong to break into this building." Alex watched the boy's reaction. "First, we'll have to find a different...hoomain... shelter for you. Second, we're going to have to figure out how you'll pay for a new lock for the building and apologize to whoever mows the church property."

"*Awww.*" Will's freckled nose wrinkled in distaste but he didn't argue. It was apparent he thought he'd gotten off easy. Alex had a hunch that this boy was accustomed to being in trouble. Still, a lesson could be learned with gentleness as well as harshness; that was his theory. And though he didn't say it out loud, he admired the boy for trying to do something about a creature in pain.

When he turned around he cleared his throat. "Did you break the lock, Will, or did one of them?"

"Me." Will's voice grew small.

"Then it is your responsibility to pay."

"I don't have any money. I spent all my money on cat food. But maybe I could borrow some from my big brother Andy. Andy and Katie always save their money. The others can't hang on to a dime. Andy says he's saving up to run away from home and my sister Katie says she's going to college. I'll bet she'll be a hunnert years old before she gets there at the rate she's going. They said she was too immature to go to school and held her back in first grade. If that keeps happening, she'll be an old lady before she gets out of that place."

Alex turned his head slightly until he could control the smile creeping across his face.

"Don't tell my pa, okay? He'd probably get out the hairbrush."

"We'll cross that bridge later," Alex said firmly, reminding himself to find out more about the Packard family dynamics. "Do you have a job?"

"Me? I'm only nine! Nobody thinks I'm good for anything yet."

"Well, I do," Alex said firmly. "I think you are good for plenty. Come to the church office tomorrow. I noticed some tarnished silver candlesticks in a closet at the church. I think you could earn a new lock by polishing them for me. What do you say?"

Will brightened. "That's it? No hollering or sending me to bed without supper?"

"Not this time," Alex said with a warning in his voice, "but if it happens again…"

The child studied him with eyes so blue and intense that he could have been running lasers over Alex. "You ain't so bad. I'm glad you came even if my pa thinks yer crazy."

"Thank you, I think." Alex made a mental note to have a conversation with Lauren, Mike or Dixon to find out more about Will's father and mother.

Alex watched the boy scamper into the ditch and come up again pushing a much used bicycle. He flung his leg over the seat and took off, pedaling hard in the gravel. The sun glinted off the boy's red hair and made it look like flames. Then he lifted one hand off the handle-bar and waved backward over his shoulder.

That had gone fairly well, Alex told himself, considering it was the first time he'd ever seen a skunk close up and personal.

"You've got a *what* in the church shed? And Will's already been over to polish the silver?" Lauren Carlsen's musical laughter rang over the telephone line like a crystal wind chime. "Those Packards! I should have warned you about them. You've just barely scratched the surface of that clan with Will. There are several more of them, a pack of red-headed, freckle-faced, angelic-looking but uncontrollable scamps. The Packard children are known to be unruly, wild, rowdy and boisterous. Plus every single one has the energy of the Energizer Bunny. They're intelligent too, in a street-smart sort of way. Good luck, Alex. You'll need it with the Packard children."

"What about their parents? Where do they fit into the picture?"

"Minnie Packard is a sweet, shy, overrun wisp of a woman. Her husband Earl is…well, let's just say he has problems with authority, alcohol and preachers."

"Will told me his father thinks I'm crazy to have come here."

There was a long silence on Lauren's end of the line. "Mr. Packard has opinions, not many of which I agree with."

"I see." Alex interpreted her hesitation. "A conversation for another time. My mission right now is to do something with the animals in the shed." He was beginning to feel a little overwhelmed.

"Don't worry about that. I'll send Mike over to pick them up. I wouldn't mind another cat, especially a good mouser, and the hen and rooster will fit right in with the batch I already have. If the roosters fight, I'm sure we can find another home for them." She chuckled again. "The whole thing is rather cute, if you don't consider the breaking and entering."

Alex laughed. "Do you have any recommendations about how to approach the parents about this?"

Lauren was silent far too long before speaking. "I'm not sure what to tell you there. The kids can be awful behavior problems, but it isn't something that can be solved with a spanking. It goes deeper than that. I'd better add Earl to my prayer list. If he ever came around, it would probably do miracles for the kids. Poor Minnie can't do it all alone.

She's got a good, faithful heart and comes to church all she can. Earl makes it difficult for her sometimes, though. There's a man who has hardened his heart. A good sermon is to him like pearls before swine."

Alex was thoughtful after he hung up the phone. Should he wait, as Lauren had suggested, to speak to Will's father? If he were a father, Alex mused, he'd like to know what his child was up to. Slowly he picked up the slender phone book that held the numbers of several of the small communities in the area. He found the Packard number and dialed.

"Yeah? Whadaya want?"

The man's voice was hoarse, belligerent and slurred. Alex realized at once that Will's father had been drinking. Not sure what else to do, he lowered the receiver to its cradle without speaking. After hearing that menacing tone Alex realized he had to think this through. He didn't want to place Will in a situation that either of them would regret.

Jonas Owens, Will and Earl Packard—how long would his prayer list for those in need grow before he was done?

CHAPTER TEN

*A*lex was surprised to reach the church before Gandy. He'd taken time to sit on the porch a little longer today, enjoying the morning. Even after just a couple days of being around her, he knew that Gandy was a gem. In all his years in academia, he'd never seen such an enthusiastic, dedicated worker. When he'd complimented her on her work habits, she'd quoted 1 Corinthians 10:31. *Whatever you do, do everything for the glory of God.* If everyone did that, she'd added, the world would be a far better place. He vowed to make a conscious effort to do just that today.

Then he stepped into an apple pie.

It was sitting just outside the door to his office, lurking in the shadows of stored folding chairs and a bevy of mops. And now it was all over his foot. He hopped on his left foot, removed the right shoe, and then jumped awkwardly to the front door of the church just in time to meet Gandy, hair flying around her head in a yellow halo. She was carrying a thermal coffee mug and a baggie containing what she'd told him was her favorite lunch, a mayonnaise sandwich.

"What are you up to so early in the morning?" she asked as she watched him beat his shoe against a concrete step and cause apple slices to fly hither and yon.

"I came in to have some prayer time. I was about to unlock the office door when I stepped into a pie someone had left there."

"Ahh." Gandy ducked into the church to put down her things and returned to pick up an envelope that was covered with sugary pie filling. The imprint of a foot was stamped on it. "It's from Irene Collins. Too bad you stepped in it. She makes some of the best pies in the county. If she'd baked banana bread there'd be less mess to clean up."

Gandy took everything in stride. She would be a good role model for him, Alex realized. This wasn't the first treat that had been left for him. He'd found monster cookies loaded with peanut butter, chocolate candies, and nuts and a note of welcome from Cherry Taylor on the seat of his car, and a package of Hilda Aadland's butter cookies on his front steps.

"I've started to write down the names of my benefactors so I can write them each a thank-you note," he said to Gandy. "If things continue like this, I may get nothing else done. Not that I'm complaining, mind you, just overwhelmed with people's generosity and kindness."

"I'll do it. Where's the list?"

Alex pulled it out of his pocket and handed it to her. Gandy stared at it intently, took a pencil out of her hair and added the apple pie to the list. Then she sat back and muttered, *"Hmm…"*

"Why do you sound like Sherlock Holmes?" Alex asked. "There's no mystery about who delivered this pie."

"Every bit of this food was brought to you by women."

"What's mysterious about that? I gather Hilltop's women are all fabulous cooks."

"That's true, but there are several single women on the list, ages twenty-seven through eighty-two. The unmarrieds have come out of the woodwork for you: Brunie Bruun, Irene Collins, Tillie Tanner and Lolly Roscoe, to name a few. Some are from Hilltop Township and a few are from Grassy Valley. If this continues we'll have a jump in our church membership. I wonder if the call committee even considered that. If they did, they're craftier than I gave them credit for being."

"You mean they hired me as bait?" Alex wasn't sure if she was joking or not.

"When you put it that way…" She scratched her chin. "Nah, they couldn't have."

"Well, I'm glad you've settled that. You had me frightened for a moment."

"You've got to realize, Reverend Alex, that this was bound to happen. There aren't many single men around here, and the ones that are, aren't too interesting."

"Why not?" He was intrigued by Gandy's kangaroo logic and the way it kept jumping around.

"Most of them think a debate about the merits of a John Deere versus a Massey-Ferguson or a New Holland is scintillating, for one thing. And a discussion of what crops to plant next year can go on for weeks. Then there's the weather—too much rain, too little rain, rain in the wrong places…"

"I see what you mean."

"Mark Nash and Dixon Daniels were the prime targets until you came along." Gandy shook her head. "I'm glad I fell in love with my high school sweetheart and married him first thing. Sure saved me a lot of time and effort."

"If everyone keeps bringing me food, I'll weigh a ton. No one will think I'm a good catch then," he said hopefully.

"They'll switch to vegetarian casseroles and low-calorie dishes." Gandy grinned up at him. "You can only hope that another single man moves into the area soon and takes some of the pressure off you."

After a futile half hour of trying to polish his first sermon, Alex wandered over to where Gandy was putting together bulletins. "I think I'll take a drive over to All Saints today." He'd left the outside door open so that he could gaze at a tabletop-flat field over which birds were wheeling and diving.

Gandy searched for a pencil in the blond frizz of her hair. She'd begun keeping them there when she realized that the curl in her hair was good for keeping writing utensils off her desk, where they tended to disappear. "Now you're running off. I shouldn't have told you that stuff about being an eligible bachelor. Nobody is going to trap you unless you want to be trapped, you know."

"I'm hardly running away. I want to get to know more about it before I appear in their pulpit next Sunday."

"Suit yourself. They aren't a friendly bunch. You may have noticed that no one has come to greet you with open arms."

"I had a nice visit with the church janitor yesterday. He said it's pretty quiet at the church during the summer. I also met the organist who was there practicing for the Sunday service." They'd both been pleasant enough.

Alex leaned against the doorjamb, and his long, lean body relaxed, but he was still feeling perplexed. "What happened between these two congregations to put them at odds?" A verse from 1 Corinthians flitted through his mind. *Now I appeal to you, brothers and sisters, by the name of our Lord Jesus Christ, that all of you be in agreement and that there be no divisions among you, but that you be united in the same mind and the same purpose.*

"Nothing happened on this side of the fence that I know of." Now Gandy searched in her Harpo Marx hair for her reading glasses. "They stirred it up all by themselves. Them and Alf Nyborg."

"Who's Alf?"

"Alf Nyborg is a bit of a sourpuss and hasn't liked Hilltop for years. He's been president of All Saints since Eisenhower was president. Or maybe it was Ford. I'm not much on US history, but my son has it in school, so I imagine I'll learn it when I help him study for his tests. Do you know the names of all the presidents in order? There's Washington, of course, but that's a no-brainer...."

Gandy had a charming—and highly annoying—way of wandering off topic. Alex felt like he was always pulling on her rope, dragging her back to shore.

"How long has this been going on?"

"I told you. Since Eisenhower was president or maybe Ford."

"So this isn't so much about the congregation as it is one man?"

"That was true in the beginning, but I can't say if it's so anymore. He's probably brainwashed them all by now." Gandy plucked the tea bag out of her cup and dangled it there to drip dry.

"All Saints is just far enough away from Hilltop that people have never done much as a larger group other than share a pastor. Too bad too. Both churches are losing young people. If they can't find jobs near home and leave to find work, our congregations will shrink faster than wool in hot water. We could use each other, you know."

"I'm sorry to pump you for information, Gandy, but I'd like to understand the situation before I visit. I don't want to put my foot in my mouth and make relations even more difficult. I'd like to understand what motivates Mr. Nyborg."

"Pure meanness, probably. He lost his first wife and child in a house fire many years ago. He's remarried, but I don't think he's trusted God or anyone else since. The people from Hilltop tried to gather around him during that time, but he told everyone he wanted to be left alone. Ever after, he's said that we aren't Christian because we didn't help him in his time of need. Funny about that. He chased my father-in-law off his property with a shotgun during that 'time of need' for bringing over a basket of baked goods the church ladies had prepared. We kept trying but gave up after six months or a year. Seemed prudent not to get one of our own shot if we could help it."

"The man must have been mad with grief."

"And now he's still mad," Gandy agreed. "He pulled himself together, remarried and continued to be on the church council at All Saints, but a trickle of evil got into him somehow and now it's a toxic spill, plain and simple."

A *trickle of evil*. One that turned into a toxic spill.

Alex sat down and opened the Bible on his desk. He felt a desperate need to pray.

∾

Some time later he was glad to see Mark Nash saunter through the office doors.

"Hi, Reverend," Mark greeted him. "Do you have time for lunch? I'm going to town for a belt for my tractor and I thought I'd eat in Grassy Valley."

Alex looked at Gandy, who made a brushing motion with her hand as if to say *"Get out of here."*

"It seems I am. I'd like to go very much. I haven't spent any time in town other than driving through and seeing that pig spill on the highway."

"That was a pretty big day in Grassy Valley," Mark said with a laugh. "I hope you aren't disappointed today."

Alex hiked himself into the cab of Mark's pickup. Every man in the area seemed to have one. Alex had never been concerned with having a new car even though he was long overdue for one. Out here, it seemed a pickup was a status symbol, like a Lexus or Mercedes was in the city. The interior was soft leather. Copies of books by several theologians lay on the seat.

"You and Dixon are both full of surprises," Alex said as he picked up the one of the tomes.

"I guess you just can't stereotype anyone around here," Mark said cheerfully as he navigated the road to town.

Even to Alex's inexperienced eye, the crops looked green and healthy…and quite beautiful. He hadn't expected the prairie to have so much variety and personality. Already he was beginning to appreciate the subtle landmarks he wouldn't even have noticed in the city—a craggy rock, a clump of saplings, a dilapidated shed left to be consumed by the elements.

"Sometimes the richest men wear the shabbiest work clothes and drive the oldest beaters. That's how they got so rich. And just because we're isolated here doesn't mean we aren't world-savvy. Lots of people travel in the winter to get away from the cold. Some of them end up in rather exotic places. Mike and Lauren were on a cruise through the Panama Canal last winter, and the Mediterranean the year before."

"How about you, Mark, where have you been? Other than your time as a stockbroker in New York, I mean."

The drive to town passed quickly as they discussed South America, Norway, England and a half dozen other places Mark had traveled.

They were pulling into a parking place when an idea occurred to Alex. "When did you complete the remodel of the parsonage?"

"It must have been close to a month ago. Lauren was on a rampage to have it done before you arrived."

"So not everyone in the congregations has seen it yet?"

"A very few from Hilltop have. No one from All Saints has been over to visit it that I know of. You could ask Gandy. She knows everything."

"I've been wondering how to open a door, get the two congregations together for a common cause."

"Good luck with that."

"Why don't we have an open house at the parsonage so that people can come and see how their hard-earned dollars were spent on the renovation? If the Ladies Aid wouldn't mind providing a few cookies and some coffee…"

"That's no problem," Mark assured him. "But why?"

"There's been something on my mind lately, something I think God put there."

"And what's that?"

He thought of the enmity between the two churches, the chasm between his old life and this brand-new one. There was even the awkward, unsettled way he and Natalie had left things. "Reconciliation. Resolution. We need to settle these things between the two churches. A good way to start might be an invitation to both congregations for…oh, I don't know, an ice cream social at the parsonage, perhaps."

Mark studied him silently. "You might be right, Alex. No one around here has ever been very optimistic about that, but we should try. I'll talk to the council and we'll get it set up. Once we find a date, we'll get in the church bulletins. The least we can do is give it a try."

They pulled up to a large, low-slung building that was part garage, part showroom and sales, and part coffee shop. Three large repair bays were open; each held a dismantled tractor. In the salesroom window was a huge John Deere that Mark said was a Series 9030—what that implied, Alex had no idea—and a small fleet of lawn tractors.

Tucked in the corner behind the big machines was a large round table with a host of chairs. A long counter held a thirty-cup coffeepot, a hot plate with two pots of hot water, an assortment of fruit leathers and snack bars, and a popcorn machine.

Mark headed for the popcorn. "Want some?" He filled a bag and salted it liberally.

"No thanks, I'll wait for the restaurant."

"Suit yourself." Mark wandered up the counter where a lean fellow in grease-stained clothes nodded laconically at him. "Hey, Roger."

"Hi, Mark. What can I do for you?"

"I need a couple belts." Mark handed the technician a scrap of paper containing the information. The fellow behind the counter nodded and disappeared into one of the long aisles that held rows of equipment parts and appeared minutes later with what Mark had requested.

Alex tried to recall the last time he'd had his own head under the hood of a car. High school or college, maybe. He'd not been one for tearing cars apart and putting them back together like some of his friends. The moment he'd earned his first paycheck he'd taken his old beater to his uncle's garage and had the oil changed by someone who knew what they were doing. That fish-out-of-water feeling was dogging him again.

Mark tipped his head in acknowledgment to Roger, and he and Alex strolled out of the shop. Less than a hundred words had been exchanged between Mark and the parts man, but they'd appeared to communicate perfectly.

"Don't you have to pay him?" Alex matched his stride to Mark's.

"Nah, he'll put it on my bill."

"You certainly didn't talk much."

"He knew what I wanted and got it. Roger's a man of few words. He's worked here ever since he graduated from high school. A lot of people reared in Grassy Valley have never left. You'll discover that for yourself, of course."

"I have a lot to discover," Alex murmured.

Mark laughed and clapped him on the back before swinging himself back into his truck. "I'm going to take you on a brief tour of Grassy Valley, and then you're about to discover the best hot beef sandwich, mashed potatoes and pie ever made."

On Main Street they passed a small building with a red-and-white barber's pole out front. "That's the ice cream parlor," Mark said.

"With a barber's pole?" Then Alex read the sign. COWLICKS & PEPPERMINT STICKS—CANDY AND BARBER SHOP.

"Our barber got the idea because his pole looks like a candy cane. He cuts hair, and his wife makes the candy."

"Of course," Alex said weakly. "Why not?"

It became quickly apparent that for Grassy Valley businesses, efficiency and cooperation were paramount. The single attorney, Alex noted by his sign, was also an auctioneer. Good Finds; Good Flowers was a combination antique and floral shop.

"There's the lumberyard." Mark pointed to a large, low building with high doors and wood stacked high around its perimeter. "You can go there for all your building needs. The fellow that owns it is also an electrician. His sister is a plumber, and his father is a carpenter. They can build you a house without going outside the family.

"And if you ever need pencils, a CD, a goldfish or a sewing needle, go to More for Less. It's our version of a dime store and has a little of everything. Oh yes, there are good burgers at the Hasty Tasty Drive-in too. Just don't order the Grassy Valley special. For some reason they put *radishes* on it."

Mark slowed the truck as they went past a large, sprawling truck stop. "That's Red's."

"That I'm familiar with. His name is on every cap in the county."

"That's because everybody in the county has reason to go there at one time or another. He sells gas and is a great mechanic, but every time he sees something that people need, he adds it. There's a nice little Laundromat in the back, a car wash, TV repair and the local insurance agent offices out of there too. One-stop shopping, I guess you'd say."

GOOD EATS HERE the red neon sign proclaimed as they neared The Cozy Corner Café. A blue neon arrow pointed to the door of the small café. It was painted white, with red and blue trim, decorated with window boxes full of red geraniums and bright blue flowers Alex couldn't identify. Through the multi-paned windows Alex could see an inviting café with maple tables and chairs, a row of red and blue vinyl-covered booths, and huge woven rugs smattered across a battered hardwood floor. The waitresses inside, most of whom were on the far side of sixty, wore ruffled white aprons and carried blue-and-white spatterware cowboy coffeepots.

As they were about to enter, Jonas Owens came out of the dry-goods store across the street. Mark lifted a hand to wave him over.

"We're going to have lunch. Want to join us?"

"For coffee, maybe. I have to go to the hardware store first. I'll come over when I get done."

Mark and Alex went inside and walked to a table in the back corner. A woman with bleached-blond hair and a face that must have once been pretty flipped over two of the white coffee mugs already at the table and began to pour. "The usual?" she said.

Mark nodded. "And the same for my friend. Mazie, this is the new pastor at Hilltop Community Church, Alex Armstrong. Alex, this is Mazie Torson."

"So you got one after all." Mazie turned to study Alex. "I'll have to bring Wally out to hear you speak. My husband always uses the excuse that the preacher is a poor speaker to stay home from church. Maybe you can put a stick of dynamite under the old guy and bring him back on Sunday mornings."

"I can't, but God can," Alex said, passing the responsibility onto broader shoulders than his own.

"Okay, then. We'll give you a try." She smiled and Alex saw the beauty she had once been. "Dinner will be right up."

Almost before they could taste their coffee, Mazie returned bearing two plates mounded high with mashed potatoes and roast beef sandwiches smothered in beef gravy. Carrot medallions provided the only other color to the meal, but steam was still coming off the plate and the aroma made Alex's taste buds quiver.

"You say the grace, Reverend."

Alex bowed his head. "I'm overcome with gratitude, Lord. For the people, the beauty, the opportunities in this place and for the food, Lord. Thank You for so many unexpected, unlikely blessings. May it sustain our bodies so we can do Your work. Amen."

Mark nodded appreciatively and without another word tucked into his meal.

As he ate, Alex gazed around the room, studying the Cozy Corner's patrons. There were two women dressed in matching blazers and name tags—bank employees, no doubt—and a table full of men in work clothes at the far back. It seemed to be a gathering place for solo diners, since chairs would empty and fill again as the others were eating. Two young mothers with toddlers were trying to have soup and pie, but their restless children kept slipping out of their grasps and running to bang plastic toys on the front of an old juke box nearby. Two booths held older women in vivid purple clothing and bright red hats. Their laughter just about drowned out any chance of conversation in the booths on either side.

Alex decided to get right down to business. "Mark, I'm concerned about Jonas. Can you tell me anything about him that I should know?"

Mazie came by and filled their coffee cups and Mark waited until she left to speak.

"Jonas's family has been here from the beginning, pioneers." Mark tapped his fork on the edge of the plate. "Jonas and his sister Gandy are very different. Gandy looks on the bright side of things and makes the best of situations."

"I know. She told me why she works at the church…it's her way of tithing. I feel a little guilty about it. If she weren't working there, she could be earning some extra money for her family."

"There aren't that many jobs to be had around Grassy Valley," Mark said. "Besides, Gandy is an expert seamstress. She makes quilt samples for a fabric store in Wheatville. They display them and sell fabric kits for the quilt, and then they sell the quilt itself. I think she makes pretty good money, and she can be home evenings with her family.

"Jonas has always been quieter and more somber, even melancholy. He takes his farming very seriously and has always tried to keep the family farm a showplace." A flicker of some emotion passed over Mark's face.

"And?" Alex prodded. "What's the problem?"

"There's talk that he took out some big loans he hasn't been able to repay and that he could possibly lose the family farm."

"So he feels he's letting down his family and his ancestors?"

"No, it's worse than that." Mark swirled the mashed potatoes on his plate. "He has the idea that he's let down the whole community of Hilltop."

"What do you mean?" Alex accepted another cup of coffee from the very solicitous Mazie, reminding himself to switch to decaf the next time around.

"Jonas believes it would be letting the entire township down if he had to sell out. It would be the first farm ever sold here. That hurts for a man like Jonas. And where would they go? He's only known farming his entire life. He has kids still in school. I doubt Jonas has ever been outside the borders of this state. It has to be tearing him apart, but Jonas never says much, and none of us knows how to help him."

"You talk as if this is practically a done deal," Alex observed. "Is it only a matter of time?"

"Rumor has it that someone has offered Jonas a good price for the land, and he's considering taking it. He's been approached by a group of outside investors who are hoping to make some money growing corn for ethanol because it's in big demand right now. It has to gall Jonas that he might have to sell out to someone so blatantly disinterested in history and so obscenely interested in money."

"Can't he sell his own corn?"

"The bank wants its money back immediately, and he's already sold the corn he grew last year. Farmers sell off crops throughout the year. If he can't make the payments or afford the cost of putting a crop in the ground next year, what's he going to do?"

Alex stared blankly at his friend. He had nothing to say. He knew plenty of people who'd fallen behind on house payments only to lose their homes. That was a tragedy. But hundreds of acres of land pioneered by one's great-grandfather? No wonder Jonas had seemed so discouraged.

At that moment the door opened and Jonas entered. He crossed the room to join them. Alex moved over so Jonas could slide into the booth next to him.

Mazie brought a menu to the table but Jonas waved her away.

"We're about to have dessert, Jonas, what do you think? I'm buying," Alex added.

They were half done with the slabs of apple pie à la mode when the bell over the café door clanged again. Jonas glanced up and blanched pale when he saw who'd come through the door.

Mark and Alex turned to see what had made Jonas react as he had.

Two men in business suits had entered. Pausing in the doorway, they looked from diner to diner until their gazes settled on Jonas. They made a beeline in his direction.

"Mr. Owens. We're sorry to interrupt, but if we could have a few minutes…"

Jonas glowered at the man who spoke.

"This is important, Mr. Owens." The taller of the two men spoke. He was a dark-haired fellow with a large nose and black eyebrows that looked like tiny wings. "You've had plenty of time to consider our offer. We need an answer. If you agree to sell the land, and I can't see why you wouldn't, we'd like to take possession as soon as possible."

"An Owens put the first spade to that soil," Jonas retorted.

"History, Mr. Owens, is all about the past," the man said in a tone that told Jonas he was beginning to try his patience. "Our offer is about the present."

"You won't even agree to leave the farmstead intact," Jonas growled. "I don't want my family homestead tilled up for cropland. If I sell it to you, there won't even be a homestead to remember my family by. You'll till it fence post to fence post."

The shorter man had pale blond hair combed straight back off his face. He put a business card on the table. "What's past, is past. We, Mr. Owens, are your future. We'll be waiting to hear from you." The men walked out of the diner without another word.

No one at the table spoke. Jonas groaned and put his head in his hands.

"Is there anything we can do?" Alex understood that being a part of Hilltop meant what happened to the community happened to him as well. And this was intolerable. His mind whirled. There must be some way, *something* someone could do.

"I'm sorry you saw that," Jonas finally murmured. "They know they've got me over a barrel, and they want the farm. They're buying land all over the tri-county area. Those guys have nothing but dollar signs in their eyes."

Mark and Jonas began to talk in low tones. Alex excused himself, and Jonas stood so that he could get by to pay the bill.

This was a case only God could solve. He'd pray about it as Jonas had asked. Bigger problems had been resolved when God was invited into the picture.

He laid his money on the counter by the cash register and looked into the eyes of a plain, pleasant woman in her early forties. To his amazement, she *winked* at him.

"Did you like the pie I delivered to the church, Reverend?" she asked, a blush staining her cheeks. "Fresh this morning. I bake all the pies for the Cozy Corner."

So that was where it had come from! Alex felt himself reddening as well. "I've never come across a finer pie," he said, wanting to be truthful without admitting that most of the delicacy had gone into the garbage. He had, however, even in the face of Gandy's disapproving expression, tasted the parts untouched by his shoe. "It's even better than my grandmother used to make. She always swore by Granny Smith apples, which I thought were a little tart."

Irene Collins—her name was prominently indicated on her name tag—beamed like a lighthouse. "I use two Granny Smiths, two Macintosh and two Honey Crisps. Of course, if all I have is Galas or even Red Delicious, that's fine too. The secret is to use more than one kind of apple. It makes a more interesting combination of flavors." She lowered her voice. "I'd even share my recipe with you if you like."

"Excellent! Thank you so much," Alex said jovially and backed out the door of the restaurant and out of sight of the glowing woman.

Mark followed him outside wearing a huge grin. Even Jonas was smiling.

"What's so funny?" Alex grumbled. "I almost put my foot in it back there." His cheeks twitched. "Actually I *did* put my foot in it." And he told the men about stepping into the pie in the dark this morning.

Mark burst out laughing. "Irene gave me a blueberry pie, and Dixon got cherry. It's one of the perks of being single around here."

"She seemed like a nice woman," Alex said. "Is she...?"

"Looking for a husband? I wouldn't go that far, but she probably wouldn't mind if one of her pies fished in a live one. Irene Collins is good-hearted woman. Everyone new to town gets a casserole except the single men. I guess she wants us to feel extra special."

"How have you managed to stay single?" Alex asked.

"Fancy footwork, mostly. I love the people around here. I just haven't found one of them I want to marry."

"Well, trust me, seminary didn't warn me about any of this."

Jonas turned to leave and Alex followed him. He cleared his throat. "I know you don't know me very well, Jonas, but if there's anything I can do…"

"Thanks. I wish I could let you go to the bank today in my place," he said grimly.

"I can't take your place, but I can go with you if you like."

Alex glanced at Mark, who gave him an almost imperceptible nod. "You two go ahead. I'm going to stop in the hardware store. I'll meet you at the truck in forty-five minutes."

Jonas looked surprised. "You'd do that?"

"I don't want to interfere, but if it would help you to have impartial backup…"

Alex was afraid he might have gone too far but when Jonas spoke, he said, "It might be okay, I guess. I've been feeling pretty alone with this. It upsets my wife too much. I've wanted her to come with me, but she just can't handle it. Sometimes I'm afraid all this trouble will drive her off."

"Then let's go."

The bank was not large, and it appeared to have been caught in a time warp, with wood-paneled walls, a patterned carpet in gold and rust, vinyl-covered office chairs, and artwork that had been new in the 1980s. The air-conditioning blasting from vents around the room made Alex wish for a jacket. There were three tellers, and they all looked up from their stations to study the newcomers as Alex and Jonas walked in.

Before Alex could figure out where to go, a portly man in a dark brown suit burst out of one of the offices that ran along one wall. "Jonas, come on in."

Alex followed, noting the sign on the man's desk: DONALD KRAMER, PRESIDENT.

"This is our new pastor," Jonas said by way of introduction. "I needed some moral support."

The banker frowned and Alex saw genuine concern on his features. "Jonas, I've worked the numbers up and down, and frankly, I can't help you anymore. It's not that I don't want you to have the land, but these are tough economic times. You know that as well as anyone."

As Alex listened he felt a sinking sensation in his gut. Jonas had been telling the unvarnished truth. If anything, he'd *understated* his predicament. Sell or be foreclosed on. Now.

By the time they left the bank, Alex supporting Jonas's arm and mumbling helpless platitudes as Jonas wilted in defeat, Alex knew that only a miracle would help this man now.

Mark was waiting in the truck, just as he said he would be, when Alex returned. "How'd it go?"

Alex swung himself into the truck and sighed. "I hate to say it, Mark, but I think Jonas might be out of options." Alex ran his fingers through his hair, his gut in a knot. "The banker was as helpful as he could be, but the fact is, it's as bad as Jonas says it is. The history of Hilltop is about to change...and not for the better."

"**W**hat's your plan for the rest of the day, Reverend?" Mark draped a wrist over the steering wheel and looked at Alex.

Alex leaned back in the seat and tried to relax. His experience with Jonas had strung taut every nerve and fiber of his body. He didn't know how Jonas withstood the pressure.

"I'd thought about going to All Saints. The organist said she'd meet with me to go over my music choices. She is also the one who prints the Sunday bulletins, so we can cover that at the same time. She told me she planned to be at the church until three."

Mark nodded and backed out of his parking place. As they drove, they passed tall grain elevators that punched into the cerulean sky. They were country skyscrapers that towered above every other building and sat in stark relief to a sky so blue that if he'd seen it in an oil painting he would have called it overdone and unrealistic. After a mile or two, Mark turned north onto a gravel road that cut through the countryside.

"Where are we going?" Alex asked when he realized that they were leaving Grassy Valley by a new route, one that headed away from Hilltop rather than toward it.

"All Saints. This is a back way. Maybe we'll even run into Alf Nyborg. He spends a lot of time over there mowing and doing repairs."

Alex nodded and noticed out the window a massive gray barn

and elaborately ornamented Victorian that was equally void of paint. "Is that place empty?" A hand-painted No Trespassing—Keep Out sign sat crookedly at the end of the drive.

"No, it just hasn't seen a coat of paint in twenty years," Mark said. "That's the Bruun place. Brunie and her sister Bessie have spent their entire lives there. Never married, either one of them. Now Brunie takes care of her sister. Bessie hasn't been well for years. The sign is Bessie's handiwork. She's not much for having company."

Alex took it all in and watched the countryside go by. "Gandy told me about Alf. According to her, Alf eats, sleeps and breathes All Saints' business, and probably isn't much interested in my input."

"It's true." Mark slid his sunglasses into place and gave Alex a brief smile. "He isn't partial to teamwork. Are you worried?"

"I've spent most of my adult life dealing with students—some of them recalcitrant, others just not interested in learning. That never stopped me in the classroom, and it shouldn't here. I've always made it a policy to treat my students with respect, firmness and love. I'll treat Alf and everyone I meet the same way whether they like me or not."

"I think you've got it, Reverend. He's an unhappy man who some-times takes it out on others. If anyone ever needed respect, firmness and love it's Alf Nyborg. If you can make peace with him, you'll be halfway to home base."

Alex could see a church spire in the distance, thrusting its way upward toward the sky, when Mark slammed on the brakes. Alex caught himself on the dash, glad he was wearing a seat belt. He'd expected sudden traffic stops in Chicago, but here…

"Sorry about that. There's a moving party going on."

Alex looked out the window to see a gray-and-black mother tabby carrying a tiny kitten across the road by the scruff of its neck. She dis-appeared into the long grass at the side of the road and then rapidly reappeared without the baby. She ran back across the road, went into the grass on that side and emerged shortly with another kitten.

"She's relocating her family," Mark explained. "Mama cats do that sometimes if they decide their babies are in danger. I had a cat birth a litter on the seat of my tractor once. Next time I looked she'd moved them somewhere safer. It turned out to be inside a pair of Carhartts I'd left lying on the floor."

Mark laughed at Alex's confused expression. "She'd left them inside the work clothes I use when it's particularly cold. I was glad those kittens grew up before bad weather set in."

"This place is a mass of little miracles," Alex said, feeling oddly sentimental. "I see now that all those years in academia took me too far away from nature. I'd forgotten that milk comes from cows and bread exists because of kernels of wheat."

"Well, if you consider those things miracles, hang on, because you're in for a lot of them." Mark put his foot on the gas pedal and nodded toward the horizon. "Here we are."

A half dozen cars were parked around the church, and the front doors stood wide open.

"Something is going on." Alex said. "It's nice to see the doors open."

Mark turned onto the drive that circled the church and parked. "Do you want me to come with you or would you rather meet your flock alone?"

"Come, of course, the more the merrier." What Alex didn't say was that he was feeling the need for a second calm head and clear mind. But maybe he was growing mountains out of molehills. Just because he'd heard very little positive about the situation at All Saints, that didn't mean it wasn't there.

"One would hope," Mark muttered as he pulled the key from the ignition and swung his long legs out of the pickup.

The front door opened onto a foyer lined with coat hooks. Beyond it was a nave considerably smaller than Hilltop's, and there were no stained-glass windows, which changed the atmosphere entirely. The light was sharp and piercing, creating an almost sterile mood. A small but beautiful altar graced the front of the church, and short pews lined either side of the aisle. An elaborately hand-carved pulpit hovered majestically to the right of the altar.

"That's a beautiful piece," Alex said admiringly.

"Alf Nyborg's grandfather carved that pulpit."

"Really?" Alex was impressed. "It's a masterpiece." The panels circling the platform depicted scriptural scenes in much the same way as the windows of Hilltop did.

"Hello, can I help you?"

Neither of them had heard the small woman ascend the stairs from the basement until she literally popped up in front of them.

"Hello, my name is Alex Armstrong, and I'm your new pastor. It's good to meet…"

The small woman, who appeared to be in her mid to late thirties, stared at him wide-eyed. "You?"

Slightly disconcerted by the greeting—or lack of it—Alex plowed on. "Yes. And your name is?"

For a moment she seemed to debate whether or not to reveal it to him. Then she came down on the side of politeness. "Amy Clayborn. Welcome, Reverend Armstrong." Her head swiveled from side to side as if she were looking for someone. "Mr. Nyborg isn't here right now. He's probably the one you should be talking to. I could call him."

Did he speak for everyone? Alex wondered wearily.

"No need. I'm sure we'll meet soon enough. We noticed several cars outside. Am I interrupting something? Or could I introduce myself to those who are here?"

There was that deer-in-the-headlights look again. Then Amy blinked, met his eyes and smiled. "It's just our quilting ladies. We meet every week, sometimes twice."

Ah yes, Gandy had mentioned a quilt competition, Alex thought. It wasn't easy to recall everything she chattered about.

"I would be delighted to meet them."

"Come, then." Amy turned and started down the steep stairs to the basement. "Mind that you don't knock yourself silly on the ceiling."

Alex immediately saw what she meant. Just like the steps at Hilltop, the stairs appeared to have been built for people less than five feet high. An outcropping of wood midway down the stairs would injure anyone who inadvertently ran into it. He hunkered down and followed Amy's receding back. When he didn't hear a clunk or a yell, he assumed Mark had navigated the passage as well.

Laughter filtered up from the basement and cheerful chatter that seemed to focus on someone's upcoming wedding. But when Alex arrived at the bottom of the stairs, he was met with seven pairs of curious eyes…and complete silence.

As he scanned the room he took a census. The youngest woman appeared to be in her twenties; the oldest, deep into her eighties.

Suddenly, he felt like he was walking in knee-deep mud.

CHAPTER THIRTEEN

The silence was as awkward as anything Alex had ever experienced.

Finally, the eldest of the group—a woman with thinning white hair pulled into a knot at the nape of her neck, rheumy blue eyes and a face seamed with wrinkles—smiled at him.

"Welcome," she said, "it is good you're here." Then she added, "We need help."

The others stared at her with shocked expressions, as if she'd just violated some unspoken law.

Finding one non-hostile face was opening enough for Alex, and he moved forward to shake hands and introduce himself.

It was like shaking warm, limp fish, as halfhearted as those handshakes were, but he pasted a smile on his face and behaved as if they'd welcomed him with a marching band.

"So this is the quilting group."

Silence.

"May I see what you're making?" He moved forward and all but the elderly woman who had greeted him shrank back in their seats. Who, exactly, did they think he was?

Amy obviously felt some obligation to act as hostess. "We're tying quilts. We've run out of fabric and will have to start collecting again so we can make more. We'll send them off to missions in the fall."

"Very nice." Alex hefted one of the quilts and found it substantial yet airy. He could imagine the joy such a gift might bring. "I'm sure they are much appreciated."

"We don't do as many as Hilltop does," a jowly, heavyset woman with a permanent crease between her brows said with a scowl.

"It's not the number that counts; it's the spirit in which it's given. Remember the poor widow who gave her last penny? What's important is that it is given out of gratitude and generosity. God knows your hearts."

They all stared at him warily. Awkward silence filled the room once again.

"So…" Alex swung his arms a bit and backed toward the bottom of the stairs where Mark had remained. "I don't want to interrupt your work. I hope to see you all on Sunday. God bless." And he quickly turned and raced up the stairs on Mark's heels, barely missing the rafter that threatened to knock off the top of his head.

"Well, that went well," Mark said, sounding amused, once they were back in his pickup truck.

"Very funny." Alex noticed his hands trembling a little, so disconcerted was he by the non-welcome he'd received.

"No, I mean it. Granted, you didn't get asked to stay for coffee, but it's a start. You don't realize how insular that group has become. It's odd that a church body would close in on themselves like that, but they've come to depend on Alf to take care of everything for them, from roof repair to the collection plate. Since Alf is a mainstay in their church and he has a bone to pick with Hilltop, the All Saints congregation has lined up behind him. We haven't been able to make amends for the perceived infraction. But you're new and fresh. They might give you a chance."

"It's going to be an uphill battle."

"One thing at a time. Now you've been there. Next time will be easier. No one can spend a lot of time around Alf Nyborg without getting a little paranoid. No doubt he's already been expressing his doubts about Hilltop's choice of a new pastor."

"But he was on the call committee too," Alex said, climbing into Mark's truck.

"True, but he stayed neutral intentionally. Now if you don't work out, it will be *our* fault, not his."

"How can two churches have such dissimilar personalities, Mark? I've experienced nothing but warmth and welcome at Hilltop. And at All Saints, if today is any indicator…"

"That's part of the reason you're here," Mark told him calmly. He started the engine and pulled out onto the road. "To bring us together. To ferret out the problems and to resolve them. We don't like it any better than you. The feeling is that if All Saints could pay for their own minister and not have to share the cost with Hilltop, they would have left us long ago. But I'm confident you can bring us back together. Like Lauren says, God wouldn't have sent you if you couldn't."

There was that bit of overconfidence in him again. Listening to Mark, Alex realized that if he had to make a choice between dividing loaves and fishes to feed the masses or finding resolution between All Saints and Hilltop, the loaves and fishes gig might be easier.

Mark dropped Alex off to pick up his van at the church, and they arrived at the parsonage just as Dixon and Lauren pulled into the yard in their separate vehicles.

"Hey!" Dixon said by way of greeting through the open window of his truck. "We've got something for you, Reverend."

Lauren jumped lithely out of her car and opened the trunk.

Alex felt cheered immediately. Here, at least, were welcoming faces. "You've given me too much already. I don't need another thing."

Lauren walked toward him, her arms full of parcels wrapped in thick, white butcher's paper. "If everybody carries a load we can get this into the freezer immediately."

Alex took a few icy packages out of her hands. "What is it?"

"Venison. Mike got a deer last fall and there's no way we'll eat it all before he goes hunting again. I called Dixon and asked him to help me deliver it."

"I don't know how to cook venison," Alex ventured, not wanting to admit that he didn't know how to cook much of anything at all.

"I'll teach you. Or one of the guys will. There are also a few packages of frozen peaches. It makes fabulous cobbler. Do you have a recipe?"

"No, can't say I do." He didn't even have a cookbook. His normal dessert was something from his stash of chocolate candy bars. When he did decide to cook something, he'd always depended on the Internet for directions. Alex had a hunch that it just wasn't done that way in Hilltop. He clutched his icy parcels to his chest and hurried after Lauren.

"Where did you say we'll store this?"

"There's a small deep freeze in the basement. You probably didn't notice it behind the pile of Christmas decorations. This will keep you from starving until at least the first of the year."

"I hadn't really worried about starving," Alex said with a chuckle. "So far the food is flowing in faster than I can eat it." He felt a little like the widow of Zarephath—his jar of meal would not empty, nor his jug of oil fail.

"Another reason to have a freezer."

Arms full, Alex, Dixon and Mark followed Lauren into the basement, where she pushed aside boxes of greenery and a plastic outdoor Nativity set. With a practiced hand, she packed the small rectangular chest freezer, even leaving room for some of those seemingly endless casseroles that kept arriving.

"There." She wiped her hands on her jeans and smiled. "I have fresh doughnuts in a container on my front seat. How about some coffee?"

There was no delayed response this time. Mark hustled to her car to get the doughnuts while Alex brewed coffee. Dixon and Lauren set out cups and napkins. The kitchen had a warm, familial feel that Alex relished. It was particularly welcome after his visit to All Saints. It was as if he'd been given two families, one healthy and the other dysfunctional. He'd be on his knees a lot over All Saints in the next few weeks.

"By the way," Mark said as Lauren dug for paper plates in the cupboard, "what would you think about having an open house for Alex? We were just talking about…"

Lauren stared at him. "Great minds must think alike. It's already in the works. The Ladies Aid is debating about the date; but as soon as it's set, we're ready to roll. I love the idea of hosting All Saints, reaching a friendly hand across the border, so to speak."

"That was easy enough," Mark said with a laugh.

"What did you guys do today?" Dixon mumbled, a doughnut already in his mouth. There was granulated sugar all over his lips, which he laid waste with a swig of coffee.

Alex and Mark filled them in on their trip into town, but kept Jonas out of it, other than saying he'd joined them for a piece of pie and coffee at the café.

Dixon leaned back in his chair with a contented sigh. "You make the best doughnuts in seven counties *and* even trump the Cozy Corner Café, Lauren. Maybe you could relieve Lila Mason of the task of bringing doughnuts to me."

"Lila brings you doughnuts?" Alex asked, astounded. "Why?"

"She's adopted me as a son," Dixon said with a smile. "I fix her roof, she gives me doughnuts. I stop the toilet from running twenty-four hours a day, she gives me doughnuts. I—"

"I get the picture."

"Unfortunately, I doubt Lila has two pennies to rub together, so she gets the day-olds or the ones they are about to throw out at the grocery store. Then she makes coffee that resembles dishwater and makes me eat a half dozen at her table." Dixon shuddered. "It's enough to make me consider retiring from the fix-it business at Lila's."

This discovery about Dixon and Lila pleased Alex inordinately, both because it proved his initial reading about Dixon's good nature and thoughtfulness, and because it meant that Lila was not completely alone in this world.

"Since you're discussing eccentrics, I have news on a couple more," Lauren said. "I saw Flossie and Charles Kennedy in town the other day. I've never seen a mother and son who are practically joined at the hip like those two are."

"What's their background?" Whenever he got the opportunity Alex was determined to learn more about the members of the community.

"Before they came to Horace Abel's so that Flossie could be his housekeeper, you mean?" Lauren thoughtfully sipped her coffee.

"Yes. Were they originally from Grassy Valley—or Wheatville?"

"No one knows," Mark said, interjecting himself into the conversation.

That was the answer he least expected. "What do you mean no one knows?"

Lauren put her cup down and twiddled with her paper napkin as she spoke. "Horace had advertised for household help in several papers. They appeared here one day when Charles was a child. Flossie said she'd come in answer to one of those ads and since she and her son were already on Horace's front step, he told them she could have a one week 'trial run.' They've been here ever since."

"She must have been a good housekeeper," Alex mused.

"She's a good cook, keeps a spotless house and knows how to drive a tractor if Horace is in a pinch. He thinks she's practically perfect."

"And he didn't mind the little boy?"

"Charles has always been bookish. When Horace bought him a computer, he disappeared into his room and has hardly come out since. Now he makes his living selling things on the Internet and pays Horace rent to stay in the house. It's worked out well for everyone."

"And no one from Flossie's past ever showed up? A friend or relative?"

"Not a soul." Lauren's expression was pensive. "Of course, it's been so long that now we assume there was no one."

The conversation hit a lull, and Alex took a sip of his coffee. It was good to hear about the people he would be living among. There were so many mysteries, so many unanswered questions.

"Hey, does anyone know that unmarked grave in the cemetery?" Alex asked, setting down his cup. "Should we be responsible for ordering something for it or…?"

Dixon's and Lauren's eyes widened as they stared at him. "A grave? What are you talking about?"

Mark leaned forward in his chair. "Are you sure it was a grave?"

Alex looked from one face to the other and could see that they had no idea what he was talking about. He must be mistaken. Maybe he was just imagining things.

"I've got something in the pickup for you," Dixon said after Mark and Lauren had driven off in their separate directions. "I hope you don't mind."

"Why should I mind a gift?" Alex asked as they strolled toward Dixon's truck.

"It's not a traditional gift, just something I thought you needed." Dixon cleared his throat awkwardly. "It's something that also needs you. You can give it back, if you like, but I hope you don't. Give it a little time and see what you think before deciding."

"I have no idea what you're talking about." Alex looked at the truck for a clue. The truck bed was empty, and no box or package was poking up to reveal itself in the front seat.

He recoiled as Dixon gave an ear-splitting whistle. He flinched again when he saw a head pop up on the driver's side of the truck like a jack-in-the-box. It was a dog, its black-and-white head suggesting a Dalmatian somewhere in its ancestry.

"Dixon, I—"

"Don't say a word, and don't pass judgment. Just meet him first, okay? His name is Tripod." The dog bounced up and down inside the truck like a trampoline had replaced the passenger seat, his smooth head bumping against the top of the cab, his rosy red tongue lolling happily at the sight of them. "He's a good dog and he needs a home. I'd take him myself if push came to shove, but I think he'd be much happier with you and vice versa. When I open the door, just stand still. He has good manners and won't jump, but he might have to let off a little steam."

Slowly Dixon opened the door and a quivering black nose forced its way through the crack. Then, as if Dixon couldn't hold the dog back a moment longer, the door flew open and a thin, muscular dog with short black-and-white fur rocketed out of the cab and made a few happy circles around the men. He stopped directly in front of Alex and sat, his black rope of a tail thumping on the hard-packed ground. He gazed at Alex inquiringly.

"Dixon, I don't know what to say!" Alex could actually think of plenty of things, but none of them seemed prudent.

"Sure you can. You think I'm crazy, you don't want a dog, and he'll eat you out of house and home and make messes in your yard. You'll have to use masking tape on every one of your black suits because there will be dog hair on them; he'll bark, scare parishioners, and make a general nuisance of himself." Dixon looked at Alex. "Should I go on?"

"No, thank you. You've covered the major ones." The dog gently put a front paw on the tip of Alex's shoe.

"Then let me remind you of some of the positive things he'll do," Dixon offered.

"Do I have a choice?"

"No." Dixon didn't even smile, so intent was he on making his point. "He'll keep you company when no one's around, keep you warm in bed at night and think you're the greatest thing on earth since sliced bread."

Alex studied at the dog at his feet. He jumped up and began to wag his tail again. It was only than that Alex noticed that the dog stood with one hip higher in the air and the other lowered, as if he were standing on the side of a deep hill. "This poor thing only has three legs!"

"Of course. What did you expect of a dog named Tripod? But if you don't tell him something is missing, he'll never know. What do you think?"

"How is he able to run?" The dog obviously could, Alex had seen it for himself.

"A chair has four legs but a stool has three, and they're both sturdy enough to sit on. Tripod's like that stool. He creates balance with the remaining leg to make up for the one that's missing. It's second nature to him. He doesn't even know he's not exactly like other dogs."

Everything in Alex told him to reject this ridiculous idea with no further discussion, but something about the way Tripod held his gaze with an almost human look of adoration held him back.

"What about the parsonage? They surely won't allow a dog in such a lovely home."

"I cleared it with the board. They're fine with it. He's housebroken and kennel trained and sheds very little."

"What if he bites someone?"

"He has a very soft mouth. I gave him a raw egg to carry, and he did it without cracking the shell. I've been working with him ever since I rescued him, and he's the easiest dog I've ever trained."

Alex searched for more questions and came up empty. "Like I said, I can keep him for myself," Dixon went on, "but I already have dogs and you don't. I think you'll be happier with him than without him, Alex. There may be times when you need someone to talk to about private things, and Tripod is an excellent listener. I guarantee he'll never reveal a word of what you tell him. Mum's the word with ol' Tripod here."

"Mutt is the word with Tripod."

Dixon grinned. "That too. So you'll take him?"

"I grew up in an apartment building in Chicago. I don't know what to do with a dog, especially a three-legged one." His arguments were feeble, Alex noticed. He wasn't trying very hard to convince Dixon to take the dog away.

"He'll teach you." Dixon dug behind the seat on the passenger side. "I brought his favorite food. Directions are on the bag. Let him out to run and do his business, and he'll be fine. The more you scratch him the better he'll like you." Dixon studied the dog, which had now lain down on Alex's shoes. "He appears to like you quite a bit already."

Dixon gave a leisurely but highly theatrical stretch and ambled to the driver's side of his vehicle. "I think I'll be going now. I know the two of you will be fine, but call me if there's any trouble."

He departed in a cloud of dust, leaving Alex and Tripod alone together in the middle of the yard.

He hoped what Dixon had said was true, Alex thought, as he stood with Tripod at his side. The dog, in order to survive life at the parsonage, would have to teach this preacher how to treat him. Suddenly laughter bubbled up inside Alex and he leaned down to scratch the black ears. "The Pastor and the Pooch, that's us, Tripod. What do you think of that?"

Chapter Fourteen

Alex and Tripod watched each other intently, neither moving a muscle. It was Alex who finally broke the stare down. "Oh, come on then. We might as well get acquainted." Alex wasn't sure if it was proper etiquette to converse with a dog, but Dixon had told him Tripod was a good listener. "Would you like a dish of water? A bone?"

Tripod matched his pace to Alex's as they moved toward the house. The dog seemed completely unaware that it was missing a leg—and if Tripod didn't care, why should he?

Inside, he took an empty five-quart ice cream bucket he found under the sink, filled it half-full with cold water and set it on the floor. Tripod sniffed the bucket, found it to his liking and lapped up most of the water in record time. Then he stood looking up at his new master expectantly, waiting for his next cue.

This was more awkward than he'd expected it to be. A living being had just moved into his home and he knew nothing of its habits or personality. Maybe Tripod was a chewer or a barker or worse yet, a biter. But surely Dixon had better sense than to give a preacher a biting dog.

Alex moved into the living room and sat down on the couch just to see what the dog would do. It moved directly in front of him and sat stone still, big brown eyes gazing longingly at the cushion next to Alex's.

"Oh, all right," Alex sighed.

With a graceful leap, Tripod joined Alex on the couch and leaned into him, his warm, solid body resting against Alex's arm and shoulder. It was a surprisingly pleasant sensation.

"Now what do you plan to do?" Alex inquired of the dog, which seemed remarkably intelligent, at least to his inexperienced eye.

Tripod lay down on the cushion, curled himself into a tight spiral like a nautilus shell and closed his eyes.

"Very well, if you insist." Finally Alex allowed himself to do what he'd been longing for all day, particularly since the latest awkward venture to All Saints. Alex put his feet on the footstool, sank into the depths of the couch and closed his own eyes.

It was getting dark when he awoke. Tripod was still there next to him, motionless, his eyes open, watching for Alex's next move.

"This is a fine way to spend a Friday night," he commented to the dog. "Maybe I should make dinn…no, supper," he said out loud and Tripod's ears went up. "You're particularly bright for a dog, aren't you?" Tripod opened his mouth to yawn and Alex could have sworn he smiled at him.

The refrigerator was full of food, but Alex, already feeling like an overstuffed couch, decided that something light appealed to him tonight.

"Tomato soup and a grilled cheese sandwich," he told the dog, who lay on the rug in front of the sink. "And I'm going to have to get over talking to you like you're human."

Out here he was forced to take full notice of the solo nature of his life. At one time, particularly before meeting Natalie, he'd relished his hours alone, away from students, classes, and the demands of both teaching and seminary; but tonight he felt a twinge of pure, unadulterated loneliness.

Dixon could read the future, apparently, for he'd brought Alex companionship even before Alex knew he would need it. Alex scratched Tripod's head and the dog's rope-like tail thumped happily on the black-and-white tiled floor. Now he would have a companion at supper.

A gas stove was something with which Alex had had little experience. His previous homes had always had electric ranges. How hard could it be? He buttered bread and peeled the wrappers off two slices of American cheese. *Turn it on, put the pan on the stove and grill the sandwich*—there couldn't be anything simpler than that. He'd put the bread and cheese on to grill just as the bell on the microwave rang, signaling that his tomato soup—made with milk, not water— was ready. He opened the door, grabbed for the bowl and sloshed steaming soup across the tops of his fingers.

"Ow!" Shaking his hand, he rushed to the sink, sending Tripod scrambling out of the way. He ran cold water on the burned spot, something he'd observed his mother doing for her own burned fingers when he was a child. *"Keep it there until it stops burning,"* she'd say. *"Put the fire out. Cool it off."*

The cool water did indeed ease the sting and he would have stood there longer if the smoke alarm hadn't begun to ring. Alex spun around to see flames licking up the sides of the frying pan, charring his grilled cheese sandwich. He was in such a rush to reach the stove he almost lost his balance on a wayward throw rug, but managed to turn off the gas and remove the pan from the burner without burning himself again.

The smoke alarm screamed in his ears until he found a step stool in a coat closet and hiked himself up to the alarm and dismantled it. When all was said and done, the room smelled as if he'd had a campfire on the countertop, gray smoke hovered in the air and his supper was up in flames. Tripod, with a keen sense of self-survival, had disappeared beneath the table to wait out the crisis.

He would reheat the spaghetti and meatballs tonight after all. If he dared chance the microwave again, that was. Alex made a decision then and there while still standing on the step stool, hand stinging and ego more than a little bruised. He would learn to cook, even if it killed him. And if tonight were any indication, it just might.

∿

Sunday morning dawned bright and clear, and Alex finally felt calm and relaxed about his initial sermon. He took a deep breath as he left the house and grew almost light-headed as a result. He'd grown so accustomed to fumes from automobiles, taxis and city buses that that air scented only with earth and its perfumes—flowers, loamy soil and cut hay—made him almost giddy.

What's more, he'd committed to running daily now that he had Tripod. The dog delighted in their early morning run and had kept pace with Alex unless he spotted a rabbit. Then he shifted into mach speed and left Alex eating his dust. When the dog tired of the chase, he returned to the relative sedateness of their jog.

It seemed amazing that he'd only been here a few days, Alex mused. The friends he'd already made—Dixon, Mark, Mike and Lauren—felt like they'd been in his life forever.

A whine behind him made Alex turn around. Tripod sat inside the house behind the screen door, head and ears drooping disconsolately.

"You can't come today. It's my first sermon, and I'm sure they don't want you lying underfoot in the pulpit. Don't worry, I'll be back soon."

Tripod slowly crumpled onto the rug in front of the door as if disappointment had dissolved his bones. Alex felt like he was leaving a child behind to fend for itself, but he knew better. The dog would be on his bed, head on a pillow, before the van left the driveway. Tripod just wanted a little sympathy first. Then he would make himself truly comfortable.

There was a single car at the church when he arrived. He could hear strains of the organ through the walls of the church. That would be the organist, Annie Henderson, whom he'd met only briefly to hand over the numbers of the hymns they would sing that day.

He rehearsed the morning in his mind as he mounted the front steps. First the service at Hilltop at nine, time for greeting the congregants and then off to All Saints for the eleven o'clock service. He had to be sure to leave Hilltop early enough in order to get to All Saints on time and without speeding.

Annie turned around the moment he set foot inside the church. "Good morning! Couldn't be any prettier out, could it?" She was a woman of rusty hues from the top of her red-brown hair to her sun-kissed skin, the generous smattering of freckles across the bridge of her nose, and the silky bronze blouse she wore. "I've been working on those new hymns. I hope you have a good, strong voice. Every time this congregation gets a new one to learn, they start to sing in whispers. I know God hears them, but it would be nice if they could hear each other too."

Alex put his sermon notes on the pulpit, opened the Bible, lit the candles and turned on the primitive sound system. Then he and Annie discussed the weather, the crops and the general topics that everyone out here seemed to feel necessary to cover before a real conversation could begin.

"You're early," he commented as he opened a couple of windows to let the breeze freshen the room.

"I've got to be. Aggie and Leonard Lundqvist always come early, as do Brunhilda and Bessie Bruun. They're usually in their pews a half hour before the service starts. Bessie doesn't go out much due to her condition, but she loves to go to church and they come when they can. I'm surprised they aren't here already. Perhaps Bessie isn't up to it today."

"About that…"

"I don't know exactly what happened to Bessie," Annie said bluntly. "I've heard that she was always a little odd. Maybe it was shyness, I don't know. I haven't lived here all my life. I married into the Hilltop family. My husband says Bessie has been nervous in crowds for a very long time and the older she becomes, the more reclusive she is. Sorry I can't tell you more."

Alex tried to process this.

"Oh yes, and I forgot to mention Lila Mason, who always comes to church either an hour early or an hour late."

"Excuse me?"

"Lila's memory is good, but short. About a minute long, I'd say. She always forgets to set her clock forward for daylight savings in the spring and back again in the fall, so she keeps a clock set to each time 'Just in case.' That way she's always got the right time somewhere. Unfortunately, she usually can't remember which clock is which, so she comes when she feels like it."

"Is she…does she suffer from…is she safe at home alone?" He tried to frame the questions as tactfully as he could.

Annie smiled at the concern in his voice. "You mean, is something wrong with her? She's just forgetful. Sometimes she just doesn't *listen* when someone is telling her something, and she gets it all bollixed up. It used to be easier when she got most of her facts straight, but now…" Annie's friendly face creased with concern. "Too bad too, since Lila loves to gossip. Now there's a font of misinformation if I've ever known one!"

"Can she be helped? There are medications…."

"Oh, Lila doesn't believe in medications. Or doctors either, although she did go to the clinic once for stitches when she jammed her hand on the knife she'd put into her knitting bag."

Alex's eyebrows rose and Annie hurried to explain.

"She put it there because she couldn't find her scissors. If Lila takes anything, she's made it herself. She self-medicates."

Alex didn't like the sound of that.

Annie saw the expression on his face. "Nothing illegal or dangerous, mind you. Just concoctions she brews up. Her house usually smells like she's been cooking hay and old shoes, but she drinks the stuff and says it helps her memory. And she takes vitamins too. Her cupboards are just as full of vitamins as the Medi-Shop's pharmacy in Wheatville."

Annie began to ruffle through the pages of her music. "She's mostly harmless—as long as you don't try to get directions from her or ask her what happened on such-and-such a date. Lila's very 'in the moment,' like people say nowadays. 'Live in the Moment,' her bumper sticker says. Unfortunately that's the only moment Lila has sometimes."

"That's very sad," Alex commented.

"Not for Lila. She's the happiest little camper on earth." Her hand flew to her mouth. "Oh, I hear a car driving in. Find your place, Reverend, the race is about to begin."

Alex was grateful for the familiar faces that walked through the door to greet him. Mike Carlsen arrived in a suit, and Lauren in a brightly colored jacket that highlighted the copper in her hair. Dixon Daniels and Mark Nash followed not long after. Dixon had forgone the Red's cap and even tamed his hair. Mark, of course, looked perfectly at home in a suit. They were early, no doubt, to give him moral support. Angels, that's what they were, Alex decided, sent to bear him up on their wings.

Ava and Ralph Johnson arrived with Ralph's mother Isabelle. Isabelle, according to Gandy, was a bit of a legend around Hilltop. Though she was remarkable in many ways, including her age, most knew her for her driving skills—or lack of them. Exceedingly independent, Isabelle refused to give up her car for fear of losing her autonomy. Others, including her son and daughter-in-law, were more in fear for her life—and their own—as long as Isabelle was behind the wheel. It was, rumor had it, a long-running battle.

Alex glanced through the door and was pleased to see a few teenagers gathering outside. Two were talking on cell phones and one was listening to an iPod. Typical teenagers in every way. Alex didn't recognize any faces, but there were a couple of redheads in the bunch, and Will Packard came to mind. He hoped to see Will in church someday—if his father ever got over thinking the new pastor was crazy.

Other members of the call committee also came early. Stoddard Bloch stomped in, spine straight as if a steel rod ran up his back, wearing a gray wool jacket that looked hot and itchy on this beautiful day. His chins waggled as he walked. His wife Edith, in a pale blue, nondescript dress and bright cobalt blue shoes, scurried behind him like a little mother hen, clucking and chirping and agreeing with every word the man uttered.

Mattie Olsen followed, beaming happily because she'd met the new pastor *ages* ago and was pleased to tell that to anyone who would listen. She wore a hat with a veil, a fashion Alex hadn't seen since he was a young boy and then only on his grandmother.

Ole Swenson of Twinkle Toes fame arrived next. Wiry and thin,

Ole wore a well-tailored navy blue suit that was shiny in the seat and at the elbows but still looked good on his sinewy frame. "You'll have to stop over and see the pigs," he told Alex as he shook his hand vigorously. His voice crackled with age but was laced with good humor. "I hear you were there when my truck tipped and Twinkle Toes made a run for it. I'd like you to meet her again, under better circumstances." His laugh, a hearty, infectious chortle, bubbled from him and he winked at Alex. "If you come at noon, we'll have a pork sandwich."

That juxtaposition nearly sent Alex's imagination into overload.

Mildred and Winchester Holmquist made a regal pair. Chester, attentive and solicitous, stood with impressive military posture by his wife's side. Mildred's hair was silver-white and her face surprisingly unlined. Her expression was serene.

Hans and Hilda Aadland, elderly Norwegian immigrants and Scandinavian to the core, entered the church holding hands. They were followed by Margaret and Dale Keller. Margaret's quick, bird-like movements and Dale's propensity not to raise his voice above a whisper made them a particularly odd pair.

A woman with platinum-blond hair tottered in on improbable but very stylish shoes. She was perfectly made up with smart, tasteful clothes. The man with her was equally well dressed. They made a striking couple.

"I'm Belle Wells, Pastor, and this is my husband, Curtis. Welcome to the community. I hear you're from Chicago—how exciting! I'm from that area myself. We must have tea and talk about the city!" She turned with bright eyes to her husband. "Isn't that right, dear?"

"Oh yes," Curtis said absently, as if he'd quit listening to his wife quite some time ago.

As they walked away, Lauren sidled up to Alex and whispered, "Belle's never quite adjusted to being a country girl. She's always looking for someone who has been away from the farm. She and Curtis met while he was in the military and he swept her off her feet and carried her to Hilltop. I don't think she's ever gotten over it. Do you remember the old television show *Green Acres*? That's Curtis and Belle."

He was going to have to start a notebook, Alex decided as he greeted person after person, for keeping track of this wide and sometimes quirky flock. The buzz of conversation filled his ears, and young children gathered in the back pew to giggle and swing their legs.

Alex recognized the home-party lady by her perfume. Lilly Sumptner swished up to him in a stylish and puffy taffeta skirt and a cloud of Citrus Sunshine. She had her curly-haired husband Randy in tow. "My daughter in Minneapolis sent me this. Isn't it something?"

"It certainly is." It was something, all right, but Alex didn't know quite what. He'd never paid much attention to women's fashions. Apparently he should have.

A pleasant-looking young couple, Nancy and Ben Jenkins, introduced themselves and told Alex they lived on "the Hubbard place." Several people had mentioned it, but Alex still wasn't certain why.

"You'll have to stop by," Nancy said warmly, her brown eyes glowing. "We live in that old barn of a place, but someday soon we hope to have a home that doesn't have clanking radiators and drafty windows. It's better in the summer, so come soon. We love to entertain."

He'd be busy until a month from February, Alex realized, if he were to take everyone up on their offers of hospitality. He looked forward to it.

There were Clarence and Lydia Olson minus brother Jacob, downhearted Jonas Owens and his family, and so many others that Alex's brain threatened to implode. Even his study of the church directory hadn't prepared him for this.

A well-dressed and -coiffed couple, Katrinka and Harris Hanson, arrived, wondering out loud whether or not there would be food served after the service. Alex heard Matt and Martha Jacobson invite them over for a noon meal at their house to salve their disappointment at not having a free meal at church.

There were others, of course, some of whom stood out more in Alex's mind than others. Inga and Jim Sorenson were particularly memorable. Inga, the local artist, arrived in something she'd created out of what appeared to be white cotton dishcloths and tempera paints. Around her neck she wore a chunky, colorfully painted necklace made of clay beads. On her feet were slip-on white canvas shoes with faces painted on the toes so that they smiled out at all the other shoes. She was in her "youth and light" phase, she told Alex by way of introduction.

Her husband Jim made even Ole Swenson and Jonas Owens look obese. He was tall and beanpole thin, a skeleton with clothing. Alex heard him make a joke to Dixon about Inga's poor cooking. Alex made a mental note to himself avoid dinner at the Sorensons' home.

Then Annie Henderson began to play "What a Friend We Have in Jesus." That was Alex's cue to get to the front of the church. The Lord would take it from there.

He'd finished his sermon, one of his better ones, he hoped, and was shaking hands, when Dixon sidled up beside him and whispered in his ear. "You'd better get going or you won't get to All Saints on time for their service."

Alex glanced at his watch. "I know. I hope I haven't spent too much time visiting. Can I make it?"

"Depends on how heavy your foot is on the gas pedal," Dixon said with a grin.

Gravel roads were not meant for speeding, Alex decided on the way to All Saints. He gripped the wheel with both hands as the car shimmied, and he prayed he would stay on the road for the next nine miles. It would be a fine mess if the new preacher landed himself in the hospital the first Sunday out.

He winced as a small stone spit up from beneath his tires and made stone chips in the paint. He took his foot off the gas pedal and realized he was still stirring up a blinding cloud of dust behind him. He careened into the parking lot of All Saints and, legs still shaking from the adrenaline pumping in his system, grabbed his Bible and sermon notes and flew up the steps.

And all for fewer than twenty people.

They were clustered in the back pews like they wanted to leave as much space as possible between themselves and the new pastor. The organist hammered out "Beautiful Savior" on the piano, and a gaunt man with narrowed eyes, obviously the usher of the day, glared at him. The clock on the wall said 11:02.

Wherever two or more are gathered, he reminded himself. It didn't matter how many pews were filled. What mattered was who was in those pews. Whom did God want to speak to today?

He recognized Amy Clayborn and the elderly gray-haired woman from the quilting group. Amy smiled tentatively and the older woman, to his surprise, gave him a thumbs-up. It wasn't much, but it was enough encouragement enough to carry on. He'd hoped to see Alf Nyborg in the pew, but apparently he'd chosen not to come today. It was discouraging, but Alex refused to allow himself to dwell on it. Alf would be able to hear him preach for many Sundays to come.

Afterward, Alex couldn't remember what he said, but he hoped he'd stuck to his notes to some extent. It was alarming and a little nerve-racking to be late, ostracized and deemed an obvious disappointment on his first Sunday, but that was exactly how the experience had made him feel.

This was only his first Sunday, and Alex felt like he'd lived a few lifetimes during it. He was very glad to be able to go home and take a nap.

CHAPTER FIFTEEN

By Tuesday, a rainy spell had settled over Hilltop and, by the look of the weather report, much of the upper Midwest.

The sky was overcast—a dreary gray that reminded Alex of the color of a tired old bathrobe his father had worn for years. Rain came in a soft, fine mist that the farmers referred to as a soaker. Some of them were even beginning to tire of the persistent mist, which they would have preferred in early June rather than now in late July. Alex felt soggy around the edges, and his shoes never seemed quite dry even though they sat on the rug overnight.

He opened a folder on his desk and found a note from the treasurer for both churches, Walter Englund, with information concerning the two new windows All Saints had purchased. Someone had left him a prayer request, and there was a jar of Lydia's strawberry-rhubarb jam.

Tripod had followed Alex to the church and lay by the front door on a rag rug Gandy had brought from home. A dog with manners, he knew enough to stay there until he'd dried off before making his way to Alex's desk, where he remained the rest of the day, encouraged by the occasional doggie treats his master slipped to him when Gandy wasn't looking.

A slamming door and boots stomping across the wooden floor announced Gandy's arrival. She breezed in with a jolt of chill, damp air, pulled off a rain hat and shook it wildly, much the way Tripod shook himself after a dip in a slough.

"M'rning," she mumbled. She didn't look in Alex's direction. Instead, she turned her back to him, hung up her raincoat, and scuttled backward to her desk, where she sat down, grabbed a folder, and held it up to her face.

This was odd behavior, even for Gandy, who'd been very forthright about her quirks, which included chewing and snapping gum when she was nervous and an addiction to Milk Duds. He'd already come to rely on her to bring a ray of sunshine into the room. Especially on gloomy days, he welcomed her ever-ready smile.

"Gandy, are you okay?"

"Yup, yup. Fine. Never better." She pulled the folder closer to her nose. Her voice sounded nasal, like an old country-and-western singer.

"Did you catch a cold?"

"Healthy as a horse." The folder never moved. "But thanks for asking."

"Is the material in that folder urgent?" Alex rose from his desk.

"Just some stuff I should have finished up weeks ago. I need to order new candles, the ones with the little fishes on them, and some pew Bibles because we're a few short. Oh yes, and Annie requested some new musical arrangements so she'd have some on hand when someone volunteers to sing a solo—*Eeeek!*"

She squawked at Alex, who had stolen up beside her and lifted the folder from her hands. Her face was red and blotchy, puffy too, and her eyes looked boiled and bloodshot, like a pair of fake glasses Alex had once worn to a costume party.

"You've been crying."

"Now why'd you do that? I would have been just fine if you'd given me a few minutes to pull myself together." Her hands flapped inefficiently at her hair, which had turned into corkscrews in the rain. "I didn't want you to see me a mess but I didn't want to be late either.

She reached for a tissue from the box on her desk and blew her nose. It was a honk to rival that of the geese in Mike and Lauren's yard.

"Would you like to talk about it?" he asked gently. "I'm a good listener."

"Not particularly, but it's going to be all over anyway so you might as well hear it from me."

"And what is that?" He pulled up a chair and sat down across the desk from Gandy. "Would you like a cup of coffee first?"

"Please."

He allowed her a few more moments to gather herself together and then handed her the coffee in the mug she'd told him was her favorite. It stated in bold black letters MOSES WAS A BASKET CASE.

She inhaled the fragrant steam and sighed.

"What is going to be all over soon?" he prodded gently. "My brother Jonas has gone insane. It's all his worries. They've finally driven him out of his mind."

"Surely not."

"Really. His wife woke up from a deep sleep to find him screaming and pulling drawers out of the chests and pictures off the walls. He was crying and wailing and carrying on something frightful. He even pulled down the curtains! He was sleepwalking and having a fit. She finally got him to wake up by throwing a glass of water in his face. When he realized what he'd done, he sat down on the bed and cried like a baby. If that's not crazy, nothing is!"

Alex didn't think Jonas was crazy at all. The man was, however, in deep trouble.

"I don't know what we're going to do about him. Maybe we should have an intervention, or something." Gandy was pale and there was a small tic jumping beneath her right eye.

"Into what would you be intervening?"

"That's just it. There is nothing. My brother doesn't drink, smoke or gamble. He's faithful to his wife, God-fearing and family-loving." Gandy's eyes began to water and her lip to tremble. She looked at Alex with a pitiable expression. "And he's still crazy! Isn't it awful?"

"I think it's admirable that your brother is that fine a man, Gandy. He's distressed about the possibility of losing his farm. Anyone would be. Last night his anxieties and frustrations manifested themselves in his dreams. He's far from crazy. If he *weren't* upset, then I'd say you should worry."

"My sister-in-law told me she found a bunch of nasty letters he'd hidden from her—credit card collection agencies and the like. It's worse than even she knew. I know he's at his wits' end, and I have no idea what to do for him. We don't have any money to loan him, that's for sure. I'm afraid if he does sell the land to those people he will never forgive himself."

Alex recalled the meeting in the café with distaste.

"Selling the land to someone he knows would be hard enough, but these strangers… You saw them, you know they're hovering overhead like vultures waiting for Jonas to get so desperate that he calls them. He has good, productive land; and there's money to be made except, apparently, by Jonas." Gandy's face crumpled and she looked as if she would cry again. "I think he's close to doing it. And if he does, I don't know what will happen to him."

"When he asked the neighbors if they were interested in buying his land, did they all say no?"

Gandy looked askance. "He didn't even let on he was having problems. He was too ashamed to admit the trouble he'd gotten into. People suspected things were going badly, but no one knew how badly until recently. Things are tight for everyone right now, and no one has extra money lying around. Jonas wouldn't approach the neighbors because he'd never put anyone in the awkward position of having to turn him down." Her entire body drooped like a wilting flower. "His troubles would still be a secret if he could help it. Jonas thinks asking for help is the same as asking for handouts."

"Buying land outright is hardly a handout."

"You don't know my brother very well yet, Reverend Alex. He's a proud man. He certainly wouldn't grovel."

Alex had seen that for himself.

"'I hate pride and arrogance,'" Alex quoted softly, more to himself than to Gandy. "'I have good advice and sound wisdom.' Proverbs 8."

"Jonas? He isn't arrogant."

"Not in the sense you mean. In this verse, arrogance is synonymous with pride. When we find ourselves wanting to do things our own way, to figure out our own answers, we're struggling with our pride, resisting God's leadership and refusing His help. God doesn't want us to do anything without Him. He wants to help. He's *waiting to help*—and we persistently thumb our noses at Him."

Gandy was silent as she pondered this.

"It would be insulting, wouldn't it? To have so much to give, yet to have those you want to help refuse it time and time again." She crossed her arms over her chest and frowned. "So by thinking his way is the only way, Jonas is refusing to let God into the picture?"

"It's something to consider."

"If Jonas were to let God handle it without any input from him, what do you think would happen?"

"I have no way of predicting God, Gandy. All I do know is that if Jonas were resting fully on God's wisdom, he'd probably sleep better at night."

She looked Alex up and down with an appraising stare. "I'll talk to Jonas." She brightened, and her persistent optimism returned.

"Maybe God's getting everything set up to help Jonas out of this mess and just waiting for the go-ahead from Jonas himself."

"Setting up? What do you mean?"

"We've been without a preacher for a long time. Now we've got one. Maybe God sent you to help Jonas through this." She smiled for the first time. "I'll bet you're it, the answer to my prayers and Jonas's too!"

"Gandy, I can't fix your brother's financial issues, all I'm saying is—"

"Pray about it, will you? See what God has to say about my brother."

∾

"I'm really in for it now, Tripod," Alex groaned after he and the dog had taken a particularly long run that evening. "I can't fix problems with a snap of my fingers."

Tripod whined in commiseration and put his head dolefully on the floor.

"Or maybe I'm being as falsely humble as Jonas has been prideful," Alex murmured thoughtfully. He'd almost immediately taken to talking to the dog, who was, as Dixon had promised, an excellent listener. Of course he couldn't fix this. But God could. He would ask God to show him exactly what part he was to play in this unfolding drama.

Alex mounted the steps to his room two at a time and shed his running clothes in a pile on his bedroom floor. Before he stepped into the shower, he decided to do the deed he'd been dreading. He ventured onto the bathroom scale and watched the needle jump and flutter until it settled on a number.

It had to be broken. He backed off, made sure it was set properly and stepped on again. The number was the same. Surely it couldn't be—he was up eight pounds. In such a brief time? And he'd thought he'd shrunk his trousers in the wash! Horrified, he turned on the shower and stepped in even before the water had time to get warm. The cold, pelting droplets brought him to his senses. If he wasn't careful, he would turn into a round-faced, chubby caricature of himself. A six-foot-tall Tweedledum was what he'd be—pants hiked past his ample stomach to his armpits and held aloft by suspenders. He shuddered at the thought. Things would have to change around here. And quickly!

He approached the refrigerator warily when it was time to prepare his meal. There was a rasher of bacon and a quart of real cream in a Mason jar from Ole, who milked a few cows in addition to raising the pigs. Half of a to-die-for chocolate cake sat on the second shelf with a casserole of fresh garden vegetables swimming in butter and a half gallon of whole milk. In the cupboard were deep fried chips, chocolate chip cookies and a dozen boxes of items containing dreaded trans fats. He made himself a bowl of instant oatmeal and watered down the milk until it had the pale blue look of skim. He tried to feed his leftovers to Tripod but even the dog wouldn't eat them. It had to have been nasty for him to reject them.

Then he picked up the phone and dialed the Carlsens. "You're sounding a little down," Lauren observed when she heard his voice. She could pick up nuances in a person's voice more quickly than anyone else Alex had ever met. "Something wrong?"

"Where's a place to buy vegetables? Fresh ones, I mean." The long silence at her end of the line surprised him. He didn't think he'd asked a difficult question.

"What about your garden? If everything isn't ready yet it will be soon. Unless, of course, you want beets, cabbage, or melons. I didn't plant any of those this year. The grocery store has things, but mostly we don't *buy* vegetables. We *grow* them."

"What about people who don't have gardens? Where do they get fresh produce? Or do they settle for canned and frozen?" He heard the judgment in his question—suggesting that these options were second best. It was ironic, since the majority of the food his mother had ever served him was either frozen or canned. But at the moment he was on a mission. The waistband cutting into his midsection was reminder of that.

"I'll have Mike run over with a bag of tomatoes. And there's still some nice lettuce even though I've had a few cuttings. And green beans—I have them coming out my ears."

"You don't have to give me anything, Lauren. I'll have plenty soon, but it makes me wonder about the people who want to buy fresh things."

"It's a good question, Alex. It's just that around Hilltop we haven't needed an answer."

"What about Grassy Valley?"

"There are gardens there too, I suppose."

"How about a farmers' market?"

"There's one in Wheatville, but no one will drive forty or fifty miles to buy radishes or even corn when it's all right here. I doubt anyone around here has ever considered that there are people who actually need to buy that stuff."

"I see. Then how about organic foods?" He was going to improve his health even if it killed him, he decided.

"There are farmers around who don't use pesticides, if that's what you mean. Jonas Owens is one of them. And there is an organic food section in the grocery store. Unfortunately it's limited to soy milk, soy yogurt, and frozen gluten-free bread. There are a couple of kids in town with allergies. What is this all about, anyway?"

He told her about the number on the scale and his dreadful oatmeal, and she burst out laughing.

"Everyone who comes to Hilltop has the same problem at first. Don't worry, people will feed you less and less, and the busier you get the more quickly you'll see the pounds fade." She lowered her voice. "And if you don't tell anyone, I'll bring you vegetable lasagna that's out of this world but is absolutely healthy and low-cal. Don't worry; you'll be back in shape in no time flat."

He could only hope.

❧

Gandy's face was long when Alex walked into the church office the next morning. She didn't even greet him with her usual cheer.

He pulled up a wooden chair in front of her desk and straddled it, his arms folded over the back of the chair. "What's wrong?"

"Jonas's telephone has been shut off."

"I'm sorry, Gandy."

"The lights were about to be shut off too, but I scraped up enough for the light bill."

Alex reached into his back pocket for his billfold. "Let me help." He pulled out a twenty dollar bill, all he had, and put it on Gandy's desk. "I can get more."

Gandy put her hand over his. "You've helped my brother so much already. It's Barbara who worries me. She's not handling this well. She told Jonas that if he couldn't figure this out, she'd take the kids and go to her mother's until he did."

"Is there anything we can do?"

"She's as bad as my brother about accepting help. Right now I think we have to wait this out."

So they settled into their work for the day. Gandy busied herself at her desk while Alex puttered around the office.

"Somebody's bellowing like they're being hog-tied and skinned out there," Gandy said, looking up from her desk where she was compiling the new church directory. She nodded toward the door.

Alex, who was on a ladder changing an overhead lightbulb, carefully descended. Because he was agile and strong, climbing usually didn't frighten him, but a ladder with legs of mismatched lengths and a broken rung put the fear of falling into him. No use cracking his head open or breaking a leg if he could prevent it.

"I'll see what's wrong. By the way, see if you can find a space in next year's church budget for a new ladder, or at least put out a cry for help in Sunday's bulletin. Maybe someone has one they aren't using and would be willing to donate."

The front door flew open, and the source of the shrieking and bawling entered. It was Will Packard, being half-pulled and half-carried by a furious Clarence Olson. Will's hands and feet were churning like little windmills. Fortunately Clarence had been blessed with long arms and could dodge most of Will's flailing.

"I found this young hooligan in my pigsty with a pail full of garter snakes, a bird with a broken wing and that wretched skunk the Packards call a pet." Clarence's face turned the color of boiled beets. "And he said you gave him permission to be there!"

Garter snakes, Alex had observed in his back yard, had long colored stripes—mostly yellow in this region—and dark blotchy stripes between the yellow. They were harmless but snakes, nevertheless.

"Me? I…" Alex looked intently at Will, who'd quit thrashing and was now staring up at the pastor with a fearful expression. "Will, I did not tell you to take your…your…humane society to the Olsons'."

"Well, you said I had to take it out of the church shed. What was I

JUDY BAER ~ 169

supposed to do?" He scowled fiercely. "I thought you were going to help me find a new place!"

"The Carlsens took the cat and the chickens, and you gave the kittens away. I thought your shelter was closed down."

"Are you kidding?" Will looked at him, aghast. "There will always be animals to rescue, don't you know? 'If it's not one thing, it's another,' my mom always says. Right now the other thing is a bunch of garter snakes that Bucky was going after with a hoe and that bird I found. I think I can patch him up good as new. I've done it before."

"I didn't think you'd start collecting again after our little talk about using the shed."

"How could I stop?" Will's small face was intent and every freckle stood out. "Hurtin' animals are just like the poor, don't you know?"

Alex blinked. "What do you mean?"

"And you call yourself a preacher!" Will looked disgusted. "It's another verse my ma taught us. 'You always have the poor with you.' Well, we'll always have hurtin' critters too."

Out-quoted by a nine-year-old. Alex liked this child immensely. Despite the trouble he seemed determined to cause, he was clever and quick-witted. If that naughty energy could be channeled into something productive, he'd be a real dynamo.

"So did you or did you not tell him to use my pigsty?" Clarence finally let go of the boy. Will tumbled to the floor.

"I did not. Will thought that up by himself. The problem is, no matter how many times we kick him out of buildings, I believe he will find a new place and start collecting animals all over again."

"Not at my place," Clarence rumbled.

"No, definitely not there," Alex agreed, "but we're open to suggestions."

Pacified, Clarence's color was beginning to return to normal. "Why can't he use his own farm?"

"Are you serious?" Will chirruped. "My pa would kill me! Don't think he hasn't been tempted already."

Even Clarence's expression softened at that. Will's father was a real piece of work, Alex thought. Poor kid.

"Well, I'll leave him with you, Reverend. Just make sure he has that bucket of snakes and company out of my shed in the next hour." Clarence stormed out.

Gandy, who'd listened to the entire exchange with rapt interest, pretended to look at the directory, a smile playing at the corners of her mouth.

Will straightened himself indignantly. "I don't know why he's so persnickety. He wasn't using that old sty anyway. And he didn't have to be so crabby either. The snakes are already out of the bucket."

A warning bell sounded in Alex's head. "Then where are they?"

Will grinned at him. His front teeth were too big for the rest of him. "I kicked the bucket over when he wasn't looking. Now they're all over his yard."

"Will..."

The boy glanced over his shoulder and saw the organist Annie Henderson mounting the steps of the church with a sheaf of music in her hands. "Gotta go, Pastor Alex. Looks like you've got company." He darted out of Alex's grasp and headed for the door.

"We're going to discuss this, Will Packard. And you aren't going to get out of it!" he called after the boy.

Will never turned around, but he waved his hand over his shoulder and disappeared from sight.

"What are you going to do?" Gandy asked. She'd cheered up considerably now that her mind was on things other than her brother.

"I'm not sure. I'm afraid that Will's father will punish him more severely than the infraction calls for, but I really can't ignore it."

"Will's mama is a good woman. Maybe you could talk to her." Gandy picked up the phone. "I'll see if she answers the phone."

Almost before Alex could gather his wits, she handed him the phone.

"Hello, Mrs. Packard, my name is—"

"Gandy told me. How nice of you to call." Her voice was sweet and mild, and Alex immediately understood why it was difficult for her to stand up to her husband.

"I'm afraid this is a bit of a business call. It's about Will."

Her sigh came across the line loud and clear. "Now what's that child done?"

Alex told her about Will's animal rescue and the bucket of snakes.

She was silent for a long time. When she spoke, there was amusement in her voice. "You know, it might even be funny if I didn't know Will's daddy would punish him terribly if he knew."

"About that—"

"My husband loses his way sometimes, mostly when he's been drinking. I keep praying that God will pick him up and shake some sense into him and scare him sober, but I don't know when that will be."

"So I should leave the conversation with Will to you?"

"I'll take care of it, Reverend, although I can't promise how much it will help. My Will has a big heart for hurting things, and I really don't want to punish that out of him."

"I know you'll do your best."

"I'll try. And by the way, I'd appreciate it if you'd pray for my husband. I can't think of anyone who needs it more."

Humbled by the woman's faith and endurance, Alex hung up the phone.

At the end of the day Alex was relieved to hear Mark Nash's calm, refined voice on the other end of the phone line. "Have you got plans for supper?"

"Not really." He had a freezer full of rich desserts and casseroles, but nothing that was going to help him shed a few pounds.

"Tonight is meat loaf night at the Cozy Corner Cafe."

"Does that place serve salads?" He looked longingly at the candy dish on his desk. Gandy had filled it with miniature chocolate bars.

"Definitely."

"Then I'll come."

"Good. I'll pick you up in ten minutes."

The café was busy; meat loaf was apparently a popular item. Despite the plates of mashed potatoes and glistening brown gravy going by, Alex ordered a chef's salad with oil and vinegar on the side. Then he told Mark about getting on the scale and the too-tight trousers.

Instead of getting sympathy or the least little bit of commiseration, Mark, like Lauren, burst out laughing. "I could have told you that would happen. Just be glad you caught it before it turned into twenty or thirty pounds. That happened to a pastor many years back. He looked like a walking heart attack before the ladies started feeding him roasted turkey breast and fruit salads instead of fried chicken and ambrosia."

Alex said nothing for a long while. His mind had wandered to something far more important than his waistband. "Have you heard how Jonas is doing?"

"Like I said before, I knew Jonas was in trouble," Mark said softly. "I'd have to be blind not to, but even I had no idea how deep it was." He looked troubled. "Maybe on some level I didn't *want* to know. There have been Owenses on that land since the 1800s."

"Isn't there any other way? Could he grow something that would bring in more cash?"

"Only thing I can think of is wind."

"Grow wind? I know you can do wonderful things out here, but isn't that a little over the top?"

"I mean wind farms. There are several in the state, big windmills that turn wind into energy, but those things cost a pretty penny. No, this has to be something quick, something that would help Jonas immediately."

"If you can think of any way I can help him other than moral support and prayer, let me know, will you?"

Mark looked at him with sympathy in his eyes. "You got thrown into the deep end of the pool here, didn't you, Alex?"

Chapter Sixteen

Mark's words resonated in Alex's head. Actually, he'd been swimming in the deep end of things for some time now.

To his relief, thoughts of Natalie and curiosity about what might have happened had they stayed together came less often now. Because he was occupied with other things, the sting was not quite so sharp. For this he was grateful. He couldn't have borne that original agony for very long. Still, he felt emotionally bruised. The wound was still tender.

He said that very thing to his sister when she called Friday afternoon.

"Are there any interesting ladies in Grassy Valley?" she'd asked hopefully.

"I have no idea, Carol. I'm not looking."

"You can't hide out there, Alex, and avoid relationships altogether. You deserve a good wife by your side."

How like Carol to worry about his heart.

"I didn't say I'm against marrying someday, Sis. But I'm hardly good husband material. I advise people all the time not to marry on the rebound. Besides, I'm not even sure what all led up to her decision. She refused to talk about it."

That bothered Alex more than anything, leaving things so open and unfinished. In his position as a pastor, the reconciliation of divided parties was practically part of his job description; yet in his own important relationship, there had been no settlement, no feeling of completion. But that was too difficult for him to attempt to explain to Carol, so he changed the subject. Carol always loved a party.

"The people here are planning an open house for me."

"How nice! When Jared got home from North Dakota, he immediately told me how nice the people were there."

"How *is* Jared? I really enjoyed having him travel with me."

"Impossible. Crabby. Angry. Irritable. Surly. Shall I go on?"

"Are we talking about the same kid?"

"I don't know what's with him. I told him he should take a preparatory class in August in order to be ready for college testing, and he hit the roof. He roared that he *wasn't* going to college and that his dad and I couldn't make him. He's hardly spoken to us since."

"Something is going on, Sis. He's never been like that."

"I wish you were here, Alex. He's always been close to you. Maybe he'd tell you something."

"Maybe," Alex said vaguely. He'd worked with college kids long enough to know that if they didn't want to talk, dynamite wouldn't get it out of them. "Tell him to call me when he's ready to discuss it."

After the call, he decided to make some calls of his own—of the face-to-face variety.

He climbed into his van. As soon as Alex was settled, Tripod leaped from the ground like a horse jumping a fence.

He soared past Alex's lap and landed on the passenger seat. He sat there looking expectant, as if this maneuver should earn him praise or at least a scratch behind the ear.

Although Alex didn't want to reward the dog for bad behavior, Tripod's strength and agility were admirable. The dog had become his personal shadow, and Alex had to admit he liked it.

Until he'd moved to Hilltop, there had been so much noise in his life—students, peers, traffic, televisions, radios, complaining staff—that it was a little *too* quiet here. But there was also more time to spend in study and prayer. And the more he did, the more he wanted. He was always hungry for the Word, and there was much more silence here with which to sate it. He was beginning to like it. Who could have predicted that Alex Armstrong would become a country boy?

But not all silence was golden. All Saints was an active volcano rumbling and churning beneath the surface, and Alex was steeling himself for an explosion. So far, however, they'd been absorbed with the installation of two stained-glass windows, gifts from two families in memory of loved ones.

Alex was eager to see them in place. It would certainly warm up the church's interior. Even that was a step in the right direction. The thaw had to start somewhere.

He'd been back to the church to visit with the quilting ladies, but never run into Alf Nyborg. Was that intentional? If so, he'd have to be the one to seek Nyborg out.

But first he wanted to visit with Mildred and Chester Holmquist. Dixon had told him that Chester understood Alf about as well as anyone could, since over the years he and Chester had occasionally driven to meetings together at the VFW in Wheatville.

"Are you ready for the open house at the parsonage this afternoon?" Gandy asked when he walked into the church on Wednesday morning. She was busying digging plastic flowers out of a large rubber tub. She held up a cluster of crimson roses. "Do you want the fancy decorations for the table, or do you prefer fresh-cut flowers?"

"Fresh-cut, I think."

"I've got five dozen cookies in the car I'd like to put in your kitchen, if you don't mind. I'll check your flowers then."

"You are a treasure, Gandy. I don't tell you that nearly often enough."

"I hope you still thank me when this thing is over. I haven't heard if anyone from All Saints is attending."

"Don't worry. We've extended the invitation. Now the ball is in their court."

The ball might be in All Saint's court, Alex mused as people began to arrive at the parsonage, but evidently they weren't interested in returning the serve. There wasn't an All Saints member in the bunch.

He found the Holmquists in his backyard, though, beneath a lawn umbrella, and he headed toward them.

It was no wonder Mildred's beauty was legendary, Alex thought. Her cheekbones were high and her face an attractive oval. Though she was deep into her eighties, her face was remarkably unlined. There'd been no long days in the sun for her. Her white hair was of a silvery cast and framed her placid face in soft wisps. Mildred's delicate, pale pink dress swirled around her ethereally, as if it were part chiffon and part cotton candy.

"My girl is lovely, isn't she?" Chester looked at her with adoring eyes. "She won a beauty pageant, you know, Miss Midwest Heartland in 1949. I'm a lucky man. Do you know how many suitors she had? Why..."

Before Alex could respond, a blushing Mildred put a hand on Chester's arm. "Now, don't go talking like a besotted teenager, dear. The reverend will think we're a silly old couple reliving our youth. Chat about something substantial. Tell him about that antique musket you just purchased for your gun collection."

That wasn't exactly what Alex had hoped to discuss, but he smiled and nodded.

Chester looked at Alex with an appraising eye. "You might think it's strange, keeping all these old guns around and enjoying them the way I do, but I've got my reasons. These guns remind me of all that has been sacrificed over the years. I spent my entire career as a military man, but now I'm a man of peace, not war."

"Me too," Alex said softly.

They stood silently, side by side, watching children playing tag on the lawn for a long while before Alex spoke. "I understand that Alf Nyborg was in the military as well. Mark Nash told me that the two of you sometimes rode together to the VFW in Wheatville. He suggested that you might be able to tell me a little more about him. I know he's very influential at All Saints."

"Alf is a funny guy," Chester murmured more to himself than to Alex. "He's probably avoiding you."

"He doesn't even know me."

"Alf holds things inside and lets them build up. He is, rightly or wrongly, upset with Hilltop. Alf carries grudges like a mule carries pack bags. Mildred compares him to a pressure cooker. When he has to, he lets off just enough steam so that he doesn't explode, but he's hot and angry inside all the time anyway. If he ever blows, he'll scald everyone around him."

"Has he always been this way?"

"No. He was a different person before the fire that took his first wife and child." Chester's expression saddened. "Always laughing, telling jokes. Cheerful as could be. Of course, I can't blame him. After a tragedy like that, I'd quit smiling too."

"How did it happen?" Alex felt a desperate need to understand this man who was so actively standing between him and one of his parishes.

"An accident, pure and simple. It started near a propane furnace in his basement. Bad luck. Propane is volatile around sparks. The furnace exploded, taking the house with it. Alf's wife and five-year-old son were inside. He was out in the barn, milking cows. He never had a chance to save them. When the fire truck arrived, he was trying to get inside and his clothes were on fire. They got to him before the burns went too deep, but he was scarred for life, inside and out."

Life had run roughshod over him, that much was clear. "He's been angry ever since. Alf remarried—a nice woman with a heart of compassion. They had another son and a daughter who are both grown. They don't come home very often, and I can't blame them. They were able to escape." Chester shook his gray head mournfully.

"All Saints wasn't so lucky. Alf emptied himself and his suffering into work for the church. It was as if he tried to fill the hole inside himself, the one left by his first wife and son. It's my theory that Alf does all he does at All Saints to help himself forget.

"It didn't sweeten him up, unfortunately, but it did make All Saints dependent upon him. He's held every office and been on every committee. He works tirelessly on the building and grounds. It's thanks to him that they have new cupboards in the kitchen. He made them by hand. And he's the one who recently started to buy and plant trees around the cemetery. When All Saints needs funds, Alf chips in. He alone likely pays half of the salary you get from All Saints."

That made Alex particularly uncomfortable.

"He's treasurer, custodian, and permanent church board member. All Saints has been relying on him for so long—and their numbers have shrunk in the past few years—that they are afraid to be without him."

"So he's the primary spokesperson for the church?" The unfortunate picture was growing clearer.

"Yes. And just about everything else. In his effort to move past his pain, he's trained those people to depend on him."

"Where does God fit into this picture?" Alex inquired softly. The noise and clatter of the party receded as they spoke.

"Alf would like to boss Him around too." The old man's expression was grieved. "I think he still blames Him for that fire. Of course, that's a lot easier than blaming himself."

A sense of foreboding spread in Alex. "What do you mean?"

"A couple of days before the fire, Alf had run a new piece of copper tubing to the furnace from the outside propane tank. Every day of his life he's wondered if he missed something when he checked the connection to the furnace for a proper seal. If he did, he was responsible for the fire. He couldn't bear that. Of course many other things could have happened. A spark inside the furnace when it kicked in, for instance. Alf's little boy was found downstairs, with the remains of the family dog. They could have set something off by accident. Who knows? It's been killing Alf slowly for years."

A shudder ran though Alex, followed by a surge of compassion. No wonder Nyborg was a difficult man, considering the pain he'd carried around inside him all these years.

Even though Gandy seemed determined to keep him busy every minute of the workdays, Alex couldn't get his mind off Alf. Neither, it seemed, could anyone else.

Although the open house was a rip-roaring success as far as Hilltop's congregation was concerned—the ladies particularly loved the new kitchen—All Saints members' notable absence cast a pall over the otherwise delightful party.

"Can you believe it?" Lilly Sumptner said, waving a spatula in the air. "Not a soul showed up from All Saints. I'll bet Alf Nyborg is behind it. How rude!" She went back to dishing up the marble cake, which was being eaten almost as fast as she could get it out of the pan.

The women in the kitchen nodded dolefully as if they'd all thought the same thing.

"More for us," Katrinka Hanson said brightly. "May I take home some leftovers?"

Katrinka, or Trinka, as most people called her, enjoyed free food, Alex had observed. It was, Lauren had told him, a money-saving measure. The Hansons were quite wealthy, but they'd never gotten over squeezing everything they could out of a penny.

In the yard, Alf wasn't faring much better.

Alex pulled Dixon aside. "Why is everyone so sure Alf is behind All Saints' absence today?"

"Because he usually is."

It was a puzzle, Alex thought, one he'd have to solve—soon.

∾

No time like the present, Alex told himself the next morning as he drove out of his yard. It was now or never. He was going to talk with Alf about the enmity he had toward Hilltop. Love, he thought, was the only antidote for what ailed this man. Ignoring the situation was out of the question, and expecting him to be rational about something that would cause anyone to become irrational was naïve. He'd depend on God for orders on this one.

His cell phone rang, startling him so much that he might have driven into the ditch had he not been crawling along at a snail's pace.

It was Gandy. "The Ladies Aid wants to know what they should serve next Sunday. We're going to have a fund-raiser for missions. Do you have any favorites?"

"Favorite missions or favorite foods?"

"Very funny. Food, of course."

"I've never been in a place that fuels everything they do with food. Tell them to surprise me."

"That could be dangerous. Last time the ladies surprised someone, they'd gotten a line on a hundred pounds of *lutefisk*. I'm not sure you're ready for that."

"Lutefisk?"

"Like I said, you're not ready yet."

"Gandy, you started this. The least you can do is tell me what lutefisk is."

"It's cod fish soaked in lye. Around here they serve it with boiled potatoes, peas, and *lefse*. My mother likes it with mashed rutabagas. When you cook it, it becomes translucent and stinks like crazy. Then you pour butter all over it and…"

"You're right. I'm not ready for that." His stomach roiled at the thought of stinky fish and mashed rutabagas.

"I thought so. I'll tell them, but you aren't going to get out of eating it forever, you know. Around here some people compare it to eating lobster."

"Gandy, pouring butter on overshoes would make them taste better too, but I'm still not interested."

"Consider yourself warned. Lutefisk is in your future." Perhaps the future was bleaker than he'd anticipated. "Anything new at church?"

"Brunie called to say Bessie was having a bad day and asked that we pray for her. Bessie's obsessive compulsive disorder is kicking up, and she has been washing her hands all day. Walter Englund called to let you know that he'd be happy to go over the church books with you any time. Sam Waters, who owns the hardware store behind the grocery store, heard our ladder was bad and offered to give us a new one. Oh yes, and Porkchop Smith has a lot more soup bones than he can sell. He wanted to know if we want some for a soup dinner or something. I told him yes. I hope that's okay with you."

"Sure, I suppose so." No one in seminary told him he'd have to decide about soup bones. "How's Jonas? Have you heard from him lately?"

"No, but I talked to my sister-in-law this morning. She said he prowled the house half the night." Gandy hesitated and Alex heard a catch in her voice. "She asked me if I knew of anyone who might rent them a house—cheap. I think it would break my sister-in-law's heart if she had to give up her house."

Gandy cleared her throat. "She also asked if I knew if the grocery store threw away expired produce."

"They're that hard up for food?"

"I told Lauren about it, and she's going to see what she can do."

"There should be a food shelf in Grassy Valley," Alex commented.

"Lauren said the same thing. Maybe she can get one up and running, but I doubt it will be in time to help Jonas's family."

Alex's mind whirled with what he'd learned about Alf's heart-break and with his concern for Jonas. He'd wanted to be a pastor of a small church where he could serve people and love them. And God, in His generosity, had given him exactly what he'd asked for.

Alex's heart felt bigger out here, like it had grown as expansive as the prairie he'd come to. That old cliché was true. God did not call the qualified to serve Him; instead He qualified the called.

Still, when All Saints Church appeared on the horizon, Alex's gut clenched.

There were cars parked around the church—the quilting ladies, no doubt, because they often met more than once a week. One of them would steer him toward Alf if he was not already somewhere in the church.

Alex walked into the sanctuary to look at the newly installed windows and found it fascinating which two scenes had been chosen—the stoning of Stephen and Daniel in the lions' den. They had been chosen, Dixon had told him, by Alf. Had he selected them because of the dark, hard places he'd been in his own life? Was that how he felt—like he was being pelted to death by grief or in mortal danger of being eaten alive by his own feelings? It was one more thing to think about.

He walked down the stairs, dodging the beam that threatened to behead anyone who walked under it, and emerged in the dining area.

The ladies were all standing around a table, a large piece of freezer paper with pencil sketches lying before them. Seven heads turned and seven pairs of eyes seemed to pierce right through him.

Ignoring the welcome, Alex strode to the table. "Good morning, ladies. Hard at work, already? Between you and the quilters at Hilltop, I don't believe I've ever seen such industrious workers."

They didn't seem to know whether to take this as a compliment or not, Alex noted. Never mind. It was his plan to put All Saints and Hilltop into the same sentence as often as possible. "We're planning a new quilt," Amy said. She pointed to the drawing. It was divided into squares, and on each of them was the name of the family who attended All Saints. The Nyborg name was squarely in the middle.

"Each of us is going to make a quilt block depicting something important to the history of our family. When we put it together, it will be a history book made of fabric. We plan to hang it right here." She pointed to an empty wall that was crying out for decoration.

"That's a great idea," Alex said, genuinely meaning it. "Then I can look at the quilt and know more about you. It's a perfect tool to introduce a green preacher to his congregation."

Smiles spread across the ladies' faces, and one woman stepped forward. "My name is Emma Bright. I'm glad you like our idea. We never thought about it that way, but you're right. It's not just for us but for everyone who comes to All Saints."

It's not just for us.

"Exactly! No church is just for its members. If a church isn't reaching out, it is dying from within." A glimmer of hope fluttered within him. "I wish Hilltop would do something similar." Then he paused. Maybe they didn't want to hear about Hilltop.

"You mean they haven't done anything like this?" Emma said.

"Not that I know of. I can ask Gandy, of course, but there's nothing on display."

"So we're the first?" Her eyes brightened and a small, *Mona Lisa* smile graced her features.

Alex could see that the women liked this idea. The little sister had finally come up with a new idea, one that deserved some attention. "You are. If you don't mind, I'd like to suggest that the Hilltop quilters do something similar. I'm sure they'd be pleased to hear of it. Maybe you ladies could advise them as to how to go about it."

The smiles were a little wider now and the tension in the room had been erased by something close to conviviality. "In fact," Alex continued, building on the small opening that had occurred. "I'd love to visit your group sometimes and hear the family stories while you work. Would you mind?"

"Not at all," Emma said, "and plan to stay for coffee."

"I'll do that. I hope you won't get sick of me. I'm very anxious to know you all better."

"You really mean it, don't you?" There was a bit of wonder in Amy's voice. "Alf always said…"

Alex decided to pretend he hadn't heard her last words. "Of course I mean it! What's more, Gandy told me that someone in this group makes something called a Sally Ann molasses cookie. Is there any chance of me tasting one of those during coffee hour some day?"

A woman in the back blushed a furious red. The maker of the Sally Anns, no doubt.

He stayed a half hour more, relishing the relaxed laughter and the chatty discussion of molasses cookie recipes. At least one door at All Saints had been opened.

When he left, it was with a sack of cookies, directions to the Nyborg farm and, at least for the moment, a lighter heart.

It seemed that the closer he got to the Nyborg farm, the rougher and narrower the road became. He thought it was rather appropriate as his tire sank into a pothole and threatened to stay there. If Alf had wanted to deter guests, he couldn't have picked a better method.

The farm itself was nice enough, tidy and well kept. There were few trees and fewer flowers. The house was large but simple, a rambler with gray shutters and pale blue siding. Most of the windows were closed, the drapes drawn tight. Maybe Alf had even expelled sunlight from his life.

"You're making things up, Armstrong," Alex muttered to himself. In his anxiety, he'd built this meeting up to be something painful and ominous. It didn't have to be that way. Still, he prayed for wisdom for the meeting ahead.

The large door was open to the machine shed. Through it, Alex could see a large green combine. A shadow moved, and a man jumped down from the cab and walked out into the sunlight wiping his hands on a greasy rag.

He was in his midsixties, a little round at the middle as if his once substantial chest had migrated southward. His legs, clad in denim, were thin, bordering on spindly, and his shoulders slightly rounded. He wore a checked cotton shirt and an old vest from which tools sprouted. On his head was a cotton bucket hat with a down-sloping brim to shield the sun from his eyes. There were harsh lines in his face, the kind that come with suffering.

"Yeah? What do you want?" was the not-so-friendly greeting. "If you're selling something, I don't want it."

That, despite the fact that Alf knew full well who he was. Nyborg wasn't going to make this easy.

"Hi. I'm Alex Armstrong, your…" He held out a hand, which Alf didn't take.

"What are you doing here?"

"Just visiting." Alex allowed his hand to drop to his side. "I'd like to get to know the members of All Saints better, and since you are currently president of the congregation, I thought that we should—"

"I've been president of our church council for years. Nobody else seems to want it."

Alex decided not to touch that.

Alf looked at him from beneath furrowed brows. "Just so you know, we're not Hilltop, and Hilltop's not us."

"That's been obvious to me since I got here. You are your own special entity. Every church has a personality, Mr. Nyborg. I wouldn't dream of trying to take that away from you."

"No?" Alf looked surprised. "Well…good."

At that moment, a woman with mouse-brown hair exited the house and came toward them carrying a large Thermos and paper cups. "You aren't much of a host, Alf. Who do we have here?" She had pleasant features and an air of kindness about her that Alex sensed immediately.

"Mrs. Nyborg? I'm Alex Armstrong."

She glanced sharply at her husband and then back at Alex. "Welcome. It's good to have a new face in the pulpit. I like fresh starts, don't you?" Her choice of words seemed directed at her husband, who ignored them completely. "My name is Betty." She reached out her hand and gave Alex's a shake with a firm, warm grip.

"I understand you were on the call committee from All Saints, Mr. Nyborg, but I didn't get the opportunity to talk to you during the interview."

"What was the point?" Nyborg didn't mince words. "Those

people were going to do what they were going to do whether I liked you or not."

"Would you like to come inside and have some of this lemonade? That way we'd be out of the sun," Mrs. Nyborg suggested in an attempt to diffuse the awkward situation.

"I can't stop working to be lollygagging around the house," Alf said shortly. "Go ahead, Reverend, if you want, but you'll have to excuse me." With that, he turned and headed back to the shop.

Betty smiled apologetically and gestured Alex toward the house. "Just because he's cranky, it doesn't mean that we can't enjoy ourselves. Come on."

The interior of the house was like that of so many ramblers built in the late 1950s and early 1960s: kitchen, living, and dining areas across the front, and a row of bedrooms and baths behind, running down a long hall. It was meticulously neat.

"Sit down. I'll get you a real glass to drink from." She set the paper cups aside and went to the cupboard. Then she sat down across from Alex, folded her hands and beamed at him. "I am *so* glad you're here."

"Tell me a little about yourself," Alex encouraged. "I'm on a mission to learn a little something about everyone in the community." He tapped his head with his forefinger. "And to keep their names and faces straight."

"Good luck with that. The older I get, the leakier my brain becomes. Some days my memory is like a sieve." She sipped her lemonade. "You want to learn a little about me? There's not that much to tell. I have lived on this farm my entire married life and have two children—Jessica and Jerome. They both work in the Twin Cities. Jessica teaches kindergarten, and Jerome is a Realtor."

"And before that?"

Betty smiled sweetly, as if he'd struck a happy nerve. "I was a missionary in South America for a number of years. I worked with an orphanage in Lima, Peru. Those were some of the best days of my life. It was difficult work and there were so many in need, but every day was gratifying. Good physical and spiritual things happened for the children. It was easy, in a sense, because we could witness the changes in them. It's harder to be in a mission field where you wonder if your voice is even heard."

Like Alf? He almost said the words out loud but stopped himself. Betty looked directly into his eyes. It was if she were reading his mind. "You're thinking that if Alf is my current mission field, I've probably bitten off more than I can chew, right?" She sighed. "It's true. Alf can be a hard man to get along with, but he has many fine qualities as well. He's generous to a fault, hardworking and a good, faithful husband." Betty smiled and soft dimples nicked her cheeks.

Then her expression grew serious. "You've heard about the fire and Alf's son and first wife?"

"Yes. How tragic." He ventured onward. "I understand that it was about that time that Alf and Hilltop had a parting of the ways."

Betty nodded thoughtfully. "From what I've pieced together from what Alf and others have said, people from both All Saints and Hilltop surrounded him, but no one could comfort him. Hilltop Church worked hard to console Alf, but he wouldn't accept it. The pastor at the time was on sick leave and his fill-in was an inexperienced student. He said some misguided and badly chosen things while trying to comfort Alf. That verse from Ecclesiastes really set him off."

Alex searched his mind for what that might be.

"It's one of my favorites but it certainly hit Alf the wrong way. 'For everything there is a season, and a time for every matter under heaven....'"

The lightbulb came on in Alex's brain. "'A time to be born, and a time to die; a time to plant, and a time to pluck up what is planted.'"

"Exactly. Alf said there was *no time* that a little boy should die. He kicked that young man out of his house, said Hilltop had done wrong by sending him over and closed his heart tight as if he'd put a lock on it." Betty put her hands behind her and kneaded her lower back.

"Of course that pastor didn't mean to say a child had to die. I believe that passage is all about timing."

Alex waited for her to continue.

"God's timing, that is. The only way to have peace is to accept that God's timing is perfect, no matter what time schedule we'd prefer for ourselves. And if we can't accept that, and discover and even appreciate His divine timing, then, like Alf, we either doubt God or resent Him."

Betty's face glowed with a peace and serenity that Alex found beautiful. "One thing I learned early is that if I move ahead before God's ready or if I resist Him, things don't work out very well."

Alex knew the feeling. "No wonder Alf feels such despair and discontent. He's disillusioned with God and God's people."

"We're complicated folk, aren't we? My husband probably can't even tell you why he behaves the way he does, at least not anymore. He's made a habit of being contrary. It stuck, and it made him a bitter man. And somehow Hilltop got mixed up in his head with that. Alf's never gotten over it."

"Pastors aren't perfect," Alex said slowly, feeling exceedingly unqualified himself. "Nothing this side of heaven can make a man faultless." How many times had his own words been taken in ways they were not intended?

"Of course not, but Alf in his grief and guilt couldn't sort that out. Everyone says he's been a different man since that awful day."

Betty studied Alex's face carefully. "Maybe you're the one who can bring him around. He's done his best to convince the people of All Saints that they can't do without him and that Hilltop is not to be trusted. It doesn't make sense, but after all these years, it's just the way it is. Seeking relief from his pain, he's made himself a one-man show around that church, and All Saints accepted what he offered. Frankly, there are those who'd like to have better relations with Hilltop but have no idea how to accomplish it without causing Alf more pain. It's touchy business."

That, Alex thought, his gut in a knot, was an understatement.

"Thank you for your honesty," he said, meaning it with his whole heart. "But how can you...?" He let the question drift away.

"Are you familiar with termites, Reverend?"

"I've never had them in my home, if that's what you mean, but I know what destruction they can do."

"My husband is like a house with termites."

She smiled at Alex's quizzical look. "From the outside, he looks sturdy and strong, but inside he's being eaten away by termites, these thoughts that just gnaw at him. His memories are eating him up inside; and when it happens, there is no way for me to reach him or to get inside his pain.

"The guilt, loss and fear are with him as much today as they were with him the day of the fire. It made him a driven man. He needs to do something to assuage the guilt he feels. In his need to do something, he's managed to take everything about All Saints onto his own shoulders and, in the process, taught its people to depend on him for everything.

"He's tried to replace his son with All Saints and thinks if he can be busy enough, he won't hurt. It doesn't work that way, of course. He needs to forgive himself and to trust that God can forgive him. He's a man of the church who doesn't know God, Pastor, at least not the loving, gentle God we know."

"What does that leave for you and your children?"

"Not much, sometimes. Jessica and Jerome avoid him if they can. It's very sad. He has a new son in Jerome, a living, breathing, healthy son that he sometimes ignores to think about the one he lost. Alf just can't let go, and he's too stubborn to believe that God can handle this without his help. I'm afraid that at the end of his life, Alf is going to have a wagonload of guilt about both the son he has and the one he lost."

"And what about you?" Alex asked gently.

Betty shrugged lightly, her eyes warm and sad. "I understand him and I love him. He can be wonderful too, you know. I'll just keep on keeping on." Then she smiled, and it lit up her face. "I suppose I do view Alf as my personal mission field. I have more hope now than I've had for some time. I've been praying for someone who can get through to Alf. Now you're here. Maybe you are my answer."

When Alex drove away, Alf didn't even come out of the shed to say good-bye.

He drove slowly down the rutted path, dodging holes and large rocks, but his mind was not on the road. Instead it was on the heavy cloak of responsibility he felt settling on his shoulders. Jonas, Will, Alf and who knew how many others? He asked again the question that had stalked him since the first time he saw Hilltop Community Church in the distance: *Now what?*

CHAPTER EIGHTEEN

Alex was so deep in thought that he almost didn't realize he was out of gas. He had no idea how long the aging van's fuel light indicator had been on. Hoping vapors could carry him as far as Grassy Valley, he headed for Red's.

The vehicle limped into the gas station and died with a sputter in front of the pump. Alex glanced around, hoping no one had seen this inauspicious arrival.

He was about to jump out of the vehicle to fuel up when a grizzled-looking man with a chin full of stubble and four prominent teeth in his upper gum line stuck his head in the window. "Fill 'er up?"

"Fill it up with gas, you mean?"

"You betcha. Fill 'er up?" The man grinned and the four teeth looked gargantuan in his mouth.

There were no self-serve signs on these pumps. It had been a long time since he'd been to a gas station with an actual attendant. "Yes, thank you. That would be very nice."

"You betcha." The man busied himself opening the gas cap. He started the pump and then hurried to the hood to check the oil.

Alex was unaccustomed to such attention. He felt a little useless. Alex got out of the van and headed toward the station itself.

"Check the tires?" called a voice from behind him.

"Please!" City folk considered themselves civilized, Alex thought, but the finer things of life—like not having to gas up your own car—happened here, at what urbanites consider the end of the earth.

The large, rambling building that was Red's appeared to have once been several smaller structures that were now joined together by halls and walkways. It was barn red with white trim. Shutters had been added, and a wooden porch ran the entire jagged front of the building. The porch rail was made to look like a hitching post, and wooden rockers, benches and tables littered the area. A soda and juice machine hummed near the front door, as did a freezer chest with ICE inscribed on the lid. Alex was sorely tempted to sit down in one of the rockers, put his feet up and watch the world go by.

Instead, he walked inside and was met by an eye-catching array that was part gas station, part fast-food restaurant, part clothing store, part gift shop and part hardware supply. To his right was a bank of coffee and soda dispensers; a rotisserie with bratwursts and hot dogs warming; a bakery case full of doughnuts, bear claws and maple bars; and a display of chips and candy that would rival any grocery store in Chicago. In the center of this were four small tables with benches, all occupied by workingmen on their breaks and a small woman behind a counter frying burgers.

The clothing portion of the arrangement included sweaters and shirts sized six months to XXXL, billed caps, rain slickers, and dreadful-looking matched scarf and mitten sets leftover from the winter stock. Fuzzy yellow work gloves, sunglasses and T-shirts with various sayings emblazoned on them filled other shelves.

There were tacky gifts—plastic horses with clocks surgically inserted into their bellies, Lava Lamps, stuffed animals—as well as WD-40, deicer for gas tanks, windshield washer fluid, motor oil, belts and wrenches. One could rent movies, play in the video arcade, shower in the trucker's shower room, do laundry in the tiny Laundromat, do one's Christmas shopping and buy enough glazed doughnuts for a large brunch, all under one roof. A sign hung suspended from the ceiling with arrows pointing in opposite directions. Under one arrow were the words INSURANCE, THE AGENT IS *In*. The arrow pointing in the other direction said TV REPAIR.

Red's was a veritable feast for the eyes and took the place of at least seven or eight separate businesses in the city.

Then he heard something smash to the floor and an eruption in the direction of the small kitchen. He moved to check it out. Two of the men he'd noticed at the tables were now on their feet, glaring at each other, fists raised. On the floor was a shattered glass plate. Parts of a hamburger and a bevy of french fries were strewn across the floor.

The woman behind the counter scooted out of the tiny kitchen carrying a spatula, waving it in the air. "Break it up, you two. Break it up! Bucky Chadwick, you know better!"

"He knocked my food on the floor." The speaker was a fellow in his late twenties. His nose was bulbous, his coloring ruddy, and acne scars ran deep across his face. His already narrow eyes slanted even further as he curled back his lips, ready for a fight. In his mouth were a set of very large teeth that appeared to have had nowhere to grow except out.

Bucky Chadwick. Will Packard's nemesis. The one who was unkind to animals and people alike.

The little woman swatted at him with the spatula, and hamburger grease splattered across his already oil-spattered clothing. "Bucky, you behave yourself. I won't have anyone picking fights in here, you understand? I'll pack you a burger and fries and bring it out to your pickup truck. You can come back when you decide to behave like a gentleman."

"Ah, Ma."

"Go!" the little woman roared. And Bucky did as he was told.

"Sorry about that," the woman said to the other diner. "Your food is on the house today." And she turned around calmly and returned to her kitchen.

Not knowing what to make of what he'd just seen, Alex turned toward the checkout and nearly ran into another man, one with flame-red hair, freckles so thick that they overlapped and a big grin. A well-chewed toothpick dangled from his mouth.

"You are a quart low on oil in your van." the big redhead said politely. "We can put in some 5W30 for you."

"Thanks. That would be great."

"Good, 'cause we already did it." The man studied Alex. "New in town, aren't you?"

"I'm the new pastor at Hilltop Community Church." Alex thrust out his hand. "Alex Armstrong."

The other took the proffered hand and shook it vigorously, like a pump handle. "I'm Red O'Grady. Welcome to our part of the world. And don't worry about that little dustup back there. Bucky is a troublemaker, but his mother is spitfire enough to keep him under control in here. Too bad she can't follow him around like a tick on a dog and make sure he behaves everywhere."

"Red, come here and look at this carburetor," a mechanic called from the doorway.

"Excuse me. Again, welcome." Red disappeared into the garage part of his mini-kingdom, leaving Alex to pay his bill.

On the way out, between the inside and outside doors, was a small vestibule with huge bulletin boards covered with sheets of paper advertising everything from Labrador retriever puppies to babysitting, housecleaning and livestock sales. He stopped to look at them and noticed he could buy an antique tractor or a prize bull. Then his eyes fell on a flyer that announced WHEATVILLE FARMERS' MARKET—EVERY SATURDAY 8–NOON. Listed were an assortment of vegetables, pastries and jams. There were even homemade quilts available.

He was still studying the flyer when a tall, sturdily built woman with white-blond hair entered the outer door and stopped beside him. "Are you looking for fresh vegetables?" she asked, seeing where his gaze was fixed.

"I just noticed the flyer for the farmers' market. Is there anything like that around Grassy Valley?"

The blonde, whose shoulders were nearly as wide as Alex's, reached up, took a stray tack off the board and posted a sign of her own. HOME GROWN VEGGIES—CALL LOLLY ROSCOE. "There isn't, but I wish there were. It would be a lot easier for me to bring my garden produce to one location and sell it. People have mentioned it over the years but no one has ever taken the bull by the horns and organized it. In the past I suppose it was unnecessary since most everyone planted a garden, but times have changed. What's more; this gas station has become pretty famous for its burgers and good service. People stop here a lot. I'll bet a few tables of vegetables would sell well if they were in Red's outlot."

"Surely it couldn't be too hard, could it?"

"I wouldn't think so. In fact, I'd help whoever started it. I just don't want to have all the responsibility." She smiled at him and he noticed her white, even teeth and bright blue eyes. "You're the new pastor at Hilltop, aren't you?"

"I am."

"I go to Hilltop sometimes. I'm Lolly Roscoe, by the way, if you haven't already guessed."

"And I'm Alex Armstrong."

She shook his hand and her fingers were warm and strong. What's more, her eyes were sharp and appraising.

"Maybe you would be interested in helping me start a farmers' market," she said lightly. "What do you think?" There was a flirtiness in her smile that set off warning flares in Alex's mind. Obviously he wasn't ready yet, not open to a relationship. When would memories of Natalie quit stalking him?

He swallowed thickly. "Not at the moment, but if I find someone who can, I'll let you know." Suddenly he felt the urge to escape her appraising stare.

He excused himself as quickly and politely as he could and headed for the food counter, which held soda dispensers and a variety of fast foods.

Carrying the foot-long hot dog and bag of potato chips he'd purchased at Red's, Alex entered the house to find Tripod standing on the area rug in the entry, tail wagging so hard it shook the whole dog. At the first whiff of the hot dog, his tail began to pound on the floor.

"Don't worry, I got you one too," Alex said, reaching into the depths of a sack and pulling out a regular hot dog with no mustard and ketchup. "But you get it only if you promise not to beg while I'm eating."

Tripod gave a sharp whine and tipped his head to one side but followed Alex into the kitchen and lay down on the floor beside his master's feet as he ate. When the foot-long was gone, however, Tripod jumped up and gazed longingly at the other hot dog.

The dog was more disciplined than he would have been, Alex thought as he tossed bits of frankfurter and bun to Tripod, who caught them midair. When he was done, Alex threw away the paper wrappings, wiped the counter and walked into the living room. He stood in front of the large picture windows and stared out at the serene scene before him as the sun lowered in the sky. The days were long here on the prairie so far north on the continent. In the summer it was still light out at nine or even ten o'clock.

Alex rambled through the house trying to shake the feelings of isolation and restiveness he was experiencing. Finally he picked up the phone and dialed his sister Carol's number.

Jared answered. "Hi, Unc. What's up? Do you miss me?"

"I certainly do. Do you want to move out here with me and go to school in Grassy Valley?" Alex asked.

Alex was joking, but Jared answered somberly, as if it were the most reasonable question in the world. "I wish I could, but it probably wouldn't help. I *hate* school."

They were both silent. Alex tried to digest the venom in Jared's voice. He decided to change the subject. "I have news. I got a dog."

"No kidding?"

"None whatsoever. His name is Tripod."

"That's a weird name for a dog."

"Not if it only has three legs."

"A three-legged dog? Are you crazy?" It was Carol. She had picked up another phone extension and was now on the line.

"No more so than usual, I don't think."

"I suppose it's nice to have company out there in the country all alone, but if you were—"

Alex closed his eyes and groaned inwardly, knowing exactly where this was going.

"—married and had a nice wife to keep you company…"

"I hear you, but let's not go into it tonight."

"If you guys are going to talk about Uncle Alex getting married, I'm hanging up."

"I'll call again and we'll leave your mother out of it," Alex promised.

"Cool." A click signaled that Jared had hung up. "How are things going? Any more outbursts?"

"The only thing I can really connect it to is school—or the mention of it. He's never loved school, but this year he's counting down the days until it starts and getting more miserable with each one that passes. He scares me sometimes, Alex."

"Maybe once it starts things will be better."

"I hope so," Carol said without much confidence, "but I doubt it. I've never seen him as agitated as this."

They engaged in desultory chatter for a few more minutes before they hung up.

The conversation hadn't eased his mind whatsoever. Now Alex's mind was whirling even faster. He felt the need to do something, to make something positive happen. He got out the slim phone book that held the numbers of everyone in the communities around Grassy Valley, found what he was looking for, and dialed. An answering machine picked up.

"Hello, Jonas? Gandy said you have a green thumb and that your garden is huge. She also said you grow everything naturally, no pesticides or the like. Is that true? Because if it is, I have an idea I'd like to run past you."

Late that afternoon, Alex and Tripod were sleeping on the living room floor and being warmed by the sun when they awoke to the sound of the church bells clanging.

"Whaaa—?" Alex jumped to his feet and shook his head to clear out the cobwebs that had lodged there during his nap. The telephone began to ring. He stumbled toward the table and picked up the receiver. "Hello?"

"Reverend Alex!" It was Gandy and her voice was even higher-pitched than usual. "There's a grass fire by All Saints and the wind is blowing it right toward the church! The fire department is on its way. Mac just drove over there. Some of the men are trying to get the pews and altar out in case the building burns, but they need help."

"I'm on my way." He didn't even pause to consider that he was still wearing the dress trousers, white shirt and slip-on loafers he'd donned before the Ladies Aid meeting this afternoon. He left Tripod whimpering inside the house and raced to his van.

He was growing accustomed to taking these gravel roads at high speeds, Alex thought grimly as his white-knuckled hands gripped the steering wheel. If he were going to stay in the Hilltop and All Saints communities, his next car would have to be something heavy like an all-terrain SUV—or a souped-up tractor.

He could see smoke rolling skyward. A chill shivered through him. It had been a dry summer, Dixon had explained.

There was not much ground moisture and the last rain had done little to allay the aridness. He saw the large pasture, parched and brittle from the heat, on fire. The flames were spreading outward and moving rapidly toward the little country church. Yellow and orange tongues of fire hungrily gobbled up everything in front of them.

There were several vehicles in the churchyard and out in the pasture, a bright red fire truck. Its crew labored to hold back the flames. Alex recognized the vehicle driven by the All Saints janitor in the mix, as well as the pickup truck he'd seen in the Nyborg yard.

Dixon loped toward the van. He was traveling faster than Alex had ever seen him. "We're moving things out. A lot of it is on Mark's flatbed trailer, which he's pulled out of harm's way. There are still a few pews left, and the pulpit."

"We can't let that burn!" Alex was horrified at the thought of the beautiful piece of art created by Alf's grandfather being reduced to dust and ashes.

"It's pretty solidly installed." Dixon glanced at the rolling flames inching their way toward them. "I don't know if we can get it out in time. Alf is inside working on it. He's determined to get it out or die trying." Dixon paused and gave Alex an intense look. "Literally."

Another chill spread through Alex although he felt sweat pouring down his sides beneath his shirt. "I'm going inside." He was surprised to hear the strength of his own voice.

It was startling how much noise a fire made. There were yells of the men from All Saints and Hilltop, for once working side by side, moving the rest of the pews and the piano out the front door. But more remarkable to Alex was the crackle and snap of dry grass and the rush of water from fire hoses dousing the flames. The scene was chaotic.

Inside the church, men were grabbing sections of altar. Someone yelled, "If they don't get it stopped soon, this place is going to go up like a tinderbox. We need to get out of here."

Alex found Mark trying to gather candlesticks and collection plates into his arms. Mark turned to Alf, who was frantically working to unscrew the bolts that held the hand-carved pulpit in place. "You'll have to leave it, Alf. It's not worth risking your life over."

"No!" was the strangled response. Alf looked up and Alex was shocked to see the tortured expression, the sheer terror, on his features. There were tears streaming down his face. "Someone's got to help me!"

In this moment, Alex realized, Alf wasn't fighting for this pulpit or even this church. Alf was reliving another place and time, fighting to change history, to somehow redeem himself for not saving his wife and son.

Without thinking, Alex dodged behind the old-fashioned altar and picked up a piece of microphone stand that was stored there and attacked the planks around the platform, prying them loose. Alf, realizing what Alex was doing, began to use his screwdriver to help Alex pry at the planks. If they couldn't get the pulpit off the floor, they'd take the floor with them.

Together they worked like madmen, chopping, prying and weeping. Somewhere in the distance Alex heard the sound of another fire truck approaching, its siren wailing.

When Mark realized what they were trying to do, he added his muscle to the job, working the massive piece forward and back until the wood creaked and snapped.

It was almost loose when a fireman appeared in the building, his thick yellow and black gear making him appear large and alien. "Out! Now!"

It was as though Alf hadn't heard him. He continued to work frantically, sweat soaking his shirt and hair, oblivious to the warning.

Alex and Mark exchanged glances and, as if of one mind, they approached Alf. Each slipped a forearm beneath one of the man's armpits and lifted him off the floor and half-dragged, half-carried him through the now-empty sanctuary as Alf kicked, fought, and screamed.

They emerged from the church and deposited him on the ground by Mark's truck. "They want us all to move. We saved most of the furniture. You have to let it go, Alf," Mark said. "It's not worth it, not for a piece of wood."

"It's not just wood!"

Alf's scream pierced a hole in Alex's spirit.

Silently, they lifted him into the truck and drove him to safety.

The men of the church stood helplessly by, staring at the scene before them. Minutes passed like hours.

It was Dixon who noticed the change first. "The wind is dying down," he said. "Feel it?"

"And I think it's turning," Alf added. "They'll be able to stop it now. Thank God."

"Let's pray," Alex said and bowed his head in prayer. "Lord, You control not only the wind but our hearts. Thank You today for a double dose of Your generosity. Thank You for sparing most of the church, Lord, and odd as this might sound, thank You for allowing us the opportunity to work together as one. Thank You for the men of All Saints and for those of Hilltop who were united in a single purpose today. You are able to bring blessing out of tragedy, Lord, as You have proved once again. You are a good and gracious God. Amen."

A chorus of *amens* erupted behind him. When Alex looked up he noticed that Alf had slipped away. He heard him start his pickup and watched him drive away. The fire must have brought every painful memory back.

One by one, the men drifted over to stare at the site, at the small miracle that had transpired.

Guided by the changing wind, the line of fire had stopped at the southwest corner of the church before burning off in another direction. The church lawn and the pasture beyond was charred black, and some of the church's siding was slightly charred; but for the most part, the little country church sat unscathed, ringed by burnt grass.

"Quite something, isn't it?" Tim Clayborn, husband of Amy, murmured as he stood next to Alex. The men of both churches had gathered together and were talking softly among themselves. "The fire somehow went all the way around the church. The siding is blistered and some sparks burned holes in the roof, but it's still here. It's as if God directed the wind to blow right around All Saints." Tim, a strong, athletic-looking man, glanced at Alex. "Do you think He can do that?"

"He can do anything He wants, Tim," Alex murmured. "I think He's done something much bigger than directing the wind."

"Huh?" Tim looked at him blankly.

Alex nodded to the cluster of people nearby. The men of the two disparate and conflicted congregations were smiling with relief and clapping each other on the shoulders in celebration, both overjoyed that the little church was safe. "The wind is nothing compared to blowing these two groups into the same place and after the same goal."

Tim took off his cap and scratched his blond head. "It was nice to see us working together for a common cause."

CHAPTER NINETEEN

The Ladies Aid is still waiting to hear what they should serve for the missions fund-raiser," Gandy said when Alex and Tripod entered the church office.

"It all sounds like a lot of work. This church must have as many meals as it has services." He thought back to the casseroles, baked goods, venison and dozens of other kind acts involving food that he'd experienced in the few short weeks he'd been at Hilltop.

"Don't try to stop a Ladies Aid member from cooking a meal they've already made their minds up about. It would be like trying to stop the Amtrak with a pile of bean bags. Like I said, I told them to hold off on the lutefisk, but you aren't out of the woods yet. You'd better be specific—meatballs, ham, tuna casserole, pot roast..."

"No tuna casserole, please."

"Okay, I'll tell them to pick one of the others." A smile played on Gandy's lips. "You're pretty popular from what I hear. No one's complained about anything you've done so far. Congratulations."

"Is that unexpected?"

"This place doesn't have a critical spirit, if that's what you mean, but to go this long without doing *anything* wrong, well, I'd say it's remarkable."

More likely miraculous, Alex thought, but didn't verbalize it. "By the way," he said, recalling the thought he'd had during his morning run, "I think it would be a nice gesture for Hilltop to invite the people from All Saints for this dinner."

"I think there goes your winning streak."

"You don't think Hilltop would like that?"

"Not after they stood us up at the open house." Gandy shook her head. "Of course things have softened up between us considerably since the fire. I've even been invited to All Saints to learn how they're putting together their history quilt. But invite them to the Ladies Aid? I don't know. "

Alex moved toward his desk, which was stacked with hymnals, Bibles, sermon notes and bags of red licorice. The licorice was Gandy's big downfall but he'd discovered for himself that it was almost as addictive as chocolate and started his own stash of the candy. He decided to move to a more neutral subject. "How's Jonas's garden this year?"

"Huge. He loves to put seed in the ground. He's Hilltop's Johnny Appleseed. Jonas subscribes to the old way, even with his crops. He rotates crops to put nutrients back into the soil and doesn't depend on fertilizer. He lets land lie fallow to rebuild itself, and he plants a variety of crops on the land so that no one crop drains the soil of its nutrients. What some crops take out of the soil, others put back in. Maybe that's part of his problem. He's *too* good a steward of the soil. He could make a lot more money dumping fertilizer, pesticides and who knows what other chemicals on his land, like everyone else does." She paused to study him. "What is this about?"

"I'm sure there is a place for both kinds of farmers, Gandy. I'm just trying to figure out the place where Jonas fits in."

She harrumphed loudly. "Jonas doesn't fit in anywhere these days."

"I'm not so sure about that. I think that Jonas just hasn't found his niche yet."

"*Neesch?* What's that?"

"It's an area that is particularly suited to someone's gifts, talents or personality. In business, it can mean a specialized market."

"I don't get it," Gandy said bluntly. "What does that have to do with my brother?"

"Niche markets specialize in a certain type of product or service."

"Like what?" Gandy was interested but unconvinced.

"Snowblowers, for example, or tree removal."

She stared at him, confusion written all over her face. Alex thought he'd lost her so he hurried to explain.

"Say that you like to fix lawn and garden tractors and lawn mowers, but you especially enjoy fixing snowblowers. In fact, you're really *good* at fixing them, better than anyone else in a hundred and fifty mile radius. People begin to hear about your work and start to bring you their snowblowers to repair. Word spreads and soon you are the most prominent and popular snowblower repairman around. Snowblower repair becomes your niche, your specialty, the thing that sets you apart from everyone else. It's the same way with tree removal. My father had to have several sick elms taken down around his apartment building, but he wouldn't let just anyone come in and start chopping. He made an appointment with the best company in town, one that had taken down more elms than any other. That was their niche."

"And Jonas's niche is…?" She cocked her head, waiting for an answer.

"Pesticide-free, organically grown crops and vegetables."

Her eyes narrowed as she thought about it. "That's true, but what of it?"

"You might take that for granted out here. I'm sure Jonas has been making a practice of it so long that he thinks of it as completely normal, but it's not. Organically grown produce, grown with no synthetic fertilizers and no pesticides, needs to meet standards set by the government. If Jonas's crops meet those standards, he can label and sell his produce as organically grown."

"So what?" Gandy was a hard sell, that was for sure.

"If Jonas could meet the qualifications and find a market for what he grows, he'd earn some decent money. Until then, he should bill himself as a chemical-free producer and consider participating in farmers' markets in the area—or start one himself."

"What's the big deal with that?" Gandy was losing interest. She started to shuffle papers around on her desk.

"People are willing to pay much more for food that is organically grown."

That caught her attention. "Here? I'm not so sure about that."

"But where I come from they do."

"But he's here and they're there."

"Then he will have to find a way to sell his product to a wider market. It would take some research and some solid business advice."

Then Alex told her about the woman he'd met in Red's, and the conversation they'd had about a farmers' market and the message he'd left for her brother.

She stirred the cup of tea on her desk. "Jonas really respects Mark Nash. Mark's got a good business head. Maybe he could talk to Mark and get some advice."

"Perfect!"

She studied him intently, her pale eyes filling with tears. "You really care, don't you?"

"Yes, Gandy, I really do. I want your brother and every other person in this community to thrive. In my business, their souls will always come first, but their success and happiness is a close second."

Her eyes narrowed again, and Alex could almost hear the wheels turning under that mop of blond hair. "Who did you say you met at Red's? The woman who was interested in a farmers' market?"

"I'm not sure if I remember her name correctly, Lolly something, but she was tall and had white-blond hair. She looked very Scandinavian."

"Lolly Roscoe?"

"Probably. I knew hers was an unusual name, but I must admit I had my mind on Jonas at the moment."

"Lolly is hard to miss," Gandy said dryly. "A lot of people think she's beautiful."

"She's very nice looking, I'm sure, but I had my mind on other things."

"She's single, you know." Gandy appeared to think this was monumental information.

Alex didn't know quite how to respond. "I see."

"And she's been single a long time. She's been engaged a time or two, but it didn't work out."

"I see."

"What is it you see, Reverend? That you just stumbled upon a beautiful single woman who wants you to help her start a farmers' market? Seems to me that you don't see at all. In fact, you're plumb blind to what's right in front of you!"

He didn't like the direction this was going, so he decided to change it. "Lolly is a very unusual name. Where did it come from?"

"There's a story about that."

"There's a story about everything around here." Alex poured coffee into a mug and prepared to listen.

"Lolly's mother wanted to name her something pretty. She read in a book that another name for Charlotte was Loleta. The trouble is, the nurse misspelled the name on the birth certificate and it came out as Lolita."

"How unfortunate."

"Exactly. Her mother was upset, but decided to make lemonade out of this particular lemon, and she's been Lolly ever since."

Alex was at a loss for words.

"Word has it that she'd like to get married. She's not getting any younger, you know." She looked him up and down in that disconcerting way she had. "Neither are you."

"I don't exactly have one foot in the grave!" he protested.

"No, not yet. But you'd better watch out. One day you'll wake up and realize you're old and alone and wonder where the time went." Gandy tapped her temple with her forefinger. "You have to watch out for these things, you know. It happened to Walter Englund and it will happen to you."

Here it was, another of Gandy's mercurial leaps from one subject to another. Alex was going to be a mental gymnast by the time she got done with him. He had to admit, however, that he enjoyed talking with Gandy immensely. She didn't mind saying exactly what was on her mind even if he was her pastor. It was enormously refreshing.

"Walter is a good man, but terribly shy. He would have made a wonderful father, but he was too bashful to ask a woman out on a date. And now he's in his sixties and alone, without anybody in the world." She furrowed her brows. "Don't you go doing the same thing."

"I'll remember that." He had an uncomfortable vision of being whisked down the aisle to the altar with Gandy on one side and Lolly on the other. "It just might be, however, that what I'm looking for in a wife is different from what you imagine for me."

"Just don't get too fussy." She waggled a finger at him. "Remember, 'he who hesitates is lost.' Is that quotation from Scripture? Proverbs, maybe?"

"It's an American proverb. Or maybe it originated on the front of a T-shirt."

"Oh." Gandy was undaunted. "All I'm saying is, if love slams you in the face, don't slap it away." She smiled proudly. "And that is a Gandy Dunn quote. Feel free to use it whenever you wish."

Alex was relieved to hear footsteps outside. It was Mattie Olsen, marching in with the same determination she'd had the first time he'd met her when she was on her mission to destroy the ant population of Hilltop Township. Her square jaw was set, her beady eyes flashed with fire and her footsteps sounded like a soldier marching in heavy boots. What had she run into this time? Wasps?

"I have just heard the worst possible news! I don't know what those two young people are thinking. It's practically a historical monument, at least around Hilltop. Desecration! That's what it is, defilement!"

She was certainly given toward melodramatics, Alex mused. What had happened now? The way she was talking, someone might have just torn down the Statue of Liberty. But there was hardly an equivalent to that in Hilltop. Was there?

"What are you jabbering about, Mattie?" Gandy got up and poured the little woman a cup of coffee. Then she dug in her drawer for a Nut Goodie, a candy, Alex had discovered, that was available primarily in the Midwest.

"Ben and Nancy Jenkins, that's who. I was in town today for a new perm"—she patted the tight ringlets haloing her head—"and I heard from the beauty operator who'd heard from one of her clients who'd been at the lumberyard and overheard the young Jenkins couple discussing tearing down the Hubbard house and building a *rambler* in its place! A plain old ranch-style house in place of that mansion? My source also said they'd visited the bank, possibly to discuss a *loan*."

Her source? Mattie was obviously well connected in the grapevine.

"Can you imagine?" Mattie was warming up to enjoy her rant.

"That house is homage to the people who settled here, a tribute to show what people can do. The Hubbards came here penniless, worked the land, made good, and built that lovely home; and now some great-great-grandchild wants to tear it down? Sacrilege, I say, disrespect!" She spun on her toes and faced Alex. "What are we going to do about it?"

He must have looked like a trout out of water, working his lips and trying to catch a breath, Alex thought. *We?* When had saving houses become his responsibility?

"Tear the house down?" Mattie snorted. "Why, that house has been a landmark here for decades. What could those children be thinking?"

Who knew, Alex thought; but he put Nancy and Ben at the top of his visitation list. Next time Mattie asked that question, perhaps he'd have an answer.

CHAPTER TWENTY

The scream nearly curled his hair.

Gandy leaped to her feet and knocked her chair backward so that it rolled across the office's sloping wooden floor and slammed into the metal file cabinet. This sent up a racket as the mug rack on top tipped over and the cups went rolling. "Is somebody being scalped out there?" she said as she hurried to retrieve the errant mugs.

"I don't know, but I plan to find out." Alex strode out of the church and paused on the top step to stare at what was unfolding before him.

Will Packard had arrived in the church parking lot with his bicycle and an old red wagon that had seen better days and probably a dozen children before Will. In the wagon was a wire cage, with a printed cardboard sign hanging off the door that said *Rose*. But the wire door on the pen was open, and the person who opened it—Bucky Chadwick—still had his hand on the wire. Rose, meanwhile, was meandering off at a surprising pace, her wide, squat body waddling from side to side as she moved.

"You get away from her, Bucky!" Will's voice was hoarse from screaming.

"Skunks should be dead, all of them," Bucky retorted in a flat voice as he raised the shotgun he was carrying to his shoulder and took aim. "I haven't got any time for skunks."

"Drop it. Right now. No guns on church property." Alex wondered for a moment if that commanding voice was actually his. Of course, he'd never before been quite this furious with someone.

From the corner of his eye he watched Will scramble to catch up with his skunk. "I could call the police if I thought that you were trying to kill someone's pet."

"It's only a dumb skunk," Bucky growled. His face flushed an ugly red that did nothing for his complexion. "Dragging that thing around in a cage like it was a prize rabbit from the fair, that's just plain stupid."

"And what would you call trying to shoot someone's pet, even if it is a skunk?"

"I was just kidding. I wanted to give the little twerp a scare."

If there was one thing Alex hated, it was bullies who hid behind the line "just kidding" when they got caught. "That's not kidding, that's cruel."

Bucky scowled and thrust a bill into Alex's hand. "I didn't follow him out here to do it, if that's what you mean. Red told me to drive out here and deliver the water softener salt you ordered. I always carry my gun, so I thought I'd do the world a favor and get rid of that rodent. I never thought a guy like you would try to protect a nasty critter like that. Those Packards are crazy, you know."

So he hadn't been kidding at all. He would have shot Will's pet, given half a chance.

Bucky slunk to his pickup and unloaded the forty-pound bags from the pickup bed, his sullen expression never changing. When he was done, he got into the pickup and drove off without an apology to either Alex or Will, who'd corralled Rose and was hugging her tightly to his chest. He stuck as closely as possible to Alex until Bucky was out of sight.

"He'd have killed Rosie if you hadn't come along," Will said bitterly. "Shot her dead. Bucky is the meanest dude in five counties, I'll bet."

"You didn't try to set up a humane society at his place, did you?"

Will looked shocked. "Of course not! That's where I *get* a lot of my rescue animals. Bucky is always picking on something."

"I recommend that in the future you leave Rose at home—for her own safety."

The boy's thin shoulders drooped disconsolately. "But she's my best friend!"

That struck Alex as terribly, terribly sad. "Will, have you or any of your family been to Sunday school?"

"Nah. My dad says that's for sissies and nerds." Will stroked the skunk gently before placing her back in her cage.

"He does, does he?" Alex made a mental note to visit with Will's parents before Sunday school started again in the fall.

"Gotta go," Will said suddenly. He darted to his bike and got on.

"Where?"

"I just thought of a great place for my hoomain society. Me and Rose are going to check it out." And before Alex could give him the third degree, Will pushed off, pedaling as hard as he could. The wagon and its load swayed and bounced behind him.

Alex pinched the bridge of his nose between his thumb and fore-finger and sighed. Who would be the next to call and complain about a *hoomain* society in one of their outbuildings?

"It's a good thing that boy has you to protect him," Gandy said. She'd come up beside him so quietly that Alex had not realized she was there. "That Bucky is a mean one, through and through."

"You talk as if Will doesn't have another soul in the world to turn to."

"That's a pretty accurate statement if you ask me. His mama is timid, his daddy is rough and it's hard to make oneself heard in a rowdy group of siblings like his."

Alex expelled a long sigh. "There's need everywhere, isn't there?"

"Yup. And it's been building up since we haven't had a preacher for so long. You walked right into a backlog of need." Gandy might not be eloquent but she certainly knew how to get a point across.

She scowled. "And speaking of need, I called over to All Saints and invited them to our fund-raiser."

"Excellent! Do you think anyone will come?" Alex couldn't keep the hope from his voice.

"Who knows? If word gets to Alf Nyborg and he says he isn't attending, it might be pretty sparse. But if Alf does attend, we can expect a houseful."

"How will the cooks prepare for that?"

"I'm not sure how they do it, but they make a lot of food and know how to spread it a long way. It's not like the loaves and fishes, of course, but meatballs do seem to come out of thin air sometimes."

"There's a vision," Alex said with a chuckle, "meatballs flying through the air like badminton birdies."

"By the way, Nancy Jenkins just called. She and her husband are going to be away on Sunday, so she asked if you could come for coffee today."

Alex glanced at his watch. "I don't know if I should be off drinking coffee when there's church work to be done."

"Reverend Alex, around here, drinking coffee *is* church work."

Alex was getting more adept at driving in the country. At first he'd thought he'd never catch on.

No one used real directions around here. He was hoping for something simple, like *"Take the Twenty-Eighth Street exit and follow it to Twenty-Third Avenue. Travel on Twenty-Third until you come to a four-way stop. Turn right onto Harrison Lane."* Here, everyone used landmarks that had been heretofore invisible to Alex.

Gandy insisted on giving him directions to the Jenkinses' home. "Go about two miles, maybe three, as if you were going away from Grassy Valley. Go past the shelterbelt that will be on your right side. It's all pine trees, you can't miss it. Then the farm is on the first road to your right after that…or is it the second? Anyway, it's marked with a huge stone that has HUBBARD engraved on it. If you go too far, you'll run into a dead end. There are two separate drives into the yard. You can use either road into the yard since it's summer, but you can only use the one on the left during the winter."

If people gave directions like that in Chicago, everyone would be lost.

When he'd inquired about the two roads leading to the Jenkinses' home, he'd received another mysterious explanation.

"The summer road is quicker because it follows the tree line and so it's shorter. The problem is that in the winter, the trees catch too much snow for the road to be useable. That makes it only a summer road. The winter road is the one they plow and keep open in the winter, but of course you could figure that out for yourself."

Not likely, Alex thought. He was learning to "speak Hilltop," but he wasn't very adept at the language yet.

The Hubbard house, Alex realized, was even more spectacular up close than from a distance. It was a grand three-story structure with a wide porch that ran around three sides of the house. Ionic columns separated the first-floor porch from the second. Large windows overlooked a sloping horse pasture. To reach the front entry, Alex mounted six steps. The double doors that greeted him were made of mahogany and intricately carved.

Nancy Jenkins threw open the door and welcomed him inside.

"I'm so glad you could come today. Ben and I feel terrible about missing the fund-raiser. I made a plate of sandwiches and a cake. I hope you can join us for lunch."

"Why, yes, thank you. I'd like that." Alex was so engrossed with studying the intricate wood carvings that graced the open staircase and the massive ceiling moldings that he could barely get the words out of his mouth. There were old, elegant rugs on the maple flooring, and much of the furniture appeared to be of the same vintage of the house. "What a lovely home you have."

"*Hmm*...I suppose it is," Nancy agreed. "If you like this sort of thing."

"And your great-great-grandfather built it?"

"Yes. Would you like to take a tour before we sit down to eat?"

"It would be wonderful...if you don't mind, that is. I don't believe I've ever been in a house quite this grand before—at least not one that hasn't been turned into a museum."

"That's what this place is," Nancy said, sweeping her hand around, "an old museum. It creaks and clanks in the night, and the rooms are drafty. You can't imagine how difficult this is to heat. I've forgotten how pretty it is because of all the upkeep and high fuel bills."

He followed her through the hall to peer in at several bedrooms, each uniquely decorated around a theme quilt on each bed.

"This is amazing. You have an eye for decorating."

"Thank you. I enjoy it. I had a wonderful time when we first moved here, making quilts and choosing accessories. But now we practically live in the kitchen area for most of the winter so we don't have to heat the whole house." She paused thoughtfully. "I wish it were fun again, but it's not."

He followed her to a closed door. She paused. "My ancestors loved parties," she said. "The bigger the better. Everyone in Hilltop wanted to come to my grandmother's shindigs, which were usually held in the ballroom."

"Ballroom?" Alex asked. Surely he hadn't heard her correctly.

"Yes. Up here, where most people have attics. We have a ball-room. It was built for my great-grandmother who also loved to give parties. Come upstairs and you'll see what I mean."

They ascended the steps, and when Nancy moved aside at the top, Alex gasped. It *was* a ballroom. And not just any ballroom either. The ceiling was arched and painted a soft blue, with puffy white clouds through which sunlight seemed to shoot. An occasional bluebird dotted the sky and hummingbirds hovered overhead. Even on a cold winter's night, it would be like standing in the sun on a summer day up here. The floor underneath their feet was parquet and Alex could imagine what it might look like if it were polished to a high gleam. In its heyday, this must have been a wondrous place indeed.

"I've never seen anything quite like this in a private home," Alex admitted. "It's fantastic."

"Yes, I suppose it is," Nancy sighed. She sounded torn, as if she believed his statement to be true yet somehow resented it.

"What's wrong?" The words slipped out of his mouth a little too abruptly. "You don't have to answer that, I mean…"

"I don't mind. Let's talk about it over lunch."

He followed her downstairs, rather sorry to leave the fantasy world on the top floor of the house. When they entered the kitchen Ben Jenkins was waiting there. He was quick to offer Alex a cup of coffee.

"We heard about the fire," Nancy said. "It's a miracle that the church didn't burn. Ben said that Alf Nyborg took it pretty hard."

"His wife says he's doing better," Alex commented. He and Betty had talked on the telephone a number of times since the incident.

He didn't, however, have time to dwell on Alf as Nancy led him into the kitchen.

The kitchen of the old house was big and sunny. There were cupboards everywhere, and they sat at a large wood table in the middle of the room, which Nancy loaded with food while her husband poured pink lemonade into tall, chilled glasses. After Alex said grace, they dug into the food and didn't speak for some moments.

"Delicious!" Alex said. "Even a sandwich out here tastes like ambrosia. I've never met so many good cooks in one place."

Nancy laughed. "I couldn't help but learn. The two things all the Hubbard women did well were food and parties." Her eyes held a faraway expression. "But it's different now."

"How so?"

"There's no extra cash for parties anymore, especially not the kind my family used to give." Her expression hardened. "This house eats up our money. It will be good when it's gone and we are living in something that isn't impossible to heat."

Alex recalled Mattie's dramatic announcement of the other day.

"What exactly do you mean by *gone*?"

Ben and Nancy exchanged a look.

"We've decided to raze this house and build something smaller. We might take it down ourselves. If we moved out I'm not sure I could bear to see it slowly crumbling before my eyes." A cloud of melancholy seemed to overcome her.

"Surely there's another way."

Nancy rubbed her stomach. "We've tried to think of one, but considering the circumstances…"

Alex raised his eyebrows.

"You're the very first to know, Pastor. Ben and I are going to have twins."

"Congratulations!"

"So you see we're pretty desperate to do something as soon as possible. The heating bills for this house nearly broke us last winter and now, with two babies…"

"I wish I could suggest another way."

"If you can think of one, let us know," Ben responded. "This is breaking Nancy's heart, but we can't go through another winter heating this place. It has so many leaks that we heat more of the outside of the house than in. I really wish there were some other way."

Another way…another way… The litany rang through Alex's head as he drove back to the church. Who was he to cruise into this place and start telling people what to do? This was his time to listen and learn, wasn't it?

Or was it? The lightbulb moment occurred as he pulled into the parking lot.

He hurried inside, glad Gandy had gone home for lunch. If he was going to stick his nose into someone else's business, he preferred to do it alone.

It took him only a moment to find his cousin Dan's phone number. He dialed quickly and then waited impatiently for someone to pick up on the other end of the line.

"Armstrong, Lerner and Cooper Architects, may I help you?"

"May I speak to Dan Armstrong?" Alex tapped the toe of his shoe on the floor.

"Who may I say is calling?"

"His cousin Alex."

"Certainly." Her tone became obsequious. "I'll put you right through."

"Yo, Cousin Alex! What's up?" Dan's cheerful voice greeted him. "How's living in Timbuktu working out?"

"It's not quite as remote as you might think it is. And it's lovely here. I had no idea what I was getting into, but so far I'm glad I'm here."

"Good, good. Then why the call? Are you going to build yourself a parsonage?"

"I have a very good one, thank you." And he told Dan about the old Hubbard house and Nancy Jenkins's grief about having to move out. "Your firm does a lot of home restoration, what would you recommend?"

"Without seeing it with my own eyes, it's hard to say, but usually there are some basic things that can seal up a building like that without destroying the integrity of the house or breaking the bank."

"Like what?"

Dan rattled off a list of suggestions.

"That still sounds expensive."

"Not all of it is. And much of it they could do themselves."

"I can't pay you for this so I can't make you do it, but if you'd be willing to write a letter telling this young couple what you've told me, I'll pass it on to them. Whatever advice you can give would be helpful, and I know they can't afford an architect. It will give them something to think about, at least."

"Consider it done. In fact, I'll overnight one to them directly."

"You don't have to do it that quickly. I am, after all, meddling in someone else's affairs, and I haven't yet got a plan as to how to present this."

"Don't waste time. If they decide to tear down the house, all is lost. If the house is the gem you say it is, you don't want it disappearing from the landscape."

Suddenly Alex was infused with a sense of urgency. "Thanks, Dan. You don't know how much I appreciate this."

*A*lex looked down upon a sea of faces as he gave the congregation a final blessing. He was shocked to feel himself close to tears.

The Hilltop congregation was out in full force. The cooks, who'd taken up the last pew in the back, had disappeared immediately after the sermon to check the roasters and coffeepots in the basement. Everything was ready to show their welcome to their new pastor.

The members of All Saints had come to the morning's combined service held at Hilltop, with Alf and Betty Nyborg leading the procession.

Alex was glad to see him. It had to make Alf feel good to be greeted here with such enthusiasm and compassion.

"Now, before we go downstairs to eat, let's sing the table prayer." Alex closed his eyes and listened to the warbling tones of older voices, Winchester's rumbling baritone, Lauren's perfect pitch, a sweet section of sopranos and a few pleasantly off-key voices rusty with disuse. It was heavenly music to his ears.

There was a bottleneck at the back of the church as people had to go single file down the narrow staircase. Already warnings of "Watch your head" and "Be sure to duck" chorused. Alex wondered anew why the two churches had been designed with such hazardous staircases.

Then Dixon Daniels cleared his throat and bellowed, "We should let the pastor go first!"

"That's quite all right. You know us pastors, we like to feed our flocks first," Alex rejoined.

"You at least have to get ahead of Dixon," Mike Carlsen advised, "or you might not get any food at all. He's got a hole in one leg, you know, and he tries to fill it every time there's a church dinner."

Mark, who'd been quiet until now, spoke up. "I think it would be nice if our guests from All Saints were the first to eat. We're glad to have you here."

Gandy was right about the ladies' meatballs having some of the loaves and fishes qualities. They seemed to come out of nowhere in endless supply, along with accompanying gravy, creamy mashed potatoes, string beans with almonds, hot and fluffy rolls, and strawberry shortcake with berries fresh from Jonas Owens's garden.

Several people stopped at Alex and Dixon's table to talk, but it was Tillie Tanner, her brightly dyed red hair clashing fashionably with her even brighter yellow sweater, who touched Alex's heart when she handed him a pint jar filled with flowers clipped from her garden.

Then the elderly woman Alex remembered from All Saints—the one with her thinning white hair worn in a bun, blue eyes, and a pleasant but wrinkled face—appeared by his side. "My name is Althea Dawson. We first met at our quilting group." Before Alex could reply she continued, "It's a blessing to have our churches sharing a meal once again. Thank you."

"Don't thank me," Alex said softly. "It's Him," and he pointed heavenward with his forefinger, "you ought to thank."

"There was a time when our two churches were very close, but we drifted apart," Althea said. "Hardly anyone remembers that now. It's ironic that it took almost losing one of the churches to bring us back together. Perhaps we can retrieve some of what's been lost over the years. Today is a start." She squeezed his hand and he felt her bony fingers and warm, fragile skin.

Alex was savoring a second cup of coffee and his strawberry shortcake when Dixon waved three people to their table. One was a bull of a man in his seventies with a dark, leathery skin and dark hair with surprisingly little gray. Despite his age, his strength was apparent. When he smiled, his teeth flashed white and even.

The other man was taller and much younger but soft looking, as if he rarely saw the light of day. His hair was light brown with a reddish cast, his eyes big behind thick glasses. His movements were choppy and awkward. The woman with them was at least five-foot-nine and looked as though she too was accustomed to heavy farm work. With her nondescript brown hair, a pleasant smile and simple cotton dress, she could almost certainly blend into any crowd of middle-aged women. Her hands were rough and reddened, the knuckles thick, the nails chewed so short that no white above the nail bed could be seen. Working hands, Alex deduced, and nervous ones.

"I'd like you to meet Horace Abel and his housekeeper Flossie Kennedy and her son Charles," Dixon said. He was forever the social director around Hilltop, and took his job very seriously.

Alex jumped to his feet. "I'm pleased to meet all of you." Horace's handshake was painfully strong, and Alex was glad he didn't have arthritis in his knuckles. Charles's grip was just the opposite, damp and limp. It reminded Alex of a rubber glove filled with tepid water.

"I think these are the hardest-working people in the township," Dixon commented amiably. "Horace keeps his place as tidy as the queen's gardens, and Flossie does the same for his house. Charles, on the other hand, sits at the computer twenty-four/seven."

Charles's lip twitched, amused by Dixon's exaggeration.

Before Alex could say more, Mattie Olsen bustled over, coffee carafe in hand. "More?" She lifted the carafe and began to pour as Horace Abel and the Kennedys slipped away.

"This is some of the best coffee I've ever tasted." Alex looked into the bottom of his white cup. "It's so," he searched for the word, "clear." That was the first time he'd ever described coffee that way.

"Egg coffee." Mattie chuckled at the pastor's expression. "Mix an egg into the coffee grounds before you make the coffee. We do it in those big white coffeepots you see on the stove. Best in the world, egg coffee. No bitterness, no acidity. It's Scandinavian, you know. The diehards mix not only the egg but also the crushed shell into the coffee before they cook it."

"It looks like wet potting soil," Dixon offered, "but it works."

So this was the egg coffee Dixon had mentioned. That would teach him to turn up his nose at things before he'd tasted them.

Eggs in coffee, fish soaked in lye—and yet these were some of the best cooks he'd ever come across. And there were all the foreign-sounding foods he'd heard bantered about for the last few weeks— rommegrot, lefse, *krumkake*, egg and anchovy sandwiches, and perhaps the oddest of all, fish balls—made like meatballs—in a can. From now on it might be wise to just eat and not ask too much about the sources of these delicious flavors.

He picked up his cup and walked to the back of the room, where Jonas Owens was standing.

"My sister Gandy told me what you said, about the organic farming," Jonas said without prelude.

"I hope you don't think I was meddling." The difficulty with being a preacher and mentor as well as friend was how to draw the line between being interfering and simply caring enough to take action.

"Meddling? Hardly. I appreciate that you care." Jonas looked down at his feet. "I've been trying to go it single-handedly, and it's been mighty lonesome these past months. I especially left God out of the equation. I've been so ashamed of myself and of what a bad steward I've been for the blessings He gave me, that, frankly, I thought He'd given up on me. Remember what He did to the guys with those talents."

It took Alex a moment to realize what Jonas was talking about. "In Matthew 25, you mean?"

"That's the one. How does it go again?"

"A master was going away so he divided money among his servants. Each was given the amount the master knew they were able to handle. Everyone got an amount that was right for his particular abilities. Each was to care for that money and use it well. All found ways to make even more for their employer by the time he returned except the one who, instead of using his money, buried it in the ground. We all have other gifts too—time, resources, skill—and He expects us to use them wisely until He returns, not let them lie stagnant."

Jonas's gloomy face grew longer still. "See? I didn't use what God gave me well. I had a farm, and now I'm about to lose it. God isn't rating us on what we have, but what we *do* with it. I'm sunk."

"Is that it? You're giving up so easily?"

Jonas smiled faintly. "Not *easily*, exactly. I did get on the computer and do a little research on organic farming." He snorted. "That's just a big fancy name for what I've been doing all along."

"That's exactly what I was thinking." Alex hoped against hope that Jonas had taken it another step.

"So I called a friend of mine. We went to grade school together before his family moved away. Now he's a county agent and he got really excited when I told him that I only used natural pesticides and the like on my farm. He said there were lots of places looking to buy organically grown stuff and that I should get approved by an office inside the Department of Agriculture. There are accredited certifying agents that see if the food you grow meets certain standards.

"There are a lot of hoops to jump through but I'm going to try— if I can find a way to hang on to the land long enough. My buddy is going to look into it for me. He says that because organics cost more, I'd earn more money on the farm."

"That's great, Jonas." Alex paused. "But what will you do for money in the meantime?"

"There's the rub, Reverend. There's the rub."

Alex had greeted several more people when a robust blond woman walked up to him. "Remember me? I'm Lolly Roscoe. We met at the gas station. I'm the one who was talking about starting a farmers' market. Gandy Dunn encouraged me to come today."

Alex reminded himself to strangle the meddling Gandy as soon as he could get his fingers around her neck.

"I'm still interested in that farmers' market concept. I've done a lot of research." She fluttered her lashes. "Could we get together one day and talk about it?"

Warning flags popped up all over his brain. Alex found himself almost relieved to hear an angry, angry voice on the other side of the room, a reason to excuse himself from Lolly's rapt attention.

Will Packard, whom he'd only realized was in church during the final hymn, was having a food fight with another, slightly older red-headed boy. A lump of mashed potatoes had just landed on Dixon's lapel.

Will was a lucky boy, Alex decided. If anyone but good-natured Dixon had taken the potatoes all over the front of his suit, Will might have been sent packing. Dixon, however, was handling it with aplomb as Alex strode up to stand next to him.

"Are you boys hungry?" Dixon asked as he scraped the potatoes, which were fortunately gravy-free, onto an empty plate.

"Yes, sir," they replied in unison.

Alex noted that the pair was definitely cut of the same cloth—red hair, freckles, high cheekbones and rascally expressions that virtually screamed *trouble*.

"Then maybe you two should grab a couple of spoons and eat these potatoes you launched at me. I wouldn't want you to go away from a church dinner hungry."

"Gross!" Will squeaked.

"Double gross!" Both boys stuck out their tongues.

"Is this how you'd behave in your own home…?" Dixon's voice trailed away, obviously realizing that it probably *was* familiar behavior to the Packards, and he changed tactics. "If you aren't inclined to eat them—and potatoes are made for eating—then think how disinclined I am about wearing them."

"I was aiming them at Ricky," Will explained. "If he hadn't ducked, they never would have hit you. Make *him* eat them. It's his fault."

"That's flawed logic if I've ever heard it. If you'd never thrown them, they wouldn't have hit me either."

Will looked dismayed. "We're sorry, Mr. Daniels. Really."

"Then your punishment is to go tell your parents what you've done and apologize to them as well as me." Dixon wiped the last remnants off his jacket.

The boys' faces went as white as sheets, and Will made a strangled sound in his throat. Alex and Dixon simultaneously saw their reactions, and Dixon smoothly interjected, "Or better yet, tell Pastor Alex about it and apologize to him."

The relief in the boys' faces was obvious. They nearly fell over themselves to get to Alex.

"We're sorry. We really are."

"We didn't mean to cause trouble, honest."

"If you let us come back, we'll be good."

Were those tears in Will's eyes? Alex wondered. Was he afraid that this little episode would get him banished from church altogether?

"Of course you can come back. That's what church is, a place for people who do wrong things to come and to be forgiven."

"Sinners, you mean?" Ricky straightened up and leaned forward, suddenly interested. "My ma told us about sinners."

Bless Mrs. Packard's heart. The woman was trying to teach her children spiritual things against what, Alex was beginning to suspect, were nearly insurmountable odds.

"Exactly."

"My pa calls me a little sinner all the time," Will admitted, cheering up. "And that's the best of the names he calls me."

Alex exchanged a glance with Dixon, who was listening with interest. "Is he here today?"

Ricky pointed to the far corner of the church basement. "Over there, with our ma."

Alex followed the direction of the grubby little finger. A hulking man with a mop of black hair, a surly expression, and a suit straining at the seams sat next to a petite red-haired woman with a carefully blank expression on her face. There were other children with them, including a baby, all redheads.

"It was nice of them to come."

"It wasn't out of nice that Pa did it," Will informed Alex. "They had a big fight over it, and for once, Ma won. Besides, he was curious."

Ricky, seeing an opening, scampered off.

"He said he wanted to see someone 'stupid enough to come out here in this forsaken place.'"

"I see." Was that what he was? Stupid?

"I told him you weren't stupid at all, but he didn't believe me. He's not much for ministers and church. He leaves that up to Ma. She's crazy about it. She probably wouldn't have gotten him here if you hadn't had food." His eyes grew wide. "He had *three* helpings."

Alex put another notation on his mental list. *Spend some time with Mrs. Packard.* The woman, he had a hunch, would welcome some support and encouragement.

Out of the corner of his eye, Alex saw a tall man in jeans and a chambray shirt dart out of the kitchen and through the back door carrying a package. "Who was that?" he asked Lauren who was collecting used water glasses from the tables.

"Oh, that was Jacob Olson. He must have come to pick up his dinner. I'm surprised too. Usually Lydia or Clarence takes it home to him."

"Why didn't he simply join us for dinner here?" He was finally getting accustomed to calling the noon meal by its locally acceptable name.

"Jacob? He doesn't socialize." Lauren said that as if it were a commonly known fact. Before Alex could inquire further, she added, "I talked to those from All Saints as they were leaving. They were thankful to be included. Alf was very quiet, however."

"Alf's wounds go deep."

"Thankfully he has a wonderful wife who encourages him to let go of the past."

"I don't get the impression she's had much success as of yet."

"Betty's a prayer warrior and she has faith. How else could she have stayed with Alf all these years?"

How indeed? He could learn a thing or two from that woman, Alex realized, particularly about refusing to give up and about honoring God's timing, no matter how impatient he was for results.

As the crowd shrank, Alex found his way toward Mark Nash. He was sitting at the end of a table with Dixon, sharing a carafe of coffee. He sank down beside them with a sigh. "You both look pretty serious. Is something wrong?"

"I was just asking Dixon what he thought of my plan." Mark reached out and poured coffee into a cup for Alex.

"For what?" He savored the coffee as it tracked across his lips and down his tongue to the back of his throat. Mildred Holmquist had shown Alex how to make egg coffee on one of his trips to the kitchen, and he'd already decided to make it a tradition at his house. He could hardly wait to show this off to his sister Carol.

"To help Jonas out of the hole he's dug himself into."

That made Alex sit up. "Do you have an idea?"

"He told me he's looking into the organic business," Mark said. "It's a great idea. He also told me Lolly Roscoe had asked him if he'd be interested in taking part in a farmers' market. He's going to need capital long before that falls into place, if it ever does. That's why I was just asking Dixon if he thought Jonas would sell me a quarter of his land."

A quarter, Alex had learned, was one hundred and sixty acres. That was large in a city, but not so very much land out here.

"There's a quarter of his land that abuts some land I farm. I don't mind offering him top dollar. It's good land, flat and with no sloughs. If he'd take it, he could use the money to pay off his bills and get his feet back on the ground."

"It would give him time to look into this organic farming thing," Dixon added. "He'd lose one-quarter of his land but not the whole farm. What do you think, Alex?"

"I think it's a great idea...if Jonas will go for it."

"Pride runs deep around here," Mark observed mildly.

"And pride goes before the fall," Dixon added.

"This is very generous of you, Mark."

The lanky man shrugged. "I'd like more land. Jonas needs help. It doesn't seem generous at all, just practical. I only wish he'd come to me months ago or that I'd known how big the problem was earlier."

"Practical, then. When are you going to talk to him?"

"I thought I'd drive over there this evening."

"I'll start praying for both of you." Praying, Alex thought, that Jonas's pride wouldn't stand in the way.

"You do that."

Dixon walked upstairs with Alex after Mark left. His expression was troubled. "What did you think of that little Packard boy's reaction when I mentioned his father?"

"Those kids turned white as sheets. Do you think something is going on in that home? Something bad, I mean."

"If Earl Packard could be thrown in jail for being mean, nasty, callous, irritable, cantankerous, belligerent, ornery and spoiling for a fight, then he'd be there already. I've never heard of him lifting a hand to those kids, but who knows? His wife is as sweet as a woman can be."

"I think I'll keep an eye out for those children."

"That shouldn't be hard," Dixon said. "They're constantly in trouble. You'd have a hard time not seeing them."

a day off. Alex hardly remembered the concept; and now that he had one, he didn't know what to do with it. He'd awakened at his usual time, six o'clock this Monday morning, despite his plans to the contrary.

He picked up the phone and set it down again. He wanted to talk to Carol and Jared, but the last two times they'd spoken, his nephew had been gloomy and negative, and his mother, frustrated.

"It's all because of school," she complained, "and it hasn't even started yet!"

"Maybe things will be better than he expects."

"You tell him that. I certainly can't get it through to him. He won't even talk to me about it anymore."

"Carol, is Jared depressed?" It was difficult even to ask the question about his easygoing, cheerful nephew. "Maybe this isn't about school at all, but something else."

But he'd wondered what could that something else be as he returned the receiver to its cradle.

Alex grew restless thinking about it and decided that only physical activity would shake the cobwebs from his brain.

"Want to go for a run, Tripod?" he asked the dog who was sleeping in the early morning sun that filtered through the eastern-facing windows.

Tripod's ears twitched; and even though he was in a deep doggie sleep, he roused himself, sat up, and his tail began to pound rhythmically on the floor. *Run* had become his favorite word and he literally jumped with joy when he saw his master's running shoes come out of the closet.

"Come on, then. Let's check on the neighborhood."

They exited through the screen door and headed east, where the sun was rising rapidly. Alex veered northward, turned east to take a loop past the Carlsens' farm, and then turned south and finally west until he had gone what Dixon called "around the block."

As he passed the Jenkinses' house—the old Hubbard place— he slowed to study it in the morning sunlight. The windows sparkled, and the flecks in the granite block foundation twinkled in the sun. It made Alex sick in the pit of his stomach to think of it being torn down. But he'd meddled enough already by talking to his cousin last week. He'd heard nothing back from Dan either. Maybe he'd asked too much of a very busy man. Now it was time to back off and let life take its course.

"Hey, Rev!"

Alex's gaze followed the path of the voice and Tripod's ears went on alert. Ben Jenkins was heading toward them, wearing jeans, a white T-shirt and slippers. His hair was still rumpled from sleep. "You're out early," Ben said as he stopped at the mailbox. He opened it to reveal the previous day's mail, which included the weekly *Grassy Valley Gazette*. "Or I slept in. Nancy's making breakfast. Want a cup of coffee?"

He was about to make his apologies when Alex realized it was his day off. If he wanted to have coffee with a neighbor, there was no reason not to. Besides, both he and Tripod could use a break.

They followed Ben to the house, where he produced a dried pig's ear snack for the dog. "I keep them on hand." Ben grinned boyishly. "You never know when one of your visitors might have four feet...or three."

"You're a fine host, Ben." Alex took the treat and made Tripod sit before he gave it to him.

"Nancy and I both like having company. It fills this big old house and makes it feel lived in."

Nancy greeted them at the door. "Did you come for breakfast?" she asked hopefully. "I'm making Dutch babies and I'd love for you to try one."

"Babies for breakfast? I don't believe they're on my diet."

"Not that kind! They're puffy pancakes I fill with apples, butter and cinnamon."

"Then how can I say no?"

Nancy set the table with lovely old china—her grandmother's, she said. She also put out linen napkins and sterling silverware before placing her centerpiece, a small bowl of fresh flowers. "In my family, we have a policy. We don't save the good dishes for guests. We enjoy them every day. It's that old adage about treating your family like they were guests and your guests like they were family, I guess."

She disappeared into the kitchen and soon reappeared with a puffy pancake in a large cast-iron pan. "Voilà! Do you want syrup or powdered sugar?"

She returned again to the kitchen and came out with a platter of thick cut, crisply fried bacon and a fruit compote. She poured the men mugs of rich, dark coffee before joining them.

"Do you cook like this every morning?" Alex couldn't help but ask.

"When Ben encourages me." Nancy spooned fruit onto everyone's plate. "I would cook like this every day if I could, but he says I'll have to open a restaurant and feed someone besides him or he'll weigh four hundred pounds."

"Nancy loves to cook and to sew. She gardens and paints too," Ben said proudly. "Miss Domesticity, that's my wife. She'd be happy if she could do that all day, every day."

Nancy blushed prettily.

"By the way, we got a letter from an architect in Chicago who said he knew you."

Alex felt his own neck redden. "I stuck my nose into somewhere it probably didn't belong. Feel free to tell me to mind my own business. It's just that I've heard so many people concerned about losing this house that I decided to ask an expert about it."

Alex explained the telephone call to his cousin Dan. "I did it without asking your permission. It was impulsive and I'm sorry."

"Don't be. It's nice of you to be concerned," Nancy said. "His letter made a lot of sense. He listed some of the most inexpensive things he recommends to people who are restoring old houses. Unfortunately I'm not sure we can afford even that."

"We spent most of January and February with temperatures in minus double digits last year. All we really know is that we can't afford another heating bill like that," Ben said bluntly.

Nancy touched her belly. "With two babies on the way we'll have lots of extra expenses, and I don't intend to keep them in a cold, drafty house either.

"We'll have to study it, I suppose." She looked at Alex. "Who knows? But thanks for caring."

"It would be hard *not* to care about the people here," Alex admitted, relieved that they'd taken his help in the spirit it had been given. At least he'd tried.

Alex collected Tripod, thanked his hosts, and resumed his run at a much slower pace now that his stomach was full. He was on the main road that ran past the church when Lauren caught up to him in Mike's pickup.

"You're out early on your day off," she commented as she rolled down the window. "Do you need something to do?"

"Not really, but what do you have in mind?"

"I've got apples that need to be used up. You can have them if you want them. To make a pie or something."

"Me?"

"Don't sound so shocked. Some of the best cooks I know are men."

"Let me think about that for a while, but thanks for the offer."

"No problem." Lauren waved cheerily and pulled the truck away.

It wasn't long after he'd showered and shaved that Alex *was* wondering what to do with himself. Then he remembered the trove of calendars and trunks Jared had found in the old garage.

The building smelled of diesel fuel. Over the years, oil had soaked into the rough wooden floorboards, leaving them with a permanent blue-black sheen. The windows were small and caked and crusty with years of grime, as if this narrow, nondescript building had been overlooked time and time again.

The old calendars on the walls beckoned invitingly, but today it was the trunks that held Alex's interest. Aged as some of them were, they could have come west with the settlers of this area on prairie schooners or sailed the Atlantic from the old country. What could be stored in here that no one had ever come to retrieve?

He pulled a flat-topped trunk that looked like it had come from the early 1900s into the middle of the space. He found a small milking stool, which he placed so that he could view into the depths of the trunk. It opened with a loud creak, as if the leather straps and metal hinges had been untouched for decades.

The inside seemed a disappointment at first. A few old books, a felt dress hat, a moth-eaten wool suit, and a strange, collapsible basket made of wire. Alex didn't know what to make of it.

He was thumbing through one of the books—a volume of Shakespeare—when he heard footsteps behind him.

"Hey, preacher man, what's up?" a cheerful and upbeat voice said.

"Dixon, I'm glad you're here."

"I just wanted to see if you were entertaining yourself properly on your day off. Otherwise I'd invite you to go with me to pick up a used garden tractor I purchased."

Alex waved him over. "I saw these trunks in here when I first arrived, and my curiosity got the best of me—who left them here? Why?"

Dixon squatted down beside him, resting on the tips of his toes. "I doubt I can explain all of them, but I do know what that one is about." He picked up the odd little basket and collapsed it in upon itself and then pulled it into shape again.

"When you looked around the cemetery did you notice a few graves at the back that had only small, flat headstones or plaques?"

"I did. I meant to ask someone why they were so different from the rest of the headstones."

"Most of those graves are those of hired men." Dixon played with the basket thoughtfully. "Men who used to work on the farms, live in the bunkhouses and sometimes die there. Usually when a hired man died, his employer would provide a small funeral and a burial plot. Very few shelled out a lot for a regular headstone and they were buried together in that section of the cemetery. Lots of times they didn't have families or their relatives couldn't be reached, so there was no one to take the belongings. One of the former pastors started storing those things in this little garage."

"Do you think that unmarked grave is one of those men?" Alex couldn't get it out of his mind.

"I doubt it. No one like that has been buried here in many years."

A wave of sadness broke over Alex as he imagined those alone and lonely men, buried in a mass plot, their life possessions limited enough to fit into a small trunk.

"Ashes to ashes, dust to dust," he murmured. "Is that in the Bible?"

"No. It's from the Book of Common Prayer, but it expresses beautifully the fleeting nature of life and the eternal nature of God."

They sat side by side, silently and companionably considering the transitory qualities of life on earth, until they heard the crunch of tires on gravel.

Shaking off the somber mood, Alex and Dixon rose to check on the new guest.

It was Lolly Roscoe with a plate of macaroons in her hands. Her smile was wide and engaging but it faltered when she noticed Dixon emerging from the shed with Alex.

"Oh, *you're* here," she said to Dixon.

"Yep. Sure am." He made no offer to leave. In fact, he seemed to plant his work-booted feet more firmly on the earth.

"What have we here?" Alex asked, uneasy with the odd conversation.

Lolly bestowed her high-wattage smile on him. "Jonas and Barbara Owens and I spent a little time together this morning to discuss the idea of a farmers' market. We set a date to try it and made a call to Red to see if we could set up in his parking lot. He said it was fine with him as long as we paid him in strawberries and peppers." She thrust the papers into Alex's hands. "Here's a sample of the flyer we want to make up."

The paper depicted a quaint-looking market with striped awnings and carts overflowing with fruits, vegetables, and flowers. There were happy vendors beside each cart. All in all, a very inviting scene. The date and time was listed.

"We're calling around. Lydia Olson said she'd bring pint jars of jam to sell. Nancy Jenkins is bringing quilted potholders. I told her she should bring her larger quilts as well. You never know what could sell. We want to have more stuff than just produce. I think it will be wonderful!"

Then she frowned. Even that didn't mar her Scandinavian beauty. "There is some hang-up about a permit. I'm going to check into it this afternoon. I hope it doesn't cost a lot of money or prevent us from moving ahead."

"I'm sure you'll figure it out," Dixon said cheerfully.

Lolly scowled at him. She seemed to want to say something, but hesitated, glanced at Dixon, and closed her lips tightly.

"Thank you, Alex. I…" Her voice trailed away and she seemed at a loss as to what to do next. "I'd better get going."

Reluctantly, she headed for her car.

When she'd driven out of the yard and onto the main thoroughfare, Dixon chuckled.

"What was that about?" Alex scratched his head, puzzled. "Why did I just feel so uncomfortable?"

"Other than the fact that Lolly's set her eyes on you for her next romance, you mean? Lolly's upset with me." Dixon appeared impish and unrepentant.

"Why?"

"Because I didn't marry her." Alex's jaw dropped.

"She's upset with Mark too. He didn't marry her either. She's looking for a man who wants a permanent relationship. Mark and I were terrible disappointments to her." Dixon eyed Alex. "You'd be wise to remember that before you get too involved with Lolly Roscoe."

"Don't worry about that," Alex said vehemently. "There's no danger of my getting involved."

"Methinks you doth protest too much," Dixon quipped, approximately quoting Shakespeare.

"Maybe, but I've got my reasons."

Dixon crossed his arms across his chest and studied Alex. "So you either had a close call or a total wreck in the romance department."

"Let's just say I was engaged once, and she found someone else." His voice sounded terse in his own ears.

"Ouch."

"You could say that." It actually felt good to tell someone his story. He'd kept his breakup mostly to himself until now.

"Are you over it?"

Alex hesitated. "I think I'm more 'over it' every day since I've come to Hilltop. I don't think of Natalie as much. It's a healing place, Hilltop."

"So you aren't interested in getting involved again?"

"Involved? Not now. I have no intention of getting caught up in another relationship."

"No? Then keep that in mind around Lolly. Otherwise you might find yourself in a marriage trap before you know it."

There were land mines everywhere, Alex thought with alarm. What would he step into next?

CHAPTER TWENTY-THREE

Alex walked his company out, and on his way back inside, he noticed a brown paper grocery bag containing apples on the porch. Lauren, he thought, determined to see him learn to cook.

He showered, made coffee, ate one of the apples out of the bag and settled at the kitchen table with a stack of catalogs that had come in his mailbox. There were a million things to be done but he didn't feel like doing any of them. He was going to have to get some new hobbies. He couldn't go out and pick up a game of basketball here, nor could he walk three blocks to see a movie or go to the library. Lauren had once told him that in the country people learned to entertain themselves, not have others do it for them. He was beginning to understand exactly what that meant.

Alex was relieved to hear a rapping on his front door, glad for a diversion from his own little pity party. He opened it to find Lydia Olson on the porch.

"Lydia, to what do I owe this pleasure?" He swung the door wide to allow her to enter.

She tittered like a young girl and walked in. "You have such a way with words, Pastor. Clarence came to work on the well. There's something that needs to be replaced in the pump, I believe. I rode over with him to weed your flower beds. I'm sure you haven't had time, especially with all that's been going on."

"That's very kind of you, but not necessary. You have work of your own to do. You people of Hilltop are too good to me. Besides, Tripod and I have been pulling intruders every time we come back from a run. I think you'll find the place surprisingly weed-free."

Lydia frowned. "Oh dear. I'm sure Clarence will be here at least an hour or two. He'd be very provoked with me if I asked him to give me a ride home now. Do you have anything else I could help you with—windows to wash? Laundry to hang on the line?"

Alex was about to offer to take her home himself when an idea struck him. "Lydia, could you teach me to cook? I've got a bag of apples crying out for a pie, and I've never made one." The little woman's face lit up like the night sky on a Fourth of July. "I'd love to help you. How about an apple crisp instead? That might be a little easier to start with."

"Excellent." Alex ushered her into his beautiful kitchen. "Show me what to do first."

It was peaceful, he realized, and comfortable, working side by side with Lydia. She bustled about humming as she set him to washing, peeling and coring the apples while she placed oatmeal, flour, brown sugar, butter, cinnamon, nutmeg, measuring utensils and a large bowl on the counter.

He was reminded of Miss Merrill, his high school chemistry teacher, a plump, meticulous woman, laying out beakers and setting up Bunsen burners and microscopes in the lab for the day's experiments.

"I've laid out everything you'll need and jotted down the recipe for you to follow. Just put the ingredients in this bowl in the order I've listed them. You'd better take the butter out of the refrigerator so it softens."

As Alex did so, Lydia picked up a paring knife and began to work on the apples, her fingers swift. The red peel went flying.

"So, Lydia, tell me more about yourself." It seemed perfectly natural to ask the question in this convivial atmosphere. "There isn't much, I'm afraid," she said wistfully as she rested her forearms on the sink. "Hilltop has always been my home but, wonderful as it is, I've always wanted to get away for a time and see the world. I've often had the feeling that there is something out there for me, but there's always too much work to do. Clarence and Jacob depend on me, you see. I even dreamed of marrying, but once our parents died, I became responsible for our house, and after that…"

The longing in her voice struck Alex as particularly sad. Lydia must have been a pretty young woman. She had a good sense of humor and a charming laugh—both of which were more obvious when her brother wasn't around to quash them. "Maybe it's not too late." Alex kept his eyes on the apple he was peeling. "You could travel. Take a cruise. Find a friend and drive cross-country. Lots of things."

"Me? Without the boys?"

It always astounded Alex that out here any man who was single, no matter the age, might be called a "boy." Clarence had passed boyhood several decades ago.

"I've never even considered that." Lydia fingers slowed as she peeled. She looked up at Alex with bright eyes. "It's something to think about. I've always wanted…" Then, deftly, she changed the subject. "Do you have a bladed dough blender for cutting the butter into the dry ingredients for the topping?"

Alex peered helplessly into the drawer that held small kitchen gadgets. He wouldn't know a dough blender if it jumped up and bit him. Lydia, however, plucked the bladed device out immediately.

He hoped he hadn't started something by encouraging Lydia to exhibit some independence. Surely she wouldn't go too far with it. Otherwise he'd have to deal with Clarence and the mysterious Jacob.

He wanted to inquire about Jacob, to unravel the puzzle of why he was so reclusive and what had caused him to be that way, but he had a feeling in his gut that it might shatter the pleasant camaraderie that he and Lydia currently shared. Instead, he picked up the recipe she'd written down at his request and pretended to be interested in reading it.

LYDIA OLSON'S APPLE CRISP

- 2 cups flour
- 2 cups rolled oats (I prefer the old-fashioned kind)
- 1 tsp. cinnamon
- ½ tsp. nutmeg
- 1½ cups brown sugar, packed
- 1½ cups butter
- 2 quarts peeled, cored apples (Whatever type you have will work. Delicious makes a more mushy crisp but it still tastes wonderful.)

Combine dry ingredients. Cut butter into mixture until it's crumbly. Pat half of mixture into bottom of 9x13 pan. Top with apples. Cover apples with the rest of the crumble and bake at 350 degrees. It will take 45–50 minutes or until apples are tender.

Delicious served with whipped cream or ice cream (vanilla or cinnamon).

Alex chuckled to himself. How could this *not* be delicious? His mouth began to water. Lydia paused to look out the window, her expression wistful. "It's funny, isn't it, how life works out? What you dream of and what you actually do are sometimes very far apart."

What were Lydia's dreams? Alex mused. And how far afield had they gone?

"It was wonderful to see Alf Nyborg at the church dinner," Lydia said. "That fire may have been a blessing in disguise. And Earl Packard and his family! I don't know that he's darkened the door of the church much since he was a teenager, and I can't imagine a man who needs it more. He's got the sweetest, meekest wife and those darling children."

Alex didn't quite know how to formulate his next question. "Is he...good...to them?"

Lydia looked at him sharply, and he saw the keen intelligence in her eyes. "Does he abuse them, you mean? Nobody has ever come out and said that, although the children are careful to stay on his good side. Earl is a bully, and in his mind the glass is never half-full, only half-empty. It's amazing, really, how bright and charming— if mischievous—the children are."

"I have a lot of unanswered questions about that family," he admitted as he measured out two cups of flour and two of rolled oats.

"It will take a while to understand everyone here," Lydia said sympathetically. "But give it time." She tossed a cup and a half of packed brown sugar into the bowl while Alex measured the cinnamon and nutmeg.

"My nephew Jared said something to that effect—that I'm surrounded by stories and I've only read the first page of each."

"You wouldn't expect to read a hundred books all at once and finish them immediately, would you?"

"Of course not."

"Then you can't learn everything about Hilltop in one sitting either. And just like books, some of the people of Hilltop are easier to read than others."

"Have patience, you mean?"

Lydia smiled at him. "You said it yourself."

"I believe I will learn a lot from you, Lydia."

"And I've already learned a lot from you," she said.

The crisp was out of the oven and they started a fresh pot of coffee brewing just about the time Clarence finished repairing the pump and came to the house.

"So my sister is teaching you to cook. You picked a good teacher, Reverend Alex. A mighty good teacher."

Lydia blushed at the compliment and gave Clarence an extra large square of the crisp and a mound of vanilla ice cream to go with it.

Alex brought his own plate to the table, but a pounding at his door forced him to set it down and check to see what the commotion was all about.

As he opened the door, Will Packard darted inside and grabbed Alex's legs. The boy was trembling.

"You've got to hide me, Pastor. I'm going to get killed!" And Alex had thought dramatic announcements were Mattie Olsen's domain.

"Surely not, you're…" Then he got a good look at the boy's face. It was filled with genuine terror.

"Bucky Chadwick spotted me trying to unleash a dog he's had tied up for days. It got its foot caught in a trap and Bucky left it there to suffer. If it doesn't get help, it's going to be just like Tripod!" Will's tear-stained face was enough to wrench Alex's heart. And the thought of what had happened to Tripod…

"He yelled that he was going to go back inside and get his gun and shoot both me and the dog." Will's body was shivering slightly less as he clung to Alex. "I got the dog loose and carried him as far as I could. I hid him in a spot where me and my brother have a fort and then took off running for here. I've got some other animals there too. If he shoots that dog…"

Clarence was on his feet with a roar. "That outlaw has got to be stopped! He's been causing trouble since he was six years old, but this is ridiculous. He can't just pull out a gun and threaten to shoot people."

"Maybe we should call the police," Alex ordered, seeing red himself.

"I'll take care of this," Clarence stormed, "and I know something that scares Bucky more than the law."

"What's that?"

"His mother."

"Will, you stay here with Lydia. I'm going with Clarence." Will didn't argue.

By the time they got to the Chadwicks', Bucky was already traversing the field near his house in the direction Will said he'd taken the dog. True to his word, he had a shotgun in his hand.

Clarence, driving his four-wheel-drive pickup, ignored the KEEP OUT signs in the driveway. He drove right across the field of wheat that was not yet ripe. He pulled up next to Bucky, who stopped to glare at him, his eyes narrowing to slits.

"Just what do you think you're doing?" Clarence boomed.

"Going hunting. What's it to you?"

"Dogs aren't in season, Bucky."

The fellow looked surprised, and then suspicious. "Who says I'm hunting dogs?"

"Will Packard, that's who."

"That little weasel has been trespassing on my land and now he's stolen my dog," Bucky snarled. "I won't let him have that dog. I'll kill it myself if I have to."

"No, you won't."

Alex marveled at Clarence's turnabout. It wasn't long ago that he'd been furious with Will and his animal rescue project. Suddenly they were on the same team.

"You're trespassing too, you know. I oughta call the police."

"Do that, please. Will you? I have quite a bit to say to Grassy Valley's finest."

Bucky, realizing that tactic wouldn't work, turned on Clarence with a snarl. "There's nobody on this green earth that's going to stop me from finding and killing that dog. And I'm going to give that kid a whupping too, once I catch him."

Clarence reached for something in his pocket. "I can think of someone who'll put a stop to this."

Bucky laughed a grating, rusty laugh. Then his expression changed as he noticed that Clarence had pulled out a cell phone. "Who are you calling?"

"The one person who knows how to put you in your place." Clarence pushed a button and a call started to go through. "Your mother."

It was gratifying to see Bucky turn ashen.

"Myrtle? It's Clarence. How are you doing? Is it busy at Red's? No? Good. Then maybe you could come home and solve a little problem for us. Your son threatened one of the Packard children and he has a gun. He wants to shoot your dog."

"Is he with you?" They could all hear Myrtle Chadwick's voice through the mouthpiece.

"Yes. Do you want to speak to—"

"Bucky, you get yourself into the house!" Myrtle yelled so loudly that Alex wondered if she actually needed the telephone. Clarence winced and pulled the phone away from his ear. "I'm on my way home right now, and if you think you're going to hurt anything, then you've got another think coming!"

Her voice calmed as she said to Clarence, "I'll be right there. Have him leave that gun with you. Take it home and get rid of it. And watch him until he goes into the house. I don't want him slipping off before

I get there." Her voice raised and she was addressing Bucky again. "If you're gone when I get there, don't bother to come home again."

Bucky flung the gun into the bed of the pickup and stormed off toward the ramshackle two-story without another word. The screen door slammed behind him, and they could hear the sound of the television being turned to high volume.

"He should stay there. He doesn't mess with his mother." They got into the pickup and Clarence backed down the driveway to return to the parsonage. "He's a difficult person, but the one person who can handle him is Myrtle. We'd better get Will and see if we can find that dog."

When they got back to Alex's, Lydia was feeding the boy apple crisp and ice cream. The tears had dried into dirty little tracks on his grubby face. Alex couldn't remember ever seeing anyone more pitiful—or worried.

"Did he get the dog?" the child asked, his voice wavering.

"No, Clarence got to Bucky before he had a chance."

The relief on the boy's face was palpable.

"We'll go look for it, if you want," Alex offered.

Will jumped to his feet. "I'll call Ricky. He knows where our secret hiding place is. He can hide the dog in our barn until I find a new place for my *hoomain* society."

"Will, about that..."

Three pairs of eyes watched him expectantly, Alex noted, as he scrambled for something more to say.

Chapter Twenty-Four

*A*lex sighed deeply, wondering what he was getting himself into. "Maybe you'd better use one of the outbuildings here at the parsonage for your 'hoomain' society until I can figure out something better—and before you get in trouble with every person around Hilltop. If, that is," he cautioned, "I can get permission from the church council."

"Consider it done," Clarence said relief apparent in his voice. At least he would not have to deal with any more critters. "I'll speak to them myself. There's the little well house that's not used for anything. It will hold a couple cages and maybe a bed or two for cats or dogs. But, Will, you had better figure out how to stay out of trouble with those animals, or this opportunity will disappear."

"You mean it? You both mean it?" Will bounded up from his chair and flung himself at Alex and then at Clarence. "This is great! Wait until I tell Ricky and the others. They'll find me lots of animals, I'll bet."

"Whoa," Alex said. "There's only room for a few. Don't go overboard. And we'll probably have to think of an alternate solution sooner or later."

Will turned shining eyes on Alex, who was struck with affection for this dirty, red-haired boy. "And I can be at your house every day!"

Alex hadn't thought of that, but he was surprised to find that the idea didn't upset him. In fact, he rather liked it. Having a little boy and his pets around might be just the remedy for some of that restlessness of his.

"You'll have to behave."

A halo practically sprang out of the top of Will's head, so innocent and sweet was his expression. "You can count on me, Pastor Alex."

Alex already knew he could count on Will. He just wasn't sure for what.

✑

"So what do you think of Hilltop so far?" Lauren asked as she, Mike and Alex shared a pizza on the picnic table outside her home. A bee buzzed in the distance, no doubt romancing a sweet-smelling flower nearby. Occasionally a hummingbird dipped close, interested in the pitcher of red Kool-Aid on the table. Tripod's tail thumped happily as he lay with the Carlsens' dog on a lawn with grass so soft and thick it must have felt like a cool, plush bed.

"In many ways it's like something out of a dream. A step into the past." Then he thought about Clarence whipping out his cell phone to report Bucky to his mother. "And yet it is totally contemporary and relevant. I feel welcomed like a family member, and yet I have so much yet to learn."

He thought of the problem of Bucky and his mother and wondered how long the little woman would be able to manage the young man before he tipped over into real criminal activities. He recalled Alf Nyborg's suffering and the toxic drift that had settled over All Saints because of it. There were the mysteries too. Why did Jacob Olson never come out in public? What made Flossie and Charles Kennedy so reclusive? What exactly were Bessie Bruun's mental problems, and was there any way to help her? He thought of Jonas, Gandy, and the

Packards, particularly the belligerent Earl and the effect he was having on his children. There was Lolly Roscoe, who made him as skittish as a deer in the forest. He wanted to know more about Matt and Martha Jacobson and their movie star daughter Amelia Jacobs, and to spend time with the delightful Ole Swenson and to hear stories about Twinkle Toes.

What's more, he hadn't yet seen Inga Sorensen's artwork or visited the Aadlands or the Hansons. He wanted to spend time with the cheerful, if slightly addled, Lila Mason and have coffee with Tillie Tanner, who brought him a little gift nearly every Sunday—wildflowers, a cookie, a colorful stone—and thanked him for becoming their pastor. And he still needed answers about that grave.

He'd barely scratched the surface, just as Lydia had pointed out.

"Happy enough to stay around for a long while?" Lauren asked. "I know you're a fish out of water here. I'm just hoping that you're figuring out how to breathe here at Hilltop and not itching to go back to the ocean." Her expression was somber. "I know that we're not the biggest, fanciest place you could have gone...."

He hadn't even considered what a concern that might be to his parishioners. "No chance, Lauren. For the first time in my life I feel... right. As if I'm in the place God wants me to be. I won't run away from that. Until I get word from Him that I should move on, I'll stay."

She heaved a sigh of relief and held up the pizza pan between them. "More pepperoni?"

Even though Lolly had managed to acquire the needed permits for the farmers' market, she hadn't been able to control the weather. It had rained all night, flooding the lot at Red's and forcing the participants—a small but determined few—to make do on the school playground.

It wasn't an auspicious beginning, Alex thought as he turned off his alarm clock. He'd set it because Jonas had warned him that the best produce was likely to be gone by eight thirty; and if he wanted any of Jonas's famous sweet peppers or burpless, seedless cucumbers, he'd better come early. What's more, Mildred had harvested lavender and was selling fragrant potpourri. Most exciting of all, according to Gandy, Lilly Sumptner had decided to have a rummage sale right there at the market and sell out all her leftover makeup, not that Alex would be interested, but Gandy predicted it would draw a big crowd.

It was already difficult to find a parking spot, Alex discovered when he arrived at the school. But why should he be surprised? People around here got up so early that they had to wake the birds. The ball field had been designated as a parking lot, so he parked on third base and walked toward the hubbub.

Red was in the middle of the crowd, waving his hat and directing traffic, his toothpick clenched in his teeth, a smile on his face.

Jonas was in his booth, bagging vegetables, while Gandy counted out change to the customers. The worry lines in her face had softened somewhat, taking several years off her features.

"By the way," Gandy said to Alex, "I'm planning to up my tithing next month. From now on I'll be in the church office a half hour more each day."

Surprise must have shown on his face because Gandy added, "We'd give more if we could. God's good, you know."

Touched and humbled, Alex could only nod.

Dixon, of course, was already meandering through the booths when Alex arrived. He was carrying a thermal mug of hazelnut-flavored coffee and shelling green peas and popping them into his mouth.

"I picked green peas for my mother every summer for eighteen years and never got one into the house to cook," he admitted cheerfully. "My mother said I'd turn green and round one day, but it hasn't happened yet."

"You're chipper." Alex sat down next to him on the bench on which Dixon had taken root.

"What's not to be happy about?" Dixon took a sip of coffee and set down the mug. "Little Will Packard has a place for his animals, Bucky's afraid to go anywhere near him, and Nancy Jenkins told me this morning that they aren't going to tear the old house down this fall like they'd planned. Her doctor told her he didn't want her messing with anything like that during her pregnancy. Instead they're going to spend a little money to seal it up like your cousin told them to. The house might still be on death row, but it has a temporary reprieve.

"Nancy also told me she'd gotten a good price for one of her quilts. Somebody from back East was passing through and saw the signs. She said it would be enough to get a new storm door for the house."

"That's good news." Alex eyed Dixon, who was grinning and waving at everyone who passed by. "But that's not why you're in such high spirits."

"You're sharp, I'll give you that." Dixon sat back on the bench, stretched and removed his cap to scratch his head. "I got a letter from my twin sister Emmy yesterday. She's coming for a visit."

"I'll look forward to meeting her."

A faraway look filled Dixon's eyes. "Emmy and I used to be inseparable, like that." He crossed his fingers. "But she left the farm and I stayed. Emmy is a nurse and she was able to go anywhere she wanted to work. The time between our visits has gotten longer and longer. Lately it's been once or twice a year. I'd give anything if Emmy would decide to come back to Hilltop. It's funny, but twins do somehow feel more complete when they're together."

"What would bring her back?"

"Nothing I can think of except a miracle. There's barely a clinic in Grassy Valley, and she loves her work. Now she's become a nurse practitioner. There would have to be something pretty tantalizing here for her to stay around. Unless a hospital springs up on Main Street, I think I'll have to settle for our yearly visits."

"There's just something special about family," Alex commented, thinking about Jared. "When is she arriving?"

"She wants to be here for harvest. Says it's the best time of the year on a farm. I have to agree with her."

"Never having experienced that, I have to ask, why?"

"Even the air changes during harvest. It's dry, crisp, fresh and dusty all at once. The nights are often spectacularly clear. And it's exhilarating. The combines and trucks roll day and night. It's the time of year that farmers are finally rewarded for their hard work. It's thrilling when they can finally bring their crops in. It's like nothing else."

Alex tried to imagine the anticipation. A year's work paying out, collecting the bounty from the fields into the bins, knowing at long last if the winter rations would be sparse or plentiful. No wonder it was electrifying.

"This is the time of year you'll see the church coffers increase," Dixon added. "After harvest, people know how much of their year's income can be put in the offering plate. When I was a kid, the church set aside a Sunday after harvest to show appreciation for the preacher and the organist."

"How so?"

"There were two offering plates, one for the preacher, the other for the organist. People dropped checks or cash in each plate, giving as much as they could or as much as they thought the two should receive."

"I hope that's stopped by now. I don't need one more thing." Alex surprised himself with his own words. Back in Chicago, he'd worried how he'd make ends meet once he took the salary Hilltop had offered, but he'd rarely thought of money since he arrived. The parsonage was everything he needed and more, he had food coming out his ears, and offers for help with everything he might ever have had to hire done in the city. He felt downright rich on half the salary he'd had in Chicago.

Jonas strode over to join them, his shoulders back and his chin high. "How do you like it? I think it's going pretty well in spite of last night's rain. It should help that the Cozy Corner is going to have its meat loaf special today. That usually draws more people into town."

"It's a good start."

The man's gaze flickered. "I'm more grateful than I can say, to all of you for your help and support." He pointed upward. "And to Him."

Gandy fluttered over to them eating fluffy cotton candy that vaguely resembled her hairdo. "There are more people asking about those burpless cukes, Jonas. You'd better get back to your stand." She looked at Dixon and Alex on the bench and popped a clump of spun sugar into her mouth. "Best day I've had in months!"

As they sat there, Alex and Dixon saw most of Hilltop and of Grassy Valley amble by, and many stopped to talk. At noon, they stood in line at the Cozy Corner to eat meat loaf and fresh green beans, and afterward they stopped at Cowlicks and Peppermint Sticks for an ice cream cone. Dixon got his hair trimmed while they were there.

When Alex arrived at home in the late afternoon, Tripod greeted him with such wild abandon that he nearly knocked Alex flat. Alex finally managed to divert him by throwing a ball across the gentle green slope of the lawn. They played the game until even Tripod was tired, and then sat together on the front steps watching a fat, improbable bumblebee hover in the flower bed. Bees defied logic and physics by being able to fly with those large bodies and tiny wings, Alex knew, but nevertheless, they flew. He wasn't much different. He seemed an unlikely candidate for helping others. And on his own, he was. But he wasn't alone.

Whatever came next, whoever stirred the pot and caused the trouble, Alex refused to worry about it today. This was the day the Lord had made. He would rejoice and be glad in it.

Surprising Grace

CHAPTER ONE

A pair of recalcitrant geese began honking beneath Reverend Alex Armstrong's bedroom window at five A.M. He grimly wadded his pillow into a ball and yearned for another hour of sleep even though the late-August sun would have him up soon enough. The duo were more like foghorns than feathered creatures and had shocked him awake at dawn with their irritating noise every morning for the past two weeks.

Alex had nine-year-old Will Packard to blame for these short nights. The boy had rescued the honkers from Hilltop Township's local bully Bucky Chadwick. Will had overheard Bucky boasting that he was going to have his mother cook a goose for dinner. Will had immediately taken it upon himself to find the birds a new home and set them up in housekeeping in a shed on the parsonage property.

Mother Goose, the goose that laid the golden egg, silly goose… None of them had prepared Alex for real live geese. They were silly enough, he supposed, with their fat rear ends, upright posture and cantankerous personalities. It all went to show how little a city fellow like him knew about rural life.

Sleep-deprived but resigned, Alex got up, threw open the bedroom window and yelled, "Shoo! Scat! Beat it!" Their weight and ungainly shapes prevented the pair from flight, but they could launch themselves a foot or two in the air when motivated. Accustomed to Alex's morning rant, they didn't even budge.

He padded barefoot to the shower to wash away the cobwebs of sleep still lurking in his brain. Once dressed, he shrugged into a jacket from the back of his closet, one he hadn't worn since he'd arrived at Hilltop three months ago, and put on a tie. Had it been only the first of May when he'd come? It seemed like a second— and a lifetime—ago.

His spirits brightened with his first cup of coffee as he and Tripod, his black-and-white three-legged mutt, sat on the porch watching the world awake. Since he'd arrived in order to pastor two small country churches in rural North Dakota, he'd watched a kaleidoscope of nature's colors morph and blend as May and June gave way to the hot peak of summer. Fields—wide ribbons of wheat, oats, beans and corn—unfurled before him like a living tapestry.

He'd had no idea what he was missing during those years in Chicago entrenched in academia and blind to the marvels of nature. Now, after only three months as a resident of Hilltop Township, he couldn't imagine leaving North Dakota again.

The colors changed daily—first, from the bright, vibrant greens of spring into the mature, deeper greens of summer. The rising sun grew molten yellow, ripening fields of oats and barley and kissing the wheat with gold, making way for the September harvest.

Getting comfortable, he stretched his long legs out in front of him. As Alex leaned back, he drew his hand across his coat, felt something in the breast pocket and pulled it out. It was a photo of him and his former fiancée, Natalie, standing beneath an ivy-covered arch on the college campus where he'd taught. Surrounded by twining vines and the picturesque campus lawn, he was beaming into the camera looking carefree and happy. Natalie, beautiful as always with her dark hair and soulful eyes, was staring at something beyond the camera. Little had he known that two weeks after the photo was taken the woman he loved would call off their wedding plans and inform him that she'd found someone else.

Her brief romance, he knew, had lasted only a few weeks, long enough, however, to destroy their relationship. Still, he'd never quite quit loving her. He'd once hung his future on their relationship—home, wife, family, all of it, on Natalie. Would he ever again find what he thought he'd had with Natalie, or was his destiny to be alone for the rest of his life?

More than anything, Alex wanted to be a family man, to have children, to love unreservedly. Without considering his actions, Alex dragged his open laptop toward him and pulled up his e-mail address book. There she was. He hadn't deleted it after the breakup. Impulsively, he hit her address and typed, "Hi, Nat. Hope all is well with you. I'm in North Dakota now and loving it. God found just the place for me. Alex."

He hit SEND before he could think about it and then sat staring at the screen, which proclaimed, "Your message has been sent."

What had he just done? he wondered. And would she respond? Probably not. Still, he'd had to try.

Alex felt a tug on his pant leg. Tripod pulled at the hem of his trousers with his teeth, urging him to get up and moving.

"Gandy has ruined you completely, hasn't she?" Alex said, forcing the photo and the impulsive e-mail out of his mind.

Gabriella Andrea Dunn, known locally as Gandy, the church secretary, kept a stash of dog biscuits in one of her file cabinets. Because of this, Alex and Tripod were getting to the office earlier and earlier so that the dog could enjoy his treat for the day. Pretty soon they'd be arriving before daylight if Tripod had anything to say about it.

Of course, it didn't hurt that Gandy usually brought doughnuts for the humans.

At Gandy's name, Tripod's rope-like tail began to bang furiously on the floorboards to emphasize his impatience. A present from Alex's friend Dixon Daniels, the dog was one of those gifts that kept on giving…and giving…and giving.

The dog looked at him with soft, intelligent eyes. Most days Tripod seemed half human. He was undoubtedly more civil than some people Alex had run across in his years in academia before becoming a pastor. "Okay, you win. Let's go. I have to take the van today." Tripod headed for Alex's vehicle and sat by the driver's side door until his master joined him.

As he drove the brief distance between the parsonage and the church, Alex relished the view before him. Hilltop Community Church, a traditional white country church like those depicted on rural winter scenes and Christmas cards, grew sweeter to him with each passing week.

It had been particularly satisfying to slowly but surely befriend his congregations. There were Hans and Hilda Aadland, a sweet couple who, even after decades of marriage, were very much in love. Curtis and Belle Welles were also in love, but often at odds. Belle, very much an urban woman, had never grown accustomed to rural ways.

He thought about Walter Englund, Mattie Olsen, Ole Swenson, owner of Twinkle Toes, the tremendous pink sow, and the reclusive and oddly reticent mother Flossie and her grown son Charles Kennedy. Nor could he forget charming, down-to-earth Matt and Martha Jacobson, whose daughter had left Hilltop for Hollywood and became the famous actress Amelia Jacobs. And that didn't include his parishioners at All Saints, his second and more reserved congregation, the one he was only now truly getting to know.

He parked in front of the church and took the concrete steps to the door two at a time.

"You look like something the cat dragged in." Gandy Dunn greeted him cheerfully when Alex walked into the church office. "Did those dirty honkers wake you again?"

"Dirty honkers is right! Will told me he read that fifty geese can produce more than two tons of droppings in a year." Experiencing this on his lawn and on the bottoms of his dress shoes had tempted him to cook a goose dinner of his own. Fortunately for the geese, he'd come to enjoy both their antics and the eggs they laid before he noticed the havoc they were wreaking on his tidy lawn.

"Will Packard has you wrapped around his little finger. Otherwise he never could have talked you into setting up that little animal shelter at your place. 'Course, that child needs someone to pay attention to him." Gandy tapped the tip of her pen against her front tooth. "How many little Packards are there now? I've lost count. Andy is the oldest, I think. Earl Junior is next. He's the poor little guy that got saddled with the name of that no-good daddy of his. Then it's Will, Katie, Daisy, who is four, the twins Liam and Ian, who must be close to three, and a two-year-old named Sebastian, if that doesn't beat all! I can't recall if Minnie is pregnant again this year or not. Those poor sweet babies. Keeping track of the Packard children is impossible. I'd rather herd chipmunks than that bunch!"

Then, tired of the Packards as a topic of conversation, she launched into a report on the quilting project she and Nancy Jenkins were spearheading between Hilltop Community Church and its sister church, All Saints Fellowship. The quilting project was a triumph of the highest order. When Alex had arrived at Hilltop Church, it and its sister congregation were barely on speaking terms.

"Nancy and I bought forty-five fat quarters for the church quilters," Gandy said. "What do you think about that?"

From Packards to quilts, Gandy was the queen of the non sequitur,

Alex had decided. Rather than fight it, he'd learned to just jump on her train of thought and let her take him for a ride.

"What is a fat quarter? Someone's chubby hips?"

She snorted loudly. "You do have an odd sense of humor, Pastor Alex. It's how you cut a yard of fabric. A regular quarter yard of fabric would measure nine inches by forty-four inches. When you cut a yard of fabric in quarters, you get a piece eighteen inches by twenty-two inches. It's fatter and more versatile—therefore, a fat quarter." She said this as if it made all the sense in the world to a man who'd never darkened the door of a fabric store in his life.

"And a fat eighth is…"

"Too much information, Gandy."

"Whatever. All I can say is that forty-five fat quarters means that we're going to be sewing together for a long while. Plus, we've decided to hand quilt it. We'll have regular quilting bees where ladies sit around the quilt, take stitches and chat. It will be the most Hilltop and All Saints have talked in years!"

One step at a time, he reminded himself. When he'd arrived, the churches had resembled quarrelsome siblings. Reconciliation didn't come quickly or easily when enmity ran as deep as it had between the two churches for so many years.

The rift between the churches had started after a house fire killed Alf Nyborg's young son. The squabble had begun when a naïve young intern Hilltop had brought in tried to comfort Alf and had, unintentionally, prodded the man in the sorest spot in his psyche.

"Alf was out of his mind for a while after that fire," Gandy commented, as if she'd read Alex's mind. "I can't blame him, really. But he shouldn't have gotten All Saints all riled up over that young fellow. They shouldn't have held Hilltop responsible either."

At Alf's behest, All Saints had stood behind its hurting congregant.

Alf's pain had turned to bitterness, which had led to hurt and division. This had never been sorted out until Alex arrived and began to slowly unwind the tangled snarl of wounded feelings. Reconciliation was on his mind a lot these days. The memory of the photo of Natalie he'd found this morning flickered on the edge of his consciousness and he willed it away. It brought up a longing in him he didn't know how to quench.

"Have I told you recently how much I appreciate what you and Nancy are doing by bringing the church ladies together to quilt?"

"A half-dozen times, at least. Don't thank me, thank God. He's the One in charge." She bobbed her head emphatically, her hair swaying along.

Gandy's tightly permed hair, an unwanted gift from her hairdresser sister-in-law Barbara Owens, had begun to grow out. It bounced when she spoke, a living thing atop her head. It reminded Alex of a particular bouquet of dried baby's breath in his sister's living room—parched, brittle and untamed. Sometimes her hair was home to half a dozen pens and pencils or, as now, a pair of glasses.

He tore his gaze away from her bird's nest of curls long enough to ask, "What's on my schedule today?"

"I've got a whole mitt full of people who've called to talk to you. I also made a list of home visits to make." Gandy's eyebrows came together in a scowl. "I put the ones that sounded the most churned up at the top of the list."

"How can you tell?" Alex studied the list written in Gandy's crabbed scrawl. "It's hard to tell sometimes what is going on with people here. They don't always show much emotion." It had been challenging sometimes to pastor people who so reluctantly revealed their feelings.

"That old adage 'still water runs deep' is just a little truer here, that's all. A good share of our population is Scandinavian, people who aren't normally given to showing their feelings. Just because someone doesn't talk much, it doesn't mean that there's nothing going on beneath the surface."

Gandy's own brother Jonas Owens had suffered a great deal over the possibility of losing the family farm, and yet it was almost too late before anyone realized how desperate Jonas had become. Though everything had worked for the best, Alex didn't take anything for granted anymore.

"Nancy Jenkins said she had something to discuss with you about the Hubbard house. She asked you to come over this morning for tea. Oh yes, she says those twins she's carrying feel like they weigh five pounds each already. That's a woman who's going to have her hands full. Why, when I had my daughter Debbie..."

Gandy, noticing the resigned expression on Alex's face, reeled herself in. "And Walter Englund called. He was looking for you but changed his mind and told me not to tell you he'd called."

"Then why are you telling me about it?"

"Because Walter is shy as a dormouse and he never asks anybody for anything. That means that if he called you—even if he changed his mind about talking to you—something's up. You'd better check it out."

Illogical as they often sounded, Alex had learned not to ignore Gandy's recommendations. He made a mental note to stop and see Walter when he went to Grassy Valley.

"Lauren left a message saying that Tillie Tanner's eightieth birthday is coming up and she thinks we should have a party at the church for her." Gandy frowned. "Trouble is, Tillie's been telling people it's her sixty-fifth birthday, not her eightieth. She just dyed her hair again. Ravishing Flame...or was it Lustrous Pomegranate? I can ask my sister-in-law Barbara. She's the hairdresser who did it. I don't know how Tillie managed it, but she talked my sister-in-law into doing it for free. Everybody knows Tillie doesn't have any money of course…."

Alex wondered when Gandy would finally pause to take a breath. The woman had such lung capacity that she could probably stay underwater for at least three minutes.

"…Anyway, Tillie isn't going to take to an eightieth birthday party, I'm afraid. She's in total denial about it. We really shouldn't lie about her age here at the church. It's not acceptable to lie anywhere, but here…well, it seems even worse, don't you think?"

Not knowing if he should agree or disagree with Gandy's rapid-fire report, Alex's head bounced like a bobblehead doll.

"At least Tillie is still sharp as a tack. Lila Mason was in yesterday afternoon to report another theft. This time it's her sewing machine that's missing."

Alex groaned a little. Lila's memory was failing and the only one who didn't realize it was Lila herself. "Why doesn't she report these things to the Grassy Valley Police Department instead of the church?"

"Because the police don't believe her anymore. Besides, there are only two of them and they can't be running out to Lila's every day. She reported that someone had stolen her car and they found it parked in her garage. Lila said it was the only place she hadn't looked because she didn't recall putting it in there. They found her 'missing' purse on the top shelf in her closet and her 'lost' cat sitting on the roof.

"I can't even tell you how many times she's been in here saying her glasses were stolen while they were riding around on the top of her head. Not that I can be too critical about that."

Then she noticed Alex's stricken expression. "Don't worry. I'll stop by her place on my way home and locate the sewing machine. It's probably carefully hidden in plain sight."

"Thank you, Gandy, you're a saint. I worry about Lila."

"Unfortunately, I think we're approaching a big problem with her. It's not only stuff Lila loses, but facts. She's a font of misinformation if I've ever met one. She's the one who spread it all over Hilltop that Lauren and Mike were expecting twins, you know, when it was really Ben and Nancy Jenkins."

He remembered. Lauren had nearly split wide open laughing when she'd heard the news. She'd said that at her age, past forty, it would be a one for the record books. Mike had taken it a bit more seriously, clutching his heart and falling backward into his recliner and demanding smelling salts and a piece of lemon meringue pie to console him.

Lila had also been the one to start the rumor that Trinka and Harris Hanson had donated a significant sum of money to the church. That rumor didn't go far since everyone knew that Harris was vehemently opposed to spending money on anything, even the gospel. Loath to waste anything, he made his wife reuse her tea bags until they were bled dry of color and flavor. He would no doubt be generous in his will, but until that time, the church coffers wouldn't grow because of him.

"Do you think Lila is a danger to herself?" Alex asked.

"You mean would she leave the stove on and go to bed or put a towel on a burner and walk out of the room? Probably. Thank the Lord it hasn't happened yet. I'm more worried about those health concoctions she brews up and drinks. Who knows what she puts in those. I hope you can't buy eye of newt anywhere around here."

The thought made him shudder. Lila, petite and birdlike, had welcomed him to Hilltop with open arms and enthusiasm usually reserved for rock stars. She occasionally brought him homemade cookies that Gandy warned him not to eat. He'd almost ignored her caveats until he noticed that even Tripod wouldn't touch them. It hurt his heart to see the dear little woman going downhill.

That was the problem with loving his parishioners, Alex had

quickly realized. Their pain became his pain. Their pain also became his prayers. He was grateful he could leave their concerns at the foot of the cross, where someone with far more wisdom than his could intercede.

"I'm open to suggestions about Lila," he said. "And call me if you can't find the sewing machine. I'll come over and help you look."

"Look for what?" Dixon Daniels had entered the church office without either Alex or Gandy hearing him. Startled, Gandy squeaked like a mouse.

Dixon, his tousled brown hair still appearing as though it had been cut with pruning shears, grinned and his white teeth flashed in his tanned face.

"Don't you come tiptoeing in on me like that!" she ordered. "You almost gave me a heart attack."

Unrepentant, Dixon poured himself a cup of coffee, opened the file drawer marked OLD SERMONS and helped himself to a cookie from one of the half-dozen packages Alex and Gandy kept stashed there along with their red licorice and chocolate. "You two are certainly intent on something."

He nodded as Alex summarized the Lila problem. "I'll keep an eye on her. I do anyway, but I'll drop by more often. She likes it when I stop in to say hello. I'll check the stove when I'm there. It can't hurt."

"Thanks, Dixon. You know, this is why I love it here. Hilltop really is a family. Everyone watches out for everyone else."

"A bunch of snoops and busybodies, if you ask me," Gandy said dourly. She pawed around in her hair for her glasses. "Now why don't the two of you go visit somebody while I type up the newsletter? Make yourselves useful."

Alex, wondering if this was what it was like to be married to a bossy woman, grabbed his coffee cup and hurried outside with Dixon close on his heels.

CHAPTER TWO

"**W**here are we going?" Dixon asked.

"On a pastoral visit to Nancy Jenkins."

"Maybe I shouldn't tag along then. She might want to talk to you in private, something just for your ears and God's."

"Gandy said she wanted to talk about their house. You probably know more about it than I do."

"We can ride in my pickup," Dixon offered. "If she doesn't want me around, I'll take a little crop tour and come back for you. She's brought up the subject of the house a lot lately. Since she found out she's having twins, she's decided that her grandparents' home might not be such a bad place to live after all—if they can just figure out how to afford it."

Not bad at all. The Hubbard house was one of the finest homes Alex had ever seen—from its expansive porches and multiple bedrooms to a vast ballroom on the third floor. It had, however, turned into a liability for the young couple who had inherited it. Heating the place in winter was, according to Nancy, like heating a barn. This spring the Jenkins had almost decided to tear the place down and build something smaller in its place. Alex hoped that wasn't what Nancy had called to tell him.

They drove north past Mike and Lauren Carlson's tree-lined

driveway and Mattie Olsen's tidy white house. The Olsen house was close enough to the road to see sheets drying on the line in the back yard.

"I hung my wash outside too," Alex said. "It's a sturdy setup. The line hangs between two metal poles sunk into the ground in concrete."

"Stoddard Bloch put that one up."

"It figures. That man would hang a picture with an iron stake. Overkill."

"Stoddard likes things well built."

When Alex had been interviewed for his position as pastor, Stoddard, a member of the call committee, had spoken in terms of hammering things out and welding things into place. Stoddard built things to last, like the clothesline.

"How'd you like air-dried laundry?" Dixon looked amused by Alex's efforts.

"The sheets were wonderful. They smelled like fresh air and sunshine. The towels were something else, stiff as plywood and scratchy as sandpaper."

"You're really getting into this lifestyle, aren't you?"

"I enjoy it. My mother never hung out clothes. Of course, we lived in an apartment building in Chicago. I suppose she could have draped them over the fire escape."

Alex rolled down his window and stuck out his head as they drove into Ben and Nancy's yard. The Hubbard house was more impressive every time he saw it. He'd grown to appreciate the finely done dentil crown molding near the eaves, the foundation made of prairie stone picked on the property, and old-fashioned wicker rockers that Nancy said had been with the house for over sixty years. There were uniquely shaped windows in every peak and horizontal stained-glass windows with a myriad of colorful designs topping each of the picture windows on the first floor. Alex and Dixon pulled into the U-shaped driveway that ran beneath the porte cochere. Even before they could exit their vehicles, Nancy Jenkins burst through the door to wave them in.

Nancy, into her fifth month of pregnancy, glowed with a striking inner light. Her dark hair was thick and lustrous, and her brown eyes bright and clear. All the tension Alex had seen in her in recent weeks seemed to have evaporated. What had happened in less than ten days' time to change her so?

Dixon reached Nancy first. "Tell me if you want to talk to Alex alone; I'll go for a drive," he said cheerily. "I just came because Gandy kicked us out of the church office."

"I'm delighted you're here, Dixon. I want to talk to you as well. Come inside."

She led them through the front door, past the formal sitting room and vast dining room filled with the heavy nineteenth- and early twentieth-century furniture her grandparents had owned and into the large, cozy kitchen. The glass-fronted cupboards were original, well maintained and painted bright white. A teakettle began to whistle. "Have a seat while I finish the tea."

She poured out the hot water with which she'd been warming the teapot and carefully placed a mesh tea infuser filled with loose tea leaves in the pot. Then she poured the barely boiling water into the vessel. "If you over-boil the water for tea it loses oxygen and tastes flat," she said conversationally. "And when the tea and the water meet, the leaves open and reveal their flavor." She smiled a little. "I've heard this referred to as 'the Agony of the Leaves.'"

"Ouch!" Dixon said, grimacing. "Do I want to drink anything that suffers that much?"

She ignored him and glanced at the clock. "It's important to time the infusion, usually three to five minutes."

Nancy ceremoniously removed the mesh infuser at the allotted time and covered the pot with a knitted tea cozy. A tray with a sugar dish full of sugar cubes, tongs and a small pitcher of milk were already on the table. Nancy uncovered the plates already on the table to reveal scones, fluffy cream, strawberry jam, a warm fruit compote and a bowl of pink, white, lavender and green Swedish mints. She straightened the vase of fresh-cut flowers at the center of the table.

Alex's mouth began to water.

"It's Devonshire, not clotted, cream, but it's a pleasant second. Cream cheese, sour cream, powdered sugar...you know."

No, Alex didn't know, but he'd get the recipe from her and show off when his sister Carol came for a visit. She'd accused him of being "uncivilized" in the kitchen—eating only things that could be purchased in cardboard. That would teach her a thing or two.

He reddened slightly, not sure if he should be asking for recipes in front of Dixon, who might never let him hear the end of it, but he forged on. "Nancy, my sister says I'm unsophisticated in the kitchen. When she comes, I'd like to show her how refined I've become. Maybe I could show off by making this for her...."

"I'll jot down the recipe," Nancy said amiably. "Everyone asks for it. In fact, I have an extra copy on the counter that I was going to give to Inga Sorenson. I'll make her another."

Before he knew it, Alex was holding the instructions in his hands.

NANCY'S DEVONSHIRE CREAM

- 3 oz. cream cheese
- 1 tablespoon sugar (white)
- 1 pinch salt
- 1 cup heavy cream (use store-bought whipped topping only if you are desperate and don't have cream on hand!)

Cream first three ingredients in bowl, then beat in cream until stiff peaks form. Chill. (For clotted cream, omit salt and cream cheese and add $1/3$ cup sour cream instead. Use confectioners' sugar rather than white granulated.)

To Alex's relief, Dixon didn't make a comment. Maybe he would start by trying it out on his friend. Dixon looked like he'd eat just about anything.

"Surely you didn't go to such trouble for a pastoral visit," Alex said.

"I love to do this sort of thing," Nancy said. "This is why I'm glad to see you, Dixon. As usual, I prepared too much food. My husband Ben complains about gaining weight. He told me to find someone else to feed." She frowned. "Can I help it that I love to cook?"

"Glad to be of service," Dixon said cheerfully. "Call me any time you have leftovers. My bachelor meals leave something to be desired."

"Good to know. Now help yourselves." Nancy fluttered around them like a perfect tearoom hostess.

After one bite into the scone, Alex closed his eyes blissfully. "Just like my mother used to make."

"The highest compliment." Nancy smiled broadly.

"Unless your mother was a cook like my aunt Alice," Dixon offered. "The woman could ruin Jell-O. Don't even get me started on the chicken she cooked. There should have been a law against it. After dinner at her house we played twenty questions to figure out what kind of meat she'd served. Sometimes we'd throw it back and forth like a Frisbee until the dog got it." He tucked into the scones.

"I'm curious to know what this visit is about, Nancy," Alex said. "The last time I saw you both, you and Ben were bemoaning the cost of insulating this house for winter. And now…"

Nancy flushed and looked a little embarrassed. "I finally did what you've been telling me to do all along, Pastor Alex. I got down on my knees and prayed. Funny, isn't it, how what should be so obvious—like prayer—is always a last resort when it should be the first. It finally sank in that the only way to know what to do with the house was to ask God to guide us. I'd been asking, of course, but, I have to admit, not really listening for an answer. About three days ago I woke up with my answer."

"God does speak through dreams sometimes. Joseph, for example…"

"I woke up from a dream in which I was serving tea just like I am today—only to a group of strangers." Nancy smiled at Alex and Dixon's confused expressions. "Not just any strangers—guests at my bed-and-breakfast. Hubbard House B&B. The idea has come up before, but never so clearly as this. I saw the entire thing in my dream." She clasped her hands together and put them to her lips, looking excited.

"You'd turn Hubbard House into a B&B?"

"If we had income from the house, it would be easier to justify fixing it up and living in it. We've already closed off the third-floor ballroom and the two draftiest bedrooms on the north side of the house. I can use my homemade quilts to warm the rooms. Yesterday I designed quilted window dressings. Cozy and pretty—and when you pull the quilted curtains closed, no draft would dare try to get in."

"Very clever," Alex said, catching her excitement.

"I've been sewing quilts for years. I have enough to put a theme quilt in every room and decorate around it. The breakfast part is no problem. I love to cook. Since there aren't many restaurants around here, I might offer dinner to my guests as well."

"Dinner too?" Dixon brightened, obviously thinking his bachelor meals could soon be over.

She looked at Alex. "What do you think? Are we too out of the way for a harebrained scheme like this? Would anybody come?"

Alex nodded. He had followed a harebrained impulse of his own this morning. Who knew what the results might be?

CHAPTER THREE

"What do you think about Nancy's B&B idea?" Dixon asked as they drove in Dixon's truck toward Grassy Valley.

"The house would make an ideal bed-and-breakfast, there's no doubt about that. But would they have any guests? That's what I'm concerned about. If there was a guest speaker for the church he or she could stay there, I suppose."

"Hilltop may look quiet to you," Dixon said, "but people come and go around here all the time. I think it would work. Whatever they earned would go toward the house for a few years, but at least it would be earning its own way. And Nancy would be able to work and still be home with her twins."

"A win-win situation?"

"Right. That would be good news for Nancy and Ben." Dixon drove without speaking for a mile or two. "Another one who could use a win-win is Walter Englund. He's a middle-aged bachelor accountant in a town of six hundred people. That poor guy must lead a dull life. I'm glad you're going to visit him."

"*You* are a bachelor living near the same town. Wouldn't your life be dull too?" Alex asked. Was this what his life would become? Dull and colorless? Alex quickly made up his mind that he wasn't going to let that happen to him.

"That's different. If I'm bored, I do something about it." He grinned impishly at Alex. "That's how I usually get myself in trouble. I like to stir things up. I'm never bored. Walter simply isn't the 'stirring-up' kind." Dixon pulled up in front of the Englund house, a small gray structure with white trim. "I'm going to run a few errands. I'll be back in an hour to pick you up. Call me on my cell if you need more time—or less."

Alex nodded, straightened his shoulders and headed for the porch. He said a quick prayer for insight and raised his hand to knock on the front door, which was painted a fanciful red. Had Walter been celebrating the end of tax season when he'd chosen such a festive color?

"Welcome, Reverend," Englund said when he opened the door. "This is a pleasant surprise. Please, come in."

The two-story house was so diminutive that there was only a kitchen, living space and sunroom-turned-office on the first floor and two tiny bedrooms and a bath on the second. The house smelled of lemon and antiseptic, as if the entire structure had just had a thorough scrubbing. It was painfully tidy and the hardwood floors were so highly polished that Alex felt as though he were walking on a piece of glass hovering over the pine floor. Even the magazines, *National Geographic* and *Reader's Digest,* were stacked in painstakingly neat piles. The only pictures on the walls were Walter's ancestors scowling down upon him.

Alex found the spartan décor intimidating, particularly after the hominess and cozy warmth of the parsonage. He was suddenly more appreciative of the work the women of the church had put into the house. The only room here with any personality was the sunroom where Walter had his office. That, at least, had a few books and papers lying about and a huge white cage that housed a pair of bright yellow canaries.

"Socrates and Plato," Walter said, pointing to the canaries. "At least I hope they are. It would be a great surprise to me if Plato turned out to be a Peggy or Patricia at this late date." He chuckled at his own joke.

Walter was as meticulously tidy and polished as the house. He wore gray trousers, a starched white shirt, a gray tie with faint yellow stripes, and shoes that gleamed with polish. His thinning hair, once a nondescript brown, was graying now, particularly at the temples. He had a slight tic at the corner of one eye that made Alex wonder if his arrival had made the man nervous. Walter's complexion was fair, almost pallid.

"I suppose Gandy told you I'd called even though I didn't leave a message."

"Gandy often puts two and two together and makes five. I hope you don't mind that I dropped by."

"Not at all. In fact, knowing Gandy, I rather expected it." Walter gestured Alex toward a chair with a straight back and a seat padded with a cushion with blue and white checks. "Coffee? Tea? Lemonade?"

Prim and proper, Walter obviously thought out every move before making it. It was probably a good characteristic for an accountant, Alex thought. He would see for himself at tax time next year.

Walter disappeared into the kitchen and returned with two tall glasses of lemonade on a tray. He put the tray down on a placemat and handed Alex his glass along with a coaster to put beneath. Again, the word *meticulous* came to Alex's mind.

"I hear the church quilting ladies are pioneering a long-awaited truce between Hilltop and All Saints," Walter commented.

"It's time to reconcile. Our churches should never have had enmity between them. If it hadn't been for the sad misunderstanding when the Nyborg boy died in that fire, they would have thrived together."

They dropped into an awkward silence.

"Do you know much about Tillie Tanner?" Walter asked.

"I don't know her as well as I'd like." He knew her to be fierce and passionate about her opinions, heavy-handed with makeup and with a penchant for brightly colored clothing. "I have a sense that Tillie is a proud woman, and lonely."

"You do know her then. She is very proud, too proud to ask for help even when she needs it." Walter looked directly into Alex's eyes. "Have you ever visited Tillie's home?"

"No. Gandy tells me that Tillie doesn't encourage company."

"She likes company well enough," Walter said, "but she's ashamed to have anyone see her place. She hasn't had money to fix anything for years and it's falling down around her head. Tillie is"—he struggled for the most delicate way to put it—"seriously strapped financially."

Alex quickly put two and two together. "And you'd like me to know because… ?"

"Tillie is a dear woman but unwilling to ask for or accept help. Did you know her eightieth birthday is coming up soon? Everyone knows that Tillie is eighty except Tillie, who won't admit to being more than sixty-five." Walter frowned. "I've been debating as to whether or not I should send her a card. I don't want her to feel forgotten, but I don't want to cause trouble either."

"I can see that might be a problem." Actually, it bordered on delusional, Alex thought, but who was he to judge? Tillie's spirit was still youthful. He'd heard it in the way she chuckled at his jokes from the pulpit and seen the joy she got from watching Tripod ride shotgun in his van. Tillie loved life.

They sat quiet for a long moment as the August sun streamed in on them. Alex tipped back the last of his lemonade and placed the glass on the tray. Walter didn't move.

Finally Alex broke the silence. "I also have a question for you,

Walter. Are you familiar with the Hilltop cemetery? The layout of the graves, I mean."

"I took care of the plat map for a few years back in the late seventies, if that's what you mean. Herman Chadwick did it for many years after that. He and his wife Myrtle were regular attendees of Hilltop at that time. When Herman passed away, his wife took over. She's done a fine job, I think. Myrtle doesn't get to church as often as she'd like because she usually works at Red's on Sunday morning cooking breakfast. She likes to make the extra money. That no-good son of hers doesn't bring in anything so she's sole support for their family now. Why do you ask?"

"I noticed an unmarked grave near the back of the cemetery. I wondered if a gravestone had been ordered."

"Near the back?" Walter frowned. "Odd. There aren't many families with plots back there. I wonder whose it could be."

"Don't worry about it. I'll find out," Alex assured him. "It's not as if whoever is there is going anywhere."

Walter smiled faintly. "Check with Mrs. Chadwick. She should be able to help you."

There was another awkward silence. Finally the question burst out that Alex had been holding back ever since Walter mentioned the Internet. "Are you lonely, Walter?"

Walter considered the question thoughtfully. "It depends on how you define lonely, I suppose. I have a good deal of interaction with people—especially between the first of the year and April 15. I have the church and several nice neighbors. God is with me, of course, and He fills much of the empty space within me."

Walter might have been describing him as well, Alex realized. Something was missing in both their lives—a special person to share it with. He'd come face-to-face with that again this morning when he'd found that photo in his jacket.

The sound of Dixon's horn outside the house prevented him from following this track of conversation any further. In a perverse way, he was relieved. He didn't relish thinking about the void in his life.

∾

Dixon grinned at him when he scrambled hurriedly into the pickup. "You look like you're running away from something."

"Not at all." Alex forced a smile. "It was a very pleasant visit."

But what Dixon had said was true. He *was* running, escaping from the vision of himself at sixty with a life as ordered and sterile as Walter's was now. No wonder the man had asked about dating Web sites. He was casting about for something—anything—to break up the monotony of his life.

"What else have you got planned today, Reverend?" Dixon slid his sunglasses onto the bridge of his nose. "Anywhere you want me to take you? Or would you rather I didn't come with?"

It was an odd regional habit, Alex thought. Everyone here said "Do you want to come with?" With whom? With what? Why didn't anyone say, "Do you want to come with *me*?" or "Do you want to go with *him*?" Everyone just assumed he would know how the question would end.

The even odder part was that Alex was already doing the same thing. Last time he'd gone to All Saints he'd asked Gandy if she wanted to "come with." He sighed. This place was catchy. He was living proof of that.

"I'd like to stop at Bessie and Brunie Bruun's house."

"Unannounced?"

"Yes. Is that okay?"

Dixon's friendly features wore a peculiar expression. "I suppose so…if you don't care what you might run into."

"What is that supposed to mean?"

"Nothing in particular. It's just that sometimes when Brunie doesn't have some warning and time to collect her sister, you might discover Bessie doing something odd."

"Like what?" Alex had never been told what, exactly, was wrong with Bessie other than that she'd had a severe nervous breakdown in her late twenties that had left her with a plethora of phobias and strange ideas.

"One day I stopped by and found her spray painting the windows of the house black. She thought someone was peeking in on them at night so she'd decided to fix the problem. Brunie wasn't home to stop her. That's when Bessie usually gets herself into trouble."

"Should she be left alone? It must have cost Brunie a lot of money to replace the glass in the windows."

"Not to mention the fact that Bessie had spray painted the frames and part of the house as well."

"What did Brunie do?"

Dixon shrugged nonchalantly. "She called me. Mark, Mike and I came over and cleaned it up for her. Bessie promised to never do that again but who knows what will happen if she sees movement in the trees or hears strange noises."

"Has Brunie ever thought of…" Alex's voice trailed off as he thought of the significance of what he was saying.

"An institution? Bessie was in one for a while but it broke Brunie's heart. Bessie isn't dangerous, just odd. Brunie always justifies her decision with James 1:27."

"'Religion that is pure and undefiled before God, the Father, is this: to care for orphans and widows in their distress….'"

"That's it. She says that caring for people like Bessie, giving without expecting anything in return, is her way of serving God. Brunie says that if Jesus could love lepers, tax collectors and all types of sinners, the least she can do is love her own sister."

Alex was humbled to think of what Brunie had done. "Maybe I should call first."

Dixon turned the wheel and the pickup swung around and headed east. "Nah, it will be fine. The ladies will be glad to see you— even if Bessie is pulling flowers out by their roots or watering weeds."

Alex stared at Dixon.

"Bessie is a real champion of weeds," Dixon said. "She says all God's creations need a chance. And you should see what she does with mice...."

CHAPTER FOUR

The driveway that led to the Bruuns' house was rutted and unkempt and the grass on either side of the road resembled a badly overgrown buzz cut. Still, the winding path was quite lovely because of the huge, overarching cottonwood trees that formed a canopy over the thoroughfare, shading them and inviting them into a wooded sanctuary.

At the center of the trees sat a small house dating back to the 1930s. The roof, overhung by old trees, was lichen encrusted. It reminded Alex of barnacles on a ship. The roofline had a wavy profile indicating that part of the foundation had caved in. Though it sagged precariously in places, the paint on the outside walls was white—thanks, no doubt, to Bessie's black paint and Dixon's subsequent repairs.

Cheerful flowers studded the front of the house, and there was, oddly, a garden full of weeds that choked out nearby tomato plants and sprawling cucumbers. Bessie's weed garden. The entire place had a hidden, closeted feel, as if the woods had already overtaken the house and were simply allowing the two women to live there until the house was absorbed by nature itself. It was a surreal place, and it wouldn't have surprised Alex a bit if a cat in a red-and-white–striped stovepipe hat or a rabbit wearing a vest and carrying a pocket watch had strolled out of the forest toward them.

A thin, wiry woman with gray hair pulled back into a tight bun sat in a rocking chair on the undulating front porch. She rocked in quick, choppy bursts, the floorboards creaking and moaning beneath her. Her shoulders were rigid, her neck straight and her scowl piercing.

Had he been alone, Alex might have jumped back into his car and driven away to wait for a more agreeable day.

"Hi, Bessie," Dixon greeted the formidable-looking older woman. "Enjoying this beautiful afternoon?" He sauntered up to the house without hesitation. Alex followed close on Dixon's heels.

"What's to enjoy?" Bessie responded with a scowl. "The mosquitoes are biting, a deer ate all my strawberries, and my bones tell me it's going to rain soon."

"Weeds, mosquitoes and deer all need nourishment," Dixon said with a smirk.

Bessie smirked back. Dixon obviously knew how to handle Bessie.

"Bessie, I'd like you to meet Hilltop's new pastor, Reverend Alex Armstrong."

They mounted the steps and Dixon plopped down into the rocker next to Bessie's. Alex reached out a hand, which Bessie didn't take.

"I heard about you." Her eyes narrowed with suspicion. "My sister told me. Are you going to be trying to convert me like half the people at Hilltop?"

"That's what we hired him for, Bessie. You'd just better get ready for some good preaching."

She glared grimly at Alex. "Well, show me your stuff."

Alex petitioned heaven for an answer to this one. "I'd like to get to know you better before I start preaching at you, Bessie. It's God that speaks to the heart, not me. I will pray for you, however."

"Well, hallelujah! A preacher who isn't in love with his own words. Refreshing, I'd say." She pointed at the porch rail. "Sit there."

Alex obeyed and gave thanks that acceptable words had come from his mouth.

"I haven't seen you in church all summer," Dixon observed. "Are you avoiding us?"

Bessie cackled. "I've been listening to Pastor Pillow these past few weeks and then I catch a sermon on the radio. I only tune in to the one station, of course." A sly expression slipped across her features as she whispered, "There are those voices on the other channels."

"Voices?" Alex echoed. Dixon, he noticed, nodded sagely, as if he was completely familiar with these verbal intruders.

"Surely you know about the voices!" Bessie sounded shocked that Alex could be so ill informed.

He was saved by Brunie walking out the front door and onto the porch at that moment. "Dixon! Pastor Alex! How good to see both of you. I just finished making sweet iced tea. Let me get you some."

Alex ignored Dixon's amused expression, grateful for the diversion.

Brunie returned with the tea and a package of chocolate cookies with cream filling and set them on a small, rickety table. "These cookies are store-bought but they are Bessie's favorites. She enjoys eating the filling out of the middle before she finishes the outside. She likes to take her time so it gives her something extra to do."

Brunie sat down in another rocker and sighed. "Now, if I were ambitious, I'd bake my sister homemade cookies. Occasionally Lydia Olson brings some over. There's a woman who can cook. Too bad it's all wasted on those two spoiled brothers of hers."

"What do you mean?" Dixon asked before taking a deep swallow of tea. "Seems to me those boys eat plenty of Lydia's good cooking. No waste there."

"That's exactly what I mean. They eat like hogs at a trough but do they appreciate the cook? I doubt it. They take that sweet little woman for granted, that's what they do. She works like a slave for them. Do you know what those two spoiled men gave Lydia for Christmas last year? A vacuum cleaner and a rag mop! That woman deserves jewels for putting up with them!"

Brunie crossed her arms over her chest and looked thoroughly disgusted. "No wonder neither of those boys ever married. The only one who'd tolerate them is their sister."

"I'd marry one of them." The voice was small, not grating and harsh as it had been when Bessie had spoken before. She had her eyes closed and was rocking smoothly now.

Alex bit his lip and waited, wondering what would happen next.

Gently, Brunie said, "Oh honey, you're too good for them. You need a man who'd treat you like a princess."

A soft smile slid over Bessie's features. "Yes, like a princess."

Then Brunie got out of her chair and came toward Bessie. She leaned over and dropped a kiss on her sister's forehead. "But for now I want you to stay here with me. I can treat you like a princess too."

Bessie nodded, her eyes still closed. "Dixon treats me like a princess. Don't you, Dixon?"

"All that I can, sweet Bessie."

Alex realized that this was a conversation that had taken place before, perhaps many times.

Then Bessie's eyelids snapped open and she stared at Alex with piercing blue eyes. "You can treat me like a princess too, you know."

"I'd be honored, Bessie."

"Thank you." She held out her hand to him, palm down, as if she expected him to kiss it.

Feeling discomfited but compelled by something bigger than himself, Alex stood up, took the withered hand in his own, and placed a gentle kiss on it. Instead of feeling awkward, a swell of affection burst through him. *Love one another as I have loved you.* Love unreservedly; love without judgment; love the unlovable. His only job was to love these people wholeheartedly and absolutely. God would guide him through the rest.

Satisfied, Bessie waved Alex back to his perch.

"Lila Mason called," Brunie said, looking troubled. "She said someone has stolen her lawn mower."

"Again?" Alex blurted.

"That would be me," Dixon said. "I took it to town to get it fixed. Lila knew I'd taken it but I'm sure she forgot."

"Poor thing, I…"

Before Brunie could continue, Bessie's eyes popped open. They were a piercing blue-gray and fixed on Alex. "Do you have a girlfriend?"

"I…ah…no…not exactly…"

"If you don't know, who would?" Bessie stared at him intently.

Feeling skewered like a bug on a pin, Alex stammered, "I used to have one, but we're no longer together." Reminders of Natalie were popping up as regular as gophers in his yard these days.

"What did you do to her?"

"Nothing. She found someone else."

"That was dumb of her." Bessie rocked a little harder in her chair.

Alex couldn't have agreed more.

Brunie followed them to their vehicle when they left. "Thanks so much for coming. It meant the world to Bessie. She's pretty blunt but her heart is good. I only wish others could see in her what I see."

Alex put his hand on Brunie's. "After today, I'll always see a princess."

"How did you think that went?" Dixon asked as they pulled out of the Bruuns' driveway. "Bessie likes you. She usually doesn't warm up to strangers so quickly. Plus, she *never* tells anyone to sit down on the porch rail on their first visit. She usually leaves them standing. And she didn't mention the voices to me until I'd known her almost a year. And she let you kiss her hand. Impressive. I'd say you were a hit."

"And she gave me the third degree about my love life—or lack of it. I didn't dream the extent of her... you should have warned me..."

"She's been to doctors and tried medication but none of it has worked very well. Most of it just made her groggy and miserable. None of us in Hilltop wanted to see her unhappy so we were all relieved when Brunie quit trying to find a cure and just let Bessie be herself."

Dixon's smile was fond. "Bessie is the most honest, forthright person I know. She can be pretty sweet if she takes a notion. Granted, everyone would be happy for her if her problems were solved, but we all love her just the same. We accept her just as she is."

"It's to Hilltop's credit that she's so well accepted," Alex murmured.

"Bessie is safe here." Dixon glanced at Alex. "Do you mind if I stop at my place to let Willy and Wonka out? Later, we'll go for a run. Those dogs were restless as Mexican jumping beans last night. They kept me awake until one A.M. I want to wear them out so they'll sleep tonight."

"You need children to take care of, Dixon. You'd be a great father," Alex commented as he exited the truck.

"I know. Have you got any I could borrow?"

"Touché. One bachelor doesn't have any business telling another what to do, but that's never stopped me from trying." He didn't think that he or Dixon was truly cut out for bachelorhood, but he let the thought ride.

Alex followed Dixon in to his one-story rambler. The furnishings were masculine—lots of leather and deep colors. The place was pleasing and homey. The artwork on the walls, Western mostly, was quite good. As Dixon worked with the dogs, Alex stared at the paintings. One piece was not a painting but a black-and-white photo of Dixon and a beautiful young woman who looked a good deal like him.

She had high, angular cheekbones, and her face was more slender than Dixon's, but they had the same broad, even smile and relaxed demeanor. The woman was the female version of Dixon himself.

"My twin sister, Emmy." Dixon walked up behind him.

"She's beautiful. Lots prettier than you."

"I've heard that one before." Dixon picked up an album full of pictures and handed it to Alex. They were photos of him and his twin over the years. Emmy's personality sparkled off the page in every photo.

While Dixon let the dogs out, Alex studied the album. When they finally returned to the church, Dixon dropped him off at the front door. "Have a good one, Rev," he said with a grin and a wave before driving off.

Alex was deep in thought as he entered the church. Finding Gandy peering at him upside down from the top of the office door nearly sent him sprawling.

"What are you doing?" Then he realized that she was not upside down after all, just hanging over the edge of the ladder and peering around the corner of the door.

"This smoke alarm has been at me all day. *Beep, beep, beep*...then it's quiet until I forget about it, then... *BEEP*! Nearly startles me out of my chair every time. Then it quits again. My nerves are jangling and I can't think straight. Pretty soon I'm just sitting at my desk waiting for the dumb thing to beep again...and will it? Oh no, not until I'm settled down and have forgotten about it. Then..."

Alex stopped her before she went into another series of ear-piercing sounds.

"Come down from there before you fall off the ladder and land on your head. I need your brain clear and undamaged to keep my life and the churches in order."

Gandy gave a small harrumph but complied. "At least you

appreciate my value. Some people, my husband included, think I'm a flibbertigibbet. I can't imagine where they get *that* idea."

It wasn't a far leap, Alex mused, but he knew better than to tell Gandy that.

Alex changed the battery himself. As he climbed up the ladder, he realized that Gandy sometimes affected him the way the smoke alarm had affected Gandy. He'd settle down to work and be deep into sermon notes when Gandy would start to talk. Just when he thought she was done, she'd start up again. Sometimes it would be like that the entire day. He wondered if there was any way to change the batteries in Gandy.

"By the way, we've had some weird phone calls today." Gandy dusted herself off and ran her fingers through her hair. "A woman. She wouldn't leave a message."

"How often did she call?"

"Once an hour. Maybe if you stick around the church she'll call again. She was obviously expecting someone else to answer—like you. It's very mysterious if you ask me."

*A*lex wasn't in the mood for any more eccentricity and fled for home soon after Gandy left the church. He was ready to sit on the porch with a glass of lemonade, put his feet up and ponder the sermon ideas that had come to him today. Several themes kept cropping up—those of servanthood, reconciliation, and a third that really prodded at him today. "It is not good that the man should be alone" (Genesis 2:18). But at least for now he wasn't ready to speak of that.

He sat back, closed his eyes and thought of his favorite stained-glass window at Hilltop Church, that of Jesus washing His disciples' feet. In that simple act, Jesus had demonstrated the depth of His love, His humility and His willingness to serve. The gospel, it said, is something to be lived, not just pondered from an ivory tower. It demands action as well as contemplation. There were people like Tillie Tanner, Bessie Bruun and Lila Mason desperate for that kind of love.

His stomach growled ferociously. Unfortunately, the meals that the church and community ladies had delivered during the first months he had been at Hilltop were long gone. New items arrived infrequently, except for those of Lolly Roscoe. Lolly's persistent campaign to find her way to his heart through his stomach caused him no end of embarrassment and indigestion. This was particularly so since he knew that there was no connection between his heart and stomach where Lolly was concerned. He could never reciprocate with what she expected—romance. She was an attractive woman and would make someone a good wife. Someone, Alex mused, but not him. It was ironic, considering that he couldn't get Natalie out of his mind today. He hoped another single man would move to Hilltop and divert her attention from him, and the sooner the better.

Then he glanced out the window to see Will Packard's battered, hand-me-down bike parked by the shed. Will spent much of his time out there cuddling and playing with the critters he dragged home. Sometimes Alex questioned whether or not he should have given Will permission to house his personal humane society in the parsonage shed. Then he thought about belligerent, bad-tempered Bucky Chadwick, who tormented everything he came across, and knew he'd done the right thing. It was not only the creatures' sanctuary but Will's as well. Bucky wouldn't dare to track Will down here. A second, smaller bike painted a fading pink was there as well. It belonged to Katie Packard, Will's little sister.

Alex left the parsonage and walked across the yard to the shed where Will had posted a succinct hand-lettered sign on the wall by the door.

Hoomain Society
ADOPT OR GET OUT

In the dim coolness of the earthen-floored building, Alex found Will and his sister Katie each holding one of the geese that had so rudely awakened him that morning. The geese, which usually ran amok in the yard, were sitting contentedly in the children's laps. One was eating out of Will's hand. The other was simply resting on the little girl's outstretched legs, enjoying her soft words and gentle petting.

Perhaps all the Packard children were animal whisperers. It wouldn't have surprised Alex to find a deer dozing outside Will's hoomain society or a wild turkey roosting next to a domestic chicken. Even now, Rose, Will's pet skunk, was sleeping in her cage, and a stray barn cat atop the enclosure was soaking up light from a small window.

The wolf shall live with the lamb, the leopard shall lie down with the kid, the calf and the lion and the fatling together, and a little child shall lead them.

But until that day came, Tripod knew enough to stay outside the little hoomain society building. He'd dropped onto the grass by the south wall and lazed happily in the sun.

Alex didn't realize he'd said the Scripture aloud until Will added, "And these geese will eat with the foxes, not be eaten *by* them." He looked up, the cowlick at the crown of his head reminding Alex of a rooster's comb. "Geese can lay a hundred and sixty eggs a year, did you know that?"

"I had no idea."

"And they are ma-nog-a-mouse too, whatever that means. I saw it in a book Randy checked out of the library in Grassy Valley."

"Ma-nog-a-mouse?" The light came on. "You mean *monogamous.* That means having only one partner, one spouse—like your mom and dad."

"Oh, I get that. It means mate for life, right?"

"Correct."

"It's kinda nice, isn't it? Knowing your mom and dad will be together forever?" Will's expression grew serious. "Then even if your mom and dad fight, you'd know they aren't going to leave you." He patted the goose fondly. "That's something really good about geese."

Alex filed away Will's comment as he sat down on a small stool. "Everything is so calm." He couldn't always say that when the Packards were around.

"Animals don't like a lot of humans fussing around," Will said sagely. "It scares 'em. They need to know we'll take care of them before they can relax."

"Even people can be like that."

Will nodded. "But people have meaner ideas than critters. You can trust a critter to act like a critter, but you can't trust a person to always act human."

Profound, Alex mused, and right on the money.

"Trouble is, I think every animal in Hilltop Township has been scared out of its wits by Bucky at one time or another." Will's freckled features crumpled into a mask of concern. "I've got my work cut out for me.

"I heard from Bucky's mother, Myrtle, that they have a barn cat about to have kittens. She's gonna try to get it off the farm for me. I think I can keep it in the barn at my place. My dad doesn't usually count the cats and I don't think he'll notice." Will stopped feeding the goose and began to pet its feathers. Amazingly, the creature tucked its beak under its wing and went to sleep.

"My dad's another one of those people you can't always trust," he said softly.

Katie looked at her brother but didn't comment. Instead, she put a very dirty thumb in her mouth.

"Are your parents home today?"

"Our ma is. She's always home. Dad had to work. He should be home tonight. Ma's going to make a special supper...and pie."

Katie stuck her arm in front of Will's nose so he could see the cheap, too-big pink plastic wristwatch she was wearing.

Will bounded to his feet. "In fact, we'd better get going now. Around our house, if you don't get there on time for meals you might not get any."

Alex made his way back to the house, his stomach growling louder than ever. He was pleasantly surprised to see a blue and white plastic cooler sitting on the porch step. He hadn't heard anyone drive into the yard, but he and Will had been involved in serious conversation. He studied it hopefully. Maybe he wouldn't have to cook supper tonight after all.

He opened the container and felt the cool air waft upward. Inside, perched on ice packs, was a small bowl of potato salad, plastic-wrapped slices of ham and two homemade buns. In a separate bag was a slice of watermelon. His stomach gave a happy lurch at the sight.

Alex carried the precious parcel inside. As he was unloading the food he noticed a white envelope taped to the side of the cooler with Lydia Olson's handwriting. She'd brought him food often enough that he was beginning to salivate at the sight of her script like one of Pavlov's dogs.

He set the table for one, made the sandwiches and said grace. Too hungry to read Lydia's letter first, he set it aside until all that was left was the watermelon.

Full and satisfied, he reached for the envelope.

Lydia's handwriting, he noticed, was less precise than usual, scrawled as if she'd written it in a hurry.

Pastor Armstrong, were you serious about wanting some cooking lessons from me? If so, let me know. I'm free tomorrow—and every day after, for that matter. I will bring everything I need to your house. What shall we do first? Pulled pork sandwiches? Chocolate cake? My secret butterscotch chip cookie recipe? A pot roast? Or should I choose?

Hoping to hear from you—soon!
Lydia Olson

Odd, Alex thought as he ate the watermelon. Though the subject matter was hardly worth fretting over, the note radiated anxiety. Whether it was the nervous lurch in her penmanship or that *Soon!* commanding him to respond, he didn't know. Something had upset Lydia badly. He'd call her in the morning.

Restless in the silence of the house, Alex picked up the telephone. The number of times he'd thought of Natalie unnerved him. He hoped it was someone who would distract him. He wanted to be distracted from his thoughts. After three rings he heard his sister come on the line.

"Alex?" Carol's voice was a welcome sound.

"I really dislike caller ID, Sis. I can't even surprise you with a phone call."

"Get into the modern world, Alex."

"I prefer to live in Hilltop Township where people might have caller ID but they never admit it."

"What do they do? Cling to the past?"

"Not all the time. Though Winchester Holmquist cleaned up the old cream separator so he could show me how his grandmother separated the cream from the milk. And his wife Mildred showed me how to churn butter."

"You're a real Renaissance man now, Alex. Will you be demonstrating that at my house when you come for a visit?"

"Ha ha. People buy their butter at the grocery store these days, but they do know how to do things the old way out here. When everything goes off grid and we don't have electricity anymore, I'll be glad I'm living where I am."

Carol burst out laughing. "I'm delighted to hear you're enthusiastic. Every time I hear your voice, you sound happier. That place is good for you. I love it. Now tell me what's new," Carol ordered. She always loved to hear his account of what was going on at Hilltop.

"We've got a little problem to solve. One of our parishioners—her name is Tillie Tanner—doesn't have any family. She's turning eighty soon. We want to have a celebration for her but she won't admit being any older than sixty-five. I'm afraid she'll be insulted if we hang up 'Happy Eightieth' banners." This was just what he needed to take his mind off himself, to focus on something other than the uncomfortable wistfulness he'd been experiencing.

"Then don't. Just give her the party."

"But eighty is quite a milestone..."

"Not if you don't want to be eighty. Give the woman a break. Let her have her fantasy."

"Perhaps you're right."

"Of course I am. I'm your sister. It would be a way around the awkwardness and you could still have a good time. Besides, it's nice to be right about something for a change. In my son's eyes I'm totally clueless."

"How *is* Jared?"

"Maybe I shouldn't have let him take time off in late April to accompany you to North Dakota. He's been surly ever since. Maybe it's his full schedule of summer school classes. He's a completely changed kid and I don't understand what's gotten into him."

Alex got up and started pacing.

"He's a bright boy, but you know how he struggles with his classes."

"Is he around? Can I talk to him?"

"No, he's off dismantling a piece of machinery somewhere. I'll tell him to phone you."

Alex had a hunch he'd never receive that call from his nephew.

CHAPTER SIX

*A*lex was up before the geese the next morning.

He'd been restless all night, stalked by dreams of Jared, Tillie Tanner and the Packard children. Meandering in and out of these dreams was Walter Englund writing personal ads on an enormous chalkboard on Main Street in Grassy Valley, Bessie Bruun watering weeds, and Lydia Olson throwing cherry pies at her brothers Clarence and Jacob. No wonder he was up before dawn.

He made coffee in his beautiful but mostly unused kitchen, picked up the Bible from the desk in his study and spread it out with his journal at the round oak table.

He'd been reading James. There was so much wisdom packed into those five short chapters that Alex made it a policy to reread it several times a year. Something new spoke to him every time. That was part of what he loved so much about the Bible. It was new, fresh and relevant every single day. What other book could manage that other than the living Word of God?

Whenever you face trials of any kind, consider it nothing but joy, because you know that the testing of your faith produces endurance; and let endurance have its full effect, so that you may be mature and complete, lacking in nothing (James 1:2–4).

These verses had been a challenge for him in the past. He wasn't any fonder of trial or tribulations than the next guy, but he knew that when his faith was tested it always grew deeper and stronger.

He hadn't really known the strength of his own character or capacity for forgiveness until Natalie had abandoned their wedding plans and called it quits with their relationship.

If it hadn't been for God's supportive hand and the knowledge that He could turn anything—even the worst possible situation—into something for His glory, Alex might have crumbled. But he hadn't. Instead he'd grown, as James said, "mature and complete, lacking in nothing." And then God had sent him here in a gesture of, Alex had begun to realize, surprising grace.

Until recently, Natalie had rarely entered his mind. He'd been too busy to dwell on the past. She had fallen further and further back in the rearview mirror as he careened full tilt into this new life—until recently, that is.

It was nearly eight A.M. by the time he'd finished James, dug deeply into 1 Peter and written in his journal. He laid down his pen and stared out the window. Was it too early to pay a visit to Minnie Packard and her brood? He didn't see how anyone could sleep past dawn with the yard full of chickens the Packards kept. But first he would stop by the church.

When he arrived, there was a detailed note taped to his coffee mug and placed front and center on his desk so he couldn't miss it. Gandy didn't believe in subtlety.

Reverend Alex—
There's more ants in the kitchen. You'd better sic Mattie
Olsen on them when she stops by to weed the flower beds.
She's got all the church's ant poison in her basement.

Hilda Aadland wants prayer for her husband Han's big
toe. His gout is acting up again. And she said if you stopped
by the house to pray she'd give you some cloudberry jam her
cousin sent her from Minneapolis.

I'm worried about Lila. I stopped by her house to look for
her sewing machine and found it on the kitchen table covered
with a bathrobe. Then she told me that Mark Nash had
broken his leg. That's not true, although he said he did take
a tumble at the café when one of the legs on the chair he was
sitting on snapped. She's getting worse, Reverend. If you can
think of anything that might help, you'd better think fast.

Yours truly,
Gandy

With a sigh, Alex stuffed the note into his shirt pocket and headed
for the Packard residence.

Driving into the Packards' yard reminded Alex of driving into a
salvage yard. There were shells of old Chevys and Fords, a rusted-out
1960s Dodge pickup truck and a variety of old scooters, motorbikes
and tailpipes. Though the center of the yard was neatly mowed—
thanks to Randy and his mother, according to Will—grass grew high
around the carcasses of abandoned vehicles.

A flock of white leghorns squawked and ran as Alex pulled up to
the door of the house. Only one cocky rooster remained behind to
scratch in the dirt of what had once been the Packards' yard.

The whole place was a study in contrasts. Rusty, abandoned
tools and shovels sat next to tidy flower beds. Pristine white sheets
hung on a clothesline that threatened to cave in on itself. Alex knew
immediately what Minnie was responsible for—and what was being
neglected by her husband.

Alex winced at the sight of a rickety ladder angled against a large tree. The ladder led to an equally decrepit platform for a tree house that the children were obviously building without adult supervision. He reminded himself to post the number for the clinic in Grassy Valley near his desk and to pray that Doc Ambrose would decide not to retire and leave the town without medical help.

Two tiny children, twins, still in their pajamas, stood on the outside stoop sucking their thumbs. Mattie Olsen had taught Alex that rather old-fashioned word for porch, and stoop seemed a more apt description of the rickety platform attached to the Packard house than "porch." Porch held the promise of reliably holding a person's weight.

Suddenly the screen door flew open and slammed against the outside wall of the house. Will, follow by his sister Katie, darted outside. Nearly toppling his younger siblings, Will flew down the steps, ran toward Alex and flung his arms around his waist.

"You came to visit us!" Will squealed.

Katie clapped her hands. Even the two little ones took their thumbs out of their mouths and stared at him.

Was a visitor such a rare occasion? Alex wondered. The thought saddened him.

"I never thought you'd come to see us!" Will chattered excitedly. "But you did. Pa said you didn't care about our family, but I knew you did. Wait till he finds out. He'll split a gut!"

Alex certainly hoped not. That would be a messy and improbable reaction, even though he thought it would be good for Earl Packard to be proven wrong. Alex cared very much.

Alex pried Will from his waist and noticed that the other children were drawing closer. All redheads, they seemed to be cut out of the same cloth as their brother Will. They'd obviously dressed themselves, judging by the mismatched colors and fabrics. One of the smaller children had his shirt on backward; another wasn't fully dressed, still in his underpants.

"Is your mom home?"

"She's baking buns. She makes the best ever. 'Light as a feather,' Pa says." Will took him by the hand and led him into the house.

The kitchen hadn't aged well, Alex noted, but was neat as a pin. There was a hearty coat of wax on the floor, bright curtains on the windows and a divine aroma coming from the oven. The nicked and marred kitchen table, a massive wooden rectangle, appeared to have been used as a chopping block over the years. A quart jar filled with fresh flowers sat in its center. Shabby but immaculate summed up Minnie Packard's domain.

Minnie's eyes brightened and she wiped her flour-covered hands on her apron. "Reverend Alex! To what do we owe this honor?" Will's bright, intelligent eyes and charming freckles obviously came from her. She was small and slender. To look at her, one would never have known that she'd given birth so many times. Except for the weariness etched into her expression, she might have been a very young woman.

"I wanted to see how you were doing. I'm using my pastoral visits to get to know the residents of Hilltop."

"You're just in time for the first batch of buns to come out of the oven. Before we talk, let me get you set up." She pointed at the chair at the head of the table. "Sit here." With swift efficiency, she brought a plate and mug from the cupboard. She put a small crock of butter, a jar of homemade strawberry jam and a knife on the table. Almost before Alex knew it, he had three warm buns and a steaming mug of coffee in front of him.

By now several of the children had gathered in the kitchen. They were standing in a row, tallest to shortest, and staring at Alex as if he'd just landed from the moon. Mrs. Packard piled more buns on a plate and handed it to Will. "You kids go outside and eat these. Reverend Alex and I are going to have a visit without an audience."

"But, Ma!" Will looked horrified. Alex was his property, Will's look said. After all, he'd found him first.

"Twenty minutes. Then you can come inside, Will. The adults need a few minutes."

One by one they trickled out of the room looking disappointed. Before they were all out, they were already wrangling over who might get more than their share of the fresh buns.

Minnie poured herself a mug of coffee and sat down across from Alex. "They're a little wild, but they are good kids at heart. I just don't have the stamina to keep up with them, that's all."

"No one would," Alex responded honestly.

"You do a good job with Will." Minnie smiled sweetly. "He's a different boy since you came. He loves having his animal rescue shelter at your place." A shadow crossed the woman's features. "I wouldn't mind him having it here, but his daddy..."

She brightened again. "I was just like Will when I was a girl, dragging home rabbits, chipmunks, and even a turkey once that had an injured leg. Of all the children, I think he's the most like me." She touched her red hair. "Of course most of them look like me."

She was a lovely woman, Alex noted, fine-featured and with a persistently cheerful expression. If life hadn't worn her down, she'd still be a good deal like her son, bright-eyed, feisty and determined.

"Do you come from around here, Minnie? Is this where you grew up?"

"Oh no. I came out here from the East Coast to go to school in Minnesota, met Earl and never left. I've always regretted not getting my degree, but you know how young girls are when they think they're in love."

Think they're in love? How did one start a conversation like this, Alex wondered, other than to jump in with both feet. "How are you doing, Minnie? I mean is everything...well...okay?"

"I'm fine. I just keep putting one foot in front of the other. God is good. He gives me superhuman strength sometimes, I think. It's my husband that isn't...what he should be." Her lips turned down at the corners and sadness crept into her face.

"Would you like to talk about it?"

Minnie sighed the sigh of a long-suffering woman. "I don't know that it will do any good, but it might help you, Reverend, to understand him. Earl isn't all bad—or he wasn't, not when I married him. Life's been a disappointment for him. He had big plans back then. He was going to take over the family farm and turn it into something special. He wanted to raise cattle and horses as well as grain. We were newlyweds and had just moved into this house when it happened."

Alex leaned forward, curious.

"When we moved in, Earl's parents still lived here. They were looking forward to retirement and planning to move into Grassy Valley into a home they'd purchased." Minnie nervously folded and unfolded the napkin she was holding. "Then Earl's mother Grace, who was as excited about the move as a kid with a new bike, fell down the stairs right here in the house. The doctors said it was a stroke that made her fall and that there wasn't anything we could have done, but we all felt awful about it."

"How tragic."

Minnie nodded absently. "That was only the beginning. My in-laws didn't have health insurance and were two years shy of Medicare. The bills for Grace's care mounted up fast. They could have managed that, but Earl's father Selmer was diagnosed with cancer within months of Grace's stroke. We cared for them here as long as we could, but Selmer ended up having to sell some of his land to pay the bills. By the time they both died, there wasn't much left of the farm except what you see here. Earl had to give up his idea of raising animals and farming. There was just enough money left to buy a used semi and start trucking. The disappointment changed him. The man I married became a stranger."

Minnie got up and poured Alex another cup of coffee before she continued her story.

"I still loved him, of course, but the kids had started coming and we could never get ahead." Minnie looked at Alex, her large eyes pools of pain. "Earl never cared much about the farm after that. Things just slid into disrepair because he was gone so much. I tried my best, but I was pregnant half the time and crazy busy the rest."

"I am so sorry."

"Me too, Reverend. I'd love to have my husband back." A faint smile flashed across her features. "First thing I'd have him do is paint this house and clean up the yard. Next thing I'd tell him is to quit being so cranky with the children. They can't help it that things didn't work out the way he'd hoped. It's his unhappiness that makes him the way he is, not their noise."

She looked at him, her eyes shining. "That's why I'm so glad Will's taken a liking to you. He needs a male role model that's not yelling at him all the time."

"Would it help if I talked to your husband? I'm willing to try."

"The only thing that's going to help Earl is if God gets him by the scruff of his neck and shakes him good. You can talk to him if you want to, if he'll listen, that is. And you can certainly pray for him. There are a lot of years of hurt and disappointment to be mended."

"Does...does your husband ever"—the words nearly stuck in Alex's throat—"hit you or the children?"

"No." She smiled faintly, as if the question was too ridiculous to consider. "He loses his temper and hollers like a grizzly bear and flaps his arms like he's going to whack someone, but he doesn't do it. Earl was raised right. It's his frustration talking, not the real man. I want my kids to know the man I knew, the one I fell in love with, not the disappointed, disillusioned one he's become."

"I will pray about it," Alex said. It might not seem like much to some in the face of all the Packards' problems, but prayer is the most powerful tool on earth.

"I'd appreciate it, Reverend Alex. We need all the help we can get."

It was time, Alex sensed, to change the subject. "By the way, Minnie, I'd like to invite your children to Sunday school this fall. I understand they haven't attended before."

"Their daddy never wanted them to go, so we usually stayed home. But since you came by personally to *invite* them…" She smiled conspiratorially. "I just don't know how he could say no to that."

"Work on him, will you?" Alex felt a swell of fondness in his chest for this amiable woman. "Would the kids be interested?"

"Do dogs have fleas? Of course they would." Her smooth brow furrowed slightly. "I'd consider it carefully if I were you. I'd understand if you thought about it and 'uninvited' them. They wouldn't harm a teacher intentionally, but they could certainly wear a few out." She looked at him with a twinkle in her eye. "Just so you know."

"I'll take that into consideration."

The children began drifting back into the house. Katie, suddenly bold, walked up to Alex, crawled into his lap and leaned against his chest. She smelled like warm sunshine and fresh bread. Alex felt his heart lurch, and a longing he'd suppressed ever since he and Natalie had parted resurfaced with a fury. He wanted to be a father.

After he left the Packards', Alex drove back to the church slowly, his mind and emotions swirling tornados within him. He'd suppressed the notion of fatherhood the day Natalie had left, but it was reemerging.

Why now? What was the point? He was forty-two years old and hadn't had a date in months.

"Lord," he prayed aloud, "this is one of those things I have to put in Your lap. If I'm not to have a wife and family, then make me content with that. And if You have some plans for me in that department that I haven't even imagined, then reveal to me what they are—in Your time, not mine. Though I am in a bit of a hurry... Amen."

Maybe he would give Natalie a call one of these days. Just to talk, of course.

Gandy was at the church when he arrived. She had the door open to the storage closet and was staring into its interior with a scowl on her face.

"What's the trouble?"

"I'm missing a box of birthday presents and I think they're in here somewhere, only somebody went and piled all this junk on top of them. Who do they think I am, Goliath? I can't lift this stuff out of here!"

"Did you say 'birthday presents'?"

"It's my daughter Debbie's birthday and I need to find those presents. I've been buying and hiding them here all year."

"What's wrong with hiding them in your own house?"

"Are you kidding? She'd have discovered every one of them by now. She's terrible, that girl. We can't even put presents under the tree on Christmas Eve. They'd be open by morning. Why, if she knew I was hiding them over here, she'd probably be by trying to sweet talk you into letting her clean the storage room. This is the only way I can keep anything a surprise from that child."

"How unusual." Alex held back his amusement. "Is this an inherited curiosity?"

Gandy had the grace to blush. "She might have gotten it from me. I used to be a lot like her, curious, impatient and all that. I'm better now, especially after I broke my leg."

"What?" This was the new and improved Gandy? That was an alarming thought. What had the old Gandy been like? "Did you say you broke your leg?"

"I knew my husband had hidden my Christmas gifts somewhere at the place he works. How was I to know there was a broken rung on the ladder they use to get to the storage area above the trucks?"

"Surely you didn't…"

"Oh, I did all right. Worst December of my life. People just wouldn't leave me alone. They teased me mercilessly about sneaking into the truck barn to find my packages. And they call themselves Christians! Where was their compassion?" She picked up a torn, coverless hymnal and smacked it down again. "What's more, the cast itched like wildfire. I must have poured a ton of baby powder down it to keep it from driving me crazy. I was living in a cloud of talc for weeks."

"As usual, you amaze me, Gandy. Your ingenuity is awe-inspiring."

Gandy decided to take that as a compliment. She put her hands on her hips and inquired, "So what are you going to do about it?"

Alex thought for a moment. "Offer to take all this stuff out of the closet so you can find what you've lost?" He knew there'd be no way around it anyway.

"You'd better get busy then."

He took off his jacket, rolled up his sleeves and got busy.

"By the way, Lauren's planning the party for Tillie. She's got a great idea too. Everyone is supposed to bring a birthday card—

not mentioning the part about being eighty years old—for Tillie and a can of something for the food shelf."

Alex could feel sweat pouring down his back between his shoulder blades and muscles burning in his arms and legs as he lugged everything from discarded vacuum cleaners to boxes of candle stubs left over from old candlelight services out of the storage room.

"I didn't know we had a food shelf."

"We don't, but Lauren's going to start one. She thought Tillie would like to be involved and it would take her mind off her age as well. 'Course Lauren figures Tillie could use the food shelf as much as anyone—except maybe Lila Mason. She'll never tell her that, of course."

"Good for Lauren." Finally, he came upon Gandy's cardboard box. DEBBIE'S GIFTS was written on it in Gandy's distinctive hand.

"Hallelujah and hip-hip-hooray," Gandy cheered. "Now I won't have to buy doubles." She pounced on her treasure and trotted it out to her car, leaving Alex to replace everything he and Gandy had removed.

He'd returned several items to the closet and made a large pile of detritus in the hall by the time she came back.

"What are you doing?" She peered into the pile and picked up a piece of mashed Christmas garland with tinsel still clinging to it.

"Cleaning out. No one will ever use these vacuums again. The dust in those bags came off the Dead Sea Scrolls—when they were new. And unless someone is planning to melt all those candle stubs into wax, it's out of here. And these broken Christmas wreaths..."

"Suit yourself," Gandy said glumly. "You know for certain that as soon as you throw something away, somebody else needs it."

"I feel like living on the edge for a change. I'll take the chance."

Gandy looked longingly at a small artificial Christmas tree with a missing top. "Okay, but I don't have to stay around to watch. Close up when you're done."

He watched her leave with a combination of relief and fondness.

After returning to the parsonage and taking a long shower to eradicate the ancient dust, Alex meandered into the kitchen and noticed the message light flashing on his answering machine. He pushed the PLAY button and heard Lydia Olson's desperate voice. He realized he'd forgotten to return her other call.

"I need to give you a cooking lesson! Call me as soon as you get home. I'll be right over."

An emergency cooking lesson? What next?

Filled with curiosity and a little dread, Alex dialed the Olsons' phone number. Lydia picked up on the second ring. "Pastor Alex, is that you?"

"Hello, Lydia. I'm returning your call...."

"Have you fixed yourself dinner yet?" she interrupted, which was uncharacteristically impolite.

"No. I was going to reheat some..."

"Don't do a thing. I'll be right over. How do you feel about chicken potpie?"

"It's wonderful, of course, but I don't have any of the ingredients."

"I do. Preheat your oven to four hundred degrees. I'll be there in ten minutes." Lydia hung up.

Alex walked into the kitchen to do as he was told. After turning on the stove, he took two plates from the cupboard and set the table. If Lydia was determined to teach him to cook, he hoped she'd also take the risk of eating his creation. It would be good to have someone with whom to share supper.

Alex stared, unseeing, out the window that overlooked the yard. Another touch of melancholy hit him. He'd thought by now he'd have the company of a family, *his* family, at mealtimes. Alex fought back the loneliness that had been plaguing him. Why now? It had been months since he and Natalie had separated. Perhaps this was the first time since their breakup that he'd allowed himself to feel all that was inside him.

He'd just put water glasses filled with ice on the table when Lydia rapped on the door. Before he could reach it, she opened it and came inside carrying two big canvas bags. She handed one to Alex and bustled to the kitchen counter with the other.

"Groceries," she said briskly. "Take them out and put them on the counter. I assumed you wouldn't have everything we needed so I brought it all."

"You were certainly sure I would be home and ready to cook tonight," Alex said mildly as he took a package of frozen peas and carrots and ready-made piecrusts out of the tote.

"I knew you'd be home and ready to cook *sometime*, I'm just glad you were available tonight." Lydia busied herself putting things in order on the counter. "I wanted to teach you my real recipe but this will have to do."

"Real recipe?"

"My everything-from-scratch version." She put her fists on her ample hips and looked at the counter appraisingly. "Tonight we're taking shortcuts." Lydia pointed to the ready-made piecrust and frozen vegetables. "The piecrust should be homemade with lard to be really tender. The peas, carrots and onions should be garden fresh, but we'll make do. I've already cooked the chicken. Next time you can do it. Here's your recipe."

LYDIA'S CHICKEN POTPIE

- 1 two- or three-pound whole rotisserie chicken (meat picked off the bones)
- 2 frozen piecrusts, thawed
- 1 can condensed cream of mushroom soup
- 1 package green peas and carrots (10 ounces, although I often use more)
- 1 teaspoon chicken bouillon
- ½ to 1 cup water to dissolve bouillon

Preheat oven to 400 degrees. Pour soup into saucepan and add peas and carrots, bouillon and water as needed. Simmer till smooth. Mix in chicken. Roll out piecrust. Pour mixture into one piecrust and cover with the other. Seal edges. Cut small steam hole in top crust. Bake 30–35 minutes or until crust is brown.

Under Lydia's watchful eye, Alex simmered vegetables in cream soup seasoned with bouillon and diced the precooked chicken she'd brought. She was nervous as a sparrow, he observed, flitting from one place to another, wiping an invisible spot from one counter and rearranging dishes on another.

Did he imagine it or were her hands trembling? "Lydia, was there something you wanted to discuss…"

"Roll out this piecrust for the bottom of the potpie," she ordered, ignoring the question. She handed him the rolling pin she'd found in a drawer. "Put a little flour down first so it doesn't stick. And don't handle the rolling pin like a baseball bat. You're holding it like you want to hit a ball over the fence."

He took it off his shoulder and grasped it by the handles.

"Use a light touch. We don't want the crust ground into the counter. There now, just flatten the dough ball slightly and turn it a quarter turn. Now do it again. If you keep turning the pastry and making sure there's a little, but not too much, flour beneath it, you'll be able to roll a nice, even crust. Now there you go, pressing too hard. Light touch, remember?"

Under Lydia's tutelage he learned how to pick up a piecrust with a long, thin spatula and transfer it to a pan, fill it with the cooked mixture and top it with the second crust. "There, how's that?" It looked promising but a little sloppy to his untrained eye.

"Crimp the edges, put a small hole in the top to release steam and it's ready to bake." Lydia looked at the potpie with a satisfied expression. "I believe I have a very bright student."

"Crimp?" he said blankly.

Lydia tucked the edges of the top crust beneath those of the bottom and, using the forefinger of her right hand and the thumb and forefinger of her left, made a ruffled pattern in the crust around the pan. "Like that."

Carefully Alex transferred his prize to the oven. With a feeling of satisfaction, he set the oven timer. He was going to have an entire repertoire by the time he cooked for his sister Carol. The idea pleased him immensely.

"You'll eat supper with me, won't you?" he asked. "You can't leave now, before you've tasted the finished product."

"Thank you. I will. My brothers can fend for themselves for once. Surely between the two of them they can figure out how to make a sandwich."

Alex turned so that Lydia couldn't see him smile. Feisty was Lydia's middle name today. As they sat across the table from each other waiting for the stove's timer to ring, Alex tried to ferret out the real reason for Lydia's visit.

"I appreciate the cooking lesson, Lydia, and I look forward to many more of them, but I have a hunch there's something else behind our session today. Want to talk about it?"

Lydia's pleasant expression crumpled.

"I tell you, Pastor, I just don't know what to do anymore!" The timer rang and Lydia erupted out of her chair like a rocket from a launch pad at NASA. "Mercy, that startled me! Could have given me a heart attack!" She hurried to the stove and withdrew a perfectly golden brown chicken potpie with steam coming out of the center hole like a little geyser. "Look at what you did!"

Alex wasn't given to unnecessary pride, but the sight of the bit of culinary perfection did fill him with an unparalleled sense of satisfaction, much like when he had first learned to ride his bicycle without training wheels. "It's lovely. Shall we see if it's edible?"

Lydia marched the dish to the table and gave it the place of honor on a wooden trivet. Then she dipped a serving spoon in the crust. Alex heard the delicate crunching of crust and smelled a fragrant aroma of chicken and vegetables. His salivary glands sprang to life.

"I'll dish up, you pray," Lydia said as she filled his plate. After she'd made a plate for herself, she sat down and looked at Alex expectantly.

After the prayer, Lydia took a bite from her plate and sampled it with the intensity of a food critic about to write an article for the *New York Times*. She laid down her fork and announced, "Delicious!"

Alex's mouth was too full to do anything but nod.

"Your brothers are lucky men to have someone like you to feed them," Alex said when he could speak. He knew immediately that he'd said the wrong thing by the grim expression on Lydia's face. "Aren't they?"

"Those two! Spoiled as the day is long! I'm so fed up with the both of them right now I could just...just"—it seemed to be taking her quite a while to think of something bad enough to say—"just barf!"

"Oh well, I..." How did one respond to that, coming from this prim and proper pillar of the congregation? It was probably as close to uncouth language as Lydia Olson had ever gotten.

"I've become those two boys' slave," Lydia fumed. "Lydia, do this, Lydia, get that, Lydia, I thought I told you to make apple pie, not cherry....' Never a 'thank you' or a 'please' anymore. I'm no different in the kitchen than the toaster or the stove, just something that prepares food for those two big bellies!"

Alex had never gotten a good look at Jacob Olson, who was a serious recluse, but he had to agree with Lydia's assessment of her brother Clarence's anatomy. Clarence looked as if his stomach had been inflated with a bicycle pump. Too many pies, no doubt.

"Are you feeling taken for granted?" Alex ventured. "Overworked? Underappreciated?"

"All of the above," Lydia said grimly. "Not only that, I feel like my life is slipping away from me! I'm sixty-two years old and I haven't had any fun yet!"

"Fun? What do you mean?"

"Fun. F-U-N, fun. I haven't traveled anywhere outside the state except for an occasional trip to Minnesota. I've never been to Los Angeles, Chicago, New York...Rome! I haven't even been to Disney World. My brothers' idea of a vacation is to go to the threshing show and watch the old-time threshers harvest grain. Then they stop at a little town that holds turtle races and bet which turtle will win. The crowning glory is to stop in Fargo on the way home and order a prime rib steak with extra horseradish. And, believe it or not, they expect me to make sandwiches to eat in the car so they don't have to spend any extra money for lunch." Lydia's face reddened. "That's not exactly *my* kind of travel."

"What is your kind, Lydia?" Alex asked gently. The poor woman was so upset that he didn't want her to have a coronary in his kitchen.

She stared at him as if he'd asked a question she'd never even considered. She took a long time to answer.

"Shopping, maybe. And the theater. Yes, the theater. And music! I'd like to go to a concert, to museums and art galleries and to take a cruise on a big ship. And I'd love to have someone to cook for me for a change." She was practically transported to a realm of bliss by the notion. "I want to eat caviar, escargot and lobster. And I want to soak in a hot tub." She said this as if she were asking for the moon and the stars.

"They are all reasonable requests, Lydia. I think you should be able to enjoy those things. What's stopping you?"

She gaped at him. "What would Clarence and Jacob think? The money…"

"Is that a problem for you?" He felt awkward inquiring into her finances.

"Come to think of it, it shouldn't be." Her jaw hardened. "I own a third of the land and I work as hard on that farm as anyone else. Why am I worrying about spending money? My brothers buy machinery all the time and I've used the same stove for twenty years. It's *time* I spent some money!"

Alex wondered if he'd be in trouble for this little counseling session when the Olson boys heard that the pastor supported their sister in running off to New York to go to the theater. Still, the look of excitement—no, transformation—on Lydia's face made it worth the risk.

Unfortunately, as quickly as Lydia's exhilaration and anticipation came, they were gone again. The brief insurgency melted away.

"Lydia?" Alex said. "What's wrong?"

"I can't do any of those things! I don't have anyone to do them with and I certainly can't go alone."

Much to Alex's surprise, tears began to run down the woman's cheeks.

"That's the real problem, you know. I'm alone. Those brothers of mine don't understand. Clarence is satisfied with everything in his life—especially my cooking. Jacob prefers not to be with people so he's happy like it is. Me? I'm the only one who wants things to be different."

She gazed at Alex with a look he recognized from personal experience, and it hit him like an arrow directly to the heart. He knew what she was going to say, even before she opened her mouth.

"I'd like to be married, Pastor Alex. Is it too late for me? Has life already passed me by?"

His physical response to her question was a sinking sensation in his gut.

Was it too late for him as well? It might have been easier to find a mate in the city where there were a lot of single women. But out here the only single woman his age was Lolly Roscoe, who terrified him with all her blond hair and blue-eyed intensity and desperation to marry. He understood her problem far better than Lydia probably imagined.

"Is it too late?" he finally said, after taking seconds on the potpie. "No, I don't believe so. It's probably more difficult now, after you've lived here so many years and there are so few newcomers to the area to meet, but it's never too late. My grandfather's best friend was widowed at seventy and remarried at eighty-two. He lived happily another ten years with a wonderful woman so I know it's possible to find love at any age."

"What about you, Pastor? You're a handsome man. Why haven't

you married?" Lydia blushed the color of the pink peonies in his garden. "I'm sorry, I shouldn't have been so bold."

"This conversation is just between us, right?" He smiled at her, trying to put her at ease. "I did plan to marry, but the lady found someone else."

"I'm so sorry." Lydia put her hand to her lips, dismayed. "That's much worse than never having found anyone at all."

"I've forgiven her. I wish her only the best. We can't close ourselves off to love, Lydia. Neither should we be foolish and start looking for it in the wrong places. All we can do is pray about it and then leave ourselves open to what God brings into our lives."

That impulsive e-mail to Natalie shimmered in his mind.

"How, exactly, does one go about doing that?" Lydia bristled with curiosity.

Alex had to stifle a laugh. "I'm not quite sure, but I think that hiding out in a kitchen on a farm won't help."

"So I should get out more?" She looked both hopeful and confused, as if she had no idea how to go about such a thing.

"Yes, I think so. Don't close yourself off to new things. Keep your heart open, Lydia. See what shows up."

Maybe he should call Natalie tonight...

She sighed. "It feels better already, knowing I've told someone how I feel." She tucked into her second helping of food with renewed gusto.

"Lydia, perhaps you should begin to wean those brothers of yours from all the good food you cook. If you decide to leave home for the weekend or go on a trip, they might starve without you."

"Good idea. I can't imagine they'd be good students like you, but I suppose I could teach them how to defrost and use the microwave. It would be a start."

"And a kindness, I'm sure," Alex said with a conspiratorial grin.

Lydia's smile twinkled back at him. "I'll begin tomorrow."

"And if they come to me for counseling, I'll encourage them in every way I can."

Pact made, they settled down to eat the banana cream pie Lydia had brought for dessert.

∾

The phone rang as Alex was drifting off to sleep. "Hullo?" he answered sleepily.

"Hi, Unc."

Alex sat up in bed. "Jared? How are you, buddy?"

"Okay, I guess."

"Just okay?"

"I wanted to know how all those people I met are doing—Lauren and Mike, that guy with the pig...."

Alex told his nephew all he could think of, and Jared seemed genuinely interested in the goings-on at Hilltop. Then Alex said, "How about you? How are you doing?"

"I dunno. I wish I'd already graduated from high school."

"I remember thinking the same thing when I was your age. I could hardly wait to 'grow up.' I didn't find out till later that it wasn't much easier than being a teenager."

"It was different with you, Uncle Alex. You're a smart guy. Things came easier for you. I'm just a dummy."

"I don't understand what you mean."

"Hey, Mom's yelling up the stairs telling me to go to bed. I'll talk to you later, okay?" The line went dead.

Alex didn't get to sleep for hours, wondering what Jared had meant.

CHAPTER EIGHT

Sometimes Alex had no choice but to follow his intuition. God-hunches, he called them, thoughts and ideas that came into his brain and wouldn't leave. This morning his God-hunch concerned Lila Mason. Dixon had said something that had provoked this particular feeling, and it was time for Alex to follow up on it.

"Lila's a little lost soul," Dixon had commented. "Not necessarily lost in the sense of being spiritually adrift, but since her memory has failed she's living her life being bewildered by most of it. She's"—Dixon had thought for a long while before choosing his next word—"forlorn."

Forlorn. It was a rather old-fashioned word when Alex stopped to think about it, a word he didn't hear much anymore. A sad, lonely, despondent kind of word that epitomized dejection and despair. As he drove up to Lila's little white house, he found that dispirited as well. The screen door was in disrepair, suspended by only one set of hinges. A plastic planter on the front porch held pink petunias badly in need of watering and dead-heading.

He knocked on the door. Inside he heard a Christian radio station playing "How Great Thou Art." He knocked again and was about to try the doorknob when the door flew open. Lila stood framed in the doorway in a brown flowered house dress and oversized men's leather slippers.

"Pastor Alex, is it?" Lila peered at him. "Sorry I can't see you very well. I've lost my glasses. In the garden, I think."

Alex lifted his hand and touched something in her hair. "How about these?"

Her hands flew to her head and she began to feel around in the spot he'd indicated. Her expression turned to delight. "There they are! How clever of you to find them. I'm glad I didn't go outside and spend the morning in the garden looking for them. It's supposed to be very warm today." She stepped aside so that he could enter.

The place smelled like something half apothecary, part rendering plant, with a smidgen of skunk den. He prayed that his breakfast of oatmeal and bananas would stay down.

"I'm cooking my health drink," Lila said. "Would you like one? You look a little puny and your color's not good."

His color had been fine until he'd walked into this house and smelled whatever was cooking on the stove. "Boiling old socks" was how Dixon had described the aroma. Maybe it was old socks, but Sasquatch had to have been wearing them for at least a year before Lila threw them in the pot.

Much to Alex's relief, Lila poured most of the concoction into a quart jar and sealed the lid. The rest she put in a large glass and swilled back like it was sweet nectar. When that was consumed, the strongest odors began to dissipate. He might not lose his breakfast after all.

"What, exactly, do you put into that mix, Lila? Are you sure it's good for you?"

"Look at me! Fit as a fiddle and it's all due to my health drinks. Yeast, lecithin, fish oil, beets, prunes, cucumbers, spinach, green tea and fresh mushrooms when I can find them. Morels."

Alex felt his gut take a dip. "Mushrooms?" Lila could poison herself. "Are you sure you should be using mushrooms? What if you picked something toxic?"

"I've been doing this for years," Lila responded. She tilted back the glass she'd been drinking from to get the dregs out of the bottom. "I know my mushrooms. Of course, I have a little more trouble identifying them when I'm not wearing my glasses..."

Alex felt a chill run through him. Glancing around the room didn't comfort him either. There were trays of unidentifiable plants drying all over the kitchen. A stew pot full of meat and gravy sat on the cold stove. A gelled skin had formed across the top, and Alex wondered how long the pan had been sitting out—overnight, at least, possibly days.

"I've been robbed again," Lila told him. "Breaking and entering. I can't believe why anyone would want my galoshes, but there you are. Maybe they needed them more than I do, but sneaking into my house to take them—that beats all!"

Alex glanced at the cooking pot Lila had used for her herbal drink and wondered if the boots might not have been cooked into broth as well. Impulsively, he bent down and looked under the table. There they were, Lila's overshoes, onion tops sprouting out of one and lacy, fernlike carrot greens out of the other. He reached down and picked them up.

"Is this what you're looking for?"

"Glory be, they're back!" Lila pulled the carrots out of one of the boots. "Why'd he bring them back filled with vegetables?"

"Are you sure you didn't put them there?" Alex asked gently.

Lila's brow furrowed. "Might have. I was in my garden picking things yesterday..." Realization dawned and she began to giggle. "How silly of me! Look at that! 'Course it's a clever way to carry vegetables, isn't it, Reverend?"

Then, as if remembering her manners, she added, "Can I make you some coffee? I've got some store-bought cookies or some nice beef stew I made yesterday…or was it the day before?"

"I had a big breakfast before I left the parsonage this morning. Thank you anyway." He gathered his nerve and plunged on. "I'm worried about you, Lila. What if you accidently picked a poisonous mushroom or left a stew pot sit out too long…"

He glanced at her, expecting some sort of eruption. Instead he saw an expression that harbored both pity and pleasure.

"Reverend, you have to know that I'm not going to stop my health potions now. I appreciate the warning about the mushrooms. I may be old but I'm not stupid! I don't want to eat a bad one any more than you want me to. And as for the stew pot, well, I think the flavors blend more when it's not in the refrigerator." She saw him eyeing the pot on the stove. "If you insist, I'll put it away. But I won't throw it away. It takes a lot of my social security money to buy groceries and I don't have any to waste."

"Thank you, Lila. All I'm thinking of is your safety." He still didn't like the thing about the mushrooms, but this, at least, was a start.

"I know and I appreciate it. There's not many left to worry themselves about me anymore so I'm grateful when I get it."

It made him ache inside. Here was this brave, befuddled little soul doing her best with what she had. Alex decided that his next stop would be at the Carlsons' to have a conversation with Lauren. He wanted to encourage her. If a community ever needed a food shelf to help the likes of Lila and the Bruuns, it was this one.

It wasn't until they'd said their good-byes that he realized that Lila hadn't imparted a single bit of erroneous gossip during their visit. That, at least, was something to be grateful for.

He didn't make it to the Carlsons' as he'd planned, however. His mistake was dropping by the church to say hello to Gandy.

"There you are!" Gandy greeted him with an accusatory tone. "I thought you'd run off on us."

"I stopped at Lila Mason's this morning. I wanted to check on her."

Gandy's face relaxed and he knew that he'd been forgiven for arriving late at the church. "How is the sweet old thing?"

"Still determined to poison herself with those concoctions. I did get her to agree to start keeping her food in the refrigerator instead of leaving it on the counter." He poured himself coffee using the mug Gandy had given him on his three-month anniversary of being at Hilltop. The mug proclaimed, IF GOD IS YOUR CO-PILOT, SWAP SEATS!

"It's a step. Next try to get her to go to the doctor for her ailments and not just self-medicate. She won't even go to Doc Ambrose in Grassy Valley. I can't imagine what it would take to get her to see a doctor. Being carried out on a stretcher, maybe."

"One thing at a time, I guess," Alex said absently as he glanced through the mail. There was a long white business-sized envelope in the mix of community flyers, church supply catalogues and bills. He put the catalogues and bills together and handed them to Gandy, grateful that she had a miser's eye for errors in bills and Scrooge's talent for squeezing the most juice from every penny.

That left a brochure about the upcoming dates for Grassy Valley's farmers' market, a flyer from Lilly Sumptner announcing that she was now selling gourmet food products, and the letter. Next he signed in to his e-mail and watched a list of unread messages pop up. He started opening them from the top of the list.

Carol had sent him several forwards—jokes, notes from family, an uplifting verse.

There was a sale of inspirational fiction at an online bookstore. Jared had sent a goofy picture of himself taken with his phone.

With half an ear he listened to Gandy discussing the problems of communion bread, white wafers versus a loaf of whole wheat, store-bought versus homemade, on and on.

"This is wheat country," he finally said, putting an end to Gandy's fretting. "Have someone bake the loaves. Jesus didn't order tasteless wafers in a plastic roll for the Last Supper."

"I'll call Lydia Olson. She makes wonderful bread."

"Why don't you ask Lauren Carlson or Nancy Jenkins?" Alex said quickly. "I think Lydia needs a break."

Gandy looked at him suspiciously but picked up the phone to do as she was told.

When she was otherwise occupied, Alex returned to his e-mail. His jaw dropped open at the sight of a familiar name: *Natalie*.

Surreptitiously he adjusted his computer monitor so that Gandy couldn't see what he was reading.

Alex—

Your e-mail was a welcome surprise. I've thought about you so much. I regret many things, particularly about the way I treated you. I realize how badly I behaved after I recently had the same experience myself. How could I have been so cavalier about your feelings?

I called Carol. So you are in North Dakota now and pastor of two small parishes? It sounds idyllic, the simple life. I just wanted you to know I will understand if you never forgive me for what I did. I had no idea how much it could hurt or, shamefully, I was too wrapped up in myself to care. That doesn't say much for me, does it? I had something wonderful in you, Alex, a strong, loyal, loving Christian man (handsome too!) and I thoughtlessly threw it away. If you can see it in your heart to forgive me, I would be so happy. If not, I understand.

Natalie

An unexpected thrill of excitement raced through him. He'd forgiven her already, of course. Christ had modeled that for him in Scripture. But what did this all mean?

"Who died?" Gandy asked. Her pink-tipped nose was in the air as if she were sniffing out whatever news was in the letter. "You look awfully serious."

Alex collected himself and tried to act nonchalant. "I just heard from someone I hadn't been in contact with for a long time, that's all."

"You don't look any too pleased about it."

He signed out of his e-mail and tried to appear unruffled. "I'm not sure how I feel about it, actually."

"It's a woman, isn't it?" Gandy looked like the proverbial cat that ate the canary. Alex could practically see yellow feathers sprouting from the corners of her mouth.

"What makes you think that?" He hated it when his voice cracked, something that only happened when he was nervous.

"Woman's in-tu-i-tion, that's what, but if you don't want to talk about it, don't. I'll be here whenever you're ready to discuss her." With that, Gandy went back to work.

That, Alex thought, was exactly what he was afraid of—Gandy, lying in wait, ready to pounce, looking for signs of weakness or hints that he'd made contact with the mystery woman. Was he up to a cat-and-mouse game like that?

"Tillie's party is on Saturday afternoon at two. We have to be done in time for everyone to get to town for Saturday night. Why don't you take a break and go for a change?"

Alex looked up from his sermon notes to find Lauren Carlson looking down at him. She had an enormous zucchini under one arm and a list in her hand. There was dirt beneath her fingernails, and her nose was red from too much sun. "I hear it's wonderful, but I usually practice my sermon and spend time praying on Saturday night. I work on Sunday mornings, you know."

"You really need to enjoy a Saturday night in Grassy Valley. It's a major social event. It's something extra special now, during harvest. The stores, all of which normally close at five thirty, stay open until nine. Everyone comes to town to do their grocery shopping, get a haircut or just hang out. There's usually a little outdoor concert that the locals pull together. The elderly folks sit in their cars and watch the people go by, and the younger ones stop to say hello to them. A group of preteens watch the younger children. The teenagers roam together in packs, oblivious to anyone over twenty-five. It's very convivial. You should come."

"Maybe I will, now that I've become more comfortable preparing for Sunday mornings. Those first few sermons were pretty nerve-racking for me."

"Good. Mike and I will look for you."

"I have a question for you, Lauren. I'd like you to tell me more about this party for Tillie Tanner." For a deceptively sleepy place, things happened in the Hilltop community at lightning speed.

"We're doing cake, coffee, mints and nuts. She likes purple so that's our theme color. We're not putting a reference to age anywhere. Oh yes, bring a can of something for the new food shelf. In fact, bring two. We're going to give one can of everything to Tillie as her birthday present."

"She needs it, I'm sure."

"Better yet, this way she won't think it's a handout. She's particularly fond of pork and beans if you can't decide what to bring."

At that moment Gandy walked to Alex's desk and handed him the Sunday bulletin to proof.

"Did you get all that, Gandy?"

"You bet. I already know what I'm bringing. I've been trying for weeks to get my family to start eating kidney beans. I make chili and what happens? At the end of the meal, everyone's bowl still has a pile of kidney beans in it. They manage to eat around those things and suck the juice right off them. I give up. If they don't want the protein or the fiber, so be it. I've got a whole case of the things to bring to the party. I'm bringing my chili recipe too. Everyone except my family says it's excellent."

"Perfect." Lauren laid the zucchini on Alex's desk. "See you two later."

She disappeared through the door before Alex could ask what he should do with the long green vegetable.

"Make bread," Gandy said, as if she'd read his mind. "Or cook it with onion, add corn and then melt cheese on top. You could buy Grassy Valley's *How to Cook Zucchini* cookbook in town on Saturday. Everyone in the community contributed their favorite. By the way, be sure to lock the doors of your car when you get to town."

"Car thefts? Robberies? What's been happening?" Since coming to Hilltop, he'd quit locking the door of his van, although he still hadn't embraced the idea of leaving his key in the ignition like so many did.

Gandy looked at him as if he'd lost his mind. "You don't lock your car to keep people from taking something out, you lock your car to keep people from putting something *in*." She picked up the zucchini and swung it around like a club. "You leave that van open and the whole thing will be filled with these and tomatoes too. Everyone who has a garden will be handing out vegetables. You, being the pastor, will be their first choice to 'gift' with their excess." She chewed on the corner of her lip as she pondered this. "Unless you really like zucchini bread. Then take it all, bake it up and buy a new freezer to store it in."

Either way sounded like more work than he wanted. "Maybe I'll just stay home and practice my sermon."

Gandy's lips turned down at the corners. "Coward."

He picked up the gauntlet she'd thrown down. "Oh, all right then, I'll go, but if I get inundated with zucchini anyway, you're helping me with it."

"Lock your doors and you'll be safe."

This was very different from his home in Chicago. Fear of vegetables had never once entered his mind there.

Saturday dawned crisp and clear…and quiet. There were no geese honking outside Alex's window. Maybe they were gone for good. Of course, if they were gone and something bad had happened to them, Will Packard would be devastated. As much as he hated the noise, he wanted the geese around for Will's sake.

The coffee was already brewed thanks to his remembering to set the clock timer on the pot last night. He poured himself a mug and meandered outside without much enthusiasm to look for the geese. They were nowhere to be seen. Not that he was looking too hard. Tripod, who'd been at his side, suddenly took off toward Will's hoomain society shed. The boy's bike was already leaning against the wall. His parents, Alex thought, probably didn't know where the boy was half the time, other than being confident that he was here, playing with the animals. Fortunately, this kept Will out of even more risky projects like launching one of the twins off the chicken coop in a homemade parachute.

Inside the shed, Will was trying to cram the geese into Rosie's empty cage and not having much success at it.

"What are you doing?"

"I found them a home. Florence Kennedy says she loves goose eggs and doesn't mind their mess so I'm taking them to her this morning."

"Good for you, buddy. I'm sure the geese will be very happy." *And so will I.*

"I need the room. There are more animals coming in all the time. If Bucky moved away, I could probably close this place up, but as long as he's kicking cats and laying out bad meat for dogs, I'll be busier than a one-legged paperhanger."

"I think you mean one-*armed* paperhanger, don't you?"

"I don't know. The whole idea sounds dumb to me. My ma says it's a clee-shay, whatever that means."

Cliché. Will had a sophisticated vocabulary today.

"Are you going to the birthday party?" Will inquired as he finally got the second goose into the cage. "Ma can't so she sent me over here with two cans of stewed tomatoes, one for Tillie and one for that other place. Can you take them?"

"Of course. Your mother is very generous." He knew Minnie needed those tomatoes for her own brood.

Will beamed up at him, his cowlick particularly rowdy and his eyes shining. "She is, isn't she?" Then, in a quick turnabout, he dragged the wagon on which the cage was sitting out of the shed. The geese honked in dismay as Will hooked it to his bike and hopped on the seat. "I'd better get going. These dumb birds are going to make me deaf if I don't get them delivered soon." Feathers flew as Will pushed off.

"Bye, Preacher!" Will pedaled away as fast as his legs could manage. As he watched the boy go, Alex wondered what kinds of scholarships would be available in years to come for young people who wanted to become veterinarians. Will was a budding animal doctor if there ever was one.

Glad he wasn't the one with the geese in tow, he went inside for more coffee. He had the morning off and planned to spend it reading some of the many books that had piled up over the past three months.

At one thirty, Dixon's pickup truck careened into the yard just as Alex was about to get in his van to drive to the church. "Want a ride to Tillie's party?" Dixon hollered out his rolled-down window. "I'm going to Grassy Valley after, if you want to ride along."

It didn't take Alex long to decide that it might be prudent to leave his vehicle at home and escape the dreaded zucchini onslaught Gandy had predicted.

"Sure." He clambered into the truck and eyed Dixon. "You look like you're going on a date." His friend was wearing a freshly starched pale blue shirt and khaki trousers. His shoes were polished and his hair was combed into something that looked like an actual haircut rather than a nasty mishap with a skinning knife.

"Big times," Dixon said cheerfully.

"You look happier than I've seen you for a while."

"I asked my sister Emmy to come for a visit."

"Soon?"

"I'm not sure. She said she'd call me. She told me it would be September so it could be any day now. Emmy's like everyone else who grew up in Hilltop Township. We all love harvest and like to be around when the combines are rolling. They'll run night and day if there isn't much humidity. Otherwise the crops get tough and we stop for the night. To store it a farmer can't have too much moisture in the grain because of the danger of spoilage. It's expensive to dry and sometimes shrinks. It's best to let nature call the shots."

"There's much more to farming than I ever realized," Alex admitted sheepishly. "I certainly had an inflated sense of what I knew."

Dixon pulled into the church yard, which already held a surprising number of parked cars. "Hey, there's Belle and Curtis Wells." He pointed at an attractive blond woman with her hair piled in a complicated arrangement on her head. She was wearing black leggings, a white poet's blouse and high heels. Not the usual Grassy Valley fare for women in their fifties. "She never misses a social event. She makes Curtis come too. He'd be happier mucking stalls, but he knows she needs to get out."

"Gandy told me that Belle wants to go back to the city."

"She'd go in a heartbeat if Curtis would come with her. The only thing she loves more than the city is Curt."

They said hello to Ole Swenson, who was leaning against the church talking to Stoddard Block. From what Alex could hear of the conversation, Ole was getting advice about how to build a solid new pigsty. He'd gone to the right place.

As Alex walked into the church basement, the sounds reminded him of a school cafeteria, flatware clanking, cups and plates chinking together and an unrestrained din of voices, each trying to out-talk the other. The room had gone purple, as Lauren had predicted. There were violets on each table, purple streamers looping haphazardly across the ceiling, lavender paper tablecloths, as well as plum-colored paper plates and plastic forks. Off to one side were two tables, each mounded with groceries—rice, canned goods, boxed cake mixes, tubs of frosting, cereals and more. Tillie and the food shelf would do well today.

Tillie, wearing an amethyst dress to match the purple theme, was ensconced behind a cake that could only be described as a boisterous combination of violet, mauve and plum. She wore a straw hat with peacock feathers erupting from the brim. Tillie waved him over for a closer look at the cake.

"This is something, isn't it, Reverend?"

"It certainly is." What, Alex wasn't quite sure. "Happy birthday, Tillie. How old are you now? Surely not sixty-five yet?"

Tillie cackled gleefully. "Believe it or not, I am!" She proudly brushed back her hair to reveal enough creases and furrows to make a bas-relief map. She lowered her voice to a whisper. "I know it's amazing, but I use a good cold cream at night and stay out of the sun."

"Good for you. You could teach us all a thing or two." Alex's spirits lifted just seeing the happy glow on Tillie's face. Sometimes delusion wasn't such a bad thing.

"There you are!" Lauren came up to him holding a plate of mints. "Sit down and have coffee. The party is in full swing."

"I see that." He glanced around the room, mentally taking roll call to see how many of his parishioners were in attendance. "Most everyone from Hilltop is here, and a few from All Saints Fellowship too." He saw Althea Dawson's white hair and trademark bun, and Amy Clayborn, the young woman who had no doubt given Althea a ride. He took another quick look at the crowd. "Bessie and Brunie

Bruun are missing, of course, and where is"—he scanned the room a third time—"Lila Mason?"

"Isn't she here? I thought I saw her. Maybe not. She's such a little thing, she could get lost in a crowd like this. Look, there's Betty Nyborg waving at you. You'd better say hello." With that, Lauren sent him off to fend for himself.

He wandered over to Lilly Sumptner, who was pouring coffee with one hand and juggling a stack of empty plates with the other. "Have you seen Lila? Has she been here and gone already?"

Lily glanced around the room. "She must be here somewhere. She always is. I'll bet she's in the kitchen dishing up the nuts and mints. She likes that job."

It sounded likely. Alex methodically made his way around the room, greeting the guests as if they were his own, particularly the ones who had arrived from All Saints.

"Good to see you, Emma. How's the work on the quilt progressing? Gandy says you are all doing a wonderful job. She's says it's going to be the finest Township history quilt ever made. Yes, she told me about the fat quarters. Amazing…"

Steeped in the merriment of the party, the time flew quickly by.

"Ready to go, Reverend…Alex?" Dixon edged up to him and spoke into his ear.

"Please. I've drunk so much coffee and eaten so many mints I'm either going to overdose on a caffeine high or develop diabetes if I stay any longer. People here just don't want to stop visiting, do they?"

"Wait until we get to town," Dixon said. "They'll all pick up where they left off here."

Saturday night in Grassy Valley was a throwback to earlier, gentler times, Alex thought as he and Dixon drove down Main Street. The thoroughfare was clogged with cars, and the sidewalks were overflowing with people milling about.

Dixon pulled into a space on Main Street just in front of Cowlicks and Peppermint Sticks, or, as every one called it, Licks and Sticks. Like so many businesses in Grassy Valley, they were doing double duty under one roof. Good Finds, Good Flowers was a combination floral and antique store. At Licks and Sticks, while the barber trimmed hair, his wife made and sold homemade candy from the back half of the building.

"I have to get a haircut, first thing. The line gets long and when the barber's feet get tired he closes up shop." Dixon ran his fingers through his hair. "Now that Emmy is coming, I have to quit cutting it myself. She doesn't like the job I do."

"I can't imagine why," Alex said pointedly. Dixon's hair often pointed a half-dozen directions at once.

"Do you have anything special to do, Alex? If not, I hear music down by the park. Sounds pretty good. Be thankful it's not Fred Dooley and his accordion or, worse yet, Harry Orberg and his musical saw."

"Would Lila Mason be in town tonight?"

"Lila never misses if she can help it. Look for her in More For Less. That's her favorite shop. That, or the grocery store."

Alex wasn't sure why he was so determined to talk to Lila, but he never ignored internal promptings when they came. After all these years of walking with God, he knew enough to listen when a name kept cropping up in his mind. He stopped and prayed for that person, no matter where he was or what he was doing. Today Lila's name had been almost continually on his mind.

After Dixon departed for Licks and Sticks, Alex strolled down Main Street, past the beauty shop and drugstore, marveling at the crowd. There were more people in town tonight than he'd known there were in a thirty-mile radius. The first couple he met was Betty and Alf Nyborg. They were moving slowly. Betty carried a bag from the hardware store as Alf struggled awkwardly with a pair of ill-fitting crutches.

"Alf, what happened to you?"

"He got what he deserves," his wife Betty said cheerfully. "I've told him a hundred times that he's too old to be jumping up and down off machinery like he does. Finally, his ankle told him the same thing."

Alf gave a guttural grunt as if he disagreed, but was wise enough not to say so.

"It's only sprained, Doc Ambrose said, but that he'd better be careful in the future. Next time something happens it will probably be a break. His bones are the same age as the rest of him. I'm glad Doc said something. I've told Alf he needs help around the farm, but he's too proud to ask for it."

By now her husband was glaring at her with such intensity that it might have made a lesser women shrink back, but not Betty. "I told him he should ask our son Jerome if he would come back to the farm and help out. Jerome thinks the realty market in the cities isn't such a good place to be these days and he's looking for another job. Why not farm?"

"He doesn't want anything to do with our place," Alf said gruffly.

"He might if you two would set things right between you," Betty answered calmly. "It would be a blessing to see father and son working together again."

Alf looked as if he were about to erupt with annoyance. "Betty, you know how it is between Jerome and me..."

"I wish you the best with that ankle," Alex hurried to intercede. "Fortunately, these decisions don't have to be made right this minute. I'm heading toward the music. Would you like to come along?"

His words defused the situation, at least for a moment. Alex had had enough run-ins with Alf to know he wasn't prepared for another one, particularly on Main Street on Saturday night.

"Thanks, Pastor, but we're heading home. Alf's ankle is hurting him. That's why he's even crankier than usual." Betty smiled at Alex. "Pray for him, will you?"

It was not just Alf's ankle she wanted him to pray for, Alex knew, but his cantankerous and stubborn spirit as well. "I will, I promise." He didn't add that Alf and Betty had been on the top of his prayer list since the day he'd moved to North Dakota and discovered that Alf was nourishing and promoting the rift between Alex's two parishes. Things were changing slowly. The history quilt about the pioneer families the ladies were making was a huge step in the right direction.

He watched Alf hobble off with his wife at his side.

Alex moved against the wall of the bank when a pack of young teens took up the entire sidewalk as they moved by, like a school of fish. Alex thought of his nephew Jared and wondered how he'd enjoy being part of such a group. Maybe he could use a few new friends. Alex recognized one bright redhead in the pack. It was Andy Packard, and he looked very happy to be away from home. He was laughing and talking and acting like a normal young teen. Andy was the Packard boy who was saving his money, according to Will, so he could run away from home.

"Hey, Preacher!" Andy moved out of the crowd and walked toward Alex as the others moved on.

It occurred to Alex that he should set up a youth group at church in the fall.

"Hi, yourself, Andy. Is your family in town tonight?"

"Nah. Just me. I weeded Lauren Carlson's garden this afternoon and she said she'd take me to town for a couple hours before she brought me home."

Alex tipped his head toward the throng moving down the street. "Are those your friends?"

"Nah, not really. A couple of them, maybe. Most of them are older than me." His voice was laced with longing.

"And you'd like to be older too?"

"Yeah, old enough so I could move out on my own. Then I wouldn't have to stay home and babysit. Will's easy, 'cause he's always out with Rose, riding his bike or over at your place. But those twins are a handful. Yesterday Ma and Pa went to get a belt for his rig and left me home with them. They weren't in the house two seconds and one of 'em stuck a dinner knife in an electric outlet." Andy scowled. "Little goof-ups."

"Was anyone hurt?"

"Nah, the breaker went off, but the knife is still in there. I wasn't about to take a chance on pulling it out just in case, you know?" Andy scuffed his sneaker-clad toe on the sidewalk. "I gotta get out of there before I go crazy."

"If you 'went' somewhere, where would that be?" Alex was curious.

Andy was far more communicative when he was away from the rest of the family.

"I dunno. I'm just a kid. Maybe someplace quiet where I could read."

That statement couldn't have surprised Alex more. "Read?"

"Yeah. About science and math mostly, and mysteries. I love mysteries."

Alex didn't even think about the words that came out of his mouth next. "It's quiet at the church. Bring a book and you can sit in the shade, if you like. If it rains, you can come inside."

"You mean it?" Andy's blue eyes, so much the color of his brother's, lit with anticipation.

"I must. I just said it." Alex felt wonderment himself. Had he just invited another little Packard into his life?

Andy dropped his eyes to the ground again. "Thanks," he said softly. "I'll see if the library is still open tonight. I've been kinda jealous of Will getting to be at your place all the time."

Alex was touched by the admission. This was an interesting child, every bit as remarkable as his little brother once one got to know him. "What do you want to be when you grow up?"

"A doctor." It was clear he'd considered this for some time.

"What kind of doctor?"

"A pediatrician maybe. I found a book on childhood diseases at the library and it was pretty interesting. I looked up baby measles because the twins got them. They're really called roseola." He pronounced each syllable separately. "There's lots of good stuff in books but there are some pretty gross pictures in them too. The mumps pictures aren't so bad but…"

"I thought you were sick and tired of kids," Alex commented.

"Yeah, well, I am."

"Then why would you want to be a pediatrician?" Alex found this entire conversation fascinating.

"'Cause I'm used to them, that's why. You've been to my house. You know what I mean. And I'm not sick of other people's kids, just ours."

The mob of teens was coming back toward them on the other side of the street. Someone yelled out, "Andy, are you coming or not?"

"Gotta go," Andy said.

"Maybe I'll see you at the church one day soon." The smile on the boy's face was a rich reward for such a simple invitation, Alex thought. "I'll look forward to it."

As he turned again to walk toward the park, Clarence Olson nearly barreled into him. Clarence's large stomach cleared away pedestrian traffic on either side of him, and the way he was swinging his arms made Alex think of the rotors of an out-of-control windmill.

"Anybody besides you in the foot race?" he inquired mildly as Clarence came to a halt in front of him.

"Sorry, Reverend, it's just that things *aren't right*." Clarence thrust a sheet of writing paper into Alex's face. "Look, a grocery list!"

Alex peered at the paper in Clarence's outstretched hand. *Milk, butter, sugar, tuna fish, macaroni, hamburger buns, instant oatmeal, vanilla wafers, chocolate syrup, frozen dinners*. "It's definitely a grocery list."

"But it's all *wrong*, don't you see?"

"Looks pretty much like mine, except I usually add orange juice and coffee."

"No, that's not it. This is just plain *wrong*."

Before Alex could inquire further, Clarence launched into the explanation. "I don't know what Lydia is thinking. We don't eat these ready-made things. Since when has she purchased buns? She bakes them every week. And instant oatmeal? What's wrong with the good old-fashioned kind she cooks on the stove? Same for the chocolate sauce. And frozen dinners? The only time we've ever had those in the house was when Lydia broke her foot. Then Jacob rigged up a stool on wheels for her to sit on so she could get around the kitchen with her cast. It worked slick. She was back to cooking in no time."

Maybe she's just *found* her mind, Alex thought but didn't say so.

Clarence's tirade sputtered to a halt. "And then she handed me this and told me I should do the shopping for once. I don't know what's gotten into my sister. She should probably have her blood pressure checked, or something. Maybe she needs a pill."

If only that were the remedy for dissatisfaction and rebellion, Alex thought. Poor Clarence was in for a rude awakening.

"Where *is* Lydia?" Alex asked. Maybe he should warn her that too many changes at once might make Clarence apoplectic and cause *him* to have the stroke.

"I have no idea. Her friend Ruby Smith wanted her to meet her cousin who is here visiting her from Minnesota. Apparently Lydia met him once at a church conference and he'd inquired after her."

Lydia was a quick learner, Alex had to give her that. She'd already managed to start the weaning process in a big way.

"Clarence, have you seen Lila Mason this evening? I've walked up and down the street looking for her."

"Sometimes she goes into the Cozy Corner Café. Did you look there?"

"No. I'll check there next." Why had Lila chosen tonight to be so elusive? "Thanks. I'll look there. If you'll excuse me…"

The Cozy Corner was packed, every seat taken. It was no wonder, as there was a PIE AND COFFEE, ONE BUCK sign in the front window. The aromas of burgers frying and coffee brewing were tantalizing. Alex's mouth began to water. Someone stood up and walked away from the counter, and Alex jumped into his place.

Mazie Torson saw him from across the room and made a beeline for him.

"Hey, Mazie."

"How are you doing, Reverend? Pie for you? I recommend the lemon meringue tonight."

"Sounds fine to me." He drummed his fingers on the counter. "Has Lila Mason been in tonight?" He was beginning to sound like a broken record, he thought, and he wasn't even sure why he was doing this.

Mazie absentmindedly swabbed at the counter with a towel, squinted slightly and looked over Alex's shoulder. "Don't quite remember. It's been especially busy today. She's usually here, I think. Sorry I can't help you."

It was as if Lila was a human apparition. Everyone thought they'd seen her, but no one could tell him where or when. She was a beloved little shadow flitting around the fringes of the community. Alex recalled the concoction he had seen on her stove, the questionable food that sat indefinitely on her counter and the sweet confusion she exhibited. He found it all troubling. "If you see her, will you tell her Reverend Armstrong is looking for her?"

"Sure thing. Don't worry. Lila's around here somewhere. She always is."

At that moment, Lydia Olson entered the café in the company of a man and woman Alex didn't recognize. They took over a just-vacated booth, and Lydia, looking as girlish as one her age could look, waved him over. She was wearing makeup, Alex realized. Lipstick. Blush. There was even more pouf in her hair. He suspected a curling iron. Astounding.

"Pastor, I'd like you to meet my friends." She gestured toward the woman. "This is Ruby Paulson. We've known each other for years. She lives in Wheatville. And this is her cousin Johann Paulson. Johann is a retired engineer. Trains, that is."

The man stood up, grasped Alex's hand and gripped it so hard that

Alex almost yelped in pain. "Glad to meet you. I haven't visited Grassy Valley for some time. It's a pleasure to be back. In fact, I'm enjoying it so much that I'm going to stay at my cousin Ruby's and do some work for her around the house. The place needs painting, for one thing." His eyes sparkled like a man content with his life. "That's the benefit of being retired. I get to do exactly what I want. How about you?"

"I'm new to town. I moved here a little over three months ago, so I'm discovering it for the first time. My job started the first of May. I'm the new pastor at Lydia's church."

The skin around Johann's eyes crinkled when he smiled. He looked fondly at Lydia. "I'm rediscovering a few things myself."

Was that a blush on Lydia's features?

Alex made a polite amount of small talk and excused himself. Odd things were happening. He couldn't find Lila. Lydia had decided to liberate herself from the tyranny of her brothers' culinary demands, and, if his instinct was correct, she'd just hooked a live one in the gentleman friend department.

In a haze, he wandered outside to find Dixon and Mark Nash outside, leaning against the side of the building. They were chatting and watching people stroll by.

"There you are," Dixon said. "Ready to go home yet?"

"Whenever you are." Alex's brow furrowed. "I just wish I'd been able to locate Lila tonight. I've had her on my mind all day." They hadn't made it even halfway down the street when Dixon's cell phone rang. Alex listened to his one-sided conversation.

"Yes, he's with me. Why? Yeah, he was looking for her. Okay, I'll tell him. Have you called Doc Ambrose? Okay, thanks." He snapped the cell phone shut and frowned.

"What's going on?"

"That was Mazie Torson. She was wondering if I knew where you were. She said you'd been asking about Lila and she wanted you to know that Lila had come into the café after you'd gone."

"Good," Alex said. "I'm glad she turned up. I couldn't get her out of my mind tonight. Everyone seemed to *think* she was in town, but no one could remember actually seeing her."

"No, not so good. She collapsed in the restroom at the café. Mazie is really rattled, and since you were concerned about Lila earlier, she thinks we should come right away."

They reached the café in less than two minutes. There were people lingering outside the door and some were inside, seated at the tables, their food untouched. Mazie was standing in the doorway of the hall that led to the restrooms. She was holding a spatula and waving away anyone who tried to come close.

She dropped her hand, however, when Dixon and Alex arrived. "Thank goodness you're here. Everybody wants to help but I didn't want anyone to move her…just in case. Did you see Doc Ambrose coming?"

"I'd like to talk to her, if I could, Mazie."

The woman stepped aside. "I'm going to get a blanket out of my car." She moved away, turning over the responsibility of Lila to Dixon and Alex.

A faint moan came through the open door of the ladies' restroom. Spinning into action, the two men were inside and by the prone body on the floor in a heartbeat.

Lila lay in a crumpled heap near the sinks. It was as if she'd tried to use one to pull herself upright. The contents of her stomach had been vomited all over the floor and the poor woman herself. "My good dress," she mewled weakly.

"What do you think it is?" Dixon asked. His face had grown very pale and a little green.

"I'm no doctor, but if I had to guess, I'd say food poisoning. Do you think Doc Ambrose called an ambulance?"

Dixon frowned. "It will have to come from Wheatville. I'll call the hospital and check." Dixon pulled out his cell phone and began to dial.

Mazie thrust a blanket through the door and disappeared. Alex focused all his attention on Lila, gently tucking the comforter around her.

Beads of sweat had broken out on Lila's brow. She tried to say something, but no words came out.

"Don't try to talk. Help is coming." Alex stood up and moved toward the single window in the room. He opened it and took a deep breath of fresh air. He felt a little like throwing up himself.

When he went back to Lila, she'd closed her eyes and her breathing was slightly less labored. Poor little thing. How frightened she must be. Now that she was getting help she could relax. God had been prompting him today, pointing him toward this vulnerable woman. Lord, never let me forget to listen to You whether or not I understand what You're saying....

CHAPTER ELEVEN

Doc Ambrose, a portly, avuncular man, arrived almost immediately.

"Hi, Doc." Dixon tipped his head toward the floor where Lila lay. She seemed to be dozing, exhausted probably. "She doesn't look good."

"Go to my car and get the two pillows out of the back seat, will you?"

The doctor bent over the tiny woman to take her pulse and listen to her heart. "I've told her a dozen times she shouldn't be drinking those concoctions of hers," Doc said grimly. "I said one of them might poison her."

Doc Ambrose shook his head and sighed. Lila groaned a little, but Doc talked soothingly to her in a low voice as he moved around the pillows Dixon had produced in order to support her body. "The ambulance will be here soon, Missy. You've got yourself one bad bellyache, don't you?"

Mazie handed a basin of warm water into the room with a small dish towel. "Will this help?"

"Indeed." As Doc Ambrose gently washed the vomit from Lila's face and hair, Alex took her hand. Silently he prayed for her and gave thanks that Lila had collapsed here and not at home where she might have lain for hours—or days.

He saw the ambulance's flashing red lights outside the café window, and in a moment the tiny room was filled with medical personnel and a stretcher. Alex and Dixon backed out the door and joined the crowd on the sidewalk.

Alex took his first deep breath.

"You were right, Alex, about looking for Lila," Dixon said. "Poor old thing. Who knows what might have happened if she'd lain at her house until someone found her?" They sank into silence, both lost in their own thoughts, until the medical crew burst through the front door with the stretcher. Lila's form was so small that it barely made a bump beneath the blankets.

Lila turned her head and saw them. She opened her mouth to speak, but then, as if it took too much effort, she closed it again and her eyes drifted shut. In moments, the ambulance pulled away.

"Do you think she'll be okay?" Alex asked Doc Ambrose as he thought of Lila's ashen complexion and shallow breathing.

"She should be...this time...but she can't risk any more close calls. I'm going to follow the ambulance to Wheatville in my car. After that I'll know more." Doc joined them, wiping his hands on a towel. "Frankly, I'm not sure what we'll do with her. Her memory is bad and she can't seem to understand the danger she puts herself in when she doesn't refrigerate her food."

"Or picks weeds from the side of the road, calls them alfalfa, cooks and drinks them." Alex hesitated. "What will happen to her? She certainly doesn't have money to pay for extra care."

"I suppose the county will have to get involved. Lila's a proud woman. Taking 'handouts,' as she calls them, will go against every-thing in her," Doc said bluntly. He sighed wearily and leaned against the wall. "I'm getting too old for this."

"Don't say that, Doc," Dixon said. "You're all we have. We can't always wait for an ambulance to come. We need someone local to call for help."

"I know that when someone's hurt or sick, waiting for help can feel like an eternity, but the fact of the matter is, I should have retired two years ago. I've only hung on because I know how much people depend on me.

"Trouble is, when I retire, I don't think the physicians' group in Wheatville will hire someone new to go into the satellite clinic in Grassy Valley."

"You think they'll shut it down?"

"I went to an administration meeting last month and that's the way it sounds. It's hard enough to get doctors for Wheatville, and there is little or no interest from new physicians to man a satellite clinic forty-plus miles from the nearest movie theater or fast-food joint—other than the Hasty Tasty, that is."

"So they aren't even going to try?" Dixon sounded dumbfounded.

"They will try, but I don't know with how much enthusiasm. It costs quite a bit to keep a doctor here."

"They don't care if somebody dies out here because medical help can't get here in time?" Dixon flushed, his tone indignant.

Doc Ambrose looked at him sadly. "They care, all right. But if finances won't support it…" He shrugged resignedly. "I'll stay on as long as I can, but my wife is nagging me to buy a motor home and start traveling. I promised her we'd start shopping for one soon. I don't know how long I can hold her off. Not that I really want to. Watching the sun set over the ocean sounds pretty good to me right now." He touched his soiled shirt. "Being a physician can be messy business."

Slowly he bent down, picked up his bag. "I have a favor to ask of you two. Will you go out to Lila's place and collect whatever it is you think she might have eaten? Food poisoning is one thing, but if she cooked something toxic into her brew, we'll need to know about it."

"We'll do it right now," Dixon said.

"Good. I'll talk to you later then."

The crowd had dissipated with the departure of the ambulance, and the café was empty.

Alex jumped when Dixon slammed his fist into the wall of the hallway. "We can't be without a doctor," Dixon said furiously. "This area is already struggling to hang on to its people. Without a doctor even more will leave. I wouldn't want to have small children in a place where I couldn't get stitches sewed, an earache treated or a broken arm set. And much of the population is elderly. What are they supposed to do? Many of them—like Hans and Hilda Aadland—refuse to drive to Wheatville already because they're uncomfortable with it. Brunie would never get Bessie to ride in a car that long." He scraped his fingers through his newly trimmed and tamed hair. "What a mess." Then he eyed Alex. "You're a big-city guy, maybe you have some ideas. What do you say?"

"I say," Alex said, "that I'm as clueless as you about this. All I know is that it seems wise for the community to start their own search for a doctor. It doesn't sound like Wheatville is going to be any help to us." And tonight was proof of how much this little town needed a physician.

He looked at his watch. "We'd better get going if we're going to get to Lila's yet tonight."

Lila's house was on the same road as the parsonage and Dixon's place so they headed north out of town, driving slowly.

"Even the air feels different here," Alex commented. "Velvety."

"Harvest nights," Dixon said as if that explained everything. "When we were kids, Emmy and I slept outside in our tent every night until Mom hauled us in. If she hadn't, we probably would have woken up one morning with snow on the tent. The only bad thing I've ever found about fall is the fact that winter is right on its heels."

As they passed the road to the parsonage, Dixon's pickup hit a rut and veered to the right. "This road needs a good grader operator and blade work," Dixon commented. "Maybe I could ask one of the county commissioners if the road crew will do it. I don't mind paying for it. This is going to turn into a cow path soon and I don't want my teeth rattling out of my head when I drive home."

They pulled into Lila's yard. The house was swathed in shadows. He swung the door of the pickup open and jumped out.

Alex followed. As he did so, he felt a sharp pain in his ankle. "Ow."

"What happened?" Dixon came around to his side of the truck.

"I fell into something. Gopher hole, I think."

"Lila had chickens a couple years ago. They dug up the yard and the holes never got filled in. I'll have to put that on my list as well."

"Helping her could be a full-time job," Alex commented, wincing. He slowly moved his foot back and forth to make sure nothing was seriously damaged.

"You've got that right. Come on."

Together they approached the house and moved onto the porch. It squealed like a banshee when they stepped onto it.

Alex tried the knob and pushed on the door. "Locked. Now what?"

Ignoring Alex's effort, Dixon pushed him aside, put a brawny shoulder to the door and pushed. It swung open with a screech. "Not locked. Stuck." He reached his hand around the door frame and flipped on a light switch.

"It could have been this." Alex lifted the lid off the pot of stew he'd seen when he'd visited the woman earlier. It was back on the stove, even after her promise to refrigerate it, still jellied and thick. It also now had a grayish cast he hadn't noticed before. "I saw it here earlier and she promised to refrigerate it, but it doesn't appear that she did."

"We'll take that with us. And this." Dixon held up the large bowl in which he'd put all Lila's drying herbs and plants. "There's a jar of something suspicious in the refrigerator."

"Are we going to drive it to Wheatville?"

Dixon studied him. "'We'? I don't think so. I'll drive it over. Right now, more than anything, you need a shower and a good night's sleep."

That, at least, was a prescription Alex could take.

∽

The next morning, he was amazed to find that everyone he shook hands with on their way out of church already knew that Lila Mason was in the hospital. The grapevine was actually faster than the Internet, he decided. One didn't even have to open one's e-mail.

To his surprise, Lydia's friend Ruby and her cousin Johann were in church. They sat in the pew behind Lydia and Clarence, and Lydia sported a sly smile throughout the sermon, which nearly caused Alex to lose his place in his sermon more than once.

Gandy followed him into the church office as he was putting the leftover bulletins in the recycle bin. "Some of the ladies are going to Lila's tomorrow to clean up her place. Even a couple from All Saints volunteered, Amy Clayborn, for one. What do you think about that?"

"Don't eat the food," he said grimly. Not that anyone would be able to stomach anything once they saw the mess. "We should open a bank account in which to deposit donations for Lila. How do you think that would go over? Dixon says she will need money to pay her hospital bills."

"Good, I think." Gandy twiddled with a pencil she'd removed from her hair. "She's got one distant cousin in the state of Washington. I called her this morning to tell her what happened. She said Lila doesn't have much of anything financially, but we already knew that. Worse yet, she said that early onset dementia runs in their family. She wasn't even surprised by Lila's troubles. She sounded resigned to it, as if she'd expected it."

"The news keeps getting worse." Alex sat down in his desk chair and put his head in his hands.

"I suppose it's a possibility she could go back to her house once she's well. I wouldn't trust her to cook, though. Somebody would have to bring in meals."

"Who would that be?"

"I have no idea. Lauren's starting the food shelf, maybe she can think of something. The people of the church are Lila's family. Maybe we can help out. We're blessed to be a blessing, right? Isn't that the way it goes?"

"It's a wonderful idea, Gandy, but I think in the long run we'll have to look for a more permanent solution. I'm planning to visit Lila this afternoon. I'll see what I learn then."

Gandy, for once wordless, nodded and left the room.

Alex glanced at his wristwatch and whistled under his breath. He was going to have to fly low to get to All Saints on time.

"You're late," commented Amy Clayborn, who was jostling a fussy baby in the foyer when he raced through the door. "The organist is running through her prelude pieces a second time."

"Has anyone noticed?" Alex ran his fingers through his hair and hoped for the best.

"Of course, but no one minds. Everyone has heard about Lila. I think everyone is doing a little extra praying."

Breathing a sigh of relief, Alex strode toward the front of the congregation. He felt a sermon on loving and caring for one's neighbor coming on.

After church, Alex lingered until the last congregant had left before driving toward home from All Saints. He felt restless, so instead of going home he stopped at the Hilltop church and took a walk around the cemetery. Oddly, it was a place that calmed rather than upset him. Green grass, beautiful flowers and stillness defined the burial ground. More than once he'd walked the rows of tombstones, reading family names and imagining how each of these people might have contributed to the community.

He was near the back when he decided to have another look at the unmarked grave he'd discovered. To his surprise, the plot had changed from the last time he'd examined it. The earth had been turned over and raked smooth. The grave was now a mound of freshly turned black soil.

Who would go to that trouble when they hadn't bothered to put up a monument or marker? It struck him as peculiar, but because his mind was full of things more pressing, he dismissed his unease.

He drove to the parsonage to change clothes before heading to the hospital to visit Lila, but he stopped at the shed when he saw Will's battered bike leaning against it. An idea flickered in his mind. He should suggest a trade to the boy. Will could use the shed if he attended Sunday school this fall. Was that an inducement—or was it bribery? He wasn't sure the seminary would approve of such methods, but on the other hand, they didn't know Will Packard.

All thoughts of ministerial chicanery left his head as soon as he walked through the door and found Will sitting against a wall, his head drooping between his knees, his clenched fists jammed into his eye sockets, weeping. He shook with sobs, as if every fiber of his being was grieving. What was so horrible that it could make a child suffer so?

"Will?" Alex edged toward him.

Will looked up; wet tracks ran down his face, and tears dripped from his jawline onto his well-worn blue shirt. Will's mouth worked for a moment before anything came out. "He killed it, Reverend Alex! I saw him do it. He ran right over it and he knew it was there under his tire. Bucky Chadwick is a murderer, that's what he is. Can we call the police or something?" Will clenched his fists. "If I was bigger, I'd beat that guy till he looked like mashed potatoes…no, pig slop. I'd beat him till he was pig slop!"

It took a few minutes, but finally Alex got out of Will that he'd seen Bucky run over a baby rabbit that had taken shelter beneath one of the tires of Bucky's truck. Not only had he run over the creature, but he'd backed up and run over it again…and again. Bucky had laughed, Will told him, as if it were the funniest thing he'd ever done. Then he'd driven off with his radio blaring, a big smile on his acne-spotted face.

Alex dropped to his knees beside Will and took him in his arms. This only made Will cry harder, and soon Alex's pristine white shirt was soggy with tears and streaked with dirt. Alex simply waited it out.

Finally, when Will was empty of tears and probably dehydrated as a piece of beef jerky, Alex helped him up and led him toward the parsonage where he poured the child a large glass of lemonade. Will gulped it down and Alex filled the glass again. After the third glass, Will gave an enormous burp, leaned back in the chair and sighed. Alex couldn't ever remember seeing a more pitiful picture.

"Feel any better?"

"Yeah, but that rabbit's still dead. Why'd he do a thing like that? It was just a little fellow…." Will's tears threatened again.

"Bucky is sick," Alex said firmly. "Mentally healthy people don't do that sort of thing." This was more alarming than anything else he'd heard about Bucky. The young man might be truly dangerous.

"So let's put him somewhere so he can get well." Will's expression darkened and his eyes narrowed. "If he can't get well, let's let him get run over. My dad says he believes in 'an eye for an eye.'"

So Earl Packard could quote Scripture too.

"That was said in the Old Testament. It's true that in Exodus there is a verse that says 'you shall give life for life, eye for eye, tooth for tooth, hand for hand.'"

"So we can give a runover for a runover?" Will sounded more animated now at the thought of violence toward Bucky. "Who can we get to run Bucky over?"

Alex couldn't tell the boy that initially he'd had a similar thought about Bucky...and had quickly asked for forgiveness for the notion. "That's not the Christian way, Will. When Jesus came, He gave us new direction. He said in Matthew, 'You have heard that it was said, "An eye for an eye and a tooth for a tooth. But I say to you, do not resist an evildoer. But if anyone strikes you on the right cheek, turn the other also."'"

"That little bunny doesn't have a cheek to turn no more," Will retorted. "So what do we do about that? What is the Christian way to get even?"

Will gave Alex more sermon ideas than anyone else Alex had ever come across. The child brought up questions so simple and profound that it sometimes blew him away.

"Proverbs says, 'Do not say "I will repay evil"; wait for the Lord, and he will help you.'"

Will tipped his chin upward and turned to stare out the window. "When's God coming to repay Bucky's evil?"

"He'll decide that."

"You mean we have to *wait*? Bucky needs to get what's coming to him *now*!"

Alex didn't disagree. He was eager to see Bucky get his comeuppance too, but he was more confident than Will that God would work

His way in Bucky. And until that time, Bucky's mother Myrtle needed to know what had happened. Clarence Olson had told him the only person who could handle Bucky was his mother. If she were losing her grip on the young man, who knew what Bucky might do?

"Tell you what, Will. Let's pray that Bucky gets what God knows he needs. God can handle Bucky."

"He's the only One then." Will scrubbed at his eyes with his fists. "God's gonna have His hands full this time."

CHAPTER TWELVE

The hospital in Wheatville was small but attractive, set on rolling grounds dotted with old trees. The original building of redbrick, ornate ironwork and double-hung sash windows had been added on to several times, each addition taking the best attributes of the old building and capitalizing on them. The result was a quaint-looking building that embraced both the old and the new.

But before Alex entered the hospital, he had something to do. He called Myrtle Chadwick. "Myrtle, this is Alex Armstrong. Do you have a minute to talk? I'd like to chat with you about your son."

"What's Bucky done now?" Myrtle asked, frustration in her voice.

He told her about the rabbit. There was a long silence at the other end of the line. "I don't know what to do with that boy anymore," she finally said. "I wish his daddy was still alive. He'd be able to keep him in line. It wasn't until after Herman died that Bucky got so bad. He was a difficult child, mind you, but this…"

"I'm just concerned…" Alex realized he was tiptoeing around the subject. "I'll ask you right out, Myrtle: do you think Bucky is prone to violence? He's hurt a lot of animals. Is there any danger he might hurt a child?" Will was always in Bucky's face over his critters. The last thing Alex wanted was for Will to be hurt by someone three or four times his size.

"I've never thought so before. There's a sweet spot in Bucky too, you know. You'd be surprised how often he brings presents home for me, things he's purchased at Good Finds, Good Flowers or the hardware store. Sam Waters carries a selection of gift items, you know."

Instead of being charmed, Alex immediately wondered where Bucky was getting the money for such things. He chose not to ask Myrtle right now. "I'm concerned that if Bucky is hurting small things, he might also, well, you know..."

She was quiet for a long time before she spoke. "Bucky's got a lot of anger inside. I don't want to think he'd hurt anyone but can't say it's impossible. I'll watch him more closely, Reverend. That's all I can do."

"I know. Don't blame yourself. Bucky's making his own bad choices. I just wanted you to be aware." He could hear Mrs. Chadwick snuffling back tears.

Feeling disconcerted and sad about his conversation, Alex tried to move it out of his mind as he took the elevator to the second floor where Lila's room was located. He walked down the long, tiled hallway to room 217 and tapped on the half-open door. "Lila? It's Pastor Alex."

A dark-haired, middle-aged nurse opened the door. "Come in. Lila has been hoping you'd come by to visit." She stepped aside and Alex walked into the small, immaculate room.

The head of the bed was raised and Lila was propped up on a bank of pillows. She was nearly as white as the bedding and looked small as a child beneath the covers. Her graying hair was pinned up with bobby pins, and she clutched a TV remote as if it was a lifeline. She appeared as frail as the gossamer strands of a spider's web.

"You came," she breathed.

As Alex moved closer Lila reached out her free hand for his. "I was so ill. I do believe I would have died if I hadn't had help." Her lips trembled.

"I'm glad you didn't do that," Alex said gently.

"I'm not afraid of dying," Lila said. "Jesus has me covered, you know. It's the process that scares me—especially after how I felt yesterday."

"Let's make it a goal not to let that happen for a few more years, Lila. You do know, however, that you'll have to give up cooking concoctions and leaving food out on the counters."

"That's what Doc Ambrose says too." Lila's small face crumpled. "I have to have my health drinks! I'll be sick all the time without them."

Alex restrained himself from pointing out that it could have been a health drink that made her so deathly ill in the first place. "Once you get well, Lila, I want you to visit the church office. I'll show you how we can find you a safer, easier way to get those nutrients you want." *No weeds included.*

"How's that?" She stared at him with suspicion. "You don't grow anything there."

"We'll look on the Internet. You can buy healthy mixtures online. I'll help you. They'll be even better for you than the ones you cook up."

"More expensive too," she said gloomily. "My drinks are *free*."

"I'll make sure these are too," he assured her. He'd buy them himself rather than have Lila go through this again.

"You're a good man. I'm glad God sent you," she said as her eyes drifted shut.

"She'll doze for a couple minutes and wake up again. Poor little thing is all worn out."

Alex had almost forgotten the nurse was still in the room. "I'll slip out now. Tell her I'll be back to visit her again."

On his way through Grassy Valley, Alex stopped at Red's to get gas. Red himself came out to fill the tank.

"How's it going, Preacher?" Red greeted him with his ever-ready smile.

"Fine, thanks." Alex jumped out of the car to clean the windows. He still wasn't accustomed to having someone pump his gas for him. Full-service stations had gone the way of dinosaurs and, thanks to cell phones, phone booths in the city. "I enjoy this area very much. It's warm and connected…and safe, as if I've walked back in time to a more civilized era."

Red scowled as he topped off Alex's tank. "I don't know if that's so true anymore. Safe, I mean. Yesterday I might have agreed with you, but today I'm not so sure. Somebody smashed my outside vending machine last night and took all the money. I'd planned to empty it yesterday but didn't get around to it. Whoever the thief is got away with a lot of coins. Same thing happened to the vending machine over by the rest home. Takes a pretty gutsy crook to do that in such public places. Anybody could have driven by and caught him."

"But no one did."

"I called the police. They said it's happened before but not recently."

"Did they catch the culprit?"

"No. We hope it was somebody passing through. No one wants to believe someone from town would stoop to such a thing." Red tilted the hat back on his flame-colored hair. "This has always been a good place to live. I want it to stay that way."

"If it was local, do you have any suspicions about who might have done it?" Alex ventured. He hated hearing what Red was saying. Alex felt as if he'd been robbed as well.

"I might, but that's all they are, suspicions." He studied Alex for a moment. "I guess it wouldn't hurt to tell you. You're not likely to pass it on, right?"

"Not likely at all," Alex said. "Part of what I do best is hold people's confidences."

"Bucky Chadwick was in here the other day. He comes in a lot because his mother works here. If Myrtle weren't such a good worker—and a gem of a woman—I'd let her go just to get Bucky out of the store. Anyway, after he left, I noticed that some items were gone from the shelves—a couple boxes of ammunition, a wrench set and a box of chocolate bars. Oh yes, and all the pennies out of that dish by the cash register, the coins people can use so they don't have to break a bill to pay what they owe."

"That's small-time, petty thievery!" Alex was surprised at how indignant he felt that someone had defiled his image of his new hometown.

"My thoughts exactly. Bucky's not bright, but hopefully he's not dim-witted enough to pull something like that." Red patted the hood of Alex's van. "I'll put this on your bill. You can pay me some other time."

That was another thing to which Alex wasn't accustomed. Around Grassy Valley, every storekeeper trusted him to pay for his purchases at the end of the month. Remarkable.

When he arrived at the church, Gandy was there. At least it resembled Gandy. She was dressed in jeans and a man's T-shirt spattered with paint, and she wore a patterned babushka-like affair on her head. Her wild mane of hair erupted out the back of the scarf. She was pale and grim and busy gathering cleaning rags from the storeroom closet.

"What's going on?" Alex asked, coming up behind her.

As she stood up, she knocked over the clump of brooms and mops leaning against the wall, and they fell around her like pick-up sticks. The largest of the mops clunked her on the head.

"Rats." She shoved at the offending cleaning equipment and it fell, scattering in all directions. "This just isn't my day."

"Whose day is it?" Sometimes Alex had to do everything in his power to keep from laughing at his secretary's antics.

"Lila Mason's, I guess. Some of the church ladies—me, Nancy, Lauren, Betty, Amy Clayborn and Lilly Sumptner—decided we should go to her house and clean things up for her for when she comes home."

Gandy made a horrible face. "Reverend, it's the worst mess I've ever seen. Although she tried to keep it tidy, the place needs a thorough cleaning from top to bottom...or to be burned to the ground. It breaks my heart to think we didn't see what was going on. Why, I was there looking for her sewing machine only days ago. Why didn't I look closer? It's no wonder the poor thing got sick. We found cucumbers fuzzy with mold and milk that had not only gone sour but was so thick we couldn't pour it out of the carton! Her clothes were hung up dirty and..." Her voice trailed off. "I'm ashamed of all of us, letting this go on."

She waved some rags in front of his nose. "I had to come here for more cleaning supplies. We used up everything we brought. Do you mind if I take the wood polish and the window cleaner?"

"Help yourself. Maybe your cleaning is premature," Alex said slowly. "Perhaps Lila can't go home after all."

"We can't let it wait. We've got it passable in there now, after throwing out everything in her cupboards. I found a can of tomatoes in there with an expiration date of 2007! Betty Nyborg is taking all the clothing, towels and linens home to wash. Lauren says she and Mike will come back and do windows. And Nancy says she has a quilt she just made that can replace the bedspread we threw out. Betty even talked Alf, of all people, into setting out mousetraps and ant traps, just in case."

So something good was coming out of this mess. Betty had actually gotten Alf Nyborg to do something for a member of Hilltop church. After the years he'd spent bitter, resentful and full of hard feelings, to have him do anything was a miracle.

"*And*," Gandy continued, "the quilting ladies from All Saints are going to make meals to put in the freezer so Lila doesn't try to cook. Althea and Amy are organizing it."

"Praise God," Alex said with feeling. Miracles sprang from the oddest places.

He stopped at his mailbox at the end of his driveway on the way home. He liked the fact that it was personally delivered to him every day. It was pleasant to open the box and see what surprises were in store for him—a book he'd ordered or a care package from Carol. Today there was a catalogue selling nuts and cheeses, a flyer from the grocery store, a coupon for an oil change from a garage in Wheatville and a package from Natalie. He blinked and did a double take. *A package from Natalie.*

He realized his hands were shaking while he opened the box. Inside it was a second, smaller parcel. The paper fell away from it to reveal a little gold box, and a smile spread across his features. Natalie had sent him the one thing she knew he couldn't resist. Carefully, he lifted the lid. There, nestled in a crimped brown cup, rested a single chocolate truffle.

The way to his heart, she'd teased him often, was chocolate.

Jt wasn't until after dinner that Alex returned his attention to the gift he'd received. That was, of course, because he was preparing Lydia's chicken potpie recipe by himself for the first time. He'd eaten an embarrassingly large amount and felt stuffed to the ears before he picked up the gold box that he'd left on the counter.

A small note was tucked into it. "Alex," it read, "I've never been to North Dakota. Is this a good time for a visit?"

It was her way of asking if he wanted to see her again, he knew. Did he want to try again to make their relationship work?

"What's going on?" Dixon asked from the doorway. "What are you concentrating on so hard that you didn't even hear me knock?"

"You could give a guy a heart attack doing that." Alex laid the note on the table, facedown.

Dixon sauntered in, noticed the remains of the potpie, took a plate from the cupboard and a fork from the drawer and dished himself a piece. "You looked like you were having a heart attack already. I thought I'd snap you out of it." He held up the portion. "Do you mind? It looks great."

"Finish it up. It's best the first meal, before the crust gets soggy. I can make another any time I want."

"Glad to hear it." Dixon dived into the food. After he'd eaten a few bites, he looked up again. "Now tell me what's going on."

"Remember my telling you about a woman named Natalie?"

"Your old girlfriend? The one who ran off with someone else? Of course."

"That relationship didn't work out for her."

Dixon nodded slowly. "I see."

Did he? Alex wondered. "I e-mailed her."

Dixon's eyebrows lifted toward his hairline but he said nothing. Instead he got up and put the rest of the potpie on his plate.

"She'll come to North Dakota for a visit if I invite her."

Dixon dropped back into his chair. "What do you think about that?" Dixon forked a bite into his mouth and closed his eyes to savor it.

"I don't know what I think." Alex scraped his fingers through his short dark hair and noticed he was ready for a trim. He'd have to go to Licks and Sticks next Saturday night. "On one hand, this is what I desperately wanted. For a long time I believed Natalie would be my wife, the mother of my children, and then she just pulled away and became very distant toward me."

Dixon went to the refrigerator and pulled out the milk.

"For a long time I prayed that God would heal our relationship," Alex said slowly. "That's what I wanted most. Finally I realized that I was praying for my wishes, not for God's will. Within days of praying that *God's* will be done, Natalie was gone. She told me she'd found someone else and left. If not for that, I might never have ended up here."

"Guess that means you'd be wise to pray for His will again, doesn't it?"

Alex laughed. "That, my friend, is the understatement of the century."

"What did she say?" Dixon put the milk on the table and went looking for dessert in the freezer. He pulled out a bucket of frozen chocolate chip cookies, put some on a plate, poured himself more milk and filled Alex's glass as well.

Alex found his friend's actions very comforting. He liked the fact that Dixon felt free to make himself at home. "She indicated that she's willing to come to Hilltop."

Dixon whistled through his teeth. "That is quite a switch from 'so long, buddy; don't let the door hit your backside on the way out.'"

"Frankly, I don't know if it's a good idea. This is my new life. I'm happy that it's not filled with old memories. Unless…"

"Unless it's what God wants and He is the One who's brought her back into your life?"

"Dixon, you could be a counselor, you know that? You're very perceptive."

"Nah, just been there, done that, where love is concerned. Be careful, my friend. If she comes, just don't let her mess up your head again." Dixon went for a toothpick in the holder on the table, then settled back in his chair and studied Alex. "Tell her not to come."

"It may already be too late for that," Alex said, feeling nervous in the pit of his stomach.

"How so?"

"I e-mailed her and told her she could come."

"Oh-oh. You're sunk, big-time." A smile tweaked one corner of Dixon's mouth. "That's the trouble with computers, you know. If you'd had to write her a letter, you'd have had time to rethink the issue and back out if you wanted."

"Don't write me off just yet. Just because she comes doesn't mean we'll get back together."

"Doesn't it?"

"Of course not!" Alex felt something akin to apprehension in his chest anyway. He'd loved her once, but could he really have confidence in her now, after what she'd done?

Dixon's cell phone rang and he dug in his pocket to find it.

"Dixon here." He sat up straighter and a wide smile flashed across his features. "Hey, sis, how are you? Good. Me? I'm sitting here with our new pastor. I just finished off his supper and now I'm counseling him on his love life." He scowled at the phone. "What do you mean you want to talk to him? You don't even know him. Okay, okay…" Dixon handed the phone to Alex. "Here. It's my sister Emmy."

Alex took the phone. He was certainly popular all of a sudden.

"Hi, Reverend Alex, this is Emmy Daniels. How are you?" There was amusement and a pleasant musical quality in the woman's voice.

"Fine, thank you. I…"

"I want to tell you to keep my brother in line. He'll eat you out of house and home, given half a chance, especially if you're a good cook. And as far as counseling? Just remember that you get what you pay for. I'm assuming my brother isn't charging you for this little talk you're having?"

"No. Of course not." Alex found himself smiling.

"My point exactly." Her laugh was rich and mellow across the miles. "Watch him for me, will you? He's the only twin brother I have, and even as big a tease as he is, I love him so much."

"I'll do my best."

"A girl can't ask for more. Now is he still there or did he run off when he realized I was going to tell you the truth about him?"

"He's a brave man, Emmy. He's still sitting right here, eating cookies. Here you are." Alex handed the phone back to Dixon and sat back to listen to Dixon's side of the banter.

When Dixon hung up, his eyes were dancing. "She's a cutie, my sister. Nosy, opinionated, stubborn and smart as a whip too, but I've forgiven her for that. Man, I miss that girl."

"You said she was coming soon."

"Not soon enough. Emmy's a good cook. You'll have to keep me from fading away before she gets here."

"There's no danger of that for a month or two," Alex said wryly. "Isn't your belt already on its last notch?"

"I'm trying to develop some 'love handles' since I'm so lovable, that's all." He stood up. "Thanks for the grub. You're getting to be a pretty good cook. I'll see you around." With a wave, he was gone.

Alex went to his office and stared at the inbox on his computer. There was something from Natalie. The note was short but it had the potential to turn his life upside down—again. *Alex, I'll be there a week from Wednesday.*

The next day, Gandy looked at him and raised one eyebrow until it disappeared beneath her hairdo. Alex, without saying a word, turned and fled from the church.

Gandy *knew* something. He could feel it. Maybe she was telepathic. Or the confusion and concern he felt were written all over his face. Whatever it was, he knew he couldn't spend any time with his secretary today or she would have him pumped dry of information within the hour. Dixon was right. He should have written her a letter and given himself more time to change his mind. What had he done?

She'd broken his heart. It was going to be awkward, at best, to have her visit. And yet... He thought about lonely Walter Englund. He'd had to do it, Alex realized, or he might have gone to his grave wondering if he should have at least tried to see if he and Natalie could make it work.

Desperately needing a change of scenery, he drove to Grassy

Valley to see the room Lauren had secured for the Grassy Valley
Food Shelf.

It was small, just a long, narrow room in the implement dealership's building, but it was all one could expect since the rent was free.
Mike had built shelves along the walls, and the newly donated staples
were tidily organized around the perimeter—cold cereal, pasta and
instant potatoes, canned goods and cake mixes—enough to get the
Bruuns, Tillie Tanner and dozens like them through a winter.

"What do you think?" Lauren came around the corner carrying
a case of baby food, which she set on the same shelf as the dispos-
able diapers.

"Great. You've already got a lot of food in here. I'm impressed."

"People have been so generous. When I get time, I'm going to
explore other means of funding, but this is a start. We have a long way
to go. We have no ability to store frozen things, for instance, or even
refrigerated items. That will come. When one does things by trial and
error, there are always a lot of trials and a good number of errors."

She pulled two stools from a closet. "I need a break. Have a chair.
What are you doing in town today?"

Alex looked at her suspiciously. Did she know something about…
no, of course not!

"You're looking rather…strained," she said. "Is something wrong?"

Apparently he was terrible at keeping secrets—everything seemed
to be written on his face whether he liked it or not.

Lauren listened carefully to his highly abbreviated and edited
explanation, and when he was done, she crossed her arms over her
chest. "So she's coming back."

"If I could somehow transport us back to when we were first
engaged—happily planning the future, talking about buying a home
and starting a family—and erase all that happened after… Still, there's

been a lot on my mind concerning forgiveness and reconciliation lately. I have to believe God's put it there." He smiled wryly. "And on a purely selfish note, do I risk being alone for the rest of my life or do I risk trying to make something work with her again?"

There, he'd said it. He'd summed up exactly what was bothering him. He didn't relish the idea of, as his grandmother had always said, jumping out of the frying pan and into the fire.

"What makes you think you'll be alone? She's not the only woman in the world."

"True." Alex glanced pointedly around the room. "But most of them aren't here either."

"I see your point. Of course there's Lolly...no?" Lauren studied his expression and chuckled. "Then maybe you're sunk, but I doubt it. You ask God to plan your days. Haven't you given Him your love life as well?"

He felt himself blush. "It always seems selfish of me...and trivial... to burden God with..." He stopped midsentence. "But I tell everyone else that nothing is too small for God to care about."

"Exactly. Take your own advice, Alex. He'll guide you through Natalie's visit. If you listen to Him, I guarantee you'll know what to do. Find His peace."

"Because things of God always bring peace," he said thoughtfully, knowing exactly what she meant.

"The old stomach test." Lauren smiled widely at him. "When I'm trying to make a decision, I tune in to my stomach. If it's calm in there, I'm pretty sure I've made the right decision. When it's roiling around in there and I feel my stomach is a volcano filled with hot lava, then I'm pretty sure I'm making a wrong one."

"So I should listen to my stomach on this one?"

"I would. Just don't eat anything strange while you're deciding.

You wouldn't want to get these things mixed up with indigestion." Sage advice dispensed, Lauren leaned down to open another of the donated boxes on the floor and picked something out. "Oh good, toilet paper!"

"Thanks for your counsel, Lauren, I feel better," Alex said. "Remind me to mention during announcements on Sunday what things you need for this place."

"Toilet paper, definitely. Peanut butter, pasta, sauce and pudding."

"I'll get right on it."

Lauren looked him straight in the eye. "And I'll start praying for you immediately."

"Thank you. I don't want to jeopardize anything now. I'm the happiest I've been in months, maybe years."

"Think about the words that just came out of your mouth, Alex." She wiped auburn hair away from her eye. "'Nuff said."

Feeling better, Alex headed to the hardware store to say hello to Sam Waters and pick up some nails. Something had possessed him as he'd seen nine-year-old Will sobbing his heart out over a dead bunny. He'd realized that there was no way Will could keep his scrappy little animal shelter going once the weather turned cold, so he'd ordered a few sheets of insulated wall board to finish the inside of the shed somewhat. It wouldn't solve all the problems of winter, but it would certainly extend the life of Will's animal sanctuary for a few months. Maybe he'd put some plastic over the window as well, just for good measure.

Sam's store was in an old building with a high tin ceiling. The tin also dropped down the sides of the walls for three feet. The hardwood floors rolled beneath his feet, and Alex wondered how Sam kept from feeling seasick in there, but the walls were full of every kind of notion or necessity anyone could need. There were bird feeders, coffeepots, paint displays and paring knives. As he looked more closely he saw that Sam was well-stocked with baking sheets, gift items, simple, inexpensive dishes and flatware, bug spray and garden supplies.

"Hey, Reverend," Sam greeted him. "What can I help you find?" Sam wore a walrus mustache and suspenders that held up a pair of faded denims. Though Sam was slender, Alex had never seen the man without the suspenders. It must be Sam's fashion statement, he'd decided, that and the heavy steel-toed boots he'd worn all summer long.

"Nails, a saw and some of that plastic people use to seal windows in the winter."

"Have you got a hair dryer?"

"No, but I'm not sure I need one. I just towel dry my hair."

Sam burst out in a hearty, knee-slapping laugh. "Not for you! For putting on that plastic. That's how you get it to seal to the window frame."

"The city slicker is caught again," Alex said, hoping his face wasn't turning too red. "I figured I'd read the directions when I got home." He'd never had a house drafty enough to worry about such a thing.

"I'll bet Lauren will lend you hers," Sam said. "Don't worry about it. If not, I'm sure the missus will let you use hers. How many nails do you want, a pound?"

Alex explained what he would be using them for. Sam nodded and shook nails onto his scale, estimating what it would take to do the job. He put them in a small brown paper sack.

"That Packard boy used to be wandering around in here every time he got a ride to town. Always asking me about building cages for animals and telling me about that pet skunk of his. I haven't seen much of him since you arrived." Sam eyed Alex. "You've been good for him, I hear. Mike Carlson told me about that shed you've let him use. Those Packard kids are smart as all get-out, but Minnie can't keep track of them all, let alone teach them much. It's a good thing you're doing for Will and for his mother too."

"I wasn't sure I'd be able to say this when I agreed to have him," Alex admitted, "but I enjoy having him and his 'critters' there. He's well-behaved because he knows I'll send him packing if he isn't, and he really keeps what he rescues in good shape. I did tell him no more skunks, though. Even now Rosie gives me the chills sometimes."

"Good idea," Sam said and handed Alex his package. "You might mention snakes are off-limits too."

With that cheerful thought, Alex walked back onto the street. The saw was awkward to carry and he was rearranging it beneath his arm when another familiar face approached him.

"Hi, Pastor. Remember me? Tina Curry, from All Saints?" Tina had a round face and round eyes that were covered by thick glasses. She wore her hair in a jaw-length bob and reminded Alex of a Dutch girl in an artist's rendering. "I wanted to tell you how excited I am to be working with Lauren at the new food shelf."

"I didn't know. Thank you, Tina. It's a great project." Another All Saints Fellowship parishioner on board a project with a Hilltop member!

"I've been wanting to do something for the community and this is perfect. I raise a big garden and I thought perhaps I could contribute fresh produce when I have it. And, if anyone who uses the food shelf is interested, I could teach them how to can so they could have healthy produce all winter."

"A brilliant idea. Be sure to talk to Lauren about it. I'm delighted you have such an interest. Offering classes is a brilliant idea."

"I want to help someone. It can't be one of my own, so I'll put my energy into this." Tina suddenly looked downcast, as if all the enthusiasm had been drained from her.

"One of your own?"

She grimaced. "I didn't really mean to say that."

"But you did."

"I'm having trouble with my son, that's all. He's eighteen running with a bad crowd from Wheatville. He won't hear a thing about it from me, and his father just says 'boys will be boys.' Being a boy is fine in my book, but being a *bad* boy is something quite different."

"Do you know what he's up to?"

"Just suspicions." Tina looked at him, her brows furrowed. "Pray for him, will you? His name is Kevin."

"I will. May we put him on the prayer lists at Hilltop and All Saints?"

"Put him on both of them. I need all the prayers we can get." Tina was silent a moment before adding, "Before our churches had this big split, we had one prayer list for both churches. Somewhere along the line I think All Saints wanted their own list. I suppose *certain people* didn't want to pray for Hilltop. Maybe we should start doing that again."

Alex hadn't even realized this was why Gandy made calls to two different prayer chains on Monday mornings. It hit him again how much he still had to learn about this complicated marriage between the two churches. "I think it's a wonderful idea, Tina. I'll do it immediately."

Tina nodded gratefully. "Thank you, Pastor Alex. You aren't nearly as bad as Alf Nyborg said you were going to be."

He took the backhanded compliment for what it was worth and bade Tina a pleasant good-bye.

It was midafternoon when Alex stopped at the church to work on a letter about the food shelf that he wanted inserted in the next bulletin. Gandy left the church just as he arrived to, as she put it, "bring All Saints into the fold, the fold of a quilt that is." She laughed at her little joke and told him she and Nancy Jenkins were driving a car full of ladies to All Saints to work on the township history quilt that told the story of their pioneers. The group included Mildred Holmquist, Mattie Olsen and Isabelle Johnson.

Isabelle, though somewhere in her nineties, usually drove her own car, a Buick she'd purchased two decades ago. It truly was one of those cars with low mileage driven by a little old lady only to church. That had sounded sweet and old-fashioned to Alex until her son Ralph told him that she had accumulated a series of warnings and tickets from the Grassy Valley police. Alex himself had seen her pull out of the church parking lot and suddenly shift into reverse without stopping the car first. If anyone could wear out an engine, it was Isabelle.

"We're doing this several afternoons in the next few weeks. Stop in for coffee," Gandy told him. "People bring cookies and they try to outdo each other. You'll like it."

He assured her he would and sent her on her way, glad for the quiet time for prayer and reflection. When Gandy was in the office, it was difficult for him to even think. Then the phone rang.

"Reverend Alex?" The voice was breathy, as if the speaker had been hurrying. "You need to learn to bake bread."

"Hello, Lydia, how are you?"

"I can't really talk now," Lydia Olson said enigmatically. "Let's just say that you're overdue for a cooking lesson."

"One of your brothers is in the house?" Alex guessed. "And you'd like to talk to me alone?"

"Exactly."

"I'm almost done here." He wasn't sure if going home to bake bread in the middle of the afternoon was considered to be a pastoral duty, but considering the state Lydia was in, he guessed the church council would approve.

He was barely out of his van when Lydia drove into the yard. She practically tumbled out from behind the wheel in her haste, grabbed a bag and waved what Alex was to learn was a packet of dry yeast in the air. She was wearing a tidy blue blouse with a ruffled collar, and her cheeks were bright pink.

There was something different about Lydia today, Alex thought. Something he should notice, like a new haircut or glasses, the kind of thing that alters one's appearance only slightly, leaving others to wonder what had changed, yet not being able to put a finger on it. Finally, it dawned on him. Lydia was wearing blue jeans and eye shadow!

They were not just any blue jeans either. A series of twinkly rhinestones ran down the outside seam of each leg. When she turned to get something out of the car, he noticed a rhinestone rose riveted on her back pocket. In the time he'd known the conservative Lydia, the briefest hint of makeup he'd ever seen her wear—not that he was an expert—was lipstick. Today she wore blue eye shadow that matched the color of her blouse and mascara that seemed to weigh down lashes unaccustomed to such gilding.

He took the bags from her hands and walked with her to the house. "You look very nice today," he said. He felt a little out of his league as to how to tactfully address the changes.

Lydia beamed at him, her expression almost playful. "I do? Thank you, Reverend. I decided to take your advice and make some changes in my life."

What advice was that? Was she saying *he'd* caused this makeup and rhinestone revolution? His mouth went dry. Whatever he'd told Lydia, this was not the intended outcome.

"My brothers, of course, hit the ceiling. They said my new jeans looked like they belonged on a teenager. When I told them I *felt* like a teenager, they nearly fell apart laughing." She frowned so that scowl lines dug themselves deeply into her forehead. "I don't see what's so funny about that. When I *was* a teen, I never felt much like one. Why shouldn't I experience it sometime in my life?"

"Good question." Alex opened the door to the house and they stepped inside. On one level, Lydia worried him a little, but he was delighted to have her in his kitchen, no matter why she'd come. He was beginning to enjoy cooking, and the little woman seemed to have magic in her hands where food was concerned. Besides, the kitchen felt more cozy and alive when they were busy chopping, beating or stirring.

"They don't want me to change, those two. All they care is that I stay their dull, boring cook and waitress. And what business is it of theirs if I wear eye shadow? None whatsoever. We're in the twenty-first century! They should be glad I didn't buy leathers and get a Harley!"

That was an image Alex didn't want in his head. "So I need to learn to bake bread?" He put bread pans on the counter and looked expectantly at Lydia.

She flushed a charming shade of pink. "I needed to talk to you and not just a batch of cookies' worth either. I hope you don't mind."

"Lydia, when my sister Carol comes for a visit, she'll be blown away by what I make for her. I'm looking forward to it."

"We'd better get started then. Do you have a dough hook for that mixer?"

He looked helplessly at the stainless-steel beast lurking in the corner of the counter. "I have no idea."

Clucking beneath her breath, Lydia ransacked the cupboards until she came up with a hook and a bowl for the mixer. The dough hook looked exactly like the hook worn by Captain Hook in *Peter Pan*.

Lydia handed him a small glass bowl. "Be sure this bowl isn't cold when you put the yeast into it. The temperature of the water can't drop below one hundred ten degrees. It can't be too high either. Yeast is very particular about temperature."

He'd had no idea.

She dumped two packets of yeast and a teaspoon of sugar into the warmed water in the bowl, stirred it and set it aside. "We need to give it a few minutes to dissolve; five should be enough."

At her direction, Alex combined milk, butter and her special ingredient, honey. Lydia operated the mixer while Alex separated eggs and measured out flour and salt. There seemed to be an art, he noticed, as to when to add flour and how much. "Just enough to keep the dough from sticking to the bowl," Lydia said. She seemed to know exactly how much that was even if he did not. He observed carefully and wondered if he'd dare try this on his own.

"We'll knead it in the mixer for a few minutes and then you can learn to knead by hand," she told him as she sprinkled flour on the counter to provide a surface.

"How will I know when I'm done?"

"When it's smooth and elastic. Then put it into a buttered bowl, swish it around a bit and turn it over so that the top of the bread has butter on it."

"I feel awkward as a ballerina in snowshoes," he muttered, but finally Lydia pronounced it done and covered the bowl with a damp towel. "Now what?"

"We let it rise for an hour, until it doubles in volume. And while we're waiting for that, we drink coffee. I brought cookies."

As they sat at the round oak table with their steaming mugs, Alex looked Lydia in the eye. "Now tell me what's up."

Her shoulders sagged. "I'm afraid I'll never get out from under the thumbs of my brothers. I love them with all my heart, mind you, but they're so bossy and so…smug. You'd have thought I'd gotten a tattoo the way they carried on about my makeup! I don't care. Johann liked it and…" Lydia stopped speaking, horror spreading across her features. "I mean… just forget I said that…. It's not like there's anything…" She put her head in her hands. "Oh dear."

"Johann? The gentleman I met on Saturday night? The one visiting your friend Ruby?"

"Yes." Her face was such a bright red now that Alex feared Lydia might suffer self-immolation at any moment. She seemed to be weighing her options before going on. "He's staying at Ruby's indefinitely and he called me on Sunday afternoon to ask me to go for a drive. Since Clarence and Jacob were glued to the baseball game, they barely noticed that I left."

She took a deep breath and continued. "We drove the countryside. I showed him which wheat was ripest and would be harvested first. We went by the Jenkinses' house and he thought it was very grand. And we sat at the top of the highest point in this very flat place and enjoyed the view."

"And each other, I presume."

"I feel so silly. Like a young teenager, really. I was never silly as a child or teen so it's quite foreign to me—and pleasant. Johann asked me if I'd come to town with him next Saturday night." She sat for a moment before adding, "What shall I do?"

"Go." The word popped out without even a thought. "Have fun. Get to know your new friend. You're a grown woman, Lydia. You're single and not committed to anyone. There's no harm in it."

"What will people say?"

"It doesn't matter. My father always used to say that whatever other people thought of him was none of his business. If you're doing nothing wrong, you shouldn't feel guilty about it."

Lydia worried the dish towel in front of her.

"What do you know about this man?"

"Only what Ruby has told me. He worked for the railroad his entire life. His wife died about ten years ago. They had no children. He goes to church, volunteers in his community and likes dogs. She says she's never known him to be anything but kind and good-natured."

"That doesn't sound like a bad date to me. Go. If you don't enjoy it you never have to say 'yes' again."

"Date? Is that what it would be? Oh my…"

Lydia looked askance when the timer on the stove rang. "Done already?" She lifted the damp towel from the bowl, and beneath it the dough had doubled in size. They divided it into two loaves and placed them in bread pans.

"Cover them again with the damp cloth and let them rise another hour. They will double again. Meanwhile, preheat the oven. Just before you put them into the oven, wash the tops of the loaves with a little egg white. Bake them for forty-five minutes. When you take the loaves out of the oven, tap the bottoms of the pans. They should sound hollow. Or do what I do, I lick my fingers and touch them to the bottom of the pan. If it sizzles, it's done."

"You're going to leave me alone with it?" Alex asked doubtfully.

"Of course. You can handle it. After the wisdom you shared with me about Johann, certainly you can manage a couple lumps of dough."

Ouch. It hurt when his words came back at him like that.

∽

Mark Nash showed up on his doorstep just after Alex had removed the bread from the oven and put it on a wire rack to cool.

"Smells great in here," Mark said as he walked through the screen door. "Look at you, a regular Barney Crocker!"

"Sit down and talk. We'll give this a few minutes to cool before cutting into it."

"You're going to make someone a wonderful wife someday, Alex."

He stopped himself from groaning aloud. That reminded him of marriage, which reminded him of Natalie, which reminded him that she was coming to see him, which reminded him of how confused he was.

Changing the subject, he asked Mark, "What's on your mind tonight?"

"I had supper at the café with Doc Ambrose tonight. He's this close" —Mark held his thumb and forefinger a sliver apart—"to retiring. He's made noises about it in the past, but this time he means it. He even showed me brochures on the motor home he wants to buy."

"He can't. What would the community do?" This was exactly what he and Dixon feared.

"But he will leave sooner or later. I think we should start a search for a new doctor. He says Wheatville won't do it, so if it's going to happen, it's up to us. Wheatville would welcome someone who said they wanted to be in Grassy Valley and nowhere else, but they will spend their current dollars searching for doctors for their own community."

"Why are you telling me all this?"

"I want you on board when I propose this to the city council that we begin our own search for a doctor. If you are in favor of this, I think it would help."

"I don't have to *do* anything?"

"Just say yes."

"If you promise me..."

"Say yes, Alex."

"If you're steering me wrong... oh, I suppose so. But what influence can I have that will bring a physician to Grassy Valley?"

"You just never know, Alex. You just never know."

Mark, his business done now that he'd extracted a promise of help from Alex, buttered another piece of bread and slathered it with Lydia's rhubarb-strawberry jam. When he was about to leave, he turned to Alex with a grin. "Call me next time you bake bread. I'll be your taste tester."

"Maybe I should just give you the recipe," Alex offered.

"Nah, I'd rather eat it at your house."

Alex stared after his friend. Mark wanted to eat here. Lydia wanted to cook here. Will would hang around 24/7 if he could. Granted, it was flattering, but also stacking up to be a lot of work.

CHAPTER FIFTEEN

*L*aundry done...check. Floors vacuumed...check. Flower beds weeded...check. Notified Will that he was not to bring Rosie the skunk into the yard for a week...check. Made a reservation with Nancy Jenkins for their first B&B guest...check. Alex glanced around the parsonage, looking for anything out of place. He'd given his home the white glove treatment in anticipation of his visitor. Now he had to stay out of the place for the next three days, so as not to undo his hard work until Natalie arrived.

They still hadn't talked to each other on the phone, as if an in-person conversation might break the tenuous string that bound them.

Why were they doing this? To test the waters between them. To see if a spark still flickered. If it didn't, then they were doing this for closure. He needed to put it to rest. To quit the "what-ifs" that haunted him. Hilltop was his new life and he didn't want any anchors tying him to the past. Though he didn't relish the idea, he needed to accept that being single was likely his lot in life.

"Come on, Tripod, we've got to get out of here so we don't mess anything up. Where shall we go?" Tripod's first choice was always to go to the church and to Gandy, who spoiled the dog mercilessly. Today, however, Gandy was quilting at All Saints again. The history quilt was taking on a life of its own. Gandy was constantly quoting one of the All Saints ladies on one thing or another, and it warmed Alex's heart to hear some normalcy entering the relationship between the churches.

"I'll bet someone would give you a cookie at All Saints."

Tripod wagged his tail at the word *cookie*.

They took the road by Mark Nash's tidy farmstead to All Saints. As he drove, his mind wandered first to Lila, then to Tillie and finally to the Aadlands. There was another pair he feared might not be able to live alone much longer even though Hans's toe was healing nicely. Then again, this was the heartiest bunch he'd ever come across. They might be living in their tidy little houses long after he'd gone from Hilltop. *Gone*. It hurt him to think about that.

The church doors were flung open and Alex could hear gospel music playing somewhere in the bowels of the building. That was Gandy's contribution, no doubt. She loved to sing along with gospel tunes at the top of her untrained but enthusiastic voice.

He parked in an available spot and opened the van's door. Tripod made for the breach, but Alex caught him by the collar. "Oh no, you don't. It's taken me weeks to convince anyone at All Saints that you can be with me when you're on a leash. I'm not having you undo all the work by running through dozens of piles of fabric now." He clipped the leash to Tripod's red collar. "Now behave like a gentleman."

Alex could hear the chatter grow louder as he descended the stairs to the basement. He paused halfway down to close his eyes and murmur, "Thank You, Lord! All Saints and Hilltop are speaking again. Bless the work we do in harmony, until people see that there is no point in doing things any other way."

"Are you going to stand there praying all day or are you coming down to say hello?" Gandy stood at the bottom of the stairs looking up at him. She wore her hair in a wild ponytail that erupted from the top of her head like a whale spout. The front of her blouse was so thick with stray quilting pins that it looked like body armor. "We're about to take a coffee break."

"Good timing." Alex maneuvered the rest of the way down the stairs, clipped Tripod's leash to a support post and walked into the midst of the ladies, who were gathered around big tables. Their greeting was gratifying. Even more so were the expressions on their faces—happy, relaxed and content.

Althea Dawson, one of the first to welcome Alex to All Saints Fellowship, was there doing some delicate stitching on her quilt block telling the story of the Dawson family. Amy Clayborn, with her shy ways, was pouring coffee. Betty Nyborg, Florence Kennedy and Belle Wells were at ironing boards. Mattie was cutting fabric with a tool that resembled a pizza cutter. The others, including Hilda and Nancy, were so intent on their jobs, they barely looked up upon his arrival.

Gandy, always in charge, said, "While we're having our break, let's show Pastor Alex some of the story squares we've put together for the history quilt. Since he's a newbie to quilting, we can educate him while he eats." She looked at him. "Is that okay with you?"

If it weren't, Alex thought, it was too late to say it now. Nancy put a napkin in front of him and handed him a plate that held mocha bars, gingersnaps, lemon bars and his favorite, fudge. "Today's offerings," she said cheerfully. "Belle, why don't you tell us about the quilt block you're working on?"

Belle stood up hesitantly. "I'm not very far." The square she held up had nothing on it. "But I have been fascinated by how my husband's family came to settle here. I've been doing a lot of reading—old letters and diaries, for example. I discovered that they hadn't planned to stop here at all. They were determined to go farther west but they had trouble with a wagon. One of the wheels broke, I think, and they couldn't replace it so they decided to stop here and put down roots." Belle smiled. "It helped me to understand why Curtis is so tied to this place. Imagine, being the first people ever to settle on a piece of land…"

Alex couldn't help but smile. It was the first time he'd ever heard Belle sound genuinely interested in why her husband chose to live here rather than move back to the city.

Florence Kennedy, who rarely put herself in front of a group, stood, holding quilted renditions of both Hilltop's and All Saints' churches. "Since I'm not from here originally, I volunteered to make the center squares." Everyone clapped.

Show-and-tell went on for some time before Alex decided it was time to leave. He was sated with enough sweets to clog every artery around his heart and put him in a diabetic coma besides.

"Reverend Alex." Nancy sat down beside him. She looked nervous, her eyes wide and darting. "I'd like to talk to you for a moment."

"Sure. I'll have another cup of coffee. The caffeine will balance out the sugar and fat in my system."

She smiled faintly at his little joke and beckoned him toward the furnace room in the back corner, the only place completely removed from quilters.

"I saw Doc Ambrose." She absently rubbed her stomach. "He told me he was retiring—sooner than he expected. I said I hoped it wouldn't be before my babies were born. What if I went into labor and needed help? Wheatville is a long drive. He told me his wife had given him an ultimatum. She's tired of worrying about *his* health. He's planning to announce it tomorrow. But what about after the twins are born? They'll probably be a lower birth weight than a single infant and I'm sure they'll need a lot of care. What would I do without Doc in town?

"The B&B will tie me down. I'll have to welcome guests and help them check out." Her eyes grew wide. "We just have to have a doctor nearby, Pastor."

"Mark is looking into it, Nancy. He has suggested that we do a search of our own, rather than depend on the Wheatville hospital to supply us with someone. Don't panic quite yet."

She relaxed and appeared relieved. "Good. I was afraid nothing was being done." Her lower lip quivered and Alex saw fear on her face. "I've never done this before, Alex, having two babies I mean. I'm nervous." She patted her tummy again. "I know that Ben can drive me to the hospital, but if something goes wrong, having Doc here would be so much better. And when they are toddlers, who knows how many earaches and upset tummies I'll be dealing with?"

She clutched Alex's wrist with a surprisingly strong grasp. "You can't begin to imagine how important this is to me."

Perhaps not, but the picture was growing clearer. In a small universe like this one, every person counted. The loss of Doc Ambrose would be devastating to the community.

"Oh yes, I almost forgot to ask." Nancy spoke again, her voice businesslike this time. "Is everything still on for my very first guest at Hubbard House? I'm so excited—only three days away! I've already got my breakfast menus planned."

For a few blissful moments Alex had forgotten the nervousness and anticipation in the pit of his stomach about Natalie's arrival. Despite the prayers he'd been sending up, that gnawing kept returning like a faint but nagging headache. "As far as I know. I haven't received a text from her recently."

"This is someone you knew back in Chicago, right?"

"Yes. She was a sociology professor at the same school I taught at."

"Nice. It will be good for you to see an old friend and colleague."

I certainly hope so.

On his way out of the furnace room, Alex sat down beside Lydia Olson. "Tell me what you're working on."

She held up the cloth. Her square told the story of her pioneer family coming across the plains of the Midwest for the very first time. "I'm trying to appliqué a covered wagon. It's not going well. I shouldn't have cut out the spokes before sewing them on. It's like trying to sew a spiderweb onto cloth." She gave an enormous sigh. "But I have tackled things more difficult, I must say."

Alex caught the reference. "How are your brothers? And Johann?"

"You'd think I'd been abusing those two," she said in a low voice, "making them heat an occasional bowl of canned soup! I thought Jacob was going to have a fit over a store-bought cookie. He's got other issues, of course, but growing emotional over food has never been one of them."

"What is Jacob's situation, exactly?" Jacob had never once come into the house while Alex was there to visit Clarence and Lydia, but had always stayed in the machine shed or barn. His behavior made Alex think of a domesticated yeti, a hairy bigfoot, lurking around the perimeter of the Olsons' yard. Jacob had to be at least six foot three inches tall, and his haircuts, from what Alex could tell from a distance, seemed few and far between. The word *recluse, hermit* or *loner* was always included in any conversation about Jacob Olson.

The expression in Lydia's eyes grew sad. "Growing up, Jacob was a perfectly normal, wonderful boy. He was the pride and joy of the family—so clever and so good with his hands. He could fix anything that was broken, from the sewing machine to the combine to the family car. But he doesn't like people. The doctor says he's agoraphobic.

"He's just more comfortable at home, with us. He tries to go out sometimes, but after a while he gets nervous and wants to go home.

Crowds are especially difficult for him. I wish it weren't so. It would be so good for Jacob to attend church. He does listen to church on the television, though, while we're at Hilltop on Sunday morning. He wouldn't miss it.

"But Clarence!" Lydia's eyes narrowed. "He's a different story. And you'd think the man had never even been in our kitchen. Everything is a new discovery. He doesn't know the difference between baking soda and baking powder or that it comes dry in a can as well as in a yellow plastic bottle! So far, he's pouring his own cereal into a bowl, but acting put out about it. By being good to them I created helpless men, Reverend. It's going to take me a long time to untrain them."

"It's for their own good. Isn't it?" *And yours as well.* "I thought you'd want to spend more time with Johann—over a meal perhaps." He had to tread gently here. He didn't want to give Lydia any more ideas than she already had. Her brothers couldn't handle it if she threw off the traces completely, at least not yet.

"So," said Dixon as he sat at Alex's kitchen table the next day and polished off the last of Alex's coffee and the lumpy, but still tasty, bread Alex had baked without Lydia's help, "now that you've been here a few months, do you still like it? What do you think of September in Hilltop?"

"Better every day," Alex said honestly. "I never thought I'd say this, but it's one of the most beautiful places I've ever been. It's a quiet beauty. A gentle wind blowing across a field of ripe grain, or the sun sinking in the west is more beautiful than I ever imagined. Hilltop is a diamond in the rough. I even understand why the people here keep talking about the horrible winters and fifty degrees below zero wind chills."

"Why? You haven't experienced that yet."

"This place is a secret you want to keep to yourself. Peaceful, beautiful, authentic, friendly… Winchester Holmquist told me that he liked to exaggerate the weather extremes to 'keep the riffraff out.'"

"I'll ask you if you still think that in the spring after you thaw out."

Alex nodded and stood up to clear the table. "Are you getting ready for your sister's visit?"

"I cleaned out my refrigerator," Dixon said. "I had some great science experiments going in there. I think one was an orange…or a lemon…or a peach. It was so furry I could have kept it as a pet."

"Don't tell me any more. If I eat at your place, I don't want to be afraid for my life."

"I also dumped out my silverware and cleaned the drawer. Emmy has a thing about silverware drawers. Hers looks like a hospital operating room. Oh yeah, and the crumbs in the toaster. Emmy hates those."

"Too much information, Dixon."

"Are you ready for *your* visitor?" Dixon stood up, went to the coffeepot and refilled his mug.

"I still have three days until she arrives. I have plenty of time to finish getting ready."

Dixon stood at the sink, looking out the window. "Maybe, maybe not."

"What's that supposed to mean?"

"A car with Illinois license plates and a very pretty dark-haired woman driver just pulled up. Anybody you know?"

Alex shot to his feet and hurried to the window. "It's Natalie! She's not supposed to be here yet!" Truth be told, it was his emotional preparation that wasn't quite complete. What if this turned into a fiasco and he'd been the one to initiate the mess?

"You're as ready as you're ever going to be, my friend. It's time to face the music."

Alex couldn't remember being this nervous since he preached his very first sermon while he was still in seminary.

They watched Natalie climb out of her car and stretch. She was thinner than she'd been last time he'd seen her, svelte. And her dark hair was longer and glinted brown-black in the sunlight. She was wearing tan slacks, a hot-pink blouse, and pink flip-flops. She looked wonderful.

Dixon whistled. "You didn't tell me she looked like *that*."

"What difference would it have made?"

"I would have felt sorrier for you if I'd known someone that beautiful dumped you."

Leave it to Dixon to keep a situation light. "Very funny."

Dixon dumped his freshly poured coffee into the sink. "Well, gotta go."

"What are you doing? You have to stay."

"Only long enough to say hello," Dixon said firmly. "Then you are on your own."

"Fine friend you turned out to be," Alex grumbled and looked in the reflection from the microwave door to see if his hair was combed. He felt nervous as a teenager on his first date.

Dixon slapped him on the back. "I'm a good enough friend to know when it's time to leave. I'll be praying for you, buddy."

"Please do. I'm going to need it." Together they went outside to meet Natalie.

She looked up and smiled when she saw them exit the house. Alex had forgotten that lovely smile of hers. *Stay cool*, he told himself. *This is just*—he searched for the right words—*an exploratory mission. I just have to know....*

Natalie quickly moved forward, met them at the bottom of the porch steps and threw her arms around Alex. "I *am* at the right place! I asked for directions in that little town but I wasn't sure I'd make it. They said something about passing a trailer court, going by a red mailbox, a big rock and turning at a shelterbelt...whatever that is."

She still wore the same perfume, Alex noted. "You're early. Three days."

"I know. I hope it is okay." She turned and fluttered her long dark eyelashes Alex's way. "I finished the things I had to get done before I could leave early—and here I am. I thought it would be fun to surprise you."

His knees were actually shaking. Rather than saying anything to Natalie, he turned to Dixon.

"Dixon, I'd like you to meet Natalie Garrison, a former colleague of mine. We taught at the same college for several years. Natalie, this is Dixon Daniels."

"Nice to meet you," Dixon said politely. "Any *colleague* of Alex's is a friend of mine." He held her hand a little too long, Alex noted grumpily.

"How sweet." Natalie, a natural flirt, fluttered her eyelashes at Dixon.

He saw Dixon hesitate, as if his friend were rethinking his offer to leave immediately. Dixon wasn't blind to the charms of an attractive woman. Then he remembered his manners. "Nice to meet you, but I've got to be going. Have a good visit." Dixon winked at Alex before bolting for his pickup and shooting out of the yard.

She stood looking at him with an appraising stare. "You look fabulous, Alex, tanned and strong. You've put on a couple pounds and let your hair grow a shade longer. It looks good on you. You are better looking than ever, which is saying a lot."

He hardly expected a compliment right off the bat and felt a flush climbing his neck to his cheeks. Feeling awkward, he pulled out his cell phone. "I'd better call the B&B and tell them you're here early. They weren't expecting you yet."

He pulled out his cell phone. The phone rang twice before Nancy picked it up. "B&B, innkeeper speaking." Nancy had begun answering that way, she'd told him, because she was so excited to begin her enterprise.

"Nancy? Hi, it's Alex. How are you doing on your preparations to open the B&B?"

"I've been ready for days." Nancy laughed. "I can hardly wait until your guest arrives."

"It looks like you won't have to wait any longer. She's come a few days early. She just drove into my yard." Alex watched Natalie as she took in her surroundings. He noticed Will's red bike leaning against the shed.

"Bring her over anytime!" Nancy sounded delighted. "I'll be waiting."

"We'll see you soon." Alex put his cell phone back into his pocket and turned to her. "We're in luck. We can go over there right now and get you settled. I'm sure Nancy wants to show off her baking too."

"I'd love to have you show me around the yard before we go." She gestured toward the pristine lawn and tidy outbuildings. Her eyes were bright and curious.

"I can introduce you to my little friend Will Packard," Alex offered, surprised at how easily they were able to talk, as if not so much had transpired between them.

As they walked, he told Will's story and that of the Hoomain Society in the shed.

Natalie laughed that throaty, husky laugh she had. "How cute! I'm glad you're humoring him, until he moves on to some other nine-year-old interest."

"I don't think Will is going to move past this. I expect this boy to be a veterinarian someday."

"Can a child know that at such a young age?" Natalie said lightly. "Look at adults. Sometimes even they can't figure out what they really want." *Like me*, she might have added. *Or me*, Alex thought. Alex turned to call Tripod.

When Natalie glanced over her shoulder to see what Alex was looking at, she gasped. "What is that?"

Tripod loped to them and slid to a stop at Alex's feet, his tongue lolling happily, his tail wagging wildly. Alex leaned over to scratch him behind his ears. "This is my dog Tripod." Alex patted him on the head. "You're a good boy, aren't you, Tripod?"

"What's wrong with him?" Natalie stared at the dog, dismay on her features. "The poor thing has been injured!"

"He lost a leg, but he doesn't care, so I don't either."

Natalie put her hand over her mouth. "Is he in pain?"

"Not a bit. Tripod is a great companion." He'd never had pets of his own when she'd known him, so it was probably a surprise to her now. That and a lot more had changed since they'd last been together.

They reached the shed and Alex knocked on the open door. "Will?"

"Hey, Pastor! Come in and see what Myrtle Chadwick gave me. It's really cool."

Will had discovered an ally in his battle against Bucky's animal cruelty. With Bucky's mother on his side, he'd sprung many more critters from Bucky's grasp.

"Some new animal," Alex told Natalie with a chuckle. "A few days ago it was a baby chick."

"How sweet." Natalie followed him into the shed.

Will was sitting on the stool holding his newest rescue. He held it out for examination. "Bucky's mom brought this over. She found it in his closet in an old fish tank. She thinks he got it from someone in Wheatville. It's just a baby. He didn't want her to know about it, but once it grows, it's going to be hard to keep a secret. Isn't he beautiful?" Will thrust his new treasure out for Alex's examination.

Simultaneously, Natalie's scream pierced his eardrums.

Alex stared at the writhing cream-and-brown prize in Will's hands. A baby boa constrictor.

"Watch it, lady, you're gonna scare him!" Will pulled the writhing creature to his chest.

With some effort, Alex edged her outside and back to her car. She was trembling, behaving as if the baby snake would follow and attack her. "You stay here. I'll go back and talk to Will."

"Don't leave me, Alex." Her eyes were wide and dark, pleading.

"I need to deal with it, I'm afraid. Fortunately it's just a baby. Please excuse me while I figure out what Will is doing with that thing. Stay here. You'll be fine."

She gathered herself together admirably and nodded.

He hurried back to the shed where Will was despondently caressing the snake. He looked up when Alex entered. There were tears in his eyes. "I didn't do anything wrong," he blurted. "It isn't going to hurt anybody. I looked it up. There are lots of people who have them as pets."

That, Alex knew, was true. "You're not planning to keep it, are you?"

"Nah. Mrs. Chadwick is going to find it a home. I won't have Slinky more 'an a couple days."

"Slinky, is it?" Up close the snake was beautiful, in an alarming sort of way, Alex noticed.

"Yeah. I didn't mean for him to scare that lady. I'm really sorry about that. Is that your company? I thought she wasn't supposed to be here for a couple days yet. Please don't kick me out 'cause of Slinky."

"She surprised me and came a few days early."

"Then it serves her right that she got surprised too." Will stood up and dropped Slinky into the fifteen-gallon aquarium sitting on the floor. Then he covered the enclosure with mesh, which he secured with discarded bread ties.

"What are we going to do about this, Will? I didn't anticipate a snake when I said you could use the shed."

Will's eyes blazed. "And I didn't 'ticipate no snakes either! That Bucky can't be trusted to do anything normal!"

"You're sure it will be gone soon?"

"I'll call Mrs. Chadwick at work. She's cooking at Red's today.

Maybe she can see if any of the truckers who stop there could take it. I'll tell her it's an emergency."

"That it is." Alex sighed and thought of Natalie out by the car.

Then Will turned and glanced in the corner. When he looked at Alex, his eyes were wide. "Oh-oh," he whispered.

"Now what?" Alex hoped he didn't have a passel of salamanders hidden somewhere to add to Natalie's distress.

"Rosie got out of her cage."

Rosie the pet skunk never wandered far, Alex knew. She was too fat and happy in Will's care. Still, today was not the day for Rosie to take a walkabout. "We'd better find her." Almost before that was out of his mouth, Natalie started screaming again.

They bolted out of the dusky shed and blinked in the bright sunlight. Alex looked at Natalie's car and saw her backed against the passenger door. "Shoo! Shoo! Go away! Shoo!"

Rosie, heavy and squat, waddled toward the car and toward Natalie. Rosie's black coat was shiny, and the white stripe made a broad swath down her back. Her tail was up as it always was when she wasn't sure of a situation, but, because she'd never lived in the wild, she was unafraid of people and obviously curious about this strange one waving her hands.

"Rats," Will muttered. "That lady had better quit yelling or she's going to scare Rosie!"

And, Alex thought, the skunk had better quit waddling toward the car or it was going to lose its hearing.

Will ran ahead and scooped his pet into his arms. Then he was petting the skunk and talking in soothing tones to the creature. Rosie settled right into his arms. They walked right past Alex, and in a moment Will had the wagon that held Rosie's cage hooked to his bike. Without a good-bye, Will pedaled off as fast as his legs could take him.

By the time Alex reached Natalie, she was crying, her face was pale and mascara was melting into black rings around her eyes. Like a raccoon, Alex thought, then told himself he'd been around Will too much. That idea never would have occurred to him in Chicago.

He pulled a handkerchief out of his pocket and wiped some of the stain from beneath her eyes. He lifted her chin and stared solemnly at her.

"We're so sorry, Natalie. Will had strict instructions to keep Rosie away from here while you were visiting. Since you came early I didn't have time to tell him to leave Rosie at home. We didn't mean for you to be frightened." Alex looked at her, worried. She was hiccupping tears. "Would you like to come inside and have something cold to drink? I've got lemonade."

She shook her head. "Maybe I should go to the B&B," she stammered. "There aren't any wild animals over there, are there?"

"Not that I know of, but I can't say for sure. This is a farming community. Every yard has some sort of wildlife, but I promise, nothing like this will happen again. Will is the only person who has a skunk and a boa constrictor, and I'm sure you scared Will as much as Rosie scared you."

Natalie looked straight into his eyes. "There was a time, Alex, that I doubt you would have tolerated this. You've changed."

For the better, Alex mused. Definitely for the better.

"You'll be the very first guest at Hubbard House," Alex said to soothe his beautiful but agitated guest as they drove to the Jenkinses'. "Nancy is a wonderful cook and she's planned the best room for you. It overlooks the grain fields. They tell me that this is the most beautiful time of year, except maybe for spring...and summer...and winter.

"People appreciate the four seasons here. I'm actually looking forward to winter. It's messy in Chicago, with all the traffic, but out here it will be different. Can you imagine all these beautiful fields as pure white? And Will told me about snowshoe rabbits. They're brown in the summer and fall but turn white in the winter so they blend in with the terrain. Nature's camouflage. Isn't that something? And they have big hind feet so that they don't sink in the snow. God's little miracles are all over...."

He was babbling and he knew it, but he didn't know what else to do. He hadn't wanted to let Natalie drive her car to the Jenkinses' place in the shaken state she was in, so he was driving it for her. Nancy or Ben could take him back to the parsonage when she was settled.

"Listen, Natalie, I am so sorry about the fiasco back there but..."

"It's my fault. If I'd stuck to my plan and arrived when I should have, none of this would have happened."

"You're hardly to blame. Neither is Will. He promised me he wouldn't have Rosie around when you were here. I know he wasn't expecting you to arrive so soon. I apologize, Natalie."

She flipped her dark hair away from her face, a habit Alex remembered with affection. She glanced at him coyly from the corners of her eyes. "Haven't you thought for just a moment that I might have been hoping for a slightly warmer welcome? A hug, maybe, or even a kiss?" she teased. "Instead I get Wild Kingdom!"

"I'm sorry, Natalie, but under the circumstances I didn't think that you would expect that. We are...estranged."

"Don't you see?" She leaned toward him. "That's why I'm here. That's why I was so excited to get your e-mail. I made a mistake...."

Alex pulled into the porte cochere, covered pillars that had once provided cover for passengers departing buggies or carriages, before they entered the big house.

Natalie was obviously so startled by this unanticipated mansion on the prairie that she was temporarily distracted from their conversation.

Nancy, Alex noted, had even scrubbed the fieldstone arch around the doorway, and swept down the siding. She'd put out a new welcome mat and a planter of geraniums.

Nancy burst onto the porch with a broad smile on her face. She wore an apron with the word WELCOME appliquéd on it. Thanks to the quilting ladies, Alex was well acquainted with the appliquéing process. Nancy beamed at them and beckoned them inside.

"You must be Natalie! Welcome to Hubbard House. I just took muffins out of the oven. You must be tired from your trip. Why don't you and Alex sit down and have tea while I take your suitcase to the room?"

The house smelled enticingly like a bakery, and every surface gleamed. Alex wouldn't have been surprised to hear a band strike up at Natalie's arrival. "I'll take her luggage upstairs, Nancy. You visit with Natalie. She's never been to North Dakota before."

"Thanks, Alex. First room on the north. I've decided to call it Tessa's Room after my great-grandmother. Everything's ready."

Alex was glad to escape to the upstairs. Natalie had come hoping to reconcile. It was what he'd hoped for when he sent that exploratory e-mail…wasn't it? Then why did he feel so confused now?

He put the suitcase on the luggage rack in the elegant room, painted in soft greens. There was a white marble fireplace against the east wall and a king-sized bed dressed in puffy white bedding. Music was coming from a small player on the bedside table next to a dish of chocolates. A comfortable-looking rocker sat near the fireplace, and on the table beside it was a stack of books and magazines.

As he walked down the stairs, he could hear Nancy and Natalie in conversation. Natalie was telling Nancy about Rosie and the snake. Nancy, accustomed to animals of all sorts, laughed gaily.

Nancy looked up and patted the empty spot on the couch next to her. "Come, join us."

"Good stuff, huh?" Alex nodded at the muffin on Natalie's plate. "I suppose we'll have to think of something for dinner tonight. I'd planned to cook but haven't been to the grocery store yet."

"You? Cook?" Natalie looked at him with wide eyes.

"He's surprising everyone," Nancy said proudly. "He even promised to bring home-baked cookies to our quilting group one day. Of course, he has an excellent teacher."

"When did you start to cook?" Natalie sounded amazed but pleased.

"I've started to do a lot of things differently, Nat." *Thanks, in part, to you.* "Life goes on. Some things even begin to improve—like my cooking."

She took in what he'd said. Were those tears gathering in her eyes?

Nancy, unaware of the currents running between her guests, said, "Why don't you come here for supper, Alex? Natalie can rest and take a shower. Ben can drive you home to get your own car. You know I'm planning to offer an evening meal to my guests eventually. I'll practice on you. How do you feel about salmon? Or would you rather have pasta?"

"Anything you fix is great with me," Alex said absently and escaped the B&B.

At home and needing to talk to someone with some objectivity, Alex went into his office, picked up his phone and dialed his friend and mentor Edward O'Donnell. While they'd been on staff at the college, he and Edward had discussed a lot of life issues. Maybe he'd have some insight on this. To his relief, Edward picked up on the second ring.

"Hey, old friend," Edward greeted him. "I haven't heard from you in quite a while. Things must be going well out there on the prairie."

"Hilltop and All Saints Fellowship are speaking again, thanks to a history quilt the ladies are making together. My nemesis Alf Nyborg has softened a bit, and my little friend Will Packard is expanding his Hoomain Society daily."

"God be praised," Edward said cheerfully. "What's up with Will? You always seem to have a good story about him to share."

"It's a whopper today." Alex told Edward about Natalie's arrival, the baby snake and the pet skunk acting as official welcoming committee.

Edward howled with laughter. When he'd finally gathered himself together, he said, "So Natalie's back. What do you think about that?"

"I don't know. Part of me is delighted. I loved her, you know. I wanted nothing more than a wife and eventually a family. And part of me is, frankly, confused…nervous. When I left Illinois, I never expected to see her again, and here she is dropping hints that she'd like to make up." The hurdles they'd had to overcome were daunting.

"I heard through our mutual friend at the college that she went through a pretty embarrassing breakup. The man she'd left you for did the same to her. That's all I know, except that I'm sure she's realized she'd passed up something special in you."

"She does seem more like the old Natalie, the one I fell in love with. What do I do, Ed? Should I consider taking her back? When I look at her, I remember how much I loved her."

"Do you want to take her back?" Edward had an annoying way of answering a question with a question. He'd always said he'd like to be a psychotherapist. "We all make mistakes. Of course, hers was bigger than most."

"There are more women besides Natalie in the world," Alex pointed out rationally.

"How many of them are in Grassy Valley?"

None…or, Alex thought, maybe that was the problem in a nutshell. Was he thinking this way only because he was lonely?

"I think I'm destined to have a family, Edward, but it's difficult without a wife. I'll have to work this out in my own mind. Pray for me, will you?"

"I always do."

When Alex returned to the Jenkinses' later, he was greeted by Nancy. "She's feeling much better after a long nap," she told him when she met him on the porch. "She's very pretty, isn't she? Gorgeous, in fact. You are a very handsome couple."

Alex shrugged, reluctant to get into a discussion that might lead to his personal life.

"Okay, don't admit it," she said cheerfully, getting the hint. "I've got appetizers ready in the living room. Ben's inside playing host." She put her hands together and held them to her face. "I'm having so much fun I can hardly stand it!"

"You've found your niche."

She studied him for a moment. "I don't know that I would have if you hadn't come to Hilltop. We were ready to give up on this house. It was sucking us dry. But when you called your cousin Dan and he suggested ways to fix up the house, it gave us renewed interest. Without you, none of this would have happened."

"I can't take credit for that, Nancy. I see God's fingerprints all over it, however."

"Maybe, but you were His messenger. Now come inside and have some appetizers."

He walked into the living room, where Ben and Natalie were sitting on the Victorian-looking couch looking at a photo album of the house over the years.

"There you are! Alex, this is such a wonderful place!" Her eyes were bright. "I already feel so relaxed that my bones might melt. Try these." She picked up a plate of stuffed mushrooms. "They're out of this world!"

He took a small plate and a couple of the mushrooms and sat down in the chair across from them. Alex watched Natalie and Ben in animated conversation, covertly observing the woman he once thought he knew so well. What did he feel now? He'd thought he might feel nothing for her, but he'd had to find out for himself. One didn't just toss love away, he was discovering. Its remnants lingered in one's heart long after the love itself had shattered. But what to do about it? Would he be a fool to let her go? Or would he be more of a fool not to?

"Dinner's ready," Nancy announced. "It's on the table. Alex, will you say the prayer?"

They gathered around the table. It took Alex a moment to formulate his prayer. "Lord, You are gracious, generous and loving beyond reason. Thank You for the gift of this meal and for our hosts. Thanks for safe travel for Natalie. I ask that You be in every moment of her visit here and that *Your will be done*. Amen."

She looked at him oddly when he raised his head. Her brows beetled together in a small frown. She'd picked up on the words he'd emphasized.

But he hadn't been talking to Natalie. He'd been speaking to God.

He was playing in reverse a game that he remembered Carol playing as a child, plucking the petals of a daisy and chanting, "He loves me, he loves me not." His version was "I love her, I love her not…" Was Natalie thinking the same about him?

He was glad for the cheerful, diverting conversation over their meal, and after dinner Alex suggested Nancy and Ben join them in watching a movie. No more conversation was required between him and Natalie for the night. Alex couldn't be more thankful.

❧

The next morning Alex found himself back at the B&B for breakfast. Natalie studied him somberly over her plate.

"What?" He helped himself to a mound of fluffy scrambled eggs.

"I hope that we'll get some time alone, Alex," she said gently. "We have things to talk about." She was wearing a rich gold-colored blouse that made her skin glow, and her brown eyes were luminous. He found it impossible to look into her eyes.

"And that is?" Alex tread cautiously.

"About us, of course."

"Is there an 'us,' Natalie? You made that very clear several months ago that there was no 'us.'" No matter how gently he tried to say it, it still sounded harsh. Harsh, but true.

Alex took a deep breath and tried soften his tone. "You can understand why I'm confused by this change of heart, can't you? I'm not even sure why you're here, Natalie. Why, really, did you respond to me?"

"Because seeing your message brought back to me what a fool I've been. I want to make up, Alex. I want us to be a couple again." She paused, and when she spoke again her voice was a whisper. "I didn't think I'd ever get the chance to say that to you."

He drew back, startled at her bluntness.

"I dreamed of looking you in the eye, and having you look at me. I fantasized that there would be something special between us if we could connect again."

He had to address the elephant in the room. "What about the other man, Natalie? He's pretty difficult to overlook."

"I was a complete and utter fool. What made me think he'd be true to me when he encouraged me not to be loyal to you? We'd dated less than six months before I caught him stepping out on me." A pained look crossed her face. "Will you find forgiveness in your heart for me and give me a chance to make this up to you?" Her voice quavered. "I love you."

"Natalie, I have forgiven you. I couldn't move ahead in my own life until I did. And my love for you didn't die completely. The problem is, you see, that when I first proposed to you I knew you were right for me. Now I'm not so sure. All I do know is that God's got me on this crazy journey...."

She closed her eyes. "I know. I don't blame you." She opened them again and they were filled with fire. "But I'm going to do everything in my power to make that happen again. All I ask is that we keep the lines of communication open. I've changed. Now I want to prove it to you. Will you let me?"

"I meant what I said, Nat. Please don't."

But judging by the expression on Natalie's face, Alex doubted she'd go down without a fight.

"What are we going to do today?" Natalie was determinedly cheerful as she followed Alex out of the B&B.

He'd been right. She was still attempting to make the relationship work.

"I thought I'd introduce you to my friends Mike and Lauren Carlson. I think you'll enjoy their farm." He glanced at the sky. The weatherman had predicted rain for later, but all was clear now. "Lauren was on the call committee and they were the first people I met in the community. Lauren grew up on the farm, but Mike, who moved here twenty years ago, still calls himself a newcomer."

"Great!" Then Natalie glanced at him. "Do they know about me?"

"Yes, they do."

"Oh." She digested that before speaking. "Am I the bad woman, right off the bat?"

"Why would you think that? I haven't been saying you're a 'bad woman' and I'm the only one who knows you."

"Sweet Alex. Always kind. I was such a fool to…" Her voice trailed away.

"'Put away from you all bitterness, wrath and anger and wrangling and slander, together with all malice, and be kind to one another, tenderhearted and forgiving one another, as God in

Christ has forgiven you.'" He smiled at her. "Ephesians. Those directions are pretty clear. How could I do anything else?"

Tears welled in her eyes and she looked away, staring toward the passing fields.

They pulled into the Carlsons' yard just as Mike exited the building that housed his woodshop. "Hey, you're just in time!" He went to his nearby pickup and grabbed a bag from the hardware store. He looked at Natalie. "And who is this?"

Alex made the proper introductions and watched Mike's face for a response. He was reaching out everywhere, Alex realized, hoping to interpret his friends' expressions and gather their opinions of this woman he'd brought into their midst. It mattered to him, he realized, that Natalie liked Hilltop, but it mattered even more that Hilltop liked Natalie.

"What are we just in time for?"

"Painting birdhouses." Mike tapped the bag with his finger. "I don't have any crop ready to pick up, so I bought new paint. Come on in." He led them into his shop where a dozen birdhouses in the shapes of an entire village—church, school and café—stood in a row. "I decided to see if I could make a set of birdhouses that looked like the buildings in Grassy Valley. I'm not sure if I managed or not, but I think the paint will help." He pointed to the largest of the birdhouses, one made for martins. "This should be Red's, don't you think?"

"They are adorable." Natalie moved along the bench examining each one in detail.

Mike handed her a small brush. "I'm serious, want to help? Lauren's been nagging at me to get them done."

She glanced at Alex, who nodded. "You wanted a taste of life at Hilltop. Here's your chance."

"You can help too, Alex. We'll just put on the base coat now.

Lauren will do the final details later. She wants to sell them at an upcoming farmers' market to make money for the food shelf."

Mike thrust the birdhouse version of the church and a small can of white paint at Alex. "You do this one. It seems only fitting." Then he handed the largest one to Natalie. "Paint this one red, okay?"

Looking pleased, Natalie set to her task.

Six birdhouses later, Lauren walked through the door to the shop carrying a pitcher of lemonade and paper cups. "Hi, I saw your van down here and thought I'd come and say hello…" Then she noticed Natalie. "I didn't realize we had an extra person. Good thing I brought four cups."

After the introductions were made, Lauren plopped herself on one of the stools. "The birdhouses look great. Thanks so much. I really hope they bring in some good money. People who need help with groceries seem to be popping up everywhere. I had no idea there was so much need. I've had several calls and we aren't even open yet." She twirled a strand of her auburn hair around her finger. "The economy isn't great, so it makes sense that people are having a difficult time making ends meet. I'm sorry we didn't think of it sooner."

"It sounds like what you are doing is wonderful," Natalie said.

Lauren stood up. "Would you like to see the shelves Mike has made? And the signs? They're in the garage by the house." The women left the building together, chatting like old friends.

Alex and Mike continued to work on the birdhouses in silence. Finally, Mike said, "Is your friend having a good visit? And are you?"

"So far, so good," Alex said mildly.

"Are you interested in rekindling the relationship?" Mike asked bluntly.

"I honestly don't know. There's a lot of baggage still between us."

Mike whistled through his teeth. "That's tough, Rev. I'd be down on my knees over that one."

"I have been, my friend, I have been."

To Alex's delight, Natalie was thoroughly enamored with not only the birdhouses, but also the Belgian draft horse, the two brown and white llamas and particularly the miniature donkey. She was also charmed by Mike and Lauren themselves. Lauren fixed dinner at about one o'clock and they sat at the table over coffee and a sour cream raisin pie until nearly three.

When they finally left, Natalie rhapsodized about Alex's lovely friends. "I can see why you like it here if everyone is like the Carlsons and the Jenkins. Delightful people and so friendly.... I'd like to get to know them better. I wish I weren't leaving tomorrow." She gasped as a big white car bore down on them. Alex turned the wheel to the far edge of the road and slowed to a stop as they were surrounded by a cloud of dirt and gravel kicked up by the passing car.

"Whoever that was could have caused us to have an accident!" she said indignantly. "She didn't look either right or left and she never took her foot off the gas pedal."

"We were fine, I saw Isabelle coming. Everyone here knows to get out of her way when she comes down the road."

"You know her?"

"Isabelle is in her nineties. Her son and daughter-in-law, Ralph and Ava Johnson, who happen to be in their sixties, have been trying to get her driver's license away from her for years, but Isabelle won't relent. Her license doesn't expire for another year because she managed to pass her last test."

"Can't they just take the license away?"

"There isn't much traffic and everybody knows to watch out for her...." There was a time not so long ago when he would have been shocked by the way the area handled Isabelle too. But the time would come soon, everyone knew, when that last bit of independence would be taken from her. Until then, everyone was willing to be patient—and very, very alert.

He realized that she was staring at him. "You've changed."

"A lot has happened."

"This place has changed you. You're more laid-back, more take-it-as-it-comes."

"Is that a good thing?" He felt as if she'd paid him a huge compliment.

"I suppose so," Natalie said slowly, thoughtfully. "You seem more mellow and peaceful here."

Ah, Alex thought, Hilltop was seeping into his bones. He liked the idea.

✺

"Here you are," Nancy said when they returned to the B&B. The place smelled like a five-star restaurant. "I'm so glad you came back. I've invited Cherry and Dan Taylor for dinner, and Lilly and Randy Sumptner. Will you join us?"

"Sure. What time?"

"Six. Just enough time for Natalie to rest and primp." She turned toward Natalie and winked.

At the bottom of the stairs before going to her room, Natalie turned to Alex.

"Are we going to have that time together alone?" Her voice was soft and unsure.

"Pray first, talk second," Alex said gently. "Okay?"

Natalie nodded but she looked worried.

✺

"So I said to myself," Lilly Sumptner said later over dessert, "why not sell gourmet foods? Everyone around Hilltop is a fabulous cook and they're probably ready for something new."

Lilly was explaining her newest business venture to Cherry and Dan Taylor, the quiet young couple who lived just north of Mattie Olsen's place. Alex didn't know them well yet, because although they came to church regularly, they always slipped out right after the final hymn. Cherry, with her head full of white-blond curls and baby blue eyes, was pretty and very Scandinavian looking. Dan, her husband, was an intense young man with black hair and dark brown eyes. Together they made an attractive couple.

Randy, Lilly's husband, was looking more bored by the minute. He'd heard his wife's spiel enough times to give it himself, word for word, no doubt.

Natalie seemed spellbound by Lilly's rapid-fire chatter. They were all learning more about organic lemon pepper and tiramisu than any of them wanted to know.

Alex sat back and observed the group. Lilly's makeup was significantly reduced since she'd stopped selling it herself and switched to her new line of merchandise. Randy's waistline was fuller, however, no doubt the result of Lilly experimenting with her new products.

Cherry's porcelain complexion was paler than usual tonight. Dan's eyebrows furrowed and his mouth tipped down at the corners. He was always rather grim looking, but tonight he appeared downright dismal. Alex made a mental note to visit this couple. He knew little about them, and since they kept mostly to themselves, they rarely came up in even Gandy's conversations.

"Tell me a little more about yourselves." Alex directed his request to Dan and Cherry. "Were your families pioneers in this area too?" All of the farms in Hilltop township, the location of Hilltop Community

Church, were descendants of pioneers, so it was an easy assumption to make.

Cherry giggled uneasily. "Not exactly. My great-grandparents homesteaded here in the 1800s. That's the farm we still live on. Dan, on the other hand…"

"I'm an outsider," he said bluntly and crossed his arms over his chest as if he were protecting himself from what might come next.

"Then you're like Mike Carlson. He told me that no matter how long he lived in Hilltop, he'd always be considered 'one of the new guys' by virtue of not having been born here."

"Yeah. There's Mike, me and Belle Wells, Curtis's wife."

"So it's like being the baby of the family—no matter what you do, you'll never be considered anything but."

Dan thought about that and smiled a little. "I never looked at it like that, but I suppose that's true."

"It frustrates Dan that everyone is always watching him, expecting him to do something silly, because he didn't live on the farm as a child," Cherry piped in.

Alex looked at the young man intently and sensed that there was a lot of emotion churning under the surface where Dan was concerned. "Perhaps you should be flattered," Alex said mildly. "The baby of the family is always very special to its older siblings."

Dan nodded slowly in agreement, as if the concept had never occurred to him before. "You mean all the un-asked-for advice I get is really pampering and spoiling?"

"And, I'd guess, affection." Alex noticed Dan's shoulders relax slightly. "Maybe you're right."

Alex would have to learn more about what made Dan Taylor tick. He had a hunch it was a complicated man that Cherry had married and brought to Hilltop.

At that moment, Nancy entered the room carrying the pièce de résistance: beef Wellington, a tenderloin coated with pate and covered with a golden crust. "Here we are, my friends. Enjoy!"

Natalie was impressed. Alex could tell as he looked at her across the candlelit table sparkling with crystal and white linen and small vases of flowers from Nancy's garden. She was particularly beautiful tonight in a slender black sheath dress. Her hair was a tumble of dark curls, and she was makeup free but for a slash of bright red lipstick. Alex liked it when a woman didn't wear much makeup. He liked women to look natural—just as God had made them.

At her neck was a small, simple gold cross, one he had given her for her birthday. It symbolized everything that was important to him, that cross. Initially, when he'd seen her walk down the stairs from her room, he'd felt warmth and pleasure rushing through him. She'd kept it after their breakup. He'd assumed she'd given it away. He remembered almost asking to have it back, but he'd changed his mind at the last minute. It was a gift he couldn't renege on. She'd needed it even more right then. When the message of Christ is sent out in any form, it does not come back empty.

But as he looked at it now, misgivings washed over him. Had she *planned* to wear it to prove her point that they should be together as a couple? She was everything he'd ever wanted—engaging, intelligent, beautiful. Despite the fact that he'd been the one to initiate their reconnection, something in him resisted. His guard was up. What would it take to overcome that? Did he even want to? An emotional tug-of-war waged, one between his desire for a wife and family and his reluctance to open himself to another disappointment or rejection.

Lord, what do You want? Have You sent Natalie here because You want us together again? Or is she here for some other reason entirely? I loved her so much once. But I've put her in the past and I'm happy now. I ask that

You make it known to me what Your will is in this. Send me a clear sign so I don't act blindly on my feelings, rather than Your wishes. Amen.

Then he realized that Lilly was speaking to him. "Do you think you'd enjoy a horseradish dip? If so, I have a wonderful packet of seasonings. Do you like salsa? Of course you do, everyone loves salsa...."

Before he knew it, he'd agreed to buy three of whatever it was Lilly was selling.

A crack of thunder banged and echoed overhead, startling them all. Natalie reached for Alex's hand. They saw lightning hit the ground in a jagged bolt almost directly. It was followed by another crack of thunder.

Dan whistled. "That's close."

"How can you tell," Natalie asked nervously, "if it's close or not, just by hearing it?"

"Thunder is actually the sound made by lightning. It's a little like a sonic boom. If you see a lightning bolt and the thunder follows it directly, it's close by. If you see the lightning bolt and a crack of thunder follows it by a few seconds, then it's farther away. Nature is amazing, isn't it?"

"Amazing," she said weakly.

Then rain started to pour and they settled in for another cup of coffee and to wait until it subsided.

When Alex glanced at his watch, he realized it was almost eleven PM. The night had flown by. Alex pushed away from the table. "I'm sorry, but I have to excuse myself. I have a very busy day tomorrow. Gandy prepared a list of home visits for me that will take all day. Don't get up on my account. I'll just slip out."

But of course they did. Nancy insisted on packing the leftovers for Alex's lunch, and Randy Sumptner trailed him into the hall and caught him by the arm.

"I'm sorry about Lilly," he said.

"Whatever for? She's the life of the party."

"That's what I'm sorry for." Randy looked at the floor. "She dominates every conversation with whatever she's selling at the moment. It's too much. Why, last Sunday when I was ushering, I went into the foyer to ring the bell and I saw Lilly putting bright orange flyers on the windshields of every car in the lot. At church! That's going too far. I took them off, of course, but I missed the first half of your sermon because of it."

"I don't mind, Randy."

"You probably should. Unfortunately, I don't think there's a way to stop her. She loves what she does. She thinks she's helping people, not driving them crazy."

"She's driving *you* crazy, Randy. Not necessarily the rest of us. I tell you what, I'll try these new things she's sold me and if I like them, you can relax because we'll know she *is* doing someone a service."

"And if not?"

"That's a bridge we'll have to cross when we come to it."

Randy slapped Alex on the shoulder. "You're a good man, Reverend. I'm glad you're at Hilltop Church."

"Me too, Randy. Me too."

Alex lay in bed that night, staring at the ceiling. Nights were dark on the prairie. No cars, no neon, no streetlamps. Just stars and the moon. When the night was cloudy, he felt as if he were cocooned inside a black velvet pouch. Tripod was draped across his ankles and emitting a soft snore. It made it easier to think when there was no distracting noise or light—even if he didn't want to.

CHAPTER NINETEEN

When he reached the B&B the next morning to have breakfast with Natalie, she was already packing her car. Her hair was pulled back and coiled loosely at her neck, which showed off the delicate lines of her profile.

"I thought we were going to eat at seven," Alex said. "Isn't that what Nancy told us? I wanted to help you with your luggage."

"It's okay. I woke up early and couldn't get back to sleep so I thought I'd get ready." Natalie shut the trunk. "You have a busy schedule and I shouldn't keep you away from your work."

"The people you've met are my friends, as well as my parishioners," he said. "You aren't keeping me away from them. They understand. They've supported me since the day I arrived. If any people are 'salt of the earth,' it's these."

"I'm glad for you, Alex. I really am. You've found a special place here."

"Then why do you seem so glum?"

She sagged against the car. "Oh Alex, I know it's my fault, but I was hoping…wishing…you know."

Gently, he took her hand and led her to the far side of the porch, where no one in the house could overhear.

"I was selfish when I allowed myself to be swept off my feet by Justin. He was handsome and romantic and insisted that he couldn't live without me. I went crazy, Alex. What I thought was love was shallow infatuation. It lasted only a few weeks before I knew what a horrible mistake I'd made. I thought that if you and I could see each other you might remember how it was…"

"It was a deep wound, Natalie."

"I know. I'm an educated woman, Alex, but very stupid when it comes to love. Frankly, I'm trying to recover what I threw away."

"I'm not a scrap of paper to be dug out of a garbage can, or a box top someone is collecting for a school project, Nat. At least I hope not."

She smiled wanly. "Is that how I treated you? Like trash?" When he didn't answer, her eyes grew wide. "It is, isn't it?" She put her face in her hands, and the coil at the base of her neck trembled as she cried. "I just want you back in my life so much!"

Alex let her cry. He'd never been afraid of tears. Sometimes they were needed to cleanse away the hurt, negativity or regret people carried. He'd shed tears himself over Natalie. He believed it was a gift to allow someone to cry and not pat them on the head and beg them to stop. Doing that would only ease his own discomfort, not Natalie's.

"Natalie, I don't think this is the time for either of us to make decisions about the future. The only thing I can promise is that if you call me, I'll answer, and if you e-mail, I'll respond. I can't guarantee anything else."

"But you'll leave the lines of communication open?" She wiped the tears from her cheeks. "You aren't telling me to go away forever?"

"No."

She grabbed his hand. "I'll prove myself to you, Alex. I'll show you that I'm not that fickle woman anymore. Wait and see."

As he watched her drive down the lane and saw her car disappear around the shelterbelt, Alex felt more confused than ever, tugged this way and that, like the rope in a tug-of-war. *Lord, give me a sign!*

Turning his thoughts to other things, he pulled a list Gandy had given him out of his pocket. It wasn't long, but definitely problematic.

> *Lydia Olson wants to talk to you about her brother*
> *Jacob. Now there's a man who needs prayer.*
>
> *Minnie Packard asked if you'd talk to Earl. He's*
> *balking at the idea of the kids going to Sunday*
> *school. I'll pray for you about that one.*
>
> *Alf Nyborg was in the church office looking for*
> *you. Must be something bothering him big-time*
> *if he actually wants to talk to you. Good luck.*
> *Gandy*

Alex had learned early to tackle the most difficult job first. Earl Packard was a difficult job if there ever was one.

He drove slowly into the Packard yard. One never knew what might pop out of the trees along the driveway. The children played a game they called "the Hatfields and the McCoys." Will made up the game after reading about the family feud that developed between the two families during the Civil War. The children had divided themselves into Hatfields and McCoys, and when the kids were bored, war could erupt between them at a moment's notice.

Alex parked and got out of the van. Not even one of the mangy dogs the Packards had came to greet him. All was quiet, except for the sound of a chain saw behind the house. He walked toward the sound.

At the back, he saw a stand of trees that had to be at least fifty years old. Many of them were lying on the ground, their roots upended, hunks of black soil still clinging to them. Earl was wielding the chain saw, carving limbs off the fallen trees. He stopped the saw, laid it on the ground and began to lift the branch he'd just removed.

"So you're the one who got hit by lightning last night," Alex called out. He studied the jagged splits in the trunks of the fallen giants. "We thought the lightning had to be very close. Can I help you with that?"

Earl Packard swung around, a startled expression on his face. "What are you doing here?"

"Just came for a visit. The house and yard looked quiet, but I heard you back here."

"Minnie took the kids to get school shoes." Earl grimaced, his expression sullen. "I could buy a hundred gallons of diesel for my rig with that money." He took the tree limb again and started to pull it toward a pile of brush.

Alex grasped another part of the limb and tugged on it with him. After they dragged it to the pile, Earl returned to the downed tree and revved up the saw. Without a word, Alex waited for the next limb to fall away and helped him haul that one to the pile as well. They worked in silence, finding a rhythm together. Soon the tree was stripped of limbs, and Earl began to cut it into chunks.

He wasn't a country boy, but Alex did know how to stack wood. As Earl sawed, Alex piled the wood into orderly heaps. When one tree was done, they went to another. What was he doing here? he wondered. He had a to-do list a mile long on his desk at church. Then he glanced at Earl's bowed back. No, this was part of his job too.

After nearly two dirty, scratchy hours, Earl stood back to survey their work. "Not bad. I'll get my loader to move those stumps and chop this wood and stack it for winter. It will have to season this winter, but it will be ready for the next."

"Season?" Alex wiped sweat from his eyes with the arm of his white shirt and realized for the first time that he hadn't dressed for heavy labor. Oh well, he had plenty of shirts and trousers. His shoes, however, might be another story.

"Dry out. Let the moisture escape. You can't burn wood until it's below twenty percent water content. Otherwise your chimney will be filled with creosote and you'll have a chimney fire." Then he looked at Alex appraisingly. "You must have wanted something when you came here. Most preachers do."

"I almost forgot," Alex said with a chuckle. "I came to ask you personally if you would be willing to send your children to Sunday school this year. I understand that they haven't come before. I think they'd enjoy it."

"If they haven't been there before, what's the point now?" Earl said bluntly.

"They could spend time with other children in the community and they would learn about Christ."

"Minnie talks about Him all the time. They already know that stuff."

"I'm sure there's even more, Earl. It would be good for them and I know they would enjoy it."

The man stared at Alex for a long time. "I'm not crazy about the idea. God hasn't done a lot for me lately. If you'd asked me before you helped me with the trees, I would have said no. But since you put out some effort for me, I guess I owe you one." His voice lowered to what Alex could only describe as a growl. "Yeah, they can come. Just make sure they don't hurt anyone."

"Thank you," Alex said, despite that ominously negative granting of permission.

Earl grunted in response. "I can't sit around gabbing all day. I've got to start chopping wood." He turned his back on Alex, picked up an ax and lumbered toward the uncut wood.

Seeing he'd been dismissed, Alex got back into his car, punched his fist into the steering wheel and said, "Yes!"

Despite Earl's lack of enthusiasm, Alex was exultant. It had only taken a few hours of backbreaking work and a change of clothes to get the Packard children to Sunday school. It was worth every painful minute.

Next stop, Lydia Olson's.

The Olson yard was tidy as a pin compared to Earl Packard's. Grass was trimmed close around the buildings, and everything sported fresh paint. Alex saw Clarence and Jacob working on a tractor in the door of the machine shed. As he pulled up to the building, Jacob disappeared into the bowels of the building. Alex knew Jacob wouldn't come out again until Alex had left. He was as elusive as a yeti or the Loch Ness monster. There were always sightings of Jacob, but no one outside his family really knew who he was.

"Good morning, Clarence," Alex said as he climbed out of the van.

Clarence glanced up and glowered at him. Then he put the wrench he was using in the back pocket of his work coveralls and said, "You've got to do something about that woman, Pastor. She's gone nuts."

Alex gave him a blank look, as if he didn't already know perfectly well who the man was talking about.

"My sister! She's off her rocker. One oar short of a canoe ride!" Clarence looked visibly shaken. Alex had never seen him so upset.

"What's wrong?"

"She's always tripping off to Ruby's on some excuse or another. Ruby asked her to a coffee party. She's going to help Ruby hem drapes. Ruby wants to learn how to make Lydia's pepper jelly. Blah, blah, blah. Her real reason is that she wants to hang around that Johann Paulson. She's acting like a teenage girl with her eye on a boy and it's"—Clarence searched for a word—"unbecoming!"

"She's hardly a girl. I met Johann Paulson. He seemed very nice."

"Hah! Ten to one, he's after Lydia's money…or worse."

Alex didn't want to know what Clarence thought "or worse" was.

"She says he's a retired train engineer and that since he's retired he's come to help his cousin. Granted, Ruby could use some help. That house of hers is way too much for her. Now Lydia says that he's considering moving back to North Dakota because he likes it here." Clarence's entire visage became a scowl.

"He's moving here because he sees a good thing and wants it. My sister cooks and keeps house like an angel, Pastor. She's Hilltop's Heloise. He's just lazy and wants her to keep house for him. Well, he can't have her—that's her job for us!"

Clarence didn't see the irony, Alex noted. Lydia could slave for her brothers—just not anyone else.

No longer able to keep back a smile, Alex said, "I'll drive up to the house and chat with her a while."

"You do that. Put her head on straight. Make her see where her responsibilities are."

Alex felt compassion for Clarence. The fact was that Lydia *was* beginning to see where her responsibilities were—and Clarence wasn't going to be happy with the answer.

Lydia was in the kitchen. Alex watched her roll out bread dough and slather it with butter, cinnamon and sugar. Then she rolled the dough into a log and began to slice it into rolls. "Pastor Alex! I'm so glad you're here. My brothers are driving me to distraction. They've gone off the deep end, both of them. They're thumping around here like big bulls, pouting and carrying on about all the meals that I'm not home to cook. Have you looked at those two? They could starve for two months and still have meat on their bones!"

Johann Paulson had certainly stirred up a hornets' nest. Rather than go right into that, Alex asked, "Lydia, tell me more about your brother Jacob. He disappeared into the shed again when I drove up."

She put the last of the rolls into a pan filled with brown sugar, butter and cream and tucked it beneath a dish towel to rise again.

"Jacob is agoraphobic. He's terrified to be in places that make him uncomfortable or make him feel hemmed in. He gets panic attacks in crowds, so now he won't go anywhere he thinks that might happen. He wouldn't dream of flying in an airplane or going to a shopping mall. A doctor told us that it's difficult to treat because one has to confront one's fears and overcome them. Jacob has never been willing to try. He's fine on the farm where there are familiar open spaces and he knows he's in control. The doctor calls those his 'safe zones.' Jacob is very dependent on Clarence and me to do for him what he can't do for himself."

Lydia moved to the coffeepot and poured Alex a cup. It was the way everyone did things in Hilltop—coffee first—but Alex wondered if any of them had considered that one day he might just float away on a river of java.

"These panic attacks he has terrify him. He avoids crowds almost exclusively now. He used to go to church, but now the closest he comes is to the back door when we're having a potluck, because he knows I'll pack a dinner for him if he picks it up and takes it home to eat."

Alex recalled the time he'd seen the man skulking in the back of the church basement.

"I feel so sorry for him. I've watched him have a panic attack. He has trouble breathing, sweats profusely and gets nauseous. Sometimes he can't even swallow. He says it feels like he's having a heart attack. I can't blame him for wanting to avoid that."

"I can't either. Is there a way to get him some help?"

"Jacob has to be the one to seek help. None of us can do it for him. I know he'd be happy if he could control himself enough to go to church on Sunday and to our neighbors' homes."

"That's not possible?"

"It's gotten so that every time he steps off the farm these feelings come over him." Lydia's eyes grew sad. "He's even tried to medicate himself with alcohol, but every time he does it's a disaster. I worry most about him, Reverend. If I were ever to leave the farm, Jacob would be lost."

"Are you planning to leave?" Alex asked slyly.

Lydia blushed the color of geraniums. "I didn't mean anything by that. You know I've been yearning to have some adventure in my life. What I've always dreamed of doing is taking a safari! And I'd love to ride in a hot air balloon."

"Do you have any smaller adventures planned? Maybe you could get a ride on Ben Jenkins's motorcycle or..."

"I do have one little thing planned." Lydia's voice grew low. "But I have to keep it a secret, or my brothers would hit the roof. Johann's asked me out for dinner on Saturday night. Isn't that exciting?"

She beamed like a teenager about to go on a first date. Maybe this *was* her first date, for all Alex knew. And no matter what her brothers thought, it was about time.

"How are you planning to break the news to them?"

"I wanted to talk to you about that." Lydia peeked under the towel to check the rolls. "I don't want to lie to them about it..."

But Alex could see she was tempted. "No, I always think coming straight out with the truth is the best idea."

She sighed. "I thought you'd say that. Maybe I should write them a note and leave it on the table for them to read when they come inside."

"Won't they see Johann drive into the yard to pick you up? It would be odd not to talk to them." He could see that Lydia was dreading the confrontation by the way her lips turned down at the corners and her brow furrowed.

"Perhaps you could come for dinner that night and eat with Clarence and Jacob after we've gone," she said hopefully. "I'll make scalloped potatoes. They keep well in the oven and I have plenty of cream on hand. And pork chops. Clarence loves them. You pick the kind of pie you like…"

"Lydia, are you trying to bribe me into being here to cushion the blow?" Alex didn't know if he was dismayed or amused.

"Frankly, yes. I can't think of any other way. Will you? Besides, it will be a good chance for you to get to know Jacob. He never misses a meal."

Sly as a fox, Lydia had him just where she wanted him. It would be easy to turn down a dinner invitation if it were just to be a buffer between her and her brothers, but the chance to visit with Jacob was very tempting. "You'll owe me a cooking lesson for this, Lydia."

She beamed at him. "Something chocolate."

The deal was sealed.

CHAPTER TWENTY

As Alex drove toward the church, he saw Mattie Olsen heading straight for him.

She slammed on her brakes at the last minute and pulled up to his van so that they sat nose to nose. She burst out of her car and trotted to his.

"I need a shotgun."

Mattie had a habit of threatening death and mayhem, Alex had discovered, while she was trying to rid Hilltop Church of ants, but as far as he knew, she'd never turned her vehemence on humans. "Now what?"

"Squirrels! Red ones! The nasty kind. If it were gray squirrels, it would be one thing, but the red ones are terribly destructive. They're eating my insulation."

Alex looked her over. She still seemed rather well padded to him.

"In my roof, I mean. Red squirrels have gotten into the inside of my house. They keep me awake all night, skritching and scratching, their little nails scraping overhead." She made little clawing motions with her fingers. "The little monsters never sleep. Pretty soon one of them is going to get through the insulation and plaster and drop right down on top of me in my bed!"

"Blowing out your ceiling with a shotgun to get them doesn't seem very practical."

"I'm beyond practical. I'm sleep deprived. Really, Reverend, the only thing I can imagine that might be worse is bedbugs!"

"How about an exterminator? Or perhaps someone could live-trap them and move them somewhere else."

"Do you think it would cost a lot of money?" Mattie watched her bottom line carefully.

"I have no idea. Why don't you stop at Red's gas station? He seems to know a little about everything."

"Good idea. Thanks, Pastor. I'm glad I ran into you." Mattie turned back to her car, climbed in, revved the engine and backed up in a spurt of dust. Then she shifted into gear and sped off, leaving Alex to, literally, eat her dust.

Red squirrels. He was finding more and more things he needed to know that he hadn't been taught in seminary.

Gandy's car was at the church when he arrived.

Inside, he found her tussling with an awkwardly shaped box about five feet long and two feet high. "What have you got there?"

She jumped like she'd been shot. "I've told you a dozen times not to sneak up on me like that." She turned to him and scraped her fingers through her frizzy hair. "When I was young, my brother Jonas used to do it all the time—only he usually had a garter snake or a lizard in his hand. You'd never know that he was such a little stinker when he was young, but he was. He could have been a Packard, for all his antics. I got him back once, though, and he quit pestering me."

"Dare I ask how?"

"Ants and honey," Gandy said proudly. "They made a terrible mess of his bed. The best part was that he jumped in bed without looking beneath the covers."

"Gandy, I didn't know you had it in you."

"It's out of me now. Jonas went crying to our parents and I got what for. 'Course, I told them it was because he kept coming after me with reptiles, so he got what-for too. Life calmed down a lot after that, but I still don't like being startled."

"I will do my best. What's in that box?"

"It's those garlands I ordered to drape from the ceiling of the sanctuary for Christmas. They were such a good price that we couldn't pass them up. I thought I'd look at them and see if they were all the catalogue said they'd be."

Alex picked up the box and carried it into the entry of the sanctuary, where Gandy could unpack the clumsy parcel, and went back to his desk.

He sat down and stared out the door of the office and directly through the open church doors to the outside. Life seemed to be running in themes these days, particularly the themes of relationships and love. Lydia and Johann were stirring the pot at the Olson household. Walter Englund was inquiring about meeting women online, and Natalie had popped back into his life with a mea culpa and a desire to pick up where they'd left off.

There was also the theme of reaching out and caring for others. Lauren was working hard to make the food shelf a success. A lot of people had their eyes on Tillie and Lila. As awareness of such needs grew, he knew there would be others to add to that list.

He was so deep in thought that for a moment he didn't realize that Alf Nyborg was standing in the doorway to the office. In the time he'd been at Hilltop, rarely had Alf sought him out.

Alex jumped to his feet. "Come in, you don't have to stand in the doorway. Have a chair. Coffee's on."

Alf shuffled in looking as though he were walking the Bridge of Sighs in Venice, the bridge prisoners walked from the interrogation room in the Doge's Palace to the prison in which they would be incarcerated. He was wringing his billed cap in his hands so that Alex doubted he'd ever get it back to its original shape.

Alex handed him the coffee and sat down. Alf had little choice but to sit down across from him.

"Anything I can help you with?"

"I don't know. My wife says she's about done with me and made me promise to talk to you." He sounded gruff and angry.

Alf's tone told Alex this wasn't promising. Betty Nyborg was the most forbearing woman Alex had ever met. For her to give up on her husband was no small matter. "Can you tell me what it's about?" *Lord, step into this situation!*

"Betty says I'm ruining the present by living in the past, one particular day of the past. She's put up with it for years and now she says it's time to choose—her or my memories."

Many years before, when Alf had lost his first wife and small son to a fire, he'd blamed himself for the their deaths, fearing he might have started it by hooking up a gas line incorrectly. Though he'd remarried and had more children, he'd never let go of that one tragic day. It had infected every day of his life since.

"Should we go back to where it started?" Alex asked gently.

Misery and resentment emanated from Alf, a misery so deep Alex could feel it himself. "I know the story of how your wife and son died. And I understand that guilt is destroying you. But it is guilt no one else believes you should have. No one in this community blames you for anything. Sometimes inexplicable things happen and the only recourse is to forgive yourself and go on."

"But if I did cause my boy's death, how can I forgive myself?" The man's voice was rough with emotion.

"No matter what happened, God forgave you long ago. He's all about forgiveness. That's what He wants most, to forgive His children. All they have to do is ask."

"Seems pretty presumptuous to me," Alf grumbled, sounding more like his normal self.

"Not at all. Holding out on God is what seems presumptuous to me."

"What do you mean, 'holding out'?"

"He asks us to lay all our burdens and problems on Him. If we don't, we're giving Him short shrift. He wants *all* of us, not just the stuff we 'decide' is good enough for Him."

"Holding out on God?" Alf sounded annoyed. "What kind of talk is that? No preacher has ever said stuff like that to me before."

"He's a jealous God. Remember the first commandment? 'I will have no other gods before Me.'"

"That's about worshiping idols." Alf was squirming and his face was flushed.

This wasn't going well. Alex knew he didn't have much time before the man would storm out and perhaps never return. He clutched the Bible lying on his desk and forged ahead, speaking the things God was putting in his heart.

"Maybe you've made your dead son, the fire and your guilt your idols." The words sounded harsh, even to Alex, but he knew without a doubt that it was what God wanted him to say. He leaned back and waited for an outburst.

But Alf didn't move. Finally, after some long moments, he found his voice. "Nobody's ever talked to me that way before. It's a rotten thing to say, Reverend, that I've been worshiping idols because I put my son's death before God in my heart and mind. Really rotten." Alf lifted his cap and slapped it onto his head. "I don't have to take this. You're no better than my wife." With that, he stormed out of the office.

Alex remained firm, his eyes following Alf, his thoughts a litany of prayers to God.

"What's wrong with you?" Gandy returned to the office a few minutes later and stood in front of his desk with strands of thick garland draped around her neck.

Alex shook himself. "I'm fine." It was Alf who wasn't fine, at least not yet. He now knew that there was another theme winding through life at Hilltop. Forgiveness. Redemption. Healing.

"Good, 'cause I need you to help me put this stuff back in the box. It's going to be wonderful during the holidays. It's thick and full, just like I'd hoped. We can make a real celebration for Jesus' birthday with this."

Alex pushed out of his chair. "I'd love to help you, Gandy. I'm ready for something to celebrate."

He'd been dreading Saturday night. Perhaps that was why it came around so quickly.

Lydia called him at eight o'clock on Saturday morning. "You haven't forgotten that you are going to drop over this evening just before Johann comes to pick me up, have you?"

"No, Lydia, I haven't, but I have begun to wonder if it's the best idea."

"Of course it is! I've made some of the boys' favorites. Pork chops in blue cheese gravy, scalloped potatoes, green bean casserole and a lemon meringue pie."

She had him at the blue cheese gravy.

"Come at five forty-five. Everything will be in the oven and the timer will ring at six. I set the table for three, as usual. The boys will never guess a thing, until they realize that you will be sitting at my place instead of me."

"I don't feel right about deception, Lydia."

"This isn't subterfuge. I'm in my sixties and I'm going out for dinner with a friend! If that's not okay with my brothers and they make me stay home that's...that's kidnapping! I shouldn't have to report my every move to them. Pastor Alex, you're helping me to be normal, that's all."

It was a powerful argument. "I'll be there."

"Good. I believe Jacob will enjoy company in his own setting."

That, Alex reminded himself, was the more important reason for visiting the Olsons. He needed to meet the mysterious Jacob.

Still, 5:45 came awfully early.

Before he could even knock on the door, Lydia threw it open. "Come in, come in." She practically towed him into the kitchen. Her face was radiant and she'd had her hair done. It framed her face in soft curls.

"You look very nice."

"Do you think so? I told Barbara Owens that I wanted it full around my face." She fingered a curl. "She said she thought it made me look younger."

"You're glowing with youth." Alex truly meant it. Lydia's excitement was catching. Maybe this wasn't such a bad idea after all. Then he heard footsteps on the porch and Clarence and Jacob burst into the room.

"Reverend Alex! Just in time for supper." Clarence stepped to one side so that Alex got a full view of Jacob Olson. He was trimmer than Clarence, weather beaten and tanned. His arms were thick with muscle and his shoulders broad. Although Jacob was timid around people, to Alex he looked as though he could wrestle a small bear to the ground and pin it. Clarence made introductions, but before he could say more, a car pulled into the yard. Lydia ran to the window.

"Who's here right at suppertime?" Clarence said peevishly. "Except you, of course, Reverend. Everybody else knows better."

Alex took the social reprimand with a grain of salt. Pretty soon Clarence would think that his arriving during the dinner hour was a minor infraction.

Lydia picked up her purse and announced, "I'll be going now."

"Going where?" Clarence looked stunned. "You've got to feed us supper."

"It's in the oven. The table is set. Alex, since you're here, why don't you take my place at the table? It will be nice for you boys to visit without me."

"But where are you going?" Jacob asked. His voice was surprisingly soft and melodic in that burly body. He sounded genuinely worried.

"I'm going out to eat with Johann Paulson. You boys have a nice meal now." With that, Lydia flitted out of the house and left Alex to pick up the detritus left by her tornado-like departure.

The "boys" appeared shell-shocked. Clarence didn't seem able to close his mouth, now that his jaw had dropped open. Jacob looked utterly confused.

"That was a nice invitation to join you for supper. I'd like that very much. Do you want me to help you put things on the table?" With that, Alex went ahead and pulled the casseroles out of the oven and put them on the trivets Lydia had placed on the table. The men never moved.

He filled the water glasses from a pitcher and wondered if he should take one of them and toss the water in Clarence's face to bring him out of his daze. Finally, Alex said, "I can't wait a minute longer to eat. Why don't we sit down and I'll say grace."

Apparently, direction was what the men were waiting for. Without their rudder Lydia, they didn't seem to know which way to turn. Alex said a grace they didn't seem to hear and began to dish up. Suddenly, every dish on the table rattled as Clarence's fist came down hard on the table.

"What is she thinking? She can't leave us here unfed! What's gotten into that woman? Ever since that Johann came around she's been out of her mind!" His complexion grew dangerously flushed.

"She didn't leave you unfed, Clarence," Alex said. "Here, have some potatoes. They look wonderful. Besides, she's not out of her mind. She's one of the sanest people I know."

"You can say that after seeing her trot off after that...that..."

"Gentleman? She's a single woman who obviously feels she's missed some things in life that she wants to experience."

"What does that mean?"

"Did Lydia have a good life as a girl?"

"I suppose so. She was always in the house working, while we were out with our father."

"Did she have fun?"

"Fun? What does fun have to do with anything? It's enjoyable to be here on the farm, working in nature, making things grow... right, Jacob?"

Jacob nodded.

"But Lydia's job was housework. Maybe it wasn't as pleasurable for her as farming has been for you."

"Makes sense to me." This was Jacob's first entry into the conversation. "Lydia's been good to us, Clarence. It's time she did something for herself." He looked over the dishes on the table. "Reverend, will you pass those potatoes?"

"Humph," Clarence grumbled. "What do we know about this guy, other than he's Ruby's cousin? He could be a real womanizer for all we know. Maybe he's got a wife stashed away at home or some secret life..."

Alex was surprised that Clarence had such a vivid imagination. "You've known Ruby for years, right?"

"Well, yes..."

"And has it ever come up that she has a relative who is a scoundrel?"

"People don't talk about those kinds, if they have them in their families."

"Ruby's family is nice," Jacob said consolingly.

Alex was surprised to find him so firmly on Lydia's side. Maybe she'd underestimated this brother.

"Well, I don't like it." Clarence slopped food onto his plate. Concern over his sister hadn't dampened his appetite.

The rest of the meal went surprisingly well. It was obvious to Alex that these men loved their sister but had genuinely never thought of her as needing any more than they themselves had. If they loved farm life, Lydia should too. He also found Jacob to be an intelligent man, sociable even.

All in all, Alex thought as he drove home, it had been an amazingly successful meeting. He hoped Lydia could say the same.

Alex got home to find three messages on his answering machine.

The first was from Lolly Roscoe. "Hi, I just wanted to let you know that we're having special music at the farmers' market in two weeks. The students from Grassy Valley High School will perform. I know you enjoy music, so I thought you might want to come. I'll be there, of course. Stop by my booth. Maybe we can listen to the music together."

Lolly was always offering up opportunities for Alex to meet with her. He was just as diligent about avoiding the invitations as Lolly was about making them. Until another bachelor moved to Grassy Valley or to Hilltop township, he was afraid he would remain the target of her affections. Although he'd never encouraged her, she persisted.

The second call was from Mark Nash. "Hi, Alex. There's a quick meeting tomorrow afternoon to discuss the news that Doc Ambrose has announced his retirement. He hasn't set a date yet. Says he wants to give people some time to look for a new doctor if they can find one. I'm sure he won't be here past Christmas, though. We've got to get a search party up and running. Can you stop by my place after church?

I'll feed you. I must have something edible in the freezer. How do you feel about pizza?"

What Alex had been worrying about since the episode with Lila had come to pass. He had no idea how he could help, but at least he could lend his support.

The third call was from Dixon. His enthusiasm was obvious in his words. "Hey, Alex! Good news. My sister Emmy just called. She's coming this week. You'll have to meet her. She's heard all about you. I'm not sure which day she'll arrive. She's in high demand where she works, but she's determined to take some vacation days. I'll let you know. Isn't this *great*?"

Dixon's enthusiasm made Alex more eager than ever to meet this Emmy he'd heard so much about.

∾

Lolly cornered him first thing after church the next morning. "Good sermon, Pastor." Her blond hair was fluffed even higher than usual.

"Thanks." Alex looked around for someone else to draw into their conversation, but everyone was busy admiring Hans and Hilda Aadland's new great-grandchild, who had come to church with their visiting granddaughter.

"I love the Beatitudes," Lolly continued. "I even took notes on the sermon."

"Wonderful, Lolly," he said brightly as he edged his way around her. "Now, if you'll excuse me, I'd better see that new Aadland baby for myself." One of these days, he realized, Lolly was apt to corner him and there would be no escape.

By the time he was done admiring the new baby, Lolly had gone home. Dixon, however, had not.

"I see she got you cornered again," he said cheerfully. "You'd better watch out. One of these days she's going to go in for the kill."

"Very funny. She's a nice woman, just…"

"Starved for love?"

"Lay off, Dixon. No matter what you think, I will not succumb to Lolly's wiles. I will, however, pray she finds someone who loves her." Alex dusted off the arm of his jacket, as if he could remove the spot where Lolly had touched him. She was a good woman. He didn't want to hurt her. Nor did he want to date her.

"Are you going to the meeting at Mark's?" Dixon asked. "If so, you can ride with me."

"Who will be there? I'm not sure what I have to do with this."

"Red's coming. He's in on everything in Grassy Valley. Some of the business owners in Grassy Valley, Lauren and Mike. Mark, you, me. I don't know who else. Gandy, maybe. She's got a way of ferreting out news and people. She'd probably have somebody lined up ASAP if we let her go at it. Might be a veterinarian or a medicine man, of course, but she'd find some sort of doctor."

∽

Dixon was right on all counts, Alex observed, as they sat around Mark's large dining table eating pizza and pouring soda out of plastic liter bottles. The only other addition to Dixon's list was Walter Englund. The mood, however, was not upbeat.

"We'll never get another Doc Ambrose," Red said gloomily. "Not in a million years. Anybody available probably isn't worth the paper their degree is written on,"

Even Lauren and Mike were pessimistic. "It would take someone very special to choose small-town life over more pay at a bigger hospital," Mike said after his third slice of pepperoni and mushrooms.

"Are you saying it's hopeless?"

Then Lauren startled them all by pounding her fist on the table. "We've got to stop talking like this! Let's just formulate our plan and go through it step by step—compiling names, contacting medical schools, finding a headhunter, whatever it takes. The only thing we need to add that hasn't been mentioned is prayer. We prayed for the perfect pastor and who arrived? Pastor Alex! Now we'll pray for the perfect medical person and wait to see who shows up, right?"

Alex leaned over to whisper in Lauren's ear. "I was the *only* person to show up for this position, remember?"

Lauren jumped to her feet. "Alex reminded me of something," she announced. "We don't need dozens of candidates, we just need one, the right one. That's where prayer comes in."

He hadn't meant it exactly like that, but it was a good point.

She turned to him again. "You'll pray for us, right? And find others who will?"

"Of course, but is that all you want me to do?"

"*All*? That's huge. Now let's start making a plan…"

"What do you think?" Dixon asked as they clambered back into his pickup so he could return Alex to the church to pick up his van.

"It sounds difficult, if not impossible," Alex admitted. "But when you throw the aspect of prayer into the mix, who knows?"

"Exactly. One thing I know for sure is that God is good at surprises. I think we do our search, pray and wait to see what happens."

It wasn't a business plan most would aspire to, but it had worked for Hilltop Community Church once before. Why not the clinic?

$Alex$ found Will in the shed the next morning. The boy was petting a tiny kitten. It appeared to be mewing, but no sound came out of its mouth. Tears were running silently down the boy's cheeks.

"Will?" Alex squatted by the child and the bit of fur in his lap.

"You gotta do something, Pastor Alex." Will's voice was so plaintive that it broke Alex's heart.

"What do you mean?"

"Look at this little feller! He's practically dead from starvation. I been feeding him with an eyedropper my mom got for me, but I don't know if he'll make it." The kitten and Will both turned wide, unhappy eyes on Alex. "You've gotta stop Bucky."

Alex's heart sank. It seemed that every few days someone he talked to had a complaint about Bucky Chadwick, be it petty thievery, trespassing or rude talk.

"What did he do to this kitten?"

"He took it away from its mama and left it to die! If I hadn't snuck over there to see if the animals were okay and noticed it, it would have been dead for sure. Nothing is safe at Bucky's house."

Alex chewed at the corner of his lip. "Maybe I could talk to his mother again."

Will snorted. "Sometimes I think she's as scared of him as I am.

When Bucky gets into one of his rages, Goliath would be afraid of Bucky, even if Goliath is a hunnert feet taller."

"Six cubits and a span," Alex murmured absently. "Goliath was nine feet, six inches tall."

"Whatever. If this kitten doesn't make it, it's all Bucky's fault."

"Why don't you come back to the house with me and I'll make you a cup of hot chocolate? Then you can come back and check on the kitten." Will, Alex had discovered, could drink hot chocolate by the bucket full.

Will nodded and laid the kitten into the nest of straw and blankets he'd made for it and followed Alex to the house. There was a weary slope to the child's shoulders, Alex noted. Bucky was getting to be too much for him...for everyone, in fact.

They were sitting at the kitchen table drinking cocoa and eating saltine crackers—a combination Will had taught him and that he found very satisfying—when there was a knock on the door.

Lydia Olson was outside, holding a pan of cinnamon rolls. "Fresh from the oven," she chirruped as Alex let her in.

"Just in time. Will you join Will and me in some hot chocolate?"

"I think that would be absolutely delightful. Thank you."

She puttered around putting the rolls on the table and finding dishes and forks in the cupboards, all the while humming to herself.

When Alex set the steaming mug in front of her she rhapsodized, "Perfect! What a marvelous aroma! My tongue is tingling already."

She was certainly talking in superlatives today. Even little Will was looking at her wide-eyed, as if she'd broken into Swahili.

"You're in a good mood."

"I am in a perfectly fantastic mood, thank you very much." She sipped the cocoa and her eyelashes fluttered. "Divine."

"So last night must have gone well." Alex had a hard time not smiling.

Will stared at Lydia like she'd lost her mind. "What's wrong with her?" Will asked Alex in a stage whisper.

Lydia laughed. "Young man, for once nothing is wrong with me, nothing at all."

"Okay…" Will swilled back the last of the liquid in his mug, took a handful of saltines and wiggled out of his chair. "Thanks. I'd better go check on my kitten." He was out the door before Lydia could alarm him any further.

"How was your dinner?" Alex asked, although Lydia's glow told the story.

"Lovely." She leaned forward as if she were about to impart some astonishing bit of information. "Lobster."

"First-class all the way."

"Oh yes. Johann is a very special man. But the real question is, how did *your* meal go?"

"Delicious, once I served it. Your brothers were too shocked to get it on the table." Alex took in Lydia's worried features. "They love you very much, Lydia. Give them time. They'll come around." *Another prayer for my list.*

After Lydia left, Alex went to the church to find Gandy in high dudgeon. The tip of her nose was pink, and he could tell she'd been crying. *Talk about opposites!* he thought to himself.

"What's happened, Gandy?" Of all the moods he'd seen her in, this was rare.

"It's been the saddest morning, Reverend. I just can't stand it! How you do this for a living, I'll never know." She pulled a tissue from the box on her desk and blew her nose until she honked like Will's geese.

"Is there something I should know?" He pulled a chair to her desk and sat down in front of her. Gandy, he'd noticed, was spending more and more time in the church office. Apparently she was upping her tithe again. The Dunns weren't flush with money, so Gandy worked as the church secretary for free, tithing the pay she'd get for hours back to the church. She'd been in the church office a lot lately. Instead of a 10 percent tithe, Alex suspected she'd upped it considerably. He was a little concerned that if Gandy decided to tithe 20 percent or more, she'd be in the church both night and day.

"Cherry Taylor was here looking for you. She wants prayer. Frankly, it was probably a good thing you weren't here. Her request was for female things, if you know what I mean."

"Not exactly. Females are complicated. That could be a lot of 'things.'"

Gandy leaned forward and whispered as if there were a horde of people milling about. "She's afraid she's infertile." She let the word hang in the air a moment before continuing. "They want a baby so badly and one just isn't coming along. She's getting depressed and Dan's not handling it very well. He's got problems of his own."

"Dan?"

"He was in Afghanistan, you know. It's post-traumatic stress or some such thing. Those poor kids have a lot on their plate."

"Are either being treated for their conditions?"

"I don't know. All Cherry asked for was prayer."

"Be sure to put them on the prayer list."

"She doesn't want that. She thinks it's too private a matter to be published in the bulletin. She just wants *you* to pray."

His list was growing.

Alex sat down to look at his unopened mail and had barely skimmed the telephone and electric bills when the phone rang. Gandy answered it.

"Hilltop Community Church. May I help you?" Gandy made a series of grimaces and facial contortions, indicating that the call was for him. Alex picked up.

Allen County Public Library
Tuesday May 19 2015 06:16PM

Barcode: 31833062735193
Title: Forever Hilltop : featuring An...
Type: BOOK
Due date: 6/9/2015,23:59

Total items checked out: 1

Telephone Renewal:(260)421-1240
Website Renewal: www.acpl.info

"Alex, is that you?" An all-too-familiar voice sang across the line. "How are you, darling?"

Natalie's question took him aback. "Fine," he finally stammered. "How are you?"

"Better, now that I've heard your voice. What are you doing in that quaint little church of yours today?"

"Opening mail, taking phone calls, researching my sermon, praying…the usual."

"It's so much fun to imagine you there, in the middle of the prairie, having little talks with that cute Gandy. Since I've been there it seems so much more real to me."

"It's real, no doubt about that." He was confused. His heart had lifted at the sound of her voice, but a trickle of doubt had also entered the pit of his stomach.

He'd once loved her with all his heart. There was a tug-of-war inside him the likes of which he'd never before experienced. He cared for her, that was undeniable, and it would be very easy to let that blossom into love.

"Are you busy, Alex? You sound distracted."

"A little, I guess. I just got in. I'm getting my bearings for the day."

"Don't let me keep you. I just wanted to hear your voice. I had a wonderful time at Hilltop. I'll talk to you soon."

A series of kissing noises sounded in his ear, loud enough to cause him to move the receiver away from his head. Then the dial tone sounded. He hung up the phone.

Another series of smooching sounds now emanated from Gandy's corner. When he looked up, she had her eyes closed and her mouth puckered like that of a fish. She opened her eyes slowly. "Now isn't that romantic?"

"Very funny, Gandy. What are you doing eavesdropping on my conversation?"

"Eavesdropping? She made so much noise I could hear it over my CD playing 'How Great Thou Art'!" She put her elbows on her desk. "What do you think, Reverend, are you going to take her back?"

Gandy was no fool. She'd figured out quickly what had transpired between him and Natalie and had demanded that he fill in the details. Knowing that Gandy could be more persistent than he was strong, he'd caved in and told her. Now it was coming back to haunt him.

"Not that it's any of your business..."

"Of course it's my business. I'm your secretary. For one thing, I need to know which calls to screen and which to let go through. Besides, I like to think we're friends, and friends are open with each other. Finally, I want to know how to pray for you. Is that reason enough? Or do you want me to go on? To tell you how much my family and this congregation love you and that we are concerned for you or that..."

"Okay, okay, I hear you loud and clear." He tapped his pen on the desk for a moment. "Gandy, since you know what's going on, what do *you* think?" Gandy loved to be asked her opinion, he knew. And while it often opened a floodgate he had difficulty closing again, she was instinctively wise and always guaranteed to give him a new perspective on things.

She sat back, crossed her skinny arms over her chest and furrowed her brow. "My take? It's your heart, Alex."

He didn't speak.

"Though if you can't get along without my opinion, I shouldn't hold back, right? I should give it to you with both barrels."

He was in for it now.

"She's beautiful, that Natalie. A real stunner. Even my brother Jonas noticed and he doesn't pay attention to much of anything, except the farm and his organic vegetables. My daughter Debbie said she looked like a model, and my sister-in-law Barbara wondered who did her hair. I can see why you fell for her…but, frankly, I'm a little unsure about something."

This, Alex hadn't expected. Gandy was often wrong, but she was *never* unsure. "Go on."

"We can all see she's lovely on the outside, but I'm not so sure about her insides, Alex. It's that verse in Luke that bothers me. The one where Jesus tells the Pharisees they are like cups, clean on the exterior, but they are dirty on the inside. Natalie definitely looks good on the outside, but I can't say about what's inside her. She left you for another man, didn't she? I worry about that."

"You do?" He was stunned by this revelation.

"I don't want you hurt. I can see that you came here for a fresh start. It was a pretty bold move too, considering that we're barely a blink in the road. Even though we aren't big or fancy, you treat us like we are. You've embraced our people like no one else ever has—or maybe even ever could."

Gandy's jaw hardened. "If you two ever got back together, I'm afraid she'd talk you into leaving Hilltop in a heartbeat." Then tears suddenly filled her eyes. "I don't want you to go. None of us do."

She grabbed for another tissue and honked again as she blew her nose. "Sorry, I didn't mean to get so upset, but you asked…"

For the first time, he realized that rekindling his relationship with Natalie had ramifications far beyond his own life. What's more, Gandy was right about Natalie. He couldn't see her being content here for long, no matter how hard she tried.

"Thank you for your honest and forthright answer, Gandy. You've given me a lot to think about."

"I have?" This seemed to cheer her immensely. Satisfied, she switched topics. "I made macaroons and fudge last night. Want some?"

"Right now I'd like nothing better."

As he and Gandy ate the fudge and drank strong cups of Dixon's Sumatra coffee, Alex considered what Gandy had said.

So many unforeseen things were happening. Not only was there Natalie's visit, but Bucky's worsening behavior, Doc Ambrose's announcement that he was leaving far sooner than they'd expected, Cherry and Dan's trouble, that crazy unmarked grave…it made his head spin.

Prayer, he decided, was the only answer.

CHAPTER TWENTY-THREE

$\mathcal{J}$ust when Alex thought that nothing more unexpected could happen, an angel arrived on his doorstep.

He was in the church basement, checking on a leak dripping water from an overhead pipe onto the life-sized Christmas manger scene kept tucked in one corner of the storeroom, when he heard footsteps above him. Sighing, he backed out of the congested space and shut the door. The pipe was a job for someone with more plumbing skills than he. Maybe Jonas Owens or Mike Carlson could handle it. As he came through the door into the dining room, he saw Dixon coming downstairs.

"What's happening?" his friend greeted him.

"A leak over the manger."

"Sounds serious."

"Nothing someone with more experience can't fix."

Dixon's eyes were twinkling and his smile was a little wider. "I brought someone here for you to meet."

"Really? Who…"

At that moment a pixie-like face surrounded by short, spiky curls peeked around the corner of the enclosed staircase. Cornflower-blue eyes with improbably long dark lashes twinkled back at him. Then the rest of the adorable sprite came around the corner. The woman was slim in stylishly torn jeans and a white button-down shirt. She wore a large turquoise necklace and sandals also embedded with the stone. She wore no makeup but glowed from an inner light that was all vivacious personality and sheer delight. "So this is the handsome single pastor I've been hearing so much about!"

Alex felt blood race to his cheeks. He turned to Dixon. "And this is…"

"My sister Emmy, of course. Can't you see the resemblance?"

Alex could, actually—the dancing eyes, the shape of their faces, their smiles—she was, indeed, his female counterpart. "She's much prettier than you are. And probably smells better too."

The pair burst into laughter. "I've been told that before," Dixon said agreeably. "Alex Armstrong, I'd like you to meet my younger sister, Emmy."

"Younger by two minutes," Emmy corrected. She turned to Alex. "He thinks he's older and wiser than I am. I haven't told him that whatever age and wisdom one can collect outside the womb in two minutes isn't enough to make a difference. I let him enjoy his little fantasy." She thrust out her hand. "Nice to meet you, Pastor Alex Armstrong."

Alex willed his right hand to move. Everything in him felt strangely paralyzed, as if he'd been shot with a cartoon stun gun. "Call me Alex. Dixon does."

"I love a man who doesn't cling to titles and strings of letters behind his name. That's so boring. *Very* nice to meet you…Alex."

He felt the warmth of her slender fingers in his hand. It seemed to bleed right through him to the tips of his toes. What on earth…?

"Emmy just got here and I wanted to bring her right over. I knew you two would hit it off." Dixon looked like a proud father.

"I haven't even unpacked, not that there is much to do. When I come to Hilltop, especially during harvest, I live in jeans and T-shirts. That's the best part of a vacation, don't you think? Maybe a clerical collar is more comfy than scrubs, but they are so boring that I can hardly stand it. Same thing, day in and day out. And the shoes are pretty unattractive too. I always try to push the edges of the envelope, but my office insists on white. You know, old lady shoes." She made a disparaging face.

Alex felt like he'd been hit with a tsunami of words and images. He wasn't thinking clearly and he must look like a clump of dirt to her, silent and bemused. He was stunned. He'd seen pictures of Emmy, but none of them did her justice. No two-dimensional image could capture the breadth and width of her personality. She'd already filled the church basement with it and she'd been here two minutes.

Emmy wandered around the room running a light finger across the tables, the piano and the serving counter. She clapped her hands at the window curtains, which she said were new since her last visit, and poked her nose into the kitchen.

"I always feel like there is the smell of brewing coffee in the air when I'm down here, even when the church is empty. Am I crazy?"

"Not at all. I sense it too." Alex's smile was coming back, and he tried to keep it from cracking his face wide open.

"After all the egg coffee cooked in that kitchen, the aroma is probably embedded in the walls," Dixon commented.

"Let's go look at the cemetery!" Emmy said. She turned to Alex. "I love to visit out there. It's like reading a family history, generation upon generation from the time this place was settled to the present. It doesn't feel like a sad place because I know that the people buried there knew Jesus." She looked at Alex with a plea in her eye. "Do you know what I mean?"

"Exactly. It affects me the same way."

"Good," Emmy said, as if he'd given just the right answer.

"I was planning to stop out there myself before I left for home.

Dixon, as long as you're here, I'd like to show you something that's been puzzling me. I believe I mentioned it to you once before."

"In a cemetery? That should be pretty straightforward."

"It should. That's why I'm puzzled."

They left the church to walk the few yards to their destination. Emmy moved ahead and began reading the names on tombstones.

"Here's Mattie Olsen's family. They were one of the first to come here. Mattie is very proud of that. And here are the Bloches. Isn't that little old Stoddard a cutie? Always trying to 'hammer' out a deal or 'saw' through the confusion. And his wife Edith—she's a 'yes' woman if there ever was one. I don't believe that woman has ever made a decision for herself. I know their daughters—lovely people."

They toured the cemetery seeing it through Emmy's eyes. Alex soaked up every word, glad to learn more about these people he served. Then, as they neared the back corner of the cemetery, Emmy turned to leave.

"No, let's go a little farther. It's back here that I have something to show Dixon."

"But there's hardly anything back there," Emmy said, but she turned around to follow them.

They arrived at the unmarked grave Alex had found. Dixon and Emmy stared down at it in confusion. "Who does that belong to?" Dixon asked.

"That's the question I've been asking myself," Alex said. "It's not an abandoned grave. The family of whoever it belongs to tends to it. The soil has been recently turned because it's fresh and black."

"Weird," Dixon said, and squatted down to look at the dirt. He picked some up and ran it through his fingers. "You're right. This topsoil is still damp. This wasn't done very long ago."

"A mystery," Emmy chortled. "I adore mysteries!"

Was there anything she didn't love? Alex wondered. She was like a human sponge, soaking up everything that came her way and delighting in it.

"I've asked around, but no one seems to know who it is."

"I find this very odd." Dixon stood up. "For now I should get my irrepressible sister home so she can rest."

"Don't be a bore, Dixon," Emmy retorted. "There's life to be lived. I can rest anytime. I want you to drive me around so we can see which fields will be harvested soon. I noticed that Mark has several swathed." She caught the confused look on Alex's face. "The grain is cut, laid down on the ground so the combine can pick it up and separate the wheat from the chaff. Sometimes it's harvested standing if the wheat is dry enough. It used to be that all grain was swathed—cut—and left to dry out before being combined. I especially love it when the nights are dry and the grain doesn't dampen. Then the combines can roll all night. Then I sit in the grain truck and drink hot chocolate and listen to country-and-western music...."

"Emmy is a harvest addict," Dixon said dryly. "When we were little, she pleaded constantly to ride in the tractor cab. Mom finally gave in, packed us lunches and we spent the day in the cab with Dad. It was crowded, uncomfortable and probably illegal, but we both thought it was worth it."

As they approached their cars, they could see a cloud of dust billowing in the distance.

"Uh-oh," Dixon muttered.

"Is Isabelle still driving?" Emmy sounded shocked.

"She appears to be. No one else in the community drives that fast."

As they watched, Isabelle Johnson sped by the church, throwing up enough sand and gravel that Alex felt a prick of sharp gravel on his forearm all the way in the churchyard.

"That shouldn't be happening," Emmy said, suddenly serious. "She's a danger to herself and others."

"The family has been trying to convince her of that. She's been the matriarch of the clan for so long, they're having a little trouble getting up the nerve to force her into it."

"They surely don't want her to kill herself or someone else while they're gathering their courage!"

Now Alex could see the professional nurse practitioner in her emerging.

"If they don't tell her, I will. Isabelle was like a second grandmother to me. I don't want her life to end in a tragedy." Her voice was steely and determined. Alex was impressed. This pixie had a spine of steel.

A second car followed Isabelle's at a much slower pace. So slow, in fact, that it, too, could cause an accident if someone driving the speed limit came upon the vehicle too quickly.

"Now what?" Dixon asked. "Did all the bad drivers in Hilltop decide to go out at once?"

Alex squinted into the distance. "This 'bad driver' is Inga Sorenson." He hadn't had a lot to do with the Sorensons yet. "Inga is, supposedly, in one of her creative phases and painting for an art exhibition."

"That explains it. Inga's not a bad driver when she's not distracted," Emmy said cheerily. "It's just that she's always got her mind on something else. At least she slows down rather than speeds up. She promised to paint a T-shirt for me. I wonder if it's done."

"What's so important that she can't drive more than twenty miles an hour?"

"She's always planning some new piece of art or hatching up a scheme to save the planet, starting with the animals."

"She and Will should get together." Alex told her about Will's Hoomain Society in the shed at the parsonage.

"How darling. I can't wait to meet this kid. I've been away long enough not to know some of the younger children at Hilltop." Emmy spun around and put the palms of her hands on her brother's face. "I am soooo glad to be back." She turned to Alex. "Dixon has some oats ready to harvest. I'm going to ride with him tomorrow. Have you ever ridden on a combine?"

"Never."

"Then you have to come too. We can take turns driving the truck and riding with him. I'll pack a lunch. What do you think?"

"Sounds great."

By noon the next day, when Alex arrived at the Daniels farm, heat was rising from the ground in shimmering waves, and the sky was a pure, cloudless blue. Emmy and Dixon waved at him from the door of the machine shed, beckoning him to them. Practically overnight Hilltop had become golden—the fields were the color of bullion, and the blazing yellow sun cast a glow over the countryside. Both the air and the people crackled with energy and anticipation, as if the beginning of harvest had infused them with eagerness and vigor they'd been missing. Alex easily understood why Emmy loved to return to Hilltop at this time of year.

"Good morning, Alex," Emmy said brightly. She was dressed in faded jeans and a shocking pink T-shirt. On her feet were equally bright tennis shoes. Her hair was tousled, as if she'd combed it with her fingers. Her sunglasses appeared to have been created in a psychedelic kaleidoscope. She flitted around excitedly. If she were in miniature, Alex might have expected to see her perched on the edge of a flower petal or having tea with Tinkerbell.

Combines looked far bigger up close. The immense John Deere hunkered in the middle of Dixon's yard like a green giant.

"I always think of Ruth in the Bible, picking up the gleanings left over after Boaz took off his crop, carrying the stalks in her arms." Dixon walked up beside Alex and stared at the machine with him.

"What would those people think of how we harvest crops today? It would be a miracle in their eyes to see this thing rolling up and down their land."

"I don't believe we have any idea how far we could go if we let God guide us all. Imagine, no arguments, no wars, no crime, no getting even—all that time could be spent creating things like these."

"Sign me up for that," Dixon said, "but for now we'll go for a spin in this particular miracle. My truck is already in the field so you'll both have to ride with me. The cab will be crowded for you, but if you sit on the training set and Emmy can sit on your knee for a couple minutes, we'll be there."

They all climbed the steps to the cab. Dixon slid in first, into a seat more comfortable looking than any Alex had in his house. There was what Dixon referred to as the command center to his right that gave him access to the machine's reading and functions.

"Impressive," Alex breathed.

"New combine," Dixon said. "Just wait until I show you how the global positioning system works. It will blow you away."

Alex felt his heart thumping with excitement. He wished his nephew Jared could be there for this. To a city boy like him, this would be high adventure.

Alex also realized that being so tightly squeezed in the cab that he was forced to put his arm around Emmy Daniels was a very pleasurable experience.

"Are many people harvesting already?" he asked, curious to know everything about this season everyone seemed to love so much.

"Mark's started, and Dan Taylor. Mike said he'd probably pick up a sample this afternoon. Most everyone will be out in the fields soon."

"A sample of what?"

Dixon chuckled. "Sorry, I keep forgetting I have a city slicker here. We pick a sample of grain and test it for moisture. If the kernels are dry enough to store in a bin without spoiling, we start picking."

"What if it's not dry enough?"

"We wait. Grain can be dried in grain dryers, but I avoid that if I can. It takes a lot of electricity, for one thing." Dixon put the machine in gear and they began to move. "I think there's more activity over by All Saints Fellowship. The Clayborns and Nyborgs are already combining. And I think Kenny Dawson, Althea's son, has been going for a couple of days too. I never judge my crops by Kenny's though. He's always in a hurry. I think he takes it off too soon."

Emmy, perched on Alex's knee, spoke. "I went to high school with him. Kenny was in a hurry even then. He's the most impatient person I've ever known. His cars had to be souped up, his papers turned in ahead of time, and he could talk a mile a minute. I always told him he was born in overdrive and didn't know how to shift down."

Dixon pulled up to the waiting truck. "Emmy, you'd better drive first. I'll let Alex get the feel of things up here and then maybe you can teach him to drive the grain truck. He might as well make himself useful."

She squirmed out from beneath his arm, opened the door and scooted down the laddered steps to the ground. With practiced moves, she got into the truck, checked the shift and turned the key in the ignition. When it roared to life, she gave a thumbs-up.

"She's done this before," Alex commented, feeling a little in awe of this tiny, capable woman.

"Ever since she could see over a steering wheel." Dixon showed Alex how he dropped the header to the ground. They moved forward, and cut wheat flowed into the machine. Alex realized that the harvested wheat was flowing into a grain tank just behind them, and the chopped stalks were spit out the back of the combine and spread across the ground they'd just covered.

"When the grain tank, or hopper, gets full, Emmy will drive up beside me and I'll dump my load into the truck. When her truck gets full, she'll take it back to the farm yard and auger it into a bin. And we keep doing it until this whole field is picked."

Mesmerized, Alex watched the combine gobble the swaths and flowing grain feed itself into the bowls of the machine. He'd caught the harvest spirit.

At six PM Dixon brought the machine to a halt. "I don't know about you, Alex, but I'm ready for some of that lunch Emmy packed. Let's take a break." He opened the door of the cab, grabbed a cooler that had been stuffed behind his seat and slid out. Alex was close on his heels. Emmy exited the truck and joined them. Without ceremony, they dropped onto the ground and into the shade of one of the gigantic wheels.

"Out here I've learned that dinner is eaten at noon and supper is eaten in the evening. Does that mean everything else is lunch?"

"You're catching on. When I was a kid my mom used to feed us three meals a day plus two lunches. One was in the morning and it was usually cookie, cake or pie and coffee. In the afternoon we got sandwiches and more cookies. When you work plenty, you can eat plenty, my dad used to say."

As the men watched, Emmy dispensed food from a cooler— sandwiches, slices of watermelon, apples, half a pie, and a healthy-sized bag of chocolate chip cookies. "Eat up, boys."

While they were eating, Alex drilled Dixon with questions. Finally, Emmy broke into the conversation with some questions of her own.

"Is Bessie Bruun still hearing voices?"

"Not so much," Dixon said, yawning. "There's only a couple of radio stations she says she has to stay away from now."

"Poor sweet thing. I just love her." Emmy toyed with her cookie, picking out the chocolate chips one by one. "And Hans and Hilda?"

"Hans has a bad toe."

"Gout again?"

Alex was amazed by Emmy's ability to keep up with all that was going on around Hilltop.

Dixon stretched out on the ground, oblivious to the sharp stubble left by the cut wheat, pulled his hat over his eyes, put his arms behind his head to cushion it and promptly fell asleep.

Alex stared at him. "How did he do that?"

"He's always done that in the field—eat, nap and wake up in fifteen or twenty minutes refreshed. It's a good habit to have if one plans to work late into the night." Emmy sat with her knees close to her chest and her arms around them. "Dixon and I have worked together in the field since we were old enough to do so. We both love it out here."

"You're a real farm girl at heart."

"I am, but my job is elsewhere and I love it, so I have to make do with this, a week or two a year out here. I usually come during harvest and then again either at Christmas or in the spring. Sometimes both, depending on how lonesome I get for this crazy big brother of mine." She smiled fondly at Dixon as he lay on the ground snoring.

"Tell me about your job."

Emmy's expression brightened. "I'm a nurse practitioner, so I see patients. I'm under the direction of a physician, of course, and leave the most complicated cases for him, but I still have a lot of patients. Some of them prefer a nurse practitioner because we're able to spend more time with each of them. A lot of people bring their children to me. I love those little kids."

Alex watched her face grow animated as she spoke. Then she frowned.

"Lately, though, I've been getting stuck with more administrative stuff—educating, observing, that sort of thing. What I really love is being with the people."

"Sounds important."

"I like to think I'm making a difference in people's lives. That's why I prefer to be in the clinic and not filling out paperwork."

"Would you ever consider moving back to the Hilltop community?" Alex asked.

"It would take a rare set of circumstances," she said honestly. "I love my job and my house and of course there's my boyfriend Bryan."

Alex felt an unexpected sinking sensation in his gut. "I didn't realize...but it only makes sense."

Emmy's laughter chimed on the wind. "Why? Do you think I'm a man magnet?"

"No, but I think you are clever, charming and beautiful. I know what men look for."

"You're rather charming, yourself, Alex. Thank you for the compliment."

Dixon emitted a large, spluttering snore.

"Maybe we should wake him up. He sounds like he could sleep all evening," Emmy commented. She was about to poke a finger into her brother's side when a new sound rang out. Church bells.

"Whaaa..." Dixon struggled awake and sat up. "What's that?"

"The church bells," Alex said. "How odd. Why would anyone be ringing them this time of day?"

"Only one reason." Dixon was suddenly on his feet and jamming his cap onto his head. "Somebody's in trouble. During harvest, if there's ever an accident or a fire, someone calls for help by ringing the bells."

Emmy, too, scrambled to her feet. "Let's drive the truck over to the church and see what's going on."

They piled into the dusty truck cab. As Dixon drove, Emmy sat in the middle, leaving the outside door to Alex. It was a wild, teeth-rattling ride. In his haste, Dixon took them over every bump and ridge in the field because it was a more direct route.

They pulled into the churchyard at the same time as four other vehicles departed, driving fast. Mike and Lauren, Mark Nash, Ben Jenkins, Dan Taylor and Curtis Wells were all so intent they didn't even seem to notice Dixon's truck. Winchester Holmquist and Gandy stepped out of the church. Both their faces were pale.

"Alf Nyborg called over here and said to ring the bell," Gandy told them. "Kenny's combine plugged up and he tried to unplug it…" The tip of her nose was bright red.

Dixon muttered something dire under his breath.

"His arm is caught. Doc Ambrose was called and the ambulance from Wheatland…"

"Get me over there," Emmy said brusquely. "I can stop the bleeding until help arrives."

"He farms right next to All Saints Fellowship. His combine is in the field next to the church," Winchester called after them.

As they sped down the dusty gravel road, Dixon turned to Alex. "This might be a real good time to start praying, Pastor."

There were already several cars in the field when they arrived. Alf Nyborg was the first to meet them. His face was a greenish color and there were blood smears on his shirt. "Emmy! I'm so glad to see you. Nobody here knows what to do except keep Kenny talking and try to calm him down. Turns out Doc Ambrose was in Wheatville for a meeting at the hospital, so he's riding back with the ambulance. I'm afraid Kenny might bleed out by the time help gets here."

"His arm?"

"Still caught. Wedged in tight. We didn't dare try to move him just in case the pressure was keeping something worse from happening."

"Good call. I don't have a medical kit here, but I imagine there's a first aid kit in somebody's truck?"

"We've got one. We threw a blanket over him. I'm afraid he might go into shock if he hasn't already."

Alex was amazed at how practical and in charge Alf was. It was no wonder others deferred to him at All Saints.

"Okay. Let's go take a look." Emmy started after Alf.

Then Alf turned back to Alex. "He's asking for somebody to pray. We're all doing our best, but I think it would be a comfort if he knew you were here."

Alex nodded and followed them.

Dixon was at his heels. "It might not be pretty, Alex, but don't show any shock or fear if you can help it. That's the last thing this guy needs right now."

Lord, be with me in this, Alex petitioned silently.

CHAPTER TWENTY-FIVE

*A*t first, all Alex could see of Kenny was his head. The rest of him was covered by a blanket and several jackets, piled over him to prevent shock. His face was ashen and with his eyes closed, he looked dead. Then his eyes flickered open to see who the newcomers were. "Emmy...Pastor Alex..."

"Shush. You don't need to waste energy greeting us," Emmy said briskly, but with surprising humor in her voice. "Let me see what's going on. I'll see if there is anything I can do before the ambulance comes. If you'd wanted attention, Kenny, surely you could have found another way to do it."

"Same old Emmy... ," the man said faintly.

"I take exception to the word 'old,'" Emmy said as she gingerly removed the coverings.

Dixon's words rang in Alex's ears. *Don't show any shock or fear... that's the last thing this guy needs.* But Dixon's admonition seemed impossible at the sight of Kenny buried up to his shoulder in the machine. Alex felt faint but then, as if buoyed by an unseen hand, his head cleared and calm returned to him.

"I'm going to apply a tourniquet..."

Alex closed his eyes and caught his breath.

"Can they get it out? My arm?" Kenny asked. "Will it have to come off?"

Alex's stomach lurched and he sensed that several of the bystand-
ers had taken an unconscious step backward.

"Not if I can help it." The grit in Emily's tone was comforting
even to Alex's ears. "We're going to fight, Kenny, and I'm going to
be by your side. You and I went to school together. You know what
a hardhead I am. I don't give up easily." She finished what she was
doing and brushed a lock of hair away from his forehead. "Remember
the year I was a sophomore and you were a senior and you asked me
to the prom?"

"Hard to forget." Kenny was trying hard to catch Emmy's spirit
even though he, too, knew it was merely a distraction. "You looked
like Cinderella in all those ruffles."

"But you were hardly Prince Charming. Remember how you went
off with your buddies and left me with a bunch of other wallflowers?"

"I was scared of you, Emmy. I thought you were too pretty for
me." As Kenny spoke, a grimace of pain shot over his features.

"Now you tell me! I thought you left me because I looked like one
of the horses that pulled her carriage...." An ambulance siren droned
in the distance. "Enough reminiscing, buddy, here comes help."

Kenny looked at Alex. "Are you praying, Pastor?"

Emmy waved Alex closer. He got down on his knees near the
man. "I'm praying like I've never prayed before," he said earnestly.

Alex was still beside the injured man when the ambulance pulled
up beside the combine. Doc Ambrose jumped out of the back. Emmy
strode over to him, gave him an update on the situation and then let
Doc and the ambulance personnel take over. Alex did the same.

He was relieved that now the ambulance blocked the accident
scene from sight. Alex wasn't sure he wanted to see exactly what had
happened to Kenny's arm. He could still hear voices giving crisp
commands and Emmy's soothing patter as she stayed by the injured

man. When the ambulance finally pulled away—in what seemed like eons to Alex and the others—Emmy turned to where Dixon and Alex were standing.

"How is it?" Dixon asked. Compassion and worry were written all over his affable features.

"Hard to tell. The arm was badly mangled. It's a good thing Alf drove by when he did or it could have done even more damage. Kenny's wife Marilyn is meeting the ambulance at the hospital."

"Pastor, Emmy, you'd better come over here," Dan Taylor shouted. "Alf Nyborg just passed out."

Sure enough, Alf had fallen like an old oak, his arms splayed out on either side of him.

"Okay, give him some air, guys, back off." Emmy took charge again and Dixon gathered the gawking men at a distance. She patted Alf's cheeks and spoke soothingly.

His eyes fluttered and he opened them, seeming surprised. "What happened?"

"You passed out."

"I did no such fool thing...." Then he realized he was flat on the ground. "I did?"

"Not surprising, considering the circumstances."

"But I never..."

"We'll give you a ride home," Dixon told Alf. "Alex or Emmy will follow behind in your pickup."

"I don't need any coddling, Dixon." The man spoke gruffly.

"No? Probably not, since you've refused it all your life, but there's a time and a place for it and this is your time and your place." Dixon helped him to his feet and steered him to the truck.

Alex and Emmy found Alf's vehicle with the keys still in the ignition. Alex drove as they followed Dixon toward the Nyborg farm.

He glanced at Emmy and realized she was trembling. The business-like nurse was finally, after everything was over, developing a case of nerves.

"Emmy?"

"It's nothing. Sometimes after a bad incident I do this. Nerves, stress, tension, fear... They all come out this way. I hope Kenny's going to be okay. We have to pray hard, Alex."

"You were amazing with him, you know."

Emmy stared at him blankly, as if she had no idea what he was talking about.

"You kept him calm and distracted and did everything that needed to be done. I heard one of the ambulance drivers comment on the fact that he was glad you'd gotten there first."

"But that's my job," she said, still sounding puzzled.

"It's also your gift, Emmy." He paused before adding, "We are concerned that after Doc retires there won't be anyone to call on when there's an accident like there was today. Everyone will have to wait for help to arrive from Wheatville."

"It won't be like that. Surely you'll find someone..." She paused. "You *have* to have someone closer than Wheatville. That would be terrible." She frowned at him. "There are no two ways about it. You guys have to bring in someone to operate that clinic."

"Who? Wheatville didn't find anyone willing to be at the satellite clinic in Grassy Valley."

"I don't care. You have to have *someone*."

"How about you? Would you come and work in the clinic?" Alex blurted.

Emmy laughed and put her hand on his arm as he drove. "You are so sweet and so funny, Alex. Of course I can't come, but thanks for asking."

Alex didn't say more. Even though the words had come from him unbidden, he realized that it was a *wonderful* idea.

They dropped a grumbling Alf off at his house and left him to Betty's ministrations.

"I'll have to go to the hospital," Alex said.

"I'll go with you," Dixon and Emmy said in unison.

Then, as they came across a rise, Emmy pointed her finger in the direction of the Dawson farm. "Look! They're at it already!"

There were a half-dozen combines rolling on the land where the accident had taken place only a couple hours before. Grain trucks were lined along the side of the field waiting their turns to catch the harvested wheat.

"Who's doing that?" Alex asked, confused. "And where did they come from?"

"It looks like Ben Jenkins's rig, Dan Taylor's and Curtis Welles's. The others are from All Saints. I see the Clayborns, for one, and there are several trucks. About half are from Hilltop, the other half, All Saints."

"What are they doing?" Alex felt like a real city slicker asking these questions.

"They are picking up that field. It will give Kenny one less thing to worry about. They'll probably have another combining bee when the rest of his crops are ready. At least that won't be on his mind while he's fighting for his life. Farmers are like that sometimes; they can't rest until the crop is in the bin."

"Shouldn't we as a church be doing something?" Alex asked. "Our people are helping, of course, but it seems this deserves more."

"Kenny and Marilyn have three little kids," Dixon said. "I don't know what his insurance situation is, but no doubt money will be tight."

"A fund-raiser then? A benefit of some sort? Would that help?"

"It certainly couldn't hurt."

"And a prayer service," Alex added. "Definitely a prayer service."

"That might be the best medicine of all."

After Dixon and Emmy dropped him off at his car, Alex immediately drove to the church.

The doors were open and Gandy's car and Lauren's pickup were parked next to the building. He walked inside to find the two women huddled together over several sheets of paper. When he walked in, their heads lifted simultaneously, and they spoke as if with one voice. "How is he?"

As Alex told them what he knew, tears began to run down Gandy's face.

Lauren could only shake her head miserably. "You know, it's something we all fear out here. The men work with big, dangerous machinery. During harvest they are always in a hurry and usually tired from working too many hours in a row. It seems that every year some accident happens. I worry about Mike too. It could happen to any of them."

Gandy hiccupped on a sob. "What if he loses his arm?"

Alex didn't want to tell her that he couldn't see any way they might save it, but he was no doctor and he could see how upset she was already. "Then we'll rally around him and help him through it. This is a praying and helping community."

Gandy nodded miserably and blew her nose.

"In fact, that's what I came to the church for. I thought we might…"

"Got it covered."

Alex was startled. "How could you? I haven't told you what I'm thinking yet."

Gandy waved a dismissive hand. "You're easy to read. Like I said, we've got it covered."

Lauren jumped in. "We assumed you'd be in favor of Hilltop

Church doing a benefit for the family, so Gandy and I have been making sign-up sheets for volunteers and planning a menu."

"Spaghetti with meatballs, garlic toast and ice cream sundaes," Gandy interjected. "Paper plates so no one has to wash a bunch of dishes. We'll have lots of sprinkles and goop for the sundaes, because the kids love that. We figure if All Saints wants to go in on this with us we can serve a lot of people. Everybody in Grassy Valley will come. Usually this type of thing even attracts people as far away as Wheatville. We'll advertise on the radio, make and hang posters and see if we can talk the paper into giving us a free ad."

Gandy looked slyly at Alex. "And I figured that we could pay for it out of the emergency fund. What do you say?"

"I say yes!"

"Good man," Gandy said approvingly. "And when do you think we should set up a prayer service?"

This was a family, Alex noted, in which it didn't take long to get things done.

Chapter Twenty-Six

*A*lex slept little and woke up early. It didn't surprise him that his sleep had been interrupted by dreams of Kenny's dreadful injury. What had kept him awake since four AM was more unexpected. Emmy's matter-of-fact statement, "He's my boyfriend," was a bad tape playing continuously in his mind.

He'd known Emmy Dixon barely twenty-four hours. Why her relationships should matter to him was a mystery. With her vivacious personality and beauty, it would be surprising if she didn't have a boyfriend—or two.

Alex was glad he had an early appointment at the church to distract him. Gandy had left a disjointed message on his answering machine telling him that someone would be in to see him, but she hadn't said who it might be. He grabbed two muffins from a plastic container on the counter, made sure there was plenty of water in Tripod's bowl, and hurried to the church.

Early morning light through the stained-glass windows made the inside of the sanctuary particularly lovely in the morning, painted with sun and bright color. Alex sat down in the back pew to have his morning talk with God as he often did when he arrived for the day. He didn't hear Myrtle Chadwick come in but jumped to his feet when she tapped him on the shoulder.

"I'm sorry to interrupt you, Reverend, but I have to be at Red's at ten o'clock to get ready for the lunch rush." Myrtle's creased face was flushed, and Alex could tell she'd been hurrying.

"No problem, just talking things out with the Boss."

Myrtle smiled faintly. "I have a few more things for the two of you to talk about."

He directed her into the office, offered her a chair and poured her a mug of coffee. She took it gratefully. "What can I do for you?"

The woman's face contorted as if she felt physical pain. "I'm not sure. All I know is that I can't do it alone anymore." She stared into the mug for a moment before lifting her head to look at him. "I can't handle my son Bucky. He's out of control. He listens to me if I'm in his face, but I can't follow him to town to keep him out of mischief. He's been stealing things, at least that's what the police think. They have never actually caught him at it, and the things that have gone missing have never shown up anywhere. Some of Belle Wells's jewelry is gone, and Sam's missed a few things from the hardware store after Bucky had been in there." She leaned forward and spoke softly.

"I'm sure Bucky is the one who's been doing it. He's tormented that little Will Packard and the animals for so long that now I think he's gone on to other things. Once you allowed Will to keep his rescued animals at your place, Bucky had to back off. He's too much of a coward to antagonize someone like you."

Alex sought a way to respond. He'd not come across something like this before. "Those are pretty harsh words, Myrtle."

She looked at him, her eyes tearing, her lips turned down at the corners. "I know, Reverend, but they're true. I hope and pray he's done nothing worse." She saw Alex's questioning gaze and continued. "Bucky's never been like other people. As a child, he'd hurt other children because he didn't seem to know his own strength. He did badly in school and dropped out early. It's been a struggle from day one with him. I love him with all my heart, but at the moment I don't *like* him very much. Is that an awful thing to say about my own child?"

"It's honest," Alex said. "We often love people but don't like their actions."

Myrtle nodded, looking relieved. "I don't know what to do about that boy. The police are on the watch. I sleep with one eye open. What more is there?"

"Counseling?"

Myrtle gave a derisive snort. "Where would I get money for that? And even if I were rolling in dough, how would I get that two-hundred-and-eighty-pound man into a counselor's office? I asked him if he'd talk to you, but he laughed. He said if I was so heated up for somebody to have counseling, then *I* should come to you."

"Mark Nash, Dixon Daniels and Mike Carlson are around the neighborhood a lot. Maybe what you need is a few extra pairs of eyes to help you watch Bucky. I'll certainly be keeping an eye out for him."

Myrtle nodded. He could see she liked the idea. "I'll talk to them. Just so it doesn't get back to Bucky."

"None of us will say anything, I'm sure."

She nodded and stood up. "It's something to try, anyway."

"And I'll pray."

The little woman nodded firmly. "Bucky can be meaner than a snake. Sometimes I think God is the *only* One who can handle him."

"You know, Myrtle," Alex said with a smile, "in my experience, that's the case with all of us."

After Myrtle left, Alex sat down in his office, put his hands behind his head and leaned back in his chair. Something nagged at him. There was a connection he was missing. It had to do with Bucky, he thought, and something out of place. But what was it? He finally put his elbows on his desk and picked up a book. It would come to him eventually, he thought. Until then, he had reading to do to prepare for his sermon.

An hour later, Gandy appeared in the office. She was wearing a straw hat, a bright cotton dress and fluorescent running shoes. Alex couldn't imagine what occasion she was dressed like that for.

"Want to see my quilt?" she asked without even saying good morning.

"Is it the history quilt All Saints and Hilltop are working on together?"

"No. That one won't be done for a while yet. This is one I made as a wedding present."

"Who's getting married?"

"Someone, eventually. I like to have them on hand for gifts. You can't just whip up one of these babies in a few hours, you know."

"I imagine not."

Before his eyes, she shook out the big square of fabric she had under her arm and unfurled it across the work table. "What do you think?"

It was as intricate as the stained-glass windows in the sanctuary. The colors were equally vivid, especially with the additions of pink, lime green and lemon yellow.

"It's called a double wedding ring quilt. They're not easy to make, but it seems so appropriate to give newlyweds because of its name." Gandy stood back and admired it. "It's one of my best."

"It's spectacular. I had no idea how talented you were, Gandy."

"Of course you didn't. You haven't seen half the stuff I can do yet." She said it not as bragging but as pure fact.

"How did you get this done plus work with the church ladies on their quilts?"

She waved her hand. "Easy peasy. They're slow, I'm fast." She bundled up the quilt and with Alex's help folded it back into a square. "I'm taking this to the quilt shop in Wheatville to put on display as a sample. Then people will see it and want to buy fabric to make their own. There's always love in the air somewhere."

Did she know about Lydia and Johann? he wondered. Gandy had a personal radar system that seemed to work nonstop, day and night. He hoped she wasn't thinking about *him*.

Unaware how she'd piqued his curiosity, Gandy asked, "How's Kenny this morning?"

"Dixon and Emmy spent some time at the hospital last night. I hope they can save his arm. It's very mangled. His mother and wife are with him. They asked that no company come today."

Gandy looked somber. "One step at a time, I guess. My brother Jonas checked out Kenny's fields. Some of the men from each church are getting together to combine later today. The women are making supper and we'll eat together in the field. You'd better come and see how it used to be between Hilltop Community Church and All Saints Fellowship before Alf's fire and the rift."

"It is healing, don't you think? A little at least?"

Gandy considered the question. "Moving the right direction, anyway, thanks to you."

Thanks to God.

"I'll be there. I'll call the hospital and inquire about Kenny before I come."

"And I plan to stop by the hospital to say hello tomorrow afternoon. I made a Bundt cake—chocolate with a coconut crème filling—for them."

Alex wasn't quite sure what a Bundt cake was, or why they needed one at the hospital, but he certainly wasn't going to ask. Food seemed to be the cure-all for everything around here.

They began discussing the number of Sunday bulletins Gandy should print. They'd been running out recently due to an increase in visitors. Then Alex decided to write a new sermon, one that addressed Kenny's accident. At two o'clock he told Gandy to go home and left the church. He needed a nap.

The phone woke him out of a deep sleep. "Hey, Alex, are you coming to the Dawsons'?"

"What's going on now, Dixon?" Alex steeled himself for more bad news.

"Did you forget? We're harvesting for Kenny. The women are cooking supper. We'll pick you up in fifteen minutes."

Suddenly, Alex's heart felt lighter.

When the Daniels arrived, he crawled into the pickup's cab. It smelled like tater tot hotdish. A large pan wrapped securely in dish towels was perched on Emmy's lap. "Should I have brought something too?"

Emmy patted the thing in her lap. "No need. I made double plus a batch of brownies. I'm not sure why I come out here and slave for my brother every fall. I think I need my head checked." Emmy wrinkled her nose and laughed. "Dixon has me under his spell."

"His 'smell,' did you say?"

"Hey, quit picking on me! Don't gang up on the driver."

Alex rolled down his window and let the wind blow in his hair. He drew in a deep, invigorating breath. "You know, I feel more alive here than I have anywhere else in my life."

"I understand," Emmy said. "I do too."

Why, then, Alex wondered, did she always leave again?

Chapter Twenty-Seven

*A*lex could see roiling dust in the air long before they reached Dawson's fields. Dixon stopped at the top of a low rise to look down upon the scene. Combines churned in the fields like prehistoric monsters, chewing up the swaths of grain. Trucks lined the sides of the fields, ready to take their turns hauling the harvested grain away.

"That's impressive," Alex breathed.

"There are so many rigs here that they should have everything that's ripe picked up tonight," Dixon said. "Believe it or not, Jacob Olson is driving my rig. He never comes off that farm, but he's comfortable in the cab of a tractor, so Clarence called me. He said that he was driving their machinery and Jacob wondered if he could drive for me. Watch, when we stop for supper, Jacob will disappear rather than eat with the rest of us. Then I'll drive for the rest of the evening."

"Emmy, are you going to haul grain?"

"No. There are plenty of trucks to keep up. I'll probably help with the meal. And you," she added, "can say the mealtime prayer."

Feeling only slightly less useless than before, Alex nodded. Everything was like a well-choreographed dance. The combines were circling, trucks were dodging purposefully this way and that, and in one corner of the field the women had gathered. They'd put out a string of card tables covered with red-and-white–checked paper tablecloths. The tables were filled with coolers, slow cookers and plastic containers.

"It's as if everyone knows exactly what to do."

Dixon laughed. "Of course they do. Those women can whip up a feast in no time flat." He parked the vehicle.

Emmy immediately saw someone she knew, and the two were hugging and chatting within seconds.

"I'll never get her home once she starts gabbing," Dixon said mournfully. "I can't see why she won't move back. I understand that she has a great job but…"

"And a boyfriend."

"Yeah. I haven't scoped that out yet. She's had him for a while, but I've never met him. Maybe it's more serious than she let's on. Too bad."

Too bad, indeed, Alex thought. Tragic, in fact. Hilltop would be an even more interesting place with Emmy Daniels in residence.

As they watched the activity, Alex's cell phone rang. He picked it up to hear Natalie's voice on the other end of the line.

"How are you? I've been waiting to hear from you forever." Natalie sounded playful and happy, which reminded Alex of the good times they'd had together. "What are you doing?"

He explained in detail the threshing bee, the pristine afternoon and the portable banquet the church women had prepared.

"Just like a scene out of a television show I saw once on public television. Did Nancy bring any of her wonderful cookies?"

"Everything she makes is wonderful."

"It's a wonder you don't weigh three hundred pounds, living out there. I'd better let you get back to what you're doing."

She was careful not to push, for which Alex was grateful.

At that moment Mattie Olsen trotted over carrying a 9x13 pan of chocolate cake. She held it out to Alex. "I know how you love chocolate. Would you like an appetizer before dinner?"

He slipped the phone into his pocket, took the napkin Mattie offered him and helped himself to cake. He took a bite and closed his eyes. Chocolate bliss. He made Mattie stand still so he could take a second piece when he finished the first.

At seven o'clock Nancy Jenkins laid on the horn of her car, signaling that it was time to stop working and start eating.

Field dust mixed with laughter and stories seasoned the meal. Alex was reminded of the loaves and fishes. The serving bowls never got empty even though everyone, stimulated by the fresh air, ate twice what they normally would. He guessed there would still be twelve baskets left over.

Emmy joined him and Dixon as they sat on the ground, leaning against the tires of Dixon's pickup. "How does it taste?"

"Like ambrosia," Alex said. "Best food I've ever tasted—and that's saying a lot."

"Oh, ambrosia," Dixon said and got to his feet. "I think I saw some of that on the table somewhere. I'll be right back."

"You'd think he'd weigh four hundred pounds the way he eats," Emmy said lightly. "I guess he works it off."

"There's an amazing work ethic out here."

"I agree." Emmy stirred a melting puddle of red gelatin and canned mixed fruit.

"Why don't you move back?"

She frowned. Even a frown looked pretty on Emmy. "I do hate to see this place without a Doc Ambrose."

"We're working on it." Sadly, the news so far was all bad. The committee members had already run into a half-dozen dead ends. They were now contacting medical schools about upcoming graduates. The only thing Alex was sure of was that this might be a long, tedious and perhaps doomed project.

She rose and held out her hand to Alex. "Come with me. You haven't even *seen* the dessert table yet."

Just as Alex took Emmy's hand and rose to his feet, Lolly Roscoe appeared. She was carrying a huge tray of cupcakes decorated with chocolate frosting and candy corn. She tripped to a halt, nearly spilling cupcakes all over the ground. Alex reached out and steadied the tray.

"Careful, those look too good to waste."

But Lolly wasn't looking at Alex. She was staring at Emmy as if she'd seen a ghost. "You," she whispered. Then she turned accusing eyes to Alex. He felt as if he'd been caught in the act of doing something wrong, but he wasn't sure what it was. Hand in the cookie jar? Then it hit him. It was worse than that—his hand was in Emmy's. That dart-filled gaze of Lolly's was jealousy!

"Hi, Lolly, good to see you. These look great." Emmy dropped his hand, took a cupcake off the tray and sauntered toward the food tables. Alex grabbed one as he hurried after her.

When he caught up to Emmy, she whistled softly. "Woo-hoo. If looks could kill I'd be on the ground. Lolly considers other women her competition. I saw how she looked at you. She's got it bad where you're concerned."

"I haven't encouraged her in any way. She just…likes me, that's all."

"You are as dense as my brother Dixon," Emmy said brightly, "no offense."

"None taken, but I don't know what you mean."

"You don't have to *do* anything. You're the right age, handsome, single, intelligent, articulate, athletic—just *existing* puts you on Lolly's list. She's a nice woman who hasn't had much luck meeting a man. When you came to town I'll bet she did cartwheels."

Alex, feeling awkward at being at the center of Emmy's appraisal, blushed. "Don't be ridiculous."

"That was jealousy in her eyes when she saw us together, Alex. Pure and simple."

He knew she was right, and he had no idea what to do about it. He followed her as they assessed the dessert table piled with pies, cakes, bars and cookies. He'd never seen so much chocolate and coconut in one place, outside a bakery or a candy store.

"What should I do?" he asked as he trailed Emmy back to their spot. "About Lolly, I mean. I don't want to encourage her. I'm not looking for a wife."

"No?" Emmy gave him a gauging glance. "Never?"

His thoughts drifted to Natalie.

"Be kind," Emily advised.

"I *am* kind. That doesn't seem to be working very well."

Emmy tipped her head back to look at him. "Then you're on your own. Just don't get your foot caught in any traps."

"You're a big help," Alex groused.

"Who's my sister helping?" Dixon asked. He was carrying a large pan with a cover.

"Not me," Alex grumbled.

"I'm giving him advice on how not to become Lolly's next boyfriend."

Dixon shook his head. "I wish she would find someone—just not me—or Mark—or Alex."

"What are you carrying?" Alex asked, hoping to change the subject. He was unaccustomed to having his date-ability assessed in such a frank manner.

"Food for Lila. She hasn't been out of the hospital long. I thought I'd run over and check on her."

"Come to think of it, Tilly Tanner isn't here either."

"I'll get another container and we'll come with you, Dixon,"

Emmy said. "It won't take long and I know both the ladies would love some of this wonderful food."

In a few minutes, they were back in the pickup, heading toward Lila Mason's place.

When they arrived, the house was locked up tight, but the porch light was burning. All the shades were pulled, but every light inside the house was on. Alex and Dixon exchanged a confused glance. They knocked on the door several times before a window shade fluttered slightly and through the sliver of an opening one eye peered. Lila.

Then, from the inside, they heard scurrying motions, and the door flew open. Lila, in a pair of men's overalls and bedroom slippers, put her hands to her heart. "I'm so glad it's you!"

"Who did you think it was?" Dixon stepped into the house and quickly surveyed the room. Alex and Emmy followed. Alex immediately glanced at the stove and counters for open food containers.

"I thought the burglar was back."

More of Lila's imaginings, thought Alex.

"I was in the basement—it's not much of one, you know, more like a root cellar and a place for the furnace, but I was seeing what canned goods I had left down there, when I heard someone walking around upstairs. I quietly closed the trapdoor to the cellar. Fortunately, I had a flashlight with me. I just waited. The footsteps moved around for quite some time and then I began to hear things crashing to the floor. Oh! It was awful! Even after the footsteps stopped, I must have stayed in the root cellar nearly two hours. I didn't know who it was or what he wanted. When I came upstairs I found this."

Lila turned and gestured toward the rest of the house. Everything was overturned, tables, chairs and lamps. Drawers were open and their contents spilled out. Pictures were tipped on the walls and even flowerpots upended. The place had been ransacked.

This was obviously not of Lila's doing. The place looked like the scene of a crime.

"Is anything missing?" Dixon asked.

"I was just going to check to see," the little woman said. "I pulled the curtains and barricaded the doors because I was afraid he might come back."

"This is one for the police, Lila. Let's leave everything as it is until they get here." Alex put his arm around the woman's shoulders. They were quaking with nerves and fear. "We brought you supper. Why don't you sit down and eat it."

"In fact," Dixon said when he got off his cell phone, "Emmy can make you a cup of tea and I'll sit with you while we wait for the police. Then Alex and Emmy can deliver food to Tillie Tanner and come right back. How does that sound?"

Lila's eyes brightened. She looked less befuddled than she had in a long while. "Very nice. Tillie isn't doing very well. She needs a good meal."

"This is the first I've heard of it," Alex said. "Has she been ill?"

"She never admits feeling under the weather," Lila said as she watched Dixon open the food they'd brought. "She thinks that makes her sound old." Lila gave a snort. "She *is* old, of course, but she won't admit it. We were in school together, but I have strict instructions not to say much about that."

Alex hid a smile. "We'll check on her while Dixon takes care of you and the police. We'll be back soon."

"Dixon told me how sick Lila made herself eating old food," Emmy said as they drove the two and a half miles to Tillie's place.

"I worry about these elderly people," Alex admitted. "They are so proud, independent and determined to stay in their own homes. Unfortunately, no one is really in charge of checking on them. Dixon's a saint as far as that's concerned, but he shouldn't have that responsibility on his shoulders alone. Besides Lila and Tillie, there's Bessie Bruun to think of. Her sister Brunie worries about her a lot."

"Maybe your church should have a nurse. Some do, you know."

"Right. I wish we could, but we can't. We're glad just to cover expenses."

They pulled into Tillie's yard. It was a hodgepodge of brightly painted birdhouses, flags and pinwheel gadgets that moved with the wind. Colorful, like Tillie herself.

The door was open and they could hear a nearby radio station reporting on hog and cattle futures in the background, but Tillie didn't appear. Finally, Emmy opened the screen door and walked inside.

As Alex glanced around the house, his chest tightened. Tillie's dishes and pillows were also bright reds, greens and purples, and she'd cut vibrant multihued pictures out of magazines and put them in cheap frames. There were lots of plants and plastic flowers decorating the space, but the furniture had many years of hard use and chairs were arranged in an attempt to hide wear marks in the rug. Everything indicated one more elderly woman was barely making ends meet, yet doing her best to keep up appearances so that no one would pity her. These dear ladies made his heart swell with affection and an urgency to do something to make their lives easier.

"Alex, come here!" Emmy called from the back bedroom.

There he saw another distressing tableau. Tillie, pale as snow beneath her bright red hair, was lying crosswise on the bed as if she'd fallen there and couldn't negotiate herself into a more comfortable position. Her lips were dry, but she was trying to speak. Alex couldn't hear what she was saying until he bent so close that his ear was just over her mouth. She looked every bit her eighty years despite her incongruous red hair.

"Heart attack, I think… Help…"

"Call an ambulance. I'll see what I can do to make her comfortable." Again, Emmy slipped into nursing mode. Alex backed out of the room as he pulled his phone out of his pocket and dialed 911.

Next, he called Doc Ambrose, but his answering machine picked up. "This is the Ambrose residence. We're out of town for a couple of days. If you have a medical question, please call the Wheatland Clinic at…" Grimly, he stuffed the phone back into his pocket. Here was another taste of what it would be like when Doc left.

"Alex, she wants you." Emmy was by the bed, holding Tillie's hand. Emmy had managed to make her more comfortable and was daubing the woman's parched lips with water.

Alex took Tillie's hand. "Don't strain yourself talking to me. We can visit when you get to the hospital."

For someone so ill, she clung to his hand with remarkable strength. "Have to tell you…" The words were faint. "Want you to know I'm okay with Jesus."

Tears sprang to the backs of Alex's eyes. Here she was, practically on her deathbed and ministering to him! "He's got you in His hands, Tillie. He loves you and He died for you."

"I know." A sweet smile spread over her features. She closed her eyes. They sat together for several minutes before she opened them again. "Pastor?"

"I'm here, Tillie."

"I want to confess."

He held her hand tighter. "Yes?"

"I'm really eighty, not sixty-five."

Alex felt as though his heart had shattered and fallen about like shards of broken glass.

The ambulance arrived, this time to carry Tillie to the Wheatville hospital.

"I'm going to ride with her," Emmy told him. "Pick Dixon up at Lila's and tell him to get me at the hospital later. I want to see that she gets everything she needs."

He watched helplessly as the ambulance sped away, growing smaller and smaller, until it disappeared.

"Lord," he prayed aloud, "be with all these dear people. You are the Great Physician and You are able to give them all they need—strength, healing and peace. And let me know what You want me to do for them. Let me minister to them in the way You would have me do it." Almost as an afterthought, Alex heard himself add, "Help."

CHAPTER TWENTY-EIGHT

With nothing left to do at Tillie's, Alex turned off the lights and closed the door and windows. Then he crawled into Dixon's vehicle and drove back to Lila Mason's place. Dixon was sitting on the front porch in a rocker drinking coffee and reading an old *National Geographic* magazine.

"Lila was so upset and exhausted after the police left that I told her to go to bed and that I'd wait outside until you came back. She said she thought it would be easier to fall asleep with me here," he explained as he crawled into the passenger side of the truck. "Either she's in the bedroom with a chain saw cutting trees or she's sound asleep and snoring. I think we can go now.

"The police took pictures and tried to get some fingerprints, but I don't know how much..." He looked more closely at Alex. "What's wrong? You look awful. And by the way, where's Emmy?"

Alex told him what they'd found at Tillie's, and Dixon's expressive features crumpled in dismay.

"What's going on? First Doc wants to leave, then Kenny's accident, a burglar, and now Tillie? This is too much. What next?"

"Hopefully Kenny will keep the arm, Tillie will improve and we'll catch the burglar," Alex said, sounding much more optimistic than he felt. "You have to remember that some pretty amazing things are happening too. Think of the people of Hilltop Community Church and

All Saints Fellowship working together to harvest Kenny's fields! And the food that came together for a beautiful meal. We found Tillie now rather than in the morning after she'd had to lie alone all night, and Lila's alerted us to a problem in the community. God's still in charge, Dixon."

Dixon took off his cap and scratched his head. "We certainly don't know what's around the next corner, do we?"

They drove to Alex's place in silence. Just as Alex was getting out of the vehicle, Dixon's cell phone rang.

"Emmy," Dixon mouthed to him. "Wait." When he hung up, he looked somber. "Not good. Tillie has had a severe heart attack. There's been extensive damage. Emmy is going to stay at the hospital with her tonight. They will provide a bed for her. She'd like you to come to Wheatville in the morning."

"*Now* it's too much."

Dixon shrugged helplessly.

"Emmy said not to arrive too early as mornings are usually busy in a hospital. Do you want me to come with you?"

Alex shook his head. "No. There's more than enough to tend to here. I'll go to the church before I leave. Check in with Gandy at noon, will you? See if anything more I should know about has come up. If she doesn't have me to push around, she'll enjoy giving you orders."

Dixon clapped a hand on Alex's shoulder and a faint smile broke through his somber demeanor. "Big stuff is going on but God will provide. Sometimes it looks like He's botching things up, but He never does, not in the end."

Alex nodded, heartened by Dixon's no-nonsense approach to what was turning into a very nonsensical time.

He got to the church by nine AM, which was not early enough to beat Gandy to work. Before he could even open his mouth to greet her, she waved several pieces of paper in his face.

"It's all done. The fund-raiser for Kenny and Lila is going to be a silent auction. Sam from the hardware store has donated a whopper of a wrench set. Red is throwing in a gas card, Licks & Sticks is providing five pounds of fudge and a haircut, and the gal from Good Finds, Good Flowers is going to give a coupon for a bouquet of fresh flowers every month for a year. I'm bringing a baby quilt I made. Everybody around here loves silent auctions. They're easy and earn good money. The café, when Kenny's wife sometimes fills in, is going to sell doughnuts, coffee and sloppy joes with pickles on homemade buns. Everything we take in will go directly toward Kenny and Lila's hospital bills. It's taking place Wednesday night at the school gym. They are waiving their fee, and the janitor will set up the tables and chairs." She waved the paper again. "Here are the flyers. Debbie and some of her friends will hang them up. Now what do you think of that?"

Alex could have hugged her. "Gandy, you are a miracle in sneakers. I was dreading the details of this benefit and you did it all."

"I did more too. We're having a prayer service right after church on Sunday. Since we want everybody to stick around, I thought we'd have hobo soup with ham and cheese sandwiches and ice cream sundaes. How does that sound?"

"Hobo soup?"

"Everybody brings a can of soup, some vegetables, a potato, whatever they want. We throw it all in the pot, cook it up and eat. You'd be surprised how good it always tastes."

"I suppose I would. You're planning a lot of food."

She gave him a pitying glance. "Aren't you ever going to learn, Pastor Alex? Nothing gets done around here without food." Then she did a double take. "Why do you look like you ran over your own foot with your van? That's the most miserable expression I've ever seen on your face."

"Did you hear about last night?"

"The threshing bee? I was there till the end. The men got most everything done. There's fall's work, of course, plowing and the like, but there's not such a hurry with that. And the food was great! When Hilltop and All Saints are in agreement, they can really cook—in more ways than one. You should have seen it, Pastor. By the end of the evening Hilltop people and All Saints people were chattering like magpies and hugging each other like they were long-lost relatives. It warmed my heart. I think we're turning a corner on the past. I hate for trouble to be the reason Hilltop and All Saints united again, but we all needed a common purpose and Kenny's accident provided it."

Then her eyes narrowed. "Come to think of it, I only got one glimpse of you and then you disappeared. Where'd you go?"

Alex explained that they'd taken food to Lila and discovered her house had been broken into and how frightened she was. The part he dreaded most came next. "Emmy and I went to Tillie's to give her some food as well." He heard a catch in his voice. "We found her lying across the bed. She'd had a heart attack. Things aren't looking good."

Gandy blanched and sat down hard on her desk chair. "Is she going to make it?"

"We don't know."

"I'd better add her name to the benefit and to the prayer service. It's family here. Even though you might think your brother-in-law is a real pain in the neck and your cousin Arthur got out of jail much too soon and you'd give your eyeteeth to get Aunt Bella to quit asking personal questions, when one of them gets hurt or sick, all that love you have for them comes flooding back and you don't find them irritating at all anymore—you know?"

Alex knew exactly what she meant. He reminded himself to inquire later whether Gandy actually *had* a cousin Arthur.

He glanced at his watch. He was too restless to stay at his desk. Worse yet, Gandy began heaving great sighs every few minutes as she folded monthly calendars to be mailed out, which made it impossible for him to think.

"I'm going to stop at Ole's before I go to Wheatville," he told Gandy. "I want to check on him. He wasn't in church last Sunday. Call me on my cell if something comes up."

"I'm praying that *nothing* more comes up." Gandy opened her desk drawer and pulled out an unopened package of red and white peppermint candies. "Give these to Tillie, will you? She loves them. I always keep a few in my desk just for her. I hadn't opened that package yet. Tell her to enjoy them."

"You do that?" Alex was a little surprised.

"Lila Mason loves caramels but won't buy them 'cause they stick in her teeth. I keep them here for her too. She stops in every time she craves them."

"You're something else, Gandy, you know that? Really special."

Gandy smiled serenely, perfectly aware of her singular ways.

Ole Swenson was walking from house to barn when Alex drove into the yard. He wore bib overalls and a straw hat. His hand came up in greeting when he saw Alex. "I've been waiting for you to come," he said as he leaned his palms on the rim of the van's window. "I figured you'd be around to see Twinkle Toes one of these days."

"She's great but it's you I came to see."

Ole chuckled and his eyes twinkled merrily. "They all say that, but I know better. You'd better say hello to her right away. You're just in time for a surprise."

Alex jumped out and followed the older man to the Taj Mahal of pigsties. Twinkle Toes had a home befitting Miss Piggy, Alex thought. "This is a four-room house!" Alex blurted. He'd seen efficiency apartments smaller than Twinkle Toes's residence.

"Pigs are very tidy, organized animals," Ole said. "They prefer separate places for eating, sleeping, playing and relieving themselves. You wouldn't want to eat and drink in your bathroom, would you?"

"A fan?" Alex said, staring at a slowly rotating fan.

"Pigs need to keep cool in hot weather. The reason they got tagged with that mistaken term 'dirty pigs' is because they roll around in the mud to get cool. I have a spot outside that Twinkle Toes uses when she wants to roll, but she's pretty fastidious and prefers to stay cool under the fan."

Alex pushed against a big beam. "This place is well built."

"She'd root her way out of here if it wasn't. She loves to dig." Ole turned toward the pig. "Don't you, sweetheart?"

Twinkle Toes tiptoed over to them and kindly allowed Alex to scratch the top of her head. The skin was thick and rough. The strands of hair were as bristly as those on the broom in his kitchen, but she grunted lovingly and nudged his hand so that he would scratch more. He did as she asked and she made a soft murmur of enjoyment that made Alex wonder if pigs could purr. Then she lifted her snout and gave his hand a strange, watery kiss with her nose.

"She likes you," Ole said, sounding pleased. "It's not everyone she takes to right away. I've always thought she might charge Bucky Chadwick one day. She hates that boy. No skin off my nose, though. He's scared of her so he stays away from my place. It probably didn't hurt that I told him she doesn't have any trouble breaking out of her pen if she thinks something out of place is going on in the yard."

"Does she?"

"I believe she could, although she hasn't done it yet. There's a reason the fences are high around her outdoor pen. You'd never know it to look at her, but she's quick on her feet if she needs to be.

"Pigs are smart, Reverend, and clean, even though they've got an undeserved bad reputation. If you give them a 'bathroom' of sorts, they'll use it. They only lie around in filth when they don't have any-place else to go. Look at Twinkle Toes, pretty as a princess."

A princess from what country, Alex didn't want to know.

"Let's go into the barn. I have something else to show you." Ole led the way into the dim recesses of the big red structure. There were stalls on both sides of the concrete alleyway. In the far back stall, Alex could hear restless bumps against the walls and heavy breathing. Ole stepped up on the slatted wood railing and peered inside. Alex did the same.

In front of him was a lovely black horse moving restlessly as if she couldn't find a place to be comfortable. She flicked her tail and looked at them with beseeching brown eyes.

"What's wrong…" His voice trailed away as he noticed that the horse's belly was rotund and heavy with foal.

"She should give birth any time now. I'm glad you'll be here to see it."

Flickers of fear and fascination danced within him as Alex stared at the horse. Gradually her restlessness increased as her labor intensi-fied. Instinctively she moved her back legs wider apart and, breathing heavily, began to push. As Alex watched in stunned amazement, a slick, wet sac began to emerge; inside he could see the perfect outline of the foal's head. Struggling, straining and breathing hard, deep breaths, the mare kept laboring until the entire sac containing the foal dropped to the floor with a thud. The afterbirth soon followed.

The foal lay there unmoving, wrapped in a filmy, translucent sac.

"Is it dead?" Alex asked frantically. "The way it fell…that film over its face…"

"Oh, she'll eat that right off but if you're worried, I'll give her a hand." Ole vaulted over the rail and landed near the foal. With a flick of his finger he opened the sac and cleared it away from the baby's nose, and it took a breath. The mother, exhausted, dropped to the ground beside her new baby and began to pull at the sac with her teeth, working over the infant's body until it was all pulled away.

As she did so, Ole cleared away the afterbirth. "She'd normally eat this, but I'd like her to start bonding with her baby right away." With herculean effort, the mare struggled to her feet and began to nudge the newborn with her nose. Poke, prod, bump, push, until she forced the baby to stand. Its legs were so small and slender that it looked to Alex like the poor baby was trying to arrange a pile of sticks into order. Gradually the colt got its front legs poked out in front. Then it started to disentangle its long back legs and with a heave hoisted itself to its feet. It stood there, swaying, looking as if a puff of wind might knock it flat. Instinctively Mama turned so that the little one had easy access to her nipples, and in a miracle the likes of which Alex had never seen, the baby began to nurse.

Alex watched in awe.

He didn't realize there were tears on his cheeks until Ole lifted a finger and wiped one away. "If I live to be a thousand, I'll never tire of seeing that," the old man said. "If you want proof there is a God, there it is."

"I'll never forget that," he told Ole as they left the barn sometime later.

"That was her first colt. A healthy little boy. She's going to be a good mother. She knew right what to do. That little feller has nice bloodlines. He's off to a good start."

"What are you going to name him?" Alex asked, his head curious but his heart still back in the barn.

"For his papers he'll get some long name that in some way is a derivative of his parents' registered names, but I also give them a name that's easier to remember. That's always what they come by when I call."

"Have you picked it out?" Alex was mesmerized by the whole process. The closest he, as a city boy, had ever come to such an experience was when he and a friend came upon newly delivered kittens in his friend's laundry room.

"I usually wait until I see the little guy's personality before I decide, but I think I've got a name for this one."

"What is it?"

Ole stopped and turned to face Alex. There was a smile on his face and that gleam in his eye as he said, "I think I'll call him Preacher Man."

Alex couldn't think of another thing that at that moment might have made him any happier.

$\mathcal{A}$t the hospital, Emmy met him at the door of Tillie's room. Her expression told him all he needed to know.

"She's hanging on, Alex, but just barely. They don't want her to have too much company. I'm sure it's okay if you go in and pray with her though. Stay only ten minutes. Then I'll go back in for ten more minutes in an hour or so. That's all she can take right now."

"Then, in the meantime you should eat, " Alex asked. There were dark circles beneath Emmy's eyes, and she was swaying on her feet.

"A bag of peanuts and a cup of tar-flavored coffee from a vending machine."

"I suspected as much. Give me a few minutes and we'll get some real food." He slipped into Tillie's room.

She was very pale and still. Her white face was framed with a sunburst of red hair against the pillow. Though she was a relatively tall woman, she seemed smaller now, as if the illness had shrunk her very being. But the worst thing of all, Alex realized, was her hair. Tillie was so proud of her bright red hair. There'd been no beauty appointment with Barbara Owens this week, and at her hairline were Tillie's pure white roots. Alex knew she would never want anyone to see her this way. A woman who refused to age past sixty-five would cringe at the sight. It was silly, he supposed, when things were so dire, but he knew Tillie. Tillie had priorities and her hair was one of them.

However, his priorities were different and that was why he was here. It was his job to remind this beloved woman that Christ's death and resurrection were real and that He was waiting for her. All Alex could do was ease Tillie's passage toward heaven.

Emmy was perched on a bench outside Tillie's room when he emerged. Tears ran down his face and he was unashamed.

"Is she…"

"No. I'm just missing her already, that's all."

Emmy took his hand in hers and held it to her cheek. "I know what you mean. Tillie has been a fixture in my life since Dixon and I were born. Hilltop won't be the same without her."

"You're trembling." Alex put his hand over hers and felt it quiver.

"Just feeling a little faint, maybe."

"Where's the best food in Wheatville?"

"Why?"

"We're going there to eat."

"Now? With Tillie the way she is…"

"If Tillie could talk, what do you think she'd say right now?"

Emmy thought for a moment and a small smile crept across her features. "She'd say, 'Don't you children be ridiculous! Go on, have a nice meal. I'll be here when you get back.'"

"Exactly."

"But what if she isn't here when we get back, Alex?"

"Then she'll be so busy laughing and singing and having time with Jesus that she won't even remember we went out for a sandwich, that's what."

"You do have a certain perspective on things."

"I know for certain that Tillie is on to a better place, Emmy. I also know you look terrible. I want to take care of you both. I'll ask a nurse to stay in the room with her until we return. I'll give her my cell number."

Finally Emmy relented.

It wasn't until she sank into one of the big leather booths at the steak house that a nurse had recommended that she seemed to relax. "Every time I come back to Hilltop I get swept up in it. The place is a force to be reckoned with. Now Dixon can't quit talking about how terrible it will be when Doc Ambrose leaves and how they need someone like me to work in the clinic. I know he's hinting that I should quit my job and come back, but I've worked hard to get to where I am and I love it. He knows he can't ask me outright because I'll say no and dash his dream. There's too much holding me where I am."

Emmy's cell phone rang. Irritation spread over her features, but she picked it up and when she saw the number her annoyance turned into a smile. "Hey, Bryan, how are you?"

Emmy's love interest was no concern of his, Alex told himself, and he busied himself with the menu. When the waitress came by, he ordered for both of them.

"Soup of the day? Vegetable beef? Fine."

Still, he couldn't help hearing Emmy's side of the conversation.

"...you should have come with me...."

"No salads."

"...I miss you too...."

"We'll have the Reubens, please. Extra sauce."

"...don't be silly! Of course I'm coming home...."

"We'll look at the dessert menu after we eat."

Emmy closed her phone. Her cheeks were flushed and she was smiling.

Alex pushed a glass of ice water toward her. "Is it serious?"

She knew exactly what he meant. "I'm not sure. It is on his part. On mine?" Mona Lisa had nothing on the smile she gave Alex. "How about you? Anyone in your life? Or are you too busy with your new job? Dixon told me this is your first church. It must be quite an adjustment."

"There was someone, but I'm not sure anymore."

A whiff of strong perfume assaulted his nostrils.

"Hello, Alex. Emmy." Lolly Roscoe's tone was cool. She stood in front of their booth holding a large cardboard box. Her full lips were turned downward and her face creased into a frown.

"Hi, Lolly," Emmy responded. "What are you doing?"

"I provide fresh produce here. I was just dropping it off."

"That's great, isn't it, Alex?" Emmy kicked him beneath the table.

"Yes, great. Definitely a good idea," he stammered.

"I have to go now," Lolly announced frostily. "Have a nice dinner." She spun away and hurried off.

Alex felt a little sick. "She looked upset."

"Lolly is lonely. She's ready to settle down. Mr. Right just hasn't come her way. Obviously she hoped it might be you. I feel sorry for her."

The food arrived, interrupting the conversation and leaving Alex to wonder if he was destined to be anyone's Mr. Right.

◌

The fund-raiser was an unusually somber affair. It was no wonder, given the number of traumatic things that had happened in the past few days.

Dixon strolled up to Alex as he helped Mike Carlson fold up the extra tables they'd needed for the steady stream of people who'd come to the benefit. "It was a big success. I just talked to Lauren and Gandy, who are counting the donations. They said everyone must have given till it hurt."

"People came from as far as Wheatville," Mike commented as he stacked the table against a wall.

"And farther," Gandy said, as she moved toward them. "Over three hundred people were here today." Her hair was exceptionally wild today, and she'd pinned it back with a series of bobby pins that were having a difficult time containing the mass of curls. "It's good to know people still care. Althea Dawson blubbered like a baby when she realized how many people had come out for her son." Gandy said it as if it pleased her. "Nothing like a good cry to make a person feel better. Releases tension and all."

Alex didn't disagree. A cry could be cathartic. It was just that they didn't need any more things to cry about.

It was a good thing that Gandy had taken the prayer vigil upon herself because, as it turned out, Alex missed it entirely. He spent those days at Tillie's side. With no relatives to speak of, Tillie had lived all alone in the world. He refused to let her die alone as well.

Emmy, equally determined that neither Tillie *nor* Alex be unaccompanied during this significant and perilous time, stayed with them despite Alex's protests. They sang every song either of them had ever learned, read Scripture until they were hoarse, and hovered lovingly over Tillie whenever she was strong enough to open her eyes.

After the prayer service Dixon and Gandy arrived at Tillie's door.

"Is she awake?" Gandy whispered.

"Yes. She just opened her eyes." Alex was beginning to feel highly unpresentable with two days' growth of stubble, wrinkled clothing and bloodshot eyes. Still, he'd had no desire to leave the hospital. God, he'd realized, had planted him here for a reason, and God would be the One to release him to go home when the time came. He wasn't so sure about Emmy's motives, but he had a hunch they were similar because each time he suggested she leave, all she would say was, "Not yet. Tillie needs us both."

He allowed Gandy past him into the room and stepped into the hall to talk to Dixon.

"You're a mess," Dixon said bluntly. "I've seen homeless bums that look better than you." He handed him a Styrofoam cup with steaming coffee in it. "Here's some decent java."

"Thank you. The stuff in the vending machine tastes like it was made sometime in the 1990s."

"Why don't you go home and get a shower and a few hours' sleep in your own bed? And why don't you tell my sister to do the same?"

"You know better than I do that you don't tell Emmy to do anything she doesn't want to do," Alex responded wearily. "I've been trying. It's like talking to a brick wall."

"Yeah, I suppose so. That little head of hers is hard as a rock sometimes. But how about you?"

"I just can't, Dixon. Tillie gets a lot of comfort from having us here. When I put myself in her place—alone in the world, without family, ready to meet my Maker—I know that I'd want someone with me. Someone who could pray with me right into eternity."

"I'm not sure this much dedication is even in your job description."

"No? But I do think it's in my *life* description. Despite the physical discomfort, my soul is tranquil. That's preferable to me any day over a soft bed."

He and Dixon walked toward the family room at the end of the hall. When they were sitting, Dixon stared thoughtfully at Alex. "You were really meant to be a minister, weren't you? In the true sense of the word, I mean, when to minister means to care for, attend and look after. I can't imagine you tolerated it as a college professor for all those years."

Alex stretched his long legs out in front of him. "Those students needed exactly the same things as the people of Hilltop. To have someone on their side, to make sure they got what they needed and to learn the important lessons. I have been a minster, of sorts, my entire life. Besides, your sister has been with me the entire way and she has no duty to do that."

"That's Emmy, though. She's the one you can count on in a pinch. If you want someone who finishes what they start, that's my sister. Besides, when she was a little girl, she was always fascinated with Tillie. She used to call her the Parrot Lady because of all the bright colors she wore. Tillie adored Emmy too."

Alex could imagine the tiny Emmy tagging along behind the vibrantly garbed Tillie. The thought made him smile. "Your sister is an amazing woman, Dixon."

"I told you so." There was an undertone in Dixon's voice that Alex couldn't interpret. At that moment Gandy arrived in the family room.

"Your turn, Dixon. The poor old dear is so pleased you're here." Tears came to Gandy's eyes. "It just makes me want to weep to see her this way."

Dixon nodded, rose and left. Gandy turned to Alex. "You are a wonderful man to stay with her like this. I don't know many who would." Gandy stood there, lip quivering, wild hair flying loose around her head, eyes filled with tears. Unexpectedly she wrapped Alex in her embrace. When she let him go, she said, "God did a *much* better job picking out a pastor for us than we would have for ourselves."

To his surprise, Alex couldn't speak. His throat was filled with tears.

Looking for less emotional ground, he finally said, "Tell me about the prayer service. I hope my absence didn't make a difference."

"Oh, you weren't absent," Gandy said. "You were very much present."

"How so?"

"Everyone was so grateful that you'd taken it upon yourself to be with Tillie that many of the prayers were for you. We also got a few more donations from people who couldn't be at the fund-raiser. Frankly, we raised a ton of money, enough to help everyone out—Kenny, Lila and now Tillie once she's out of the hospital." She glanced at Alex. "She is going to get out, isn't she?"

"I don't know."

"Well, we'll divvy it up the fairest way possible. And I wish you'd heard the prayer service! Lauren and Mike led it off and people just got up one by one and gave the most beautiful petitions this side of heaven. Kenny's family was there. You should have seen his mother Althea Dawson cry! Tears of joy, she said. And the singing! The organist let out all the stops. We praised God till we were hoarse. You would have thought we were the heavenly host, the way we were singing. God heard it all. It was almost...divine." Gandy leaned back with a sigh and a blissful smile.

"Were there a lot of people from All Saints present?" Alex asked cautiously, hoping not to be disappointed by her answer.

"Lots? Every single one! We were packed in like sardines in oil. We sang together, prayed together, held hands.... Why, I even hugged Alf Nyborg, if you can believe it, and he let me do it! Miracle upon miracle, I'd say. All we needed was to find a joint mission that was bigger than either of us alone. I don't think either church will ever be the same again. I even saw Alf kiss Lila Mason on the cheek. I didn't know he had a pucker left in him!"

Alex burst out laughing and Gandy joined him.

The joy was short-lived, however. A few moments later, Emmy came to get them. "It's time," she said softly. "Tillie wants to go now."

With Gandy on Alex's left and Emmy on his right, they made their way back to the room to say good-bye for the last time.

"She was smiling when she died, did you notice?" Emmy said as they drove back to Grassy Valley together.

"She said she saw an angel. No wonder she smiled."

"It was rather wonderful, in a way. And the singing…"

During Tillie's last breaths, they had burst into "Amazing Grace" in four-part harmony, a miracle in itself considering Gandy was given to singing off tune and Dixon's voice was completely untrained. Still, their voices came together to usher Tillie into a place far better than the one she was in. Then they'd cried together and laughed together and made their peace with her passing. Alex had never experienced anything more beautiful in his life.

"We were part of a miracle, weren't we?" Emmy's eyes were still big with astonishment.

"I believe we were."

She grabbed his right hand as he steered with his left. "I'm so glad we could share that, Alex. I've never been so moved…." They made the rest of the trip in silence, but she did not let go of his hand.

CHAPTER THIRTY

The days he'd been gone from the church office seemed like an eternity. When Alex finally got back to the office, Gandy had compiled a to-do list that would discourage the most intrepid of pastors. Still, he felt the need to keep busy, to tend to the living. Tillie was in good Hands. It took him the entire day to proof mailings to go out, return phone calls and visit with the people who came to talk.

His phone was ringing when he reached his house at four PM. Alex picked up the receiver.

"You're finally there!" Lydia Olson's voice on the other end of the line was excited. "You need a cooking lesson now!"

That, Alex knew, was Lydia's code for having to talk to him. "I do? What am I planning to make?"

"*Rommegrot.* We always make it for a church dinner sometime in the fall. It will be good for you to know what it is in advance."

"Rumor grout? What is it? Something for sealing bathtubs or stopping rumors?"

"A Scandinavian pudding. You'll enjoy it."

"And it's an emergency that I learn how to cook it?" Alex felt as if he were conversing in a secret dialect.

"You have no idea." There was an ominous pause. Then Lydia added, "I've got the ingredients. And your supper."

If Lydia hadn't sounded so serious, he might have laughed out loud. This was the only place he knew where food was an effective bribery tool—one that he, at least, fell prey to every single time.

"I'll set the table." He could hear a sigh of relief on Lydia's end of the line.

"I'll be right over."

He'd barely put on water for Lydia's tea when she drove into the yard. She knocked once and walked inside. She went straight to the kitchen counter and began unloading a grocery bag. Milk, sour cream, half-and-half, butter, flour, sugar and cinnamon appeared. Alex noticed that her hands were shaking as she put out the ingredients.

"There are two ways to make this, one with sweet cream and one with sour cream. We'll make the one with sour cream first. If there's time we can make a second batch. I can't quite decide which I prefer. I know Clarence likes it with the sour cream but..."

This was a new twist. Alex put his hand on her arm, hoping to stop her mile-a-minute nervous chatter. "Slow down, Lydia. You'll be better off cooking once you get whatever is bothering you off your chest."

She turned to look at him with stricken eyes. "Oh, Reverend Alex, it's worse than I thought. I'm falling in love!"

Alex thought back to the few times he'd met Johann. He was a nice-looking man, pleasant, mild, not exactly what Alex pictured as a love interest, but then again, he wasn't a sixtysomething single woman either.

"That's wonderful, Lydia...isn't it?"

"Wonderful and terrible. He's so kind and dear. Johann's got a good sense of humor and has traveled so much. I could listen to him for hours! We *laugh* together. That's something that my brothers and I don't do much of at our house. Jacob never talks unless prodded, and Clarence prattles endlessly about combines, tractors and the weather. I didn't realize how lonesome I've really been until I met Johann."

"That is wonderful."

"But the boys! What will my brothers say? I've practically had to sneak out to meet Johann because Clarence puts up such a fuss when he comes to the farm. 'Look at that old fool,' he says. 'Thinks he can go a-courting just like a young buck! Where's his sense of decency?'" Lydia's face reddened. "He makes it sound like Johann's practically senile to have the idea of enjoying my company."

"Lydia, has Clarence ever had a girlfriend?"

"When he was younger. He even dated Mattie Olsen for a while. We all had to work on the farm back then and eventually our parents needed care. We were too busy to go out much. Those things just took on less importance, I guess."

Clarence and Mattie Olsen? That was a picture he'd have to consider for a while. "So he's suppressed all that 'foolishness' for all these years?"

"I suppose he did."

"Do you think he's missed it?"

"He probably hadn't even thought about it until I and Johann started seeing each other...." She stared at him wide-eyed. "Do you think he's jealous?"

"I don't know. I'm sure he's terrified of losing the best cook in the county, though."

"He should love me enough to let me go," Lydia said firmly. "I need to have a talk with that man right now."

"Now?"

Lydia's jaw was firmly set and there was a glint in her eye. Poor Clarence, Alex thought.

"You'll have to make the rommegrot by yourself," she told him. "I know he's in the yard working on machinery right now."

"But I..." Alex began to protest but Lydia paid no attention. She marched out of the kitchen and back to her car, leaving Alex holding the recipes in his hand. He was supposed to cook something he couldn't even pronounce?

LYDIA'S NORWEGIAN ROMMEGROT

- 1 quart heavy cream (nothing else will do!)
- 1 quart whole milk (scalded)
- 1 cup flour
- ½ teaspoon salt
- 2 tablespoons sugar
- Cinnamon and sugar

Bring cream to boil. Cook slowly 15 to 20 minutes, stirring constantly. (I prefer to use a wooden spoon.) Stir until butter comes out of the cream and forms on top. Skim this off for later use. Add scalded milk until it's an acceptable consistency. (You might not use all of it. You can thicken this with flour if you add too much milk.) Add sugar and salt. Serve warm with the melted butter, cinnamon and sugar.

Just reading the recipe made Alex's arteries clog.

CHAPTER THIRTY-ONE

Sunday morning Alex woke up energized. The air was brisk and cool, although it was predicted to become hot as a kiln in the afternoon. There was a difference in the air now as fall flourished. The sun had moved in the sky, and the colors of the world had changed along with the crops. They had taken on a crisp, sharp edge, as if someone had adjusted a pair of heavenly binoculars and everything had come into perfect view.

Alex prayed aloud as he made his breakfast. Tripod lay on his cedar chip bed and listened raptly as if Alex were discussing chasing rabbits with God.

It was going to be a wonderful day, Alex thought. He straightened his tie and glanced in the mirror. He was wearing his hair longer now. He'd been getting it cut at Licks & Sticks. Alex enjoyed watching the barber's wife making candy behind the glass wall that separated the two unlikely businesses. Occasionally she would come to the barber shop side through a door at the back and make recommendations as to how her husband should cut hair. Amazingly, he often listened. Hence, Alex's new, softer look. Even Gandy approved, which was really saying something.

A little of that optimism faded when he arrived at church, however. The organist was already doing her early morning warm-up. And the early birds started to drift in because they knew Alex always plugged in the coffeepot in the foyer. They could have morning coffee and be in their pews before the other latecomers began to arrive. The big surprise, however, the one that made Alex nervous, was an overflowing old Buick driven by Earl Packard.

Alex did a double take at seeing the entire Packard family pour out of the big four-door. They were as clean as he'd ever seen them. Even the twins had shoes on, and someone had caught Earl Junior long enough to comb his hair. Will bolted out and headed toward Alex at a dead run. He hit Alex's legs and flung his arms around his waist. "We're coming to church! We're coming to church!"

"I see that. Welcome. I'm glad you're here."

"Mom and Dad had a big fight about it this morning but Mom won. She made a peach pie for dinner and she said if Dad didn't take us to church she was going to give it to the pigs. He loves peach pie more than anything, even us kids maybe. She was halfway to the pigsty by the time he gave in." Will seemed delighted about the whole affair. "Cool, huh?"

"Very." Alex would have to talk to Minnie and Earl about marriage counseling somewhere down the road, but for the moment he chose to be grateful that the whole family had gotten to church in one piece.

One by one, the rest of Will's siblings exited the car and came to stand around him. The little Packards had a tendency to put their thumbs in their mouths and simply stare, Alex had noted, as if he were a coat of armor or an Egyptian mummy in a museum. He picked up one of the identical twins to break the ice.

"I'm so glad to see you children here," he said. "There are going to be cookies in the foyer...."

That was a mistake he'd never make again. At the word *cookies*, all the Packard children headed for the church. Even the one in his arms slithered out like a wet seal and dashed off. He hoped Gandy had stocked up well on cookies this week.

"Sorry about that," Mrs. Packard said with a sympathetic smile. "Say the word *cookie* and it's like waving a red flag in front of a bull. I probably should have warned you."

"And I should have guessed. It's fine. I'm just glad you're all here."

"It was a fight, but worth it." Minnie's expression grew puzzled. "I didn't have quite as much trouble convincing Earl to come this time, however. I usually get all the way to the pigsty before he relents. Once or twice I have given a pie to the pigs so he knows I'm serious."

Alex simply couldn't think of a response to that. He didn't have to speak, however, because Minnie was voluble this morning. She leaned forward to speak into his ear. "I saw Lydia out driving around with that Johann Paulson yesterday. It's happening quite a bit lately. Isn't that sweet?"

Sweet? It surprised him, considering Minnie's own situation, that she'd think that, or any other romantic goings-on, to be sweet. Earl didn't appear to be a romantic man.

"I'm happy for her, you know? Like God said in Genesis, it's not good that man be alone. Such a dear woman. Of course you know that, with her giving you cooking lessons and all." She sighed and looked dewy-eyed. So Minnie believed in romance even now.

Alex's first order of business for the morning was, as always, the announcements.

He looked out across the congregation for Andy Packard's eye. "I want to mention the formation of a new organization here at Hilltop. I understand it's been a few years..." *since Hilltop and All Saints split,* he thought, "...since you've had a youth group that met regularly here at church. When we combine the teenagers from Hilltop with those of All Saints, we'll have a good number of potential participants. There's a sign-up sheet on the office door. If those of you who are interested would add your name and e-mail or phone number to the list, Gandy will be contacting you about the time and place of the first meeting."

Alex noticed that Andy's eyes widened when he mentioned teenagers. A good sign.

Then Annie Henderson gave it her all on the organ, making it sound, in the little church, like a gigantic pipe organ. The congregation sang with more gusto than Alex had heard in some time, particularly "Onward Christian Soldiers" and "Faith of Our Fathers." Stoddard Block sang out particularly loudly on "Onward Christian Soldiers." Alex supposed it was that line "marching off to war" that got to Stoddard. Marching sounded purposeful and productive, like hammering, sawing and shoring up, some of his other favorite words. Winchester Holmquist stood straighter at the mention of soldiers, and his wife's voice sang out sweet and clear.

"Now please turn to hymn number..."

He realized that he had more fun being in the pulpit and looking out over his flock than he would have if he'd had to sit in the pew and look up at someone like himself. Alex's chest grew tight. He loved these people more every week. If things continued at this rate, he wasn't sure his heart could take it. It might just explode one day. Could one die of too much loving? If he could, that would be the way he'd choose to go.

"Let us give thanks...."

Not all was well in the pews, he noticed.

"Let us pray...."

Wisely, Minnie Packard had chosen to seat her brood in the back two rows of the church. With Earl present, the children had enough sense not to be noisy, but behind their father they indulged themselves in making garish faces, waving their arms, and playing the can-you-touch-your-tongue-to-your-nose game. It was highly distracting.

Alex chose to look the other way during his sermon.

There was a smattering of All Saints Fellowship people in attendance. Those who preferred the earlier service of the day had started coming to Hilltop, and the late sleepers from Hilltop—like Belle Wells and Inga Sorenson—now went to the All Saints' service. They were finally melding their congregations and truly becoming one again.

As soon as Annie started playing the parting song, "Blest Be the Tie That Binds," Alex walked down the aisle to begin greeting people at the door. The Packards swarmed into the aisle and made a dash for him. Katie got there first.

"You look lovely today, Katie. Is that a new dress?"

"No, but I got new underpants."

Minnie, blushing, scooped the little girl out of Alex's arms before the child could demonstrate. "That's not appropriate to tell people, honey. That's..." Her voice died away as she hurried the little girl outside.

"You're pretty good," Andy commented on his way by. "Maybe I won't run away until I check out this youth thing."

"An excellent idea. In fact, bike over to my office one day. I'd like to have a little conversation about...things." *Like how to get you to stop toying with the idea of running away.*

The boy shrugged. "Sure, I guess."

The twins stopped to stare at him, eyes wide, thumbs in their mouths. Finally Earl Packard shooed them on like a flock of chickens.

Alex caught him by the arm. "I'm glad you came."

"You helped me cut trees. I thought I'd give you a chance. Besides, Minnie threatened to...never mind."

"I hope you'll come back again soon." Sincerity rang true in Alex's words. "And enjoy the peach pie."

Earl looked up, startled, and a small grin tilted his lips for a moment. Then he bobbed his head, picked up a child under each arm like logs of wood and carried them out.

"Glad to see you here today, Bessie, Brunie." Bessie had worn all her favorite clothes to church—at once. She had on a bright red sweater with a reindeer on it, a yellow cotton cardigan, navy blue pants and her gardening shoes. She'd topped it off with a scarf sewn with sequins. He thought both sisters looked tired. Brunie looked especially exhausted, but with the crush of people behind him, Alex didn't have time to ask more.

Shouting and yelling in the churchyard interrupted the pleasant chatter inside. Excusing himself, Alex turned and hurried out to see what the problem was.

Dixon and Bucky Chadwick were squared off in the middle of the churchyard. Bucky had a scrap of lumber about two feet long, and he was poking it at Dixon like a sword. Dixon was deftly dodging the makeshift weapon and not backing down. Men were yelling for Bucky to stop but he ignored them, his eyes intent on Dixon.

Emmy ran up to Alex and grabbed his arm. "You've got to stop them."

"What happened?"

"Dixon decided to water the flower beds while we were in church. We slipped out early to turn the sprinklers off so no one would get sprayed when they came out after the service. He caught Bucky rummaging through his pickup truck. Bucky had some of Dixon's tools on the ground, and it looked like he'd planned to put them in his own truck and take off."

Emmy's eyes were wide with worry as the awkward dance between Bucky and her brother continued. "He was right, because when he confronted Bucky, Bucky's face got red and like that"—Emmy snapped her fingers—"he was enraged. He told Dixon, well, I won't tell you what he said, but he also told Dixon to hand over the tools. What's wrong with him, Alex? Bucky is acting like a crazy man."

"I'm afraid he might *be* a little crazy, Emmy. Call his mother Myrtle at Red's place in town. She's cooking breakfast there. I'll get Mark or Mike and we'll try to separate them."

As it turned out, it took Alex, Mark, Mike, Ben Jenkins and Alf Nyborg—who, despite his age, was strong as a bull—to wrestle the infuriated Bucky to the ground. He was still lunging at them, trying to break free, when they heard the police sirens in the distance.

Alex looked at Emmy and mouthed, "Did you call the police?"

Emmy shook her head and gestured with her hands. "No."

Right behind the police car was Myrtle Chadwick. She jumped out of her car, still in the white apron and hairnet she wore at work. She marched over to where the men had restrained Bucky, took a look at her son and kicked him in the ankle.

"Bucky, what's come over you? Have you lost your mind? Digging through people's cars when they're at church? Hasn't anything I've ever told you sunk in?"

"They called the police, Ma," he whined. His face was red and blotchy.

"They didn't call anybody, *I* did. I can't manage you anymore, Bucky. Trying to kill animals and that little Will Packard to boot, stealing from my friends and neighbors, ignoring everything I've ever tried to teach you? I need help, Bucky, and so do you."

"Ma..." The young man's voice turned into a pitiful bleat, and suddenly the fight went out of him.

Then Grassy Valley's finest took over, and Alex, Mark and Dixon turned back to the crowd and tried to disperse it.

"Man," he heard a childish voice chime from the direction of the Packard vehicle, "if this is what church is like, I want to come every week!"

By the time the churchyard was empty, Alex was spent. All he wanted to do was go home, lie on the bed, read for a few hours and pray for Myrtle and Bucky.

Sometimes his sister Carol told him she worried that he would die of boredom out here on the prairie. Alex chuckled. Die of boredom? Anything but!

CHAPTER THIRTY-TWO

"It's the police on the phone." Gandy pronounced the word so it sounded like *po-leece*.

"I was hoping they wouldn't call." Reluctantly Alex picked up the phone. "Reverend Armstrong here."

"This is Chet Ralston of the Grassy Valley Police. We picked up a young man at your church yesterday."

"Yes, Bucky Chadwick."

"Mr. Daniels said he wouldn't press charges, but that means we have to let him go. I was wondering if you had any complaint... trespassing...you know."

"I don't want to start a habit of kicking people off church property if I can help it," Alex admitted, "but Bucky is trouble, there's no doubt about that."

"That was Mr. Dixon's reasoning too. Since Chadwick got caught before he actually stole something, there aren't a lot of charges that will stick."

"He needs to be watched."

"I agree, but there are only two of us in Grassy Valley, so watching someone like Bucky is going to take more eyes than ours. We'd like to catch him red-handed at something, but he's sneaky. Guys like him, bullies, seem to have eyes in the back of their heads."

"I promised his mother I'd watch out too." Alex didn't feel very heartened by the conversation. Was Bucky going to slip through their fingers so easily? "But I do think he could seriously hurt someone." He told him about the incidents Will had experienced with Bucky.

"I think our best bet is at Red's place." The policeman sounded troubled. "Those vending machines are about ready to be emptied again. If we could catch Bucky…"

"Good luck."

"Thanks, sir. And let us know if you see something."

Gandy was looking at him expectantly when he hung up the phone. "Well?"

"Nothing, really."

"You mean that good-for-nothing lowlife is just going to walk around like nothing happened?" Gandy bristled.

"I suppose so, unless someone catches him at something. Bucky didn't have time to actually put Dixon's stuff in his truck."

"It should be easy enough to watch him."

Alex looked at Gandy sharply. "What do you mean?"

"He wanders around the church a lot. He's probably casing the joint."

"You watch too much television, Gandy. What do you mean, 'casing the joint'?"

"He always shows up when you aren't here. He never comes inside. He's always hauling himself over here with a scraggly bunch of wildflowers. He goes out and visits his daddy's grave. You can see if you want. He's got a quart jar out there and he changes the flowers. I've even seen him there in the evening. He parks so you can't see him from the parsonage because my husband and I checked. It gives me the creeps having that boy around, but he's never come into the church and bothered me." She shivered a little. "A psychopath, that's what he is, I'll bet. I saw it in a movie. Crazy as a loon, that guy was…"

Alex interrupted her before she could go into a movie review. "Bucky visits the graveyard?"

"Even more than his mother, and she's there often. She and her husband had a good marriage. It had to have been strong to stay together even after all the heartache that boy of theirs gave them."

It didn't fit. Bucky, the bully, the killer of small animals and verbal and emotional abuser of children, was constantly putting fresh flowers on his father's grave? Alex got up and walked outside. Sure enough, there in the graveyard was a measly—but fresh—bunch of wildflowers in the vase on the Chadwick grave plot.

Stymied, he walked back to the church, his mind racing. Something was up, but he didn't know what. Deep inside, he felt like he should be able to figure it out.

When he got back into the church, all thoughts of Bucky left him. Belle Wells was visiting with Gandy and she looked upset. She was fluttering her hands in the air as she talked to Gandy, and her usually pleasant demeanor was gone. Gandy picked herself up and went to the file cabinet in Alex's room.

"Hi, Belle, are you here to pick up your Sunday school supplies? The books look very good this year. I think you and your class will enjoy them."

"About that…" Belle was so nervous she actually began wringing her hands. "I don't think I'll be able to teach after all. I'm so sorry but I just can't."

"Is something wrong?" Alex's mind immediately jumped to Belle's health or that of her husband.

"Not in the way you think, Pastor. I'm a coward, that's all." Belle chewed on her lip.

"What is it you think you have to be brave about during Sunday school?" he asked cautiously.

"I just heard…I mean, I didn't realize…nobody ever told me that…I just can't handle it, don't you see?

"Handle what, Belle?"

"Having little Packards in my class, of course! I'm not that strong a teacher. They'll nail me to a wall!"

Alex stared at her dumbfounded. The woman was serious.

"I told you so." Gandy's words drifted out from the back office where she'd been eavesdropping. "I told you it would be harder to get teachers if the Packards came, but you didn't believe me."

Alex closed his eyes. Gandy *had* told him that. She was right. He hadn't believed her.

"They might be naughty and unruly on occasion, but they aren't dangerous. In fact, as you get to know them, they're very sweet children. Just unsupervised."

"What if Will brings his skunk to church? I'm terrified of skunks!"

Belle, like Alex, had grown up in the city. Skunks very seldom ventured near highly populated areas, and he'd been told all his life that they sometimes carried rabies. He, too, had been put off by Rose at first, but now he rather enjoyed watching her scamper around the yard when Will allowed her to do so. "I'll make him promise that he can't bring Rose or any other animal to church."

"What about birds and reptiles?"

"Those too."

"Anything that breathes?" Belle thought for a moment. "Or anything that breathed once but has now…quit?"

"No animals, dead or alive. I promise. Besides, Will is mostly interested in living ones."

"And the other Packard children?"

"I'll talk to them as well."

"And I can quit if they don't behave?"

Belle was driving a hard bargain.

"I'd like you to give me a chance to correct any situation that might arise before you leave, Belle. If I can't, you are certainly free to go."

"I don't know…"

The poor woman looked guilty and fearful at the same time, Alex noted. "If you don't find the children funny, charming and actually very well-versed in Scripture, I'd be surprised."

"Versed in Scripture? How could that be?"

"Their mother."

Light dawned in Belle's eyes. "Minnie, of course." She squared her shoulders and lifted her chin. "Minnie does try with those kids. I'll try it, Pastor, but if something goes awry…"

"Let me know immediately. I can handle the Packards."

After Belle left, Alex wondered if he'd told the 100 percent truth. He *thought* he could handle the Packards, but could he? That would have to wait to be seen.

∾

"Alex? This is Dixon. Do you want to come over for dinner tonight?"

"Who's cooking?"

"Very funny. Emmy, of course. She wants to say good-bye."

"She's not leaving already, is she?" Alex was dismayed and, crazily enough, dismayed about being dismayed.

"It's about her work. She says she'll come back as soon as she can, but it will be a few weeks. Some juggling of administrators and no one left who knows what's going on or something like that. She's not happy, but she doesn't have much choice."

"I'm sorry to hear that."

"Come about six."

Alex was surprised at how hard it hit him that his newfound friend was already departing. He even answered absently when Mattie Olsen called to tell him that the annual *lutefisk* dinner had to be pushed back to November because there was something about not getting the "good lutefisk" until then.

Good lutefisk was, as far as Alex had determined, an oxymoron. Lutefisk was a white fish soaked in lye until it was clear and jelly-like, soaked again, cooked, and then served with butter, potatoes and green peas. Whether he first sampled it in September or November was immaterial to him.

Emmy probably liked lutefisk. She liked everything else about this place.

The phone rang again. This time it was Natalie. "How are you, Alex?"

"Okay, I guess."

"You don't sound okay. What's wrong?"

He wasn't sure. He wanted to be happier to hear Natalie's voice. He wanted to feel pleased that she'd called. What he *didn't* want was the nagging doubt she unearthed in him or the lack of trust he felt toward her.

Natalie wouldn't give up. "Something's bothering you, Alex. Tell me what it is."

"Nothing that needs to be discussed right now. I was just invited out for supper so I'd better get going...."

"Alex!" Her chiding tone reminded him of his fifth grade teacher. "Tell me!"

He drew a deep breath. Okay, he'd tell her but she wouldn't like it. "I don't think that we should talk about you and me getting back together right now. I'm not sure when...or if...I'll ever really trust you again. I need space—and time. I'm sorry, Natalie, but I'm simply being honest with you."

There. He'd said it—the things he hadn't even been able to admit fully to himself until now. An icy chill settled around him as he imagined what Natalie must be thinking.

"I won't beg, plead or make a fool of myself, Alex," she said finally. Her tone was more sad than angry. "You know how to reach me." Quietly she hung up.

Alex stood very still, amazed at what he'd just done as he mulled over their conversation in his mind. He didn't feel he'd made a mistake, he realized, just done the honest thing. Unexpectedly, he felt only relief.

∽

"Meat loaf, green beans, mashed potatoes, squash and apple pie," Emmy said after Alex had said grace and she was about to serve. "This is Dixon's favorite fall meal. It's not fancy but I hope you like it."

"It's wonderful. Lydia Olson has been giving me cooking lessons so I'm getting better in the kitchen, but I'm getting really sick of chicken potpie."

Emmy laughed and the bright, sparkling sound made Alex smile.

"That reminds me!" Dixon put his knife down on the table so hard that it shook. "I heard some big news in town this morning."

"I don't think Alex likes gossip," Emmy reminded him gently.

"I don't think it's gossip if everyone and their sister is talking about it, do you?"

"That's probably one of the *better* descriptions of gossip," Alex said as he mounded mashed potatoes onto his plate.

"Okay, then don't let me tell you that Johann Paulson cooked dinner for Lydia Olson last night and that he fed her caviar, escargot and a fillet of beef that cost twenty-five bucks a pound. Don't let me tell you it was by candlelight either, or that when he left after dinner, he kissed her." Dixon dug into his food while he shook his head. "No sir, don't let me tell you any of that."

Now, of course, it was all too late. Emmy poked at his arm with a serving spoon. "Now that you've blabbed it all, tell us more."

Dixon looked up, innocent as a lamb. "That would be gossiping."

"How'd you find this out? I'll bet your sources aren't reliable."

"Practically from the horse's mouth," Dixon retorted. "I ran into Clarence in the Cozy Corner this morning and he was fit to be tied. He reminded me of an irate father about to pull together a shotgun wedding to protect his daughter's besmirched reputation. Of course, the *last* thing Clarence wants Lydia to do is move away so he'd be in a fix. He can't chase Johann off without chasing Lydia away too. Poor guy. We men who have old, unmarried sisters certainly do have to suffer a lot."

Emmy poked him with the spoon again. "Caviar? Really?"

"He got it in Wheatville. We might never have known, but Clarence's friend works at the meat counter and he called and told Clarence that some fool had just spent an enormous amount of money on fillet, caviar and escargot. He also told him that the fellow who spent the money must be a friend of his sister's because Lydia was right there with the guy when he bought the stuff. I guess Clarence nearly popped a blood vessel. They went to Ruby's place and found Johann in the kitchen, wearing an apron and serving Lydia caviar on toast points.

"Poor old Clarence didn't have the time to say anything before Lydia chased him out so she and her 'friend' could have some private time. I guess she came home late with a goofy grin on her face, and he got it out of her that Johann had kissed her. This morning he was drinking coffee, eating cinnamon rolls and crying in his java."

"A soap opera!" Emmy said gleefully. "I wish I didn't have to go before seeing how this all turns out."

Alex felt as though he were swinging on the end of a bungee cord, his emotions rocketing this way and that, devoid of tempo or logic. One moment he was laughing, the next reliving his conversation with Natalie. Then he felt sad about Emmy's departure. It was too much for the sensible, logical man that he was...or used to be.

"When are you leaving?" he asked.

"Six AM. This is probably the last time I'll see you this visit," Emmy said. "It's been fun, hasn't it?"

It had been fun, and knowing that the fun was almost over darkened Alex's mood to indigo.

CHAPTER THIRTY-THREE

When his alarm rang at six thirty the next morning, Alex knew that Emmy was gone. She had come to Hilltop like a ball of light and energy, touched everyone and vanished again. How had she affected him so much in the brief amount of time she was here? he wondered. He already felt her absence. A light had been switched off and he craved the brightness.

Melancholy drove him out of bed and into jeans and a work shirt. He had no business feeling so bereft over a woman he barely knew, he told himself. The only antidote was to get busy. He knew just what he'd do.

Cool weather wasn't that far off, and Will's Hoomain Society was little more than a board shack. Though it would keep the wind out, it was hardly enough for the days to come.

Alex got in his vehicle and headed to Grassy Valley's lumberyard.

"What can I do for you today?" A pleasant woman in her late thirties greeted him.

Alex stuck out his hand. "Alex Armstrong, the pastor at Hilltop Community Church and All Saints Fellowship."

"I've been wondering when I was going to meet you." She took his hand and shook it firmly. "'Course I've been working on a big plumbing project in Wheatville most of the summer. Just finished it, in fact. My name is Margaret Ames. I'm partners with my brother and father in this business. Dad's a carpenter, I'm a plumber, and my brother, who owns the lumberyard, is an electrician. Build, flush and electrify, that's us."

"Then I've come to the right place. I need a few sheets of insulated wall board to finish the inside of a shed. I have a neighbor boy who keeps a few animals at the parsonage and I thought with winter coming perhaps I could insulate it for him. It wouldn't solve all the problems of winter, but it would certainly extend the life of his animal sanctuary for a few months."

"Will Packard, right?"

"You know Will?"

"Everybody knows the Packard kids. All smart as whips and wild as fox kits. Minnie is a good friend of mine."

"So you know about his little project with the animals?"

"Minnie thinks you're the best thing ever, to take an interest in her boy. Will could be something special if someone paid more attention to him. She's got her hands full, poor woman."

"I enjoy him and his older brother Andy, and sister Katie too. I don't want him discouraged when cold weather sets in and he can't find a place for his rescues."

Margaret nodded and went directly to some samples of insulation board and pulled one out. "I'd recommend this. Then I'd put some cheap paneling over it. That will cozy it up a lot. It won't cost much since that's a small shed."

"You know it?"

"Sure. I've done work on the parsonage off and on over the years. So have my dad and brother. In fact, if my memory serves me correctly, that little shed is wired for electricity too. Maybe we could put a warming light of some sort in there and he could use it all winter." She looked up and grinned at him. "By 'we' I mean I'll give you everything you need. I'd like to do something for one of Minnie's kids, if you know what I mean."

Again, Alex was flummoxed by the generosity he found here. "That's not necessary. I don't mind."

"I'm sure you don't, but I want to do it. Don't worry. Next time we'll charge you." She grinned. "Now let me figure out how much you'll need."

Almost before he knew it, he had a van full of materials, nails and a brand-new hammer and saw.

Thanks to a how-to book he'd found in the parsonage and some skills he'd picked up at his uncle's garage, he'd already measured, cut and installed the insulation and was starting on the paneling when Will and Andy rode up on their bikes.

"Whatcha doing?" Will asked as he swung off his bike.

"Insulating the shed."

"Why?"

"So you can keep animals warm in the winter."

Will's face lit up. "You mean it? You aren't going to kick me out like my dad said? He said you wouldn't want any frozen critters at your place and that I'd have to quit dragging stuff over here."

Alex could just hear Earl. He sighed. "Margaret, the plumber…"

"My mom's friend, you mean?"

"She said there was electricity in here so I looked. Sure enough, there's one outlet. It's on a rafter and I missed it earlier. I got a warming lamp. It may not work in the coldest months, but it will give your critters a little nicer life for a while. Maybe we'll put some plastic over the window too. That should help keep it warm."

Alex staggered and nearly fell as Will attached himself to his waist and hugged with all his might. When he looked up, the boy's eyes were shining. "You did all this for me and the animals?"

"I guess I did."

Will, overcome with appreciation, didn't seem to know what to say.

"Cool," Andy said, "or, since there's a warming light, hot! You're lucky, Will. Thank the preacher."

"Thank you," Will choked out.

A warning bell went off in Alex's brain. "You're lucky," Andy had said. Alex didn't want to be known as playing favorites with these kids. They needed every positive adult role model they could get.

"There are two spots on the plug-in, Andy. If you want to come over when Will does, I'll connect the second one to a light so you can read while you keep him company. I told you I have books you might like."

Andy's face brightened even more than Will's had done. It almost hurt Alex to look at him. It was such a simple thing he'd offered. Andy responded as if he'd been given a palace.

"I'd like that, sir," Andy said.

Sir? How many times had that much politeness come out of a little Packard's mouth? Alex felt as though *he* had been given the biggest gift of all.

∾

Mark Nash roared into the yard just before noon. Alex could tell by the way he stalked to the house that he was angry. Alex met him on the porch. "Trouble?"

"One roadblock after another. The committee has run up against dead ends everywhere they search for a new physician. Nobody wants to come to a small town in the middle of North Dakota. Sometimes the doc will be interested, but his wife says no—too little shopping, or civilization, or whatever. Besides, everybody is specializing these days—where did all the general practitioners go? We'll keep trying, of course, but it's discouraging."

"Sorry. I'm not doing much to help, am I?"

"Do you know anyone back where you're from who might be interested?"

"My college roommate is a physician, but he has a big practice just outside Chicago and loves it there. I can give him a call if you like. And there's Emmy Dixon, if you can convince her to move home."

"Don't I wish," Mark sighed. "I told her that again yesterday. She just smiles and doesn't say a word."

"I'm sorry. Everyone loves Emmy. She could fill Doc's big shoes."

"Well, that's not what's got me so riled up right now anyway."

"There's more? You'd better come inside." Alex led the way and handed Mark a glass so he could help himself to the lemonade on the table.

"Someone broke into the library and made a real mess of it. Scribbled with markers on several of the books, tipped over plants, cut holes in the chair seats with a knife. Pure vandalism."

"Who'd do a thing like that?"

Mark scowled. "The police think it was Bucky Chadwick getting revenge for being thrown in jail overnight, but there's no way to prove it. They had someone outside Red's watching his vending machines. They thought he might strike there but he didn't. They missed him again. They interviewed Bucky and he said he was home, in his room, all night."

"What does his mother say?"

"She doesn't know. She was watching television and didn't hear him go out, but he could have gotten by her. She can't tell the police anything."

"The poor woman must be beside herself."

"It might be good if you talked to her, Alex. She needs support."

"Got it. I'll go right now."

Mark nodded and stood up. "And if you think of anyone who could talk Emmy Dixon into coming home, call me."

Alex got the heebie-jeebies just driving into the Chadwick yard. Old car carcasses, empty oil cans, piles of moldering hay, and discarded machinery parts littered the place. Bucky wasn't much of a steward of anything he touched. He parked by the house and was walking up the path when Myrtle came out.

"You've heard," she said, her expression grave.

"Yes."

"What am I going to do with that boy? I've tried everything I know." Tears started down her cheeks and she beckoned him inside. Myrtle's house was clean and tidy though showing its age. The furniture was covered with towels and strips of plastic, protecting them from both dirt and sun. Her Formica table was so out of style that it was almost back in style again.

There was coffee in the pot on the counter and two mugs. Absently Myrtle filled one of them and handed it to Alex.

He could see her hands shaking and the distress on her plain features.

"I'm not sure. Someone probably has to catch him at something in order to intervene."

"He's sly, that boy. Street smart. I sometimes wonder if Bucky had turned to doing good things instead of bad, how much positive influence he could have had on this community. It's as easy to be good as it is to be bad. Criminals sometimes work harder to carry off their crimes than honest people do to make a living. I just don't know what got into Bucky. His father and I tried to raise him right."

They sat quietly, each in their own thoughts, until Alex decided it was time to change the subject to something Myrtle might actually have an answer to.

"I have a question to ask you about the Hilltop cemetery."

Myrtle looked puzzled but got up from her chair at the table and went into the other room. When she came back she was carrying a large but plain picture frame. Inside it was a map of all the graves at Hilltop. She laid it down in front of Alex. "Like I told you, it's hard for me to get to church when I work at Red's on Sunday mornings, but it's up to date. My husband was meticulous about keeping track and I've tried to do the same. It's funny how these jobs get handed from family member to family member." There was a choke in her voice. "Too bad I can't trust Bucky to take on the responsibility when I'm not able."

Alex studied the picture laid out before him. It was much as he'd expected. Tidy rows with names printed in boxes that indicated family plots. He pointed to the back portion of the cemetery. "There's not much here."

"A few hired men who had no families. Sad, isn't it, to have no relatives? The church donated those plots."

"What about the one that should be right here?" Alex pointed to a spot on the paper. "Or haven't you put it in yet because it's relatively new?"

Myrtle frowned. "What are you talking about? No one is buried there."

"But there is. I've seen the grave. The soil is fresh."

"It couldn't be," Myrtle said firmly. "I would have known. That wouldn't have gotten by me."

"But I saw it."

Myrtle stood up. "Then I want to see it for myself."

Now what had he gotten into? Alex wondered as he drove Myrtle to the church. He was relieved to see both Gandy's and Dixon's vehicles parked in the yard. They both walked out of the church and onto the top step as Alex and Myrtle got out of the van.

"What are you doing here?" Gandy asked. "It's your day off."

"It's your day off too."

"I forgot my purse," Gandy countered.

"And Dixon?"

"I stopped at your place and you weren't there so I thought I'd look for you here. Looks like I found you too."

Alex explained the conversation he and Myrtle had just had about the graveyard. "Myrtle wants to see this grave for herself. She insists it shouldn't be there."

"Then we'll all look," Dixon said. "Since I've seen it too, I can vouch for you, Reverend. Gandy can be the final deciding factor if we're imagining something or not."

They trooped across the grass, through the graveyard gate and into the far corner. Myrtle muttered all the way. "There can't be anything. It must have been just a lump of dirt or…" She gasped. "There *is* a grave!"

Everyone stared down at the freshly dug soil. It had been turned again since Alex and Dixon had seen it last. The soil was again damp and black.

"What I can't figure out," Alex said, "is why whoever tends to this keeps turning over the soil instead of seeding grass and putting up a headstone. It doesn't make sense."

"It doesn't make sense unless…" Dixon paused, turned and jogged back to his pickup. When he returned, he was carrying a spade.

Without a word, he put the spade to the ground, pushed it into the earth with his foot and turned up the soil.

"Dixon, you can't!" Alex protested.

"Wait!" Gandy yelped. "You're not a gravedigger!"

"Let him do it," Myrtle said, a strange calmness in her tone.

As Alex watched, horrified, Dixon put the spade to earth again and again. Just as he was about to physically stop his friend, Alex heard a soft thump.

"Oh, mercy! He's hit a casket!" Gandy screamed, clasping her hands to her chest.

"No, he hasn't. He's not even two feet below ground," Myrtle told her.

Alex moved closer. Dixon had hit something, but what? The women hovered over the open ground as well, terrified to stay beside the hole yet too fascinated to move away.

A few more shovelfuls and Dixon revealed the top of a plastic tote box, the kind in which people store their winter clothing.

Gandy groaned this time. "Somebody buried their loved one in a rubber box!"

Everyone glared at her, and she remained quiet.

"Should we open it?" Dixon asked.

"No! I'll go call the county sheriff. If it's a dead body, let them do it." And before anyone could stop her, Gandy galloped off to the church.

It wasn't long before an official car pulled into the churchyard.

Quickly, Alex explained what they'd been doing and what they'd found. "We thought about opening it."

"It's probably good that you didn't. We might be able to get a few fingerprints off the box." The man went back to the car and came back wearing a pair of latex gloves. Gingerly, he knelt down over the shallow hole, leaned in and, with one finger, lifted the lid of the box. Bits of dirt fell away as it popped open. The inside was filled with a hodgepodge of goods—coins, jewelry, trinkets and even a little statue Alex remembered seeing at Lila's house before her break-in.

"Loot!" It was Gandy again, this time hovering over the hole and trembling with excitement. "Just like on television."

The officer dropped the lid. "Does anyone have any idea who this might belong to?"

Silence hung in the air. Finally Myrtle said, "My son," and burst into tears.

CHAPTER THIRTY-FOUR

*A*fter the call had been made to arrest Bucky Chadwick, Alex and Dixon sat with Bucky's mother until they were notified that he'd been found. Myrtle seemed relieved. Bucky, she guessed, had gotten the idea to bury the things he stole in the graveyard from the plat map hanging on the wall of his house. Since the time his father Herman Chadwick had become church sexton many years before, Bucky had used the back end of the cemetery as his secret hideout. It was only natural that when he turned to petty thievery, he would hatch a plot to bury it in a grave. No one ever looked inside a grave, after all.

No one, that is, until Dixon Daniels.

"Am I a bad mother to think it's a good thing my son got caught?"

"Bucky needs help. Until he sees that he can't get away with his behavior, he will continue to do what he was doing."

"He was getting worse, you know. And Will Packard drove him wild, coming to me and asking me to help him with the animals Bucky injured. He could have really hurt that little boy." Myrtle daubed at her eyes. "At least now I'll sleep at night, knowing he's not out getting into mischief."

It was a sorry state, Alex thought, to have that as solace, but while Bucky couldn't hurt others, he was also protected from himself.

Gandy drove Myrtle home, and Dixon followed Alex back to the parsonage.

"Emmy called today," Dixon said when they met in the yard. "She said I should be sure to tell you hello."

"How is she?" Alex's heart skipped a beat.

"Busy and tired but happy. She loves her job. She's anxious to get back here again too."

"When might that be?" Alex tried to sound casual.

Dixon glanced at him slyly. "I don't know yet, but you'll be the first one I tell."

"What's that supposed to mean?"

Dixon gave him his most innocent angelic look. Unfortunately, this angel's halo was tipped and tarnished.

Alex decided to ignore him. "Come inside. Lydia brought me a box of cookies that will take me weeks to eat."

"Not with me around it won't."

In the house, Dixon got glasses and poured milk while Alex checked the answering machine. He turned the sound up and they both listened. The first was from his sister Carol.

"Hi, bro. I wanted to let you know that we've decided to come for Thanksgiving. Jared's being a pill but he's settled down in school for the time being so I don't want to rock the boat. Looking forward to seeing you. Love you. Bye."

"That's nice, company for the holiday," Dixon said as he dug in the box for his favorites. "And she'll get to go to the lutefisk and *lefse* dinner. What about Natalie? What do you hear from her?"

"Not much." He wasn't ready to share his last conversation with her quite yet.

Dixon tapped a spot on his forehead, as if that were where his stores of wisdom were kept. "You want what Natalie *represents,* my friend—a wife, kids, family and home. But she's not the only one who can give you that, you know."

Alex rolled his eyes while Dixon kept digging in the cookies.

"You've got a lot on your hands, don't you?" Dixon asked.

If only he knew, Alex thought. Not only was there the mess with Natalie—which he would tell Dixon about later—there was Lydia Olson's attraction to Johann Paulson and her brothers' concern about losing her. There were all the Packard children, so bright and yet starving for a father able to give them the attention they needed. They were only a few of the people Alex cared about. There was also Lila Mason, sweet and befuddled; Bessie Bruun, who was given to painting windows black and watering weeds; Cherry Taylor, who feared she was infertile, and her husband Dan's battle with post-traumatic stress syndrome. He still didn't know much about the mysterious Kennedys, whom he'd found it almost impossible to get to know, or the slow softening of Alf Nyborg. Kenny Dawson and his worried family needed his support. The list went on and on. He was thankful for the people who seemed able to make it through their lives without too much daily upset—Lauren and Mike, for instance, or the Holmquists or Walter Englund.

His thoughts were interrupted by the ringing of the telephone.

"It's like a circus around here," Dixon commented as he stood up and went to the refrigerator. "I need more milk."

"Hello, this is Alex."

"Alex, this is Clarence Olson."

The man cleared his throat nervously.

"Clarence, are you okay? You don't sound like yourself."

"What are you doing this evening?"

"Not much. Dixon is here. Is there something you need?"

"I was going to ask you to come over, but if you have company I don't want to bother you."

"Dixon isn't company," Alex said with a laugh. "He's just Dixon."

"He could come too," Clarence said, an odd note in his voice. "He'll know sooner or later anyway."

Know what? "We'll drive over right away."

"Yes, maybe you should do that." Clarence hung up the phone without a good-bye.

"Now what?" Dixon asked. "Is it about Bucky?"

"No, Clarence Olson wants us to come over to see him. Put the lid on the cookies, Dixon, we're going for a drive."

Dixon swiped two more before he followed Alex out the door.

Every light in the Olson house was on when they arrived.

"The Olsons have gone wild and crazy wasting all this electricity," Dixon commented. "Clarence usually doesn't turn on any lights till he can hardly see."

The door opened as they approached, and Clarence hurried them inside, as if he were in a hurry to talk to them.

"I'm glad you came, Pastor. You too, Dixon. There's a family matter that's come up…." He winced a little, as if it hurt to talk. "Jacob and I never dreamed…I mean, how could we know? We're just God-fearing farmers, not psychiatrists or mind readers!"

Alex and Dixon stared at him.

"Clarence, spit it out," Dixon demanded.

"Lydia has run off and eloped!" The words came out in a wail. "She left us for another man!"

❧

After they returned to the parsonage, Alex and Dixon sat on the porch a long time, staring up at the sky, not speaking. It was Dixon who broke their stunned silence.

"Lydia, eloping? Can you believe it? Timid little Lydia?"

He'd been forewarned, Alex thought. She'd been restless and dissatisfied with her life and determined to make something interesting happen. He just hadn't believed Lydia would *elope*. "I hope she and Johann are happy."

"Me too. But they've only known each other a short while," Dixon marveled. "They're both adults, Dixon. At Lydia and Johann's age, maybe they feel they have to act quickly, that their time might be running out."

"So practically the first time they meet, they decided to get hitched? Who does that?"

"Wildly spontaneous Lydia and Johann, apparently."

"Lydia Olson and Johann Paulson, married before either of us," Dixon mused. "Who'd have guessed?" He searched in his pocket until he found a toothpick. Then he leaned back and stared at the sky.

They burst out laughing at the same moment, uproarious laughter that made Tripod look up from his position on the porch rug to stare at them. Slowly at first, then faster, the dog began to wag its tail.

"I love this place," Alex said as he took a gulp of air. His side was beginning to hurt.

"Me too." Dixon wiped tears of laughter from his cheeks.

"Never in a million years would I have thought…"

"Never in a *trillion* years!" Dixon said.

When they'd recovered, Alex said, "You know, Dixon, when I came out here I really expected Hilltop to be boring, even stagnant. I was sure it couldn't be alive and vibrant like the city. But, frankly, this is the most fascinating place I've ever been. Lydia and Johann are just one more reminder for me to expect the unexpected."

"You've got that right," Dixon said amiably.

"I came out here with a broken heart and a lot of trepidation. And now? I can't imagine being anywhere other than Hilltop Township."

"Speaking of expecting the unexpected," Dixon commented, "I've had a little of that myself today."

"What's that? Something that could make Hilltop even more interesting?" Alex said it lightly, expecting that Dixon had news he'd picked up in town.

"You might say that. Emmy told me she'd like to move back to Hilltop if she can find a way. I never thought she'd really consider it, but she just found out her job is changing. It's going to involve even more paperwork and fewer patients. I'll believe it when I see it, but I'd love to have my sister back here...back home."

"What about her boyfriend?" Alex didn't know if he wanted to hear the answer.

"They aren't too serious, she says. She doesn't seem to be worried about it."

Alex glanced down at his hands, needing the moment to absorb what Dixon had said.

Emmy. In Hilltop.

He settled back in his chair and looked at the black velvet blanket of night scattered with stars.

Emmy was the one possible thing that could make this wonderful place even better.

Alex smiled in the darkness. The future was bright in Hilltop.

ABOUT THE AUTHOR

JUDY BAER is the author of more than seventy-five books. She won the Romance Writers of America Bronze Medallion and was a RITA finalist twice. Judy is a North Dakota native and lives in Elk River, Minnesota, with her husband.